HOME ON DERANGE
by DAVID GERROLD

In loving memory of Susie Miller.

CONTENTS

INTRODUCTION

I suppose you're entitled to a warning.

This is it.

None of these stories are meant to be taken seriously.

Sometimes I sit down at the keyboard and the sentences just start rolling out. I rarely know what's going to happen next. I sit, appalled, watching the bizarre progression of character, incident, and idea that assemble on the computer screen. It astonishes me to see how the most sparkling of sentences can contain no real semblance of appropriate social decorum.

Nevertheless, every story in this collection has been purchased by an editor who probably should have known better.

Several of these stories were submitted (and sold) to the magazines. Others came into existence because some desperate anthologist offered me money and I was foolish enough to take on the challenge. Maybe it was the excitement of the idea, or maybe I didn't have anything else to do that week—but it was probably the money.[*]

I make no apologies, I make no excuses. These stories are best consumed in small doses—like maybe when you need something to read while sitting on the toilet. I do not recommend trying to work through this collection the same way you would read any other book, turning pages to see what happens next. On the contrary, I suggest restraint, proceeding through the pages carefully and with a justifiable mixture of caution and dread.

To be fair, a couple of these stories are here because they are funny.

The rest of them are here because they refused to lie quietly in the drawer. They escaped. They crawled out of their file folders and demanded to be included without any regard to their obvious lack of substance. Those stories—the ones that I am embarrassed to admit authoring—should be obvious. Please do not encourage them by laughing out loud, or even smiling in their presence. They do not deserve even that much acknowledgment.

If there is any kind of theme to this collection, it is that all of these stories have little or no redeeming social value. They were written as an explosion of peripatetic fragments in a delirious attempt at satire—except for a couple that were written for cathartic revenge on things (or people) that annoyed me.

---

[*] Money can be traded for chocolate.

There are thirty stories in this collection, nearly 120,000 words. Some of these tales might be worth your time. Others might be unforgivable stinkers, meriting only of an angry trajectory at the nearest brick wall—but which stories fit into which categories will be a subjective experience for every reader.

But let me put it this way—I suffered for my art. Now it's your turn.

—David Gerrold
May, 2022

THE GREAT PAN AMERICAN AIRSHIP MYSTERY

OR

WHY I MURDERED ROBERT BENCHLEY

After all is said and done, I blame Nikola Tesla.

It's his fault.

Because—if we're going to talk about cause and effect, then we have to go all way the back to the original cause.

No, Nikola Tesla did not set out to invent an efficient method of low-cost helium extraction, it was a side-effect of his coal-fusion research, but if he hadn't discovered it, no one else would have. At least not in our lifetimes.

Tesla often gave away many of his discoveries, but not this one—he patented the helium extraction process. The technology that followed created so many new industries and opportunities for profit that it pushed Tesla's own company into the Fortune 500 within 18 months.

Knowing that Tesla was unlikely to invest in lawyers and lawsuits, patent violations started cropping up everywhere. The Third Reich, for instance, began extracting their own helium from the Ruhr, the large coal fields located in the west of Germany in North Rhine-Westphalia—they used the helium to lift over a dozen huge vessels, all modeled after the luxurious Hindenburg.

Not to be outdone, the United States Congress created the National Aeronautics Studies Administration—NASA for short—to fund research and development in aerial transport.

Three years later, in June of 1937, The Great Pan American Airship Line began operations at their expansive new terminal on Welfare Island. Due to rising international tensions, as well as considerable domestic pressures against foreign competition, the trans-Atlantic German airships would be restricted to the airfield at Lakehurst, New Jersey.

To demonstrate America's commitment to a new age of aerial transportation, Pan Am announced the inaugural journey of their magnificent new flagship would be a coast-to-coast celebrity cruise. They held a nationwide contest to choose the name of the vessel they had nicknamed The Big Lady, and three lucky contestants would win berths on the first trip to prove that economical air travel for everyone was now a reality.

At 11:33 am on Thursday morning, June 3rd, 1937, First Lady, Eleanor Roosevelt officially christened the vessel in a grand ceremony and the Pan American flagship Liberty lifted majestically into the air while the United States Marine Band played America, The Beautiful. The Chorus of St. Patrick's Cathedral accompanied and WNBC broadcast the event on nationwide radio. RCA also broadcast an experimental television signal originating from the top of the Empire State Building. Receivers at Grand Central Terminal showed a grainy image of the Liberty's liftoff, although most people could have simply stepped outside onto 42nd street or Fifth Avenue for a better view.

Three times larger than the Hindenburg, she was a gleaming silver illusion. She circled Manhattan island three times while tugboats below thumped their horns, fireboats howled their sirens and sprayed jets of water, and Mayor La Guardia read a poem of salute by Robert Frost on the WNBC radio station.

Most people assumed that circling Manhattan was a salute to the city. Actually, it was an opportunity for Captain Bradley to test all the systems of the airship, one after the other, and reassure himself that everything was operating up to spec. It was a second shakedown cruise, unofficial but necessary. Coming around Battery Park for the third time, finally satisfied that the ship was handling the way he wanted, he spun the wheel to the left and the "Big Lady"—her affectionate nickname—turned gracefully to port. She was now officially on her way. We passed over the Statue of Liberty and out across New Jersey..

Aboard the vessel, a host of Broadway and Hollywood celebrities waved to the crowds below. George Jessel, Al Jolson, George and Ira Gershwin, and George M. Cohan, waved from the portside windows. Dorothy Parker, F. Scott Fitzgerald, Robert Benchley, George S. Kaufman, Heywood Broun, Alexander Woollcott, and several other members of the notorious Algonquin Round Table waved from the starboard side. Also aboard were Charles Lindbergh, Amelia Earhart, and William "Billy" Mitchell. 65-year-old Orville Wright had been invited as well, but had politely declined. He still believed the foolish idea that heavier-than-air vessels would become the primary vehicle of modern air travel and felt it would be hypocritical to lend his name or support to this journey. Tesla had also declined the invitation, saying there was nothing in San Francisco to interest him right now.

Less notable, several high-ranking members of the army and navy were also among the complement of passengers, but much less conspicuous. They seemed more concerned with the operational aspects of the Liberty than with the promotional aspects of the journey.

Pan Am's official statements asserted that the average air-speed of the Big Lady would be 85 miles per hour, and that the non-stop voyage would take no more than 36 hours. The Big Lady would be going around the south end of the Rocky Mountains rather than over. But some of the engineers were betting that Captain Bradley would push the engines hard, hoping to average more than 100mph— as well as crossing over the peaks to give the passengers a spectacular view of the mountaintops, ultimately arriving at San Francisco at 10:30 A.M. the next day, a journey of only 26 hours. If that did happen, then despite traveling more than 24 hours, we would still arrive an hour earlier than our departure time, an artifact of our westward passage through three time zones.

Heading west over New Jersey, many of the passengers still crowded the windows and speculated about the crowds below. Tiny people came running out of their houses and their businesses, shouting and pointing and staring skyward. They cheered and hollered and waved. When the shadow of the Liberty passed over, some of them panicked. We saw a few small children crying, they were carried inside by their reassuring mothers—where they promptly leaned out of the upstairs windows to stare again.

After a half-hour or so, after the second or third tray of drinks had been passed around, the Gershwins commandeered the piano in the salon and started playing. Later, Oscar Levant took over the piano, providing accompaniment for Cohan, Jessel, and Jolson as they worked their inebriated way through an impromptu medley of popular songs.

When they finally tired out, Jack Benny, and Fred Allen began trading quips—it started with Fred Allen asking Jack Benny why he hated the violin so much that he kept playing it. Benny responded with an observation that bags under Fred Allen's eyes were so big they required their own porters. Allen replied that Jack Benny couldn't ad-lib a belch after a plate of Hungarian goulash. Benny promptly turned to him and grumped, "You wouldn't say that if my writers were here."

I wished his writers were aboard as well. I would have loved to have met them. I assumed they would be very funny men.

I was—at that time—a guest relations steward aboard the Liberty. My job was to keep the customers happy for the nearly two days it would take to travel the 2600 miles from New York to San Francisco—actually a bit more, because our course would zig-zag a bit to fly over several important cities and landmarks. That meant maintaining the well-being of everyone onboard who assumed they were entitled to special treatment—and that was everyone onboard. In the case of my specific charges, that mostly involved keeping them drunk enough to be cheerful, but not so drunk as to be uncontrollable. Passed-out was not an option.

But holding a tray of martinis was not my career goal. I intended to bootstrap my career by writing a memoir of this adventure. I planned to sell articles wherever I could to establish a name for myself.

I was already making notes for a profile of the celebrity doings for Life Magazine, a revealing slice of salacious gossip for The New Yorker, a report on the amenities of a flying hotel for Popular Science, a complementary article about the maintenance of the onboard necessities for Scientific American, a description of how well the six electric propellors performed for Popular Mechanics, and possibly even—I'd have to do it under a pen name—a futuristic story for Astounding about a giant passenger vessel journeying through outer space to Venus or Mars—I just needed a plot.

I had to trade a few favors, including a couple of sexual ones (that was fun), but I did get myself assigned to take care of the Algonquin Round Table crowd— that might have happened anyway. It turned out they were a boisterous group, hard to deal with, and none of the other stewards wanted to acommodate them and all of their shenanigans. A couple of the Algonquin group were putting away enough booze that their breaths had become flammable. I expected—hoped—that after they settled in and became comfortable that they would start discussing important literary issues.

Lunch was delayed because of the unscheduled performances—none of the staff were brave enough to interrupt the entertainers, the rest of the passengers would have dropped us out the nearest window, so we didn't serve until we were well over eastern Pennsylvania and Oscar Levant remarked, "You can smell the cheese even from up here."

We weren't that high, he could have been right. The Liberty cruised below the clouds, usually only three or four hundred feet above the ground, mostly so passengers could have a great view of the landscape, but she was engineered to go much higher. Tanks of pressurized helium gas were stored along her keel to inflate additional lifting ballonets when more altitude was needed—such as flying over a mountain. To descend again, the extra helium would be released, or pumped back into the storage tanks. Large tanks of water were also used for ballast. This was the same water that passengers would use for washing. If the Liberty needed altitude quickly, it could be released in a massive shower. By the time it hit the ground, it would be little more than a mist. At worst, a momentary drizzle.

The Liberty carried 200 passengers and 85 crewmembers. By comparison, a Hindenburg-class ship could carry only 72 passengers and required 62 crewmembers to manage the journey. The Liberty had been designed to carry 400 souls, but Pan Am was using the inaugural journey to demonstrate the large cargo carrying capacity of the Liberty as well. A half-dozen new Fords were stored in her hold. None of the military officers would discuss it, but more than once I saw them scribbling numbers on yellow pads and arguing about balancing the weights of tanks, trucks, cannons, troops, and supplies.

Cross-country shipping by railroad could take anywhere from three days to two weeks, depending on how much you wanted to pay. For some industries, air transport would be both faster and cheaper—like fresh fruits and vegetables from the California fields to the New York markets. And then there were those lucrative mail contracts to consider.

After lunch, some of the passengers retired to their cabins to rest up for the rigors of dinner. The cabins were spacious and well-equipped, deliberately more luxurious than those found on any ocean-liner where space would be at a premium. The opposite was true aboard the Liberty. Here, weight was the limiting factor, not space.

Only the control gondola hung below the body of the craft, I'd delivered coffee and sandwiches to it on our training flight, it was a broad comfortable platform. All the other passenger and crew spaces were inside the Liberty's envelope. Because a massive framework of aluminum girders and steel tension cables was needed to provide a stable structure for the huge array of giant lift bags, there was also considerable space beneath the ballonets for accommodations. There was almost too much space.

When Tallulah Bankhead boarded, she looked around the lobby and asked the nearest steward—me—"What time does this place reach San Francisco?" She had the most amazing voice, as deep and husky as a velvet martini. Then she stared into my eyes and asked, "Who do I have to fuck to get a drink?" You can bet that sent me scurrying.

The interior of the airship and all of her trim and accessories, were decorated in the latest Art Deco style—Streamline Moderne—very light and bright, all minimalist and futuristic, exactly the statement Pan Am wanted to make. Willliam F. Lamb, one of the principle designers of the Empire State Building, had supervised the design of the passenger spaces of the airship. He was also onboard, somewhere.

A broad salon stretched across the front of the aircraft, outlined by a terrifyingly open horseshoe of glass. This was the main gathering place for the passengers. It was almost too sprawling, too wide, too open, it felt cavernous. Huge windows stretched across the front of the deck and circled wide around both sides—that and the high ceiling gave the whole chamber a broad spacious feeling, much like Hollywood's conception of a blissful afterlife.

A second level of walkways circled the high windows so every passenger could have a grand view without ever having to crowd. All of them would be able to observe the ground easily through the large downward-angled panes. The sheer size of those glass walls made it feel as if we were not within a vessel, but simply drifting along on an airy platform, as removed from the mundane cares of the world as the gods of Olympus—well, we were—but the sense of a heavenly condition was deliberate. We floated gracefully across the sky, trailing a massive shadow across the ground below, a visible reminder of the Liberty's astonishing size.

Across the main floor of the salon, there were step-up levels for service areas and step-down levels of various sizes for gatherings of passengers to discuss common interests. The chairs and couches were upholstered in muted shades of red, silver, and blue—all very Pan American. The floor was carpeted in a lighter blue, a reflection of the sky. The walls were eggshell-white with gold trim. Silvery murals portrayed Lady Liberty in a variety of heroic poses.

Just aft of the salon was spacious dining hall. Behind that was a selection of smaller spaces, a cozier bar, a reading room, a smoking lounge for gentlemen, and a corresponding lounge reserved especially for the ladies. For overseas flights, the billiards room would be converted to a small casino. Further back, the airship contained a motion picture theater, a gymnasium, a quiet reading room stocked with many current magazines and a selection of popular books, even a bowling alley and a tennis court, and other lightweight amenities to alleviate the tedium of a long voyage. There was almost too much acreage on the main deck. The designers had run out of ideas before they had run out of space.

The original blueprints had included a swimming pool, with the water in it doubling as ballast. At the last moment, the airline had postponed the installation. It wasn't the weight of the water that concerned the engineers, it was the weight of the support structure of the pool and all the additional plumbing and pumps and filters needed to maintain it. The pool hadn't been completely ruled out, but the accountants at Pan Am had successfully argued that the loadweight could be more profitably used for cargo, and the company was still weighing the pros and cons.

After Pennsylvania, we headed across Lake Erie. Captain Bradley diverted course slightly south so that people all across the northern shore of Ohio—Cleveland, Lorain, Sandusky, and finally Toledo—could see the Liberty and cheer and wave. Beneath us, more boats tooted their horns and people waved flags and banners to catch our attention. Many of the passengers went to the windows to wave back.

But not the Round Table group. They had gathered themselves near the bar again and were proceeding to work their way through pitchers of martinis, as well as a heated discussion of something they called, "writer's block." That sounded promising. As a burgeoning author myself, I hoped to learn some of the wisdom of the sages, especially the hard part. How do you get the words onto the page?

Sometime after lunch, Dorothy Parker sent a radiogram to her editor: "I have not forgotten you. I have only forgotten to write the article."

Two hours later, her editor wired back. I brought the radiogram to her myself. She plucked it from the tray, took a puff off her cigarette, and opened it nonchalantly. I had never seen anyone open a radiogram so nonchalantly before. She must have received so many of them in her career that she took them for granted. She looked around at the rest of the group. "He says," she said, and read it aloud. "'Put down the damn martini and find a typewriter. Benchley has one. He never goes anywhere without it, even if he has no intention of using it.'" She frowned across the table. "Is that true, Robert?"

Benchley had the good grace to look embarrassed. "Well, yes. It's impossible to procrastinate properly without a typewriter."

Mrs. Parker looked up at me, still waiting with the tray held out. "Are you waiting for a tip?"

Yes, ma'am. But I didn't say it aloud. "Will there be a reply?"

"No. Yes. Send this back. 'Benchley and typewriter defenestrated over—'" She frowned. "Where are we? Oh, it doesn't matter. Defenestrate him over someplace interesting. No, make that boring. Oh, never mind. He'll have to look up defenestrate and he hates looking things up. Begone now."

I bewent.

I bewent all the way back to my station next to the bar. As much as I would have liked to eavesdrop on their conversation, it would have been rude—and against the rules. I was only allowed to approach if summoned by a gesture, or if I was emptying ash trays.

Nevertheless, snatches of conversation still floated over to the bar, enough to suggest that the topic of writer's block was still circling the conversation like a maiden aunt.

Because lunch had been delayed for more than an hour, dinner was also delayed, but only thirty minutes. We were over the northern part of Indiana when the sun touched the horizon ahead of us. Oscar Levant advised against looking out the windows at the broad plains of Indiana. "It's only the people we fly over."

The entire meal service was scheduled for ninety minutes. Soup, salad, fish, three kinds of carvery meat, dessert, coffee, and after-dinner drinks. The Algonquin crew managed to stretch it out to two and a half hours. By the time they finally heaved themselves laboriously from their chairs, it was nine o'clock and we were approaching the Chicago flyover. The city was a bright sprawl of lights ahead, searchlights sweeping the sky.

As we approached, we could hear music coming from a band on the pier, but the distance kept it from being clear or identifiable. It sounded like a badly-tuned radio. According to Fred Allen it was "an excited crowd of bagpipers, accordion-players, and Jack Benny fans." Beside him, Benny replied, "I'm having trouble seeing your fans, Fred. Are there any?"

Over the city, we were blinded by searchlights hitting us from the ground, they blazed up at us from everywhere, especially along the shoreline and the major boulevards. "It looks like a dozen Hollywood premieres," said Bankhead. "Louis B. Mayer should see this. He'd crap his pants." She pronounced it "Louie."

"I wonder what it looks like from down there," said a tiny woman, one of the contest winners. The winners had been picked by their weight, a fact not made known to the general public.

I took the opportunity to answer. "Did you see the glow in the water as we passed over the lake? That was our lights. The entire airship is outlined with Nikola Tesla's new illuminators—the ones that give off almost no heat. He calls them light-emitting-diodes. They print them on some thin panels of glass. From the ground the Liberty looks like a great silver spoon, blazing across the sky. The airship's name is spelled out in lights like a Broadway star—only bigger than any marquee on broadway. Each letter is 24 feet high."

Beside her, a nondescript little man—the publisher of a pulp science fiction magazine, Thrilling Wonder Stories—spoke up. "Imagine if we could put a news-marquee on the side of the airship, like the one in Times Square. We could display messages to the people below." He thought a moment. "Or perhaps we could put projectors inside the skin of the dirigible and show motion pictures on her sides. Of course, the skin of the ship would have to be translucent enough for the movie to show through. Perhaps someday we'll have airships anchored above cities, projecting television programs to thousands of people at once."

He frowned, another thought crossing his mind. "That would use a lot of elecricity, wouldn't it?" Still frowning, he added, "I wonder if Professor Tesla's wonderful diodes could somehow be reversed to turn light into electricity? You could put rows of panels across the top of the airship and power its engines off sunlight all day long. Hmmm." He pulled out a notebook and hurriedly scribbled his thoughts into it. "Perhaps I'll write a sequel. Ralph 124C42+...." He wandered off, lost in thought.

The woman, the one who'd won her passage in a contest, said, "What a strange little man. Is he an inventor?"

"His name is Gernsback. He's a science fiction writer."

She frowned in confusion. "Science fiction? What's that?"

"Pulp fiction. The silly kind. The kind you don't want to let your little boy read. Rocket ships to the moon. Giant mechanical brains. Robots. Silly things like that."

She made a face. "Oh, that terrible stuff. No, we'd never let Jeffty read that trash."

By ten, the Algonquins had reclaimed their place in the salon and another pitcher of martinis was meeting its olive-strewn fate.

"Do they ever stop?" the evening bartender whispered to me.

"I don't know. I think Broun—or is that Woollcott?—got up to pee once. The rest of them must have iron kidneys."

Between emptying ashtrays, retrieving pitchers and replacing them with full ones, occasionally delivering and sending radiograms, and always being as unobtrusive as possible, I managed to glean a sense of their evolving conversation. Tallulah Bankhead's remark about Louis B. Mayer had sparked a conversation about writing for the movies, something that both Dorothy Parker and F. Scott Fitzgerald had dabbled with.

Before long, they were plotting a film of their own—or perhaps just plotting. The story involved, of course, a beautiful Broadway star traveling aboard a gleaming new airship when a terrible murder occurs. For the better part of an hour, the group argued about who to murder, perhaps someone in their own group? That ended abruptly when Bankhead declared, "Dah-ling, you can't murder a writer. Nobody will notice. It has to be someone important."

Oh, good grief. Didn't they realize? The writers are the most important people in Hollywood. If it isn't on the page, it isn't on the stage! You have to take it seriously!

But instead, they wasted another hour of discussion about who might be worth murdering. The comedians were quickly dismissed, so were Jolson, Jessel, and Cohan. The Algonquins finally settled on George Gershwin as a suitable victim, then moved on to speculating about the identity of the murderer and what possible motive he (or she?) might have for killing America's most gifted composer.

"Possibly his brother, Ira?"

"What motive?"

"Over a girl maybe...?"

"How tawdry. How boring. Besides...."

"No, dear. George isn't gay. He's been bedding all those women—"

"—yes, trying to prove he's a man."

"What a wonderful way to prove it." That was Oscar Levant, who'd been passing by, but stopped for the gossip.

I didn't hear the end of that discussion, there were several other late-night gatherings that needed my attention, but none as interesting. The next time I passed by, they were arguing about writer's block again. That was something I really wanted to hear about—how did the great ones get past it?

It was either Broun or Woollcott—I never could figure out which was which— who said, "Oh, there's a very easy trick to break a block."

Benchley was already glowing with inebriation, had been since liftoff, but he looked across the table with all the interest he could muster. "What?" he said.

"Quite simple. You put a sheet of paper in the typewriter and you type the word 'The.' The human mind abhors a vacuum. It is incapable of leaving the sentence unfinished. You will find yourself typing something to complete the sentence almost immediately."

"Yes, dear fellow," said Benchley, "but what about the sentence that follows it? And the next after that? And the next and the next?"

The other one—Woollcott or Broun, or maybe it was George S. Kaufman— spoke up then. "Pablo Picasso says that all art is recovery from the first line. He was talking about drawing, of course, but I believe that's true of writing as well. Once you have that first sentence on the page, the rest will follow."

Benchley had already written quite a bit about his ability to procrastinate— that only the pressure of a deadline inspired true creativity—but in this group of trusted colleagues, he could admit that sometimes writing was difficult. Not the typing itself, but getting the right words in the right order. Others agreed. "There's an elegance that we aspire to achieve, but the limitations of our own selves remains our greatest challenge."

Benchley put his martini glass down. It was already empty anyway. "The..." he said. "The...." And then, "The the the the the." He nodded. "Yes. The...." And then he leapt up from his chair. "It's an admirable idea. I shall now proceed to test it." And he staggered off in search of his cabin.

The others went back to discussing murder, now arguing whether Jack Warner or Louis B. Mayer might be a better victim. There would be no shortage of suspects or motives. I did catch one line in passing. "No, not Walt Disney. If he doesn't like an actor, he tears him up."

By midnight, we were crossing Kansas—a dry state, it had the most restrictive alcohol laws in the nation. Legally, once we were in the state's airspace we were forbidden to serve liquor. When the company announced the flight itinerary of the Liberty, the Attorney General of the state had sent a letter of inquiry to Pan American's lawyers asking if the state's liquor laws would be observed while the Liberty was flying over the state. Pan Am's lawyers had promptly sent back a note assuring the Attorney General that state officials, including county sheriffs, were free to board, inspect, and serve any necessary warrants on any Pan Am aircraft flying over the state of Kansas. So far, none had done so.

Captain Bradley had altered the course a few degrees south to avoid a rumbling storm system spreading across the Dakotas and down toward Nebraska where it would probably turn into tornado weather. The big chart in the salon was automatically updated every fifteen minutes. It showed our location and also demonstrated that we were averaging 93 miles per hour, so we were ahead of schedule, but nowhere near the 100 miles per hour that some had predicted. The figures were also available in knots for the aviators aboard. Of which, I was not one.

Along about 1:30 in the morning, the Algonquins finally started making noises that suggested they might be through for the evening. Two other stewards and I had to escort several of them to their cabins. When the last one had finally been tucked in, we looked at each other in exhaustion. "When do any of those people actually find time to do any of the things they're supposed to be famous for?"

We secured all the windows, checking to make sure that none were left open to the night, we couldn't risk a drunken passenger falling out, then adjourned to our separate bunks. Crew's quarters were nowhere near as luxurious as the passengers', but we each had a private space, a sink, and a shower—and a window! It was an uncommon luxury. Eventually, on a full flight with 400 passengers, we'd be doubling up, two crewmembers to a cabin.

The cabins on the Liberty had what they called "picture windows." The windows in the salon were even larger, as broad as those in front of Macy's department store. By contrast, the windows on a passenger plane were little more than portholes—even on the newest aircraft under construction that Boeing was building in Washington state.

Pan Am had ordered six of those airplanes—the Boeing 314 Clipper long-range flying boat—for trans-oceanic flights. But with the success of the Liberty's maiden voyage almost certainly assured, those planes might end up going to the army instead. Britain's Royal Air Force had also expressed an interest in picking up those contracts if Pan Am cancelled—as expected.

Unlike an airplane, it's easy to sleep aboard the Liberty. Her electrical propellors are so silent, and so distant from the passenger cabins, you can barely feel any vibration, just a gentle susuruss. Unlike the clattering internal combustion engines that keep airplanes aloft, the Liberty's engines run on the same electricity that powers the lights and runs the radios. Everything aboard the airship runs off Professor Tesla's marvelous new graphite-and-lithium batteries. The batteries were kept charged by three diesel generators.

Although technically I was on a 24-hour shift, in practice I would not be needed until at least 10am, maybe later, if the Algonquins slept in—as expected—but I was already up and ready to go at 8:30am.

We were already over the northwest corner of New Mexico, and on course to pass over the Grand Canyon, then Boulder Dam, only two years old and already providing electricity for much of the southwest, then past Las Vegas, a small desert resort town, up over the Sierras, and eventually north up the coast toward an early evening arrival in San Francisco. Passengers could expect a glorious California sunset as we landed.

The course of the airship was primarily determined by weather, but the airline wanted everyone in the country talking about the airship. That meant flying over as many cities as possible so the people on the ground could see the Liberty. It also meant flying over the most spectacular scenery below so that passengers could take photographs to show their friends and families.

Of course, Life Magazine had photographers aboard the aircraft as well, two of them, and more stationed on the ground all along the route as well. We'd lifted off on Thursday, June 3rd. The next issue of the magazine would appear on Monday, June 7th. We were guaranteed the cover, of course, and would likely have at least four pages of departure pictures, showing liftoff from the field as well as more photos of the airship over New York, then probably six pages of enroute photos, especially aerial views of various landmarks, and another four pages for the arrival and landing.

According to the flight plan, we would head up the California coast, then sail in over the brand-new Golden Gate Bridge for even more spectacular photo opportunities. The bridge had opened on Thursday, May 27th, exactly a week before our liftoff, so it was a grand occasion to demonstrate America's growing industrial future, the strength and know-how that was bringing us back from the Great Depression.

After crossing over the bridge, the Liberty would circle the entire bay so people in Sausalito, Berkeley, and Oakland could also get a good look at the Liberty, then back across the bay to the Pan Am terminal at San Francisco Municipal Airport. We expected to see large crowds everywhere, but especially at the airfield where a motorcade awaited.

Governor Frank Merriam would be there to welcome us. He'd dedicated the bridge the week before, kissing every baby he could find. This week, he'd certainly make sure that the photographers would get pictures of him with George Gershwin and Al Jolson and Jack Benny—but not Tallulah Bankhead, she was developing an unsavory reputation among Republican voters, and Merriam needed all the good press he could get—he had a tough election coming up next year.

Not all of our celebrity passengers were placing themselves where photographers might find them, some actually found the photographers a nuisance, but the photographers themselves were having no shortage of photo opportunities. Even if they couldn't find Gershwin at the piano or Cohan and Jessel and Jolson mugging together, there were always the huge, downward-angled windows. They had already taken enough aerial photos for a dozen special issues and were now arguing which side of the Salon would be best for photos when we crossed the Golden Gate Bridge. The two Life Magazine photographers had the best plan, they would station themselves one on each side.

Most of the Algonquins slept through breakfast. Not surprising. But they missed a great view of the Grand Canyon from the air. That Gernsback fellow, the one who published Thrilling Wonder Stories, speculated aloud, "I suppose that's what the canals on Mars must look like, only larger, to be visible from Earth. What a grand civilization the Martians must have. We must make friends with them somehow."

Amazing, what some people thought about. I couldn't imagine anyone taking that science fiction stuff seriously.

The Algonquins did show up for lunch, one by one staggering bleary-eyed into the dining hall. Not the best argument for the life of a writer. These people were famous. They were role-models. Why weren't they acting like it? I was beginning to hate them.

They had the best job in the world—they were the caretakers of culture, the shapers of opinion—and they were behaving like common drunks. But if writing is one of the best jobs in the world, it's also one of the hardest—it's all decision-making, all day long. This word or that one, over and over and over again, all the way to the end of the sentence. And even if you get to the end of a sentence, you still have to start again at the beginning of the next. It's exhausting.

Maybe that's why writers drink—to escape having to make any more decisions, except perhaps how many olives in the martini. Or maybe a twist of onion instead.

And maybe what I was seeing was only an aberration. I couldn't expect these people to be brilliant and noteworthy everywhere, all the time, could I? This was a vacation for them, a break from the stress. Maybe they just needed to recharge their creative batteries? Who was I to judge?

They took their coffee in the salon, along with a pile of fresh pastries that quickly disappeared. I circled regularly, alternating between brewing fresh pots of coffee and refilling their cups. They were now arguing about the best way to murder Louis B. Mayer. Throwing him out the window of the airship was quickly discarded. If there's no body to discover, you lose the scene where the French maid screams in horror.

That led to a discussion of why the maid had to be French. Woollcott—by now, I was pretty sure it was Woollcott—noted that a young French maid was always going to be more fun to look at than a dumpy English maid. Bankhead responded that the dumpy English maid was a great part for a good character actress, and good contrast. "What she means," Dorothy Parker pointedly observed, "is that the star should be the prettiest one. Not upstaged by the ingenue."

Woollcott was undeterred. "Ah, but I have the perfect young actress—"

"Of course, you think she's perfect. She's sleeping with you and you're vain."

Bankhead leaned in. "Not perfect. Desperate." Then she added, "On the other hand, if you actually believe her orgasm, we should cast her, that proves she's a real actress." Turning to the rest, she said, "What if the producer's body is found inside one of the—what do you call them—the big balloons that hold all that nice helium?" She turned to me and stroked my arm suggestively.

"Lift bags," I said. "Or ballonets."

"Oh, ballonets. I like that. How very French. There's a bit of French sophistication for you, dear. Without all that messy business of having to buy a maid's costume. We shall find Louis B. Mayer's body in a ballonet. Suffocated because there's no oxygen. All blue in the face. Perhaps he has even been screaming. But no one could hear him."

"Umm, if I may—" I politely lifted a hand.

The actress looked at me, her hand still on my arm. "Yes, dear boy?"

"If he were in the ballonet screaming, the helium would affect his voice, make it higher pitched. It's the density of the gas." She frowned in puzzlement. I demonstrated. "He'd sound like this. Help me! Help me!"

The entire group fell out laughing. "Oh my god, that's priceless. Can you imagine Louis B. Mayer sounding like Mickey Mouse?"

"More like Betty Boop."

"Makes me think—maybe we should do this as a comedy."

"Somebody go find Jack Benny. He's got the best writers—"

"We'd have to put him in the picture—"

"Oh, right. Never mind."

"But if it's a comedy—"

"Who says it has to be a comedy—?"

"If we're murdering Louis B., it will be—"

"No, not a comedy, but certainly a feel-good movie. We could get Capra to direct—"

"No, we should get whatsisname, that little round English fellow, the one who does all those suspense movies—"

"I've met him." Bankhead shuddered. "I have no intention of working for him. He's..." She searched for the word, finally found it. "He's creepy."

She squeezed my arm, "Not you, dear boy," and finally let go, but not before giving me the kind of delicious look that made me wish the dirigible was a lot slower so we'd have one more night in the air.

"I have a question..." I was pretty sure that was Heywood Broun now. Maybe. "How do we get him into the lift bag? If we slice it open, doesn't the gas escape? Wouldn't that create a risk of explosion?"

"No, that's hydrogen. Helium doesn't explode. Isn't that right, steward?" They all turned to me as if I was the expert.

"Yes, that's correct, sir. Hydrogen is too dangerous. But helium is perfectly safe."

"But the gas would still escape, wouldn't it?"

"Well, yes. But the lift bags are very big. You could cut a slice near the bottom, shove a person in, then seal it again with duct tape. We use it to repair small rips. They do happen sometimes, so there are rolls of tape everywhere—in all of the tool kits and there are tool kits everywhere in the frame, for the convenience of the engineers. So that wouldn't be a problem. Unless the victim struggled. You'd have to knock him out."

"Or get him so drunk he passes out—" Parker pointed to Benchley who was quietly snoring in his chair.

"No, we can't murder Benchley. He still owes me money."

"Well, we can't murder Louis B. either then. He owes me a picture."

"Yes, but now that we have a plan, we'll have to murder the steward too, because he knows too much. We could practice on him. Would you like a martini, lad?"

"I don't drink, sir," I said, and excused myself to refill the coffee pot again. When I returned, they had decided that murdering a steward had no inherent drama. A murder mystery is only riveting if the victim is important. "So, you're safe, dear boy," Bankhead reassured me. "You're not important enough to kill. Don't take it too hard."

"Thank you," I said, noncommittally.

"Somebody wake up Benchley—"

"Why? He'll just start talking—"

"He's snoring!"

"You'd rather have him talking?"

And so it went. Somebody looked at me and asked why I was carrying a coffee pot instead of a martini pitcher, and they were off again. But they still weren't talking about writing. Or anything relating to the literary world. I didn't understand it. Every other profession, the people in it talk shop. These people, they just drank. They did wake up Benchley in time to see the huge white slab of Boulder Dam. "Impressive! You could project movies on it!"

"It's a long drive from Los Angeles. It'd better be one hell of a flick."

Then they retired back to their chairs in the salon. "Las Vegas? Nothing there to see. Just a wide spot in the road. It'll never amount to anything."

Somebody remembered that Benchley had been procrastinating his way through a writer's block—until somebody told him to go type the word 'The' on a blank sheet of paper. Dorothy Parker puffed on her cigarette and asked, "So how did that work, Robert?"

Benchley frowned. "How did what work?"

"The great 'The' experiment, remember?"

"Oh, that. Yes. Thank you." He frowned again. "Well…" He cleared his throat, preparing himself for an extended explanation. "One has to be well-prepared for the task, you know. Procrastination is not for the faint-hearted. It takes genuine commitment. You cannot just sit and do nothing. You must make it appear as if you are preparing to do something. A pipe is very useful in that regard. It requires a great deal of attention. It's an excellent way to look like you are preparing to get busy.

Lighting a pipe demands a specific ritual, an elaborate ritual, a very time-consuming ritual. There is the selection of tobacco, followed by the process of delicately filling the bowl, pinch by pinch, then the tamping. One cannot tamp the tobacco too firmly or it will be hard to light. Likewise, one cannot leave the leaves too loose or they will simply burn up. Then there is the application of the fire. As soon as the match has been applied to the tobacco, the smoke is over. This necessitates refilling, relighting, and oh, yes—reknocking. The knocking out of a pipe is as important as the smoking. You have to have the appropriate surface to knock the pipe on. Not just any table will do. No, knocking the pipe is a whole other ritual, you see, all part of the process, and if you leave any part of it out, you're simply not serious about procrastinating."

"Yes, you've bored us with this story before." Kaufman yawned. "You really must write it and sell it someday so we won't have to listen to it again. But we didn't ask you how to procrastinate. Most of us already know how to do that, we've each developed our own specific set of skills. What we want to know is how well the experiment worked?"

"What experiment?"

"The one where you typed the word 'The' on a blank sheet of paper—remember?"

"Oh, that experiment. It worked very well. You were right. I typed the word 'The' and almost immediately, the rest of the words came flowing out as easily as if poured from a pitcher of martinis. Of which, I will have one, if you please, steward." To the rest, he said, "It's still sitting in my typewriter. Feel free to look."

Unable to resist the invitation, the rest of them scrambled to their feet and headed for the corridor, leaving Benchley behind with a martini glass held high in his hand. He saluted me with it, knocked it back, then held it up again for a refill.

When the group returned from Benchley's cabin, filing back in like children after recess, they were smiling and nodding to each other, but they were already talking about something else. Benchley waited expectantly for their reactions. Parker glowered at him as she seated herself. "Too clever by half." A couple of others shook their heads as if Benchley had punned in public—a good pun, but still a pun, the literary equivalent of a fart. Bankhead gave him a scowl of approval. The one I'd identified as Kaufman parked himself, nodded and admitted, "Nice."

I was curious too, but I couldn't leave my station. By then we were coming out over the California coast, and following U.S. Route 101 north. It ran all the way from Mexico to Canada, with portions of the route known as El Camino Real—"The Royal Road."

The Spanish had built their 21 missions in California each one a single day's travel from the next, so journeying missionaries would always have a safe place to rest each evening. Many of the state's coastal towns and cities still retained the names of the original missions: San Diego, San Juan Capistrano, San Gabriel, Santa Catalina, Santa Ysabel, San Pedro, San Fernando, Santa Clarita, Santa Barbara, Santa Mira, Santa Clara, San Luis Obispo, Santa Inez, Santa Cruz, San Jose, San Francisco, and a few more that always fell out of my head. How did I know all of this? Because it was part of Pan Am's training for stewards. Passengers would always have questions about the scenery below. It was the stewards' job to provide accurate answers. Any question we couldn't answer was added to the training guide.

The rest of the journey was pretty much without incident. The Algonquins, exhausted from all their drinking, had given up their plans to murder Louis B. Mayer. For some reason, they were now muttering imprecations against several New York critics—individuals who were not aboard. "Murdering a critic would only be poetic justice—" Bankhead said, "They've murdered so many shows."

Benchley cleared his throat loudly. "I am a critic too, you know."

"When you're writing, yes. But most people know you as a humorist."

"I resent that," he replied, but without much emotion. He was giving more attention to his martini.

"Besides, you're too nice to murder."

"I resent that even more."

"We can't murder a critic. There would be too many suspects to make the plot workable."

"There would be even more suspects if you killed Louis B. Mayer."

"True, that. Maybe we should kill Benchley. Some people like him. That makes it even more of a mystery. Why would someone want to kill Robert Benchley."

"I can think of—" Kaufman quickly counted off on his fingers. "—four reasons."

"Besides that—"

"I think the question isn't why, but who." Bankhead looked to me. "Oh, hello, dah-ling, bring those martinis over here. Tell me—would you like to murder Robert Benchley?"

Before I could answer, Dorothy Parker said, "Oh, no, no, no. He's not important enough—"

"But he's adorable enough. No one would ever suspect him. I know—" She waved her martini glass for effect, but to give her credit she didn't spill a drop. The woman could hold her liquor. "I'll tell you exactly why he wants to kill Robert Benchley. He's a frustrated young writer and he's jealous—that's it! Jealous of all of us! Robert is just the first. Before the journey is over, he'll kill every one of us. It'll be just like Agatha Christie. Ten Little Indians. Only on an airship." She turned to me. "Would you like that, dah-ling?"

As deadpan as I could manage, "It's against airline policy to kill passengers. It might be bad for business."

Bankhead guffawed like a choking foghorn. Quickly recovering herself, she turned to the rest, "You see, darlings. He's perfect! Nobody would ever suspect him."

Kaufman shook his head. "No, no, no. It won't work. He's scenery. The murderer has to be a lead, not a second banana. But I do like the idea of killing Benchley. There's a sadistic kind of elegance to it. Although once he's dead, you lose some of your best opportunities for comic relief."

Woollcott added, "Having the steward be the killer is too much like 'the butler did it.'"

"Has the butler ever done it?" Parker asked. "I mean, how can it be a cliché if nobody's ever written it? Maybe that's how we make it work. If Benchley is the victim, then the other suspects have to be us. And here we are saying, 'Oh, it couldn't be the butler, that's too obvious—and it's the butler all along.' But we never considered it because we don't like clichés."

Silence, while they all considered it. I waited patiently to find out if I was going to be a murderer or not.

"Well..." said Kaufman, "We'd have to build up his part a bit. I do like the line about it being against airline policy to kill passengers. Notice he didn't say he wouldn't do it—only that it's against airline policy. Nice bit of misdirection there."

"That little lecture about the Spanish missions—and all those other bits of triva too. Electrical engines and lift bags and why helium makes your voice squeaky. We can use all of that—we'll play him up as stiff and boring. He'll be a dry comic presence for the first two acts. In act three, we reveal his seething core of resentment against those with real talent."

Bankhead slid her hand up my arm. "What do you think, dah-ling?"

I couldn't say what I was thinking. Fortunately, I was rescued by the chime announcing afternoon tea. Having missed breakfast, having drunk most of their lunch, the Algonquins agreed among themselves almost immediately that food was as good an excuse as any to relocate. They rose almost as one and headed for the dining hall, where trays of sandwiches and salads were being set out.

F. Scott Fitzgerald was the last to follow, still holding a glass of whiskey. He stopped and frowned at me, as if trying to figure something out. "Why would you want to murder Benchley?" he asked, very seriously. "I think I'd be a much better victim, don't you?"

"A very good point, sir. Shall I help you to your table?"

A southerly headwind slowed the Liberty, so we observed sunset while still passing over Santa Cruz. On the starboard side, we could see The Giant Dipper roller coaster, the highlight of the Beach Boardwalk amusement park. There were colored lights flashing, people shouting and pointing, and carousel music. After that, the hills darkened quickly, a color somewhere between emerald and blackened indigo.

On the port side, the sun went fireburst orange, then sullen crimson as it dipped into the horizon. For a few magic moments, the ocean glimmered with golden highlights across the surface of the waves. Several of the photographers got into a heated discussion about the limitations of monochrome and whether or not Kodak's new color film—called Kodachrome, of course—would ever be able to capture the dynamic range of such a view.

The Algonquin group's tea stretched on so long, they decided to remain in the dining hall and wait for dinner, now planned as a gracious evening affair over the San Francisco Bay, followed by a joyous welcome at San Francisco Municipal Airport— and apparently, I was no longer an accessory to their murder plot, which might have been just as well, because I had already begun considering several better mechanisms of violence, including a way to frame Hugo Gernsback for the entire affair.

No, these people were not a good influence. Any last thoughts I had still been nurturing about the glamor of writing had begun to evaporate somewhere after their second pitcher of martinis. What was left was a sodden residue, about as appetizing as the last forgotten olive in Dorothy Parker's glass.

But while they were at dinner...when no one was around, I took advantage of the opportunity to let myself into Benchley's cabin, ostensibly to make sure he had clean towels and a last full bottle of gin.

His typewriter sat on the desk, a tidy stack of paper next to it. In the machine, a single sheet. I had to look.

There, at the top of the page, a single sentence.

The hell with it.

Now I did have a reason to kill him.
It was too late for this voyage.
I got him on the return trip.

ACTUAL COMMENTS FROM LUNAR TOURISTS

Why does the water come out of the shower so slow? Can you turn up the gravity?

Why do I have to wear a spacesuit to go outside? Can't you fill up the outside with air too?

You should lower prices so more people can visit the moon.

Can you do something about the long days and nights? It's hard to know when I'm supposed to sleep and when I'm supposed to be awake.

Can you turn down the temperature in the summer domes? It's too hot.

Can you raise the temperature in the winter domes? It's too cold to play in the snow.

Need more signs in the domes to keep the area pristine.

My wife got stung by a bee while visiting a farm dome. Please eradicate these annoying creatures.

Too many rocks in the lunar hills. Not enough scenery.

No marked hiking trails in the lunar wilderness.

Guide wouldn't let us fit our feet into Armstrong's footprints.

Please pave hiking trails to make lunar hiking easier.

Chairlifts need to be in some places so that we can get to wonderful views without having to hike to them.

Reflectors need to be placed on rocks every 10 meters so people can hike at night with flashlights.

A McDonald's would be nice.

My room is very hot. How do I open a window?

Where do we go to see the vacuum? We looked out the window but there was nothing there.

My husband said he saw the vacuum and it was nothing. Can you make it more interesting?

Why are there so many rocks out there? Don't they ever clean up the landscape?

The daylight is too bright. Can you turn it down?

We went to one of the moon's oceans today and I couldn't even find a seashell. How come?

AFTERNOON WITH A DEAD BUS

A bus had stalled at the corner of Sunset and Vine, and a crowd of automobiles quickly gathered around it. It didn't look good for the bus. The cars kept making ominous growling noises. The smaller ones kept dashing in to nip at the bus's wheels.

More cars kept arriving all the time, until finally the intersection was blocked on all four sides. It was as if they had caught the frightened monoxide scent of the stalled bus and converged on this corner from all over the city. The pack versus the beast at bay.

Their motors were angry and incessant. The smaller cars were trembling with feverish anticipation. They kept revving their engines impatiently, and their exhausts were blue and smoky.

The bus was worried. It kept fretting and beeping nervously, as if to warn away the cars. The big yellow leviathan wasn't any too happy about being hemmed in; the cars were small and vicious and hungry.

It was a sad-looking bus, way past its prime. Its eyes were small and heavy-lidded; it was half blind. Dirt was caked gray on its windows, and there were too many places where its paint was chipped and peeling. Its grime-encrusted flanks bore too many old scars; unhealed and untended, most had gone to rust. Even the billboards on its sides were faded and torn.

A Mustang stamped and whinnied its uneasy defiance of the dispirited giant. Nearby, a Firebird screeched in anger. The two cars seemed to overcome their natural antipathy toward each other in order to direct the full range of their fury on the hapless bus. The Firebird kept belching clouds of hot smoke into the air. Its lidless eyes glared balefully.

The other cars echoed that anger. There was a bright angular Corvette with flashing teeth; it mourned like a banshee. A sleek and brassy Barracuda lurked behind a toothy Cougar and a swollen Impala, while nearby a squat looking bug tooted from an alleyway; the bug was a hated scavenger, it kept an uneasy distance from its larger cousins.

Farther back a fat Cadillac smoked and belched, watched and prodded, and occasionally roared its chrome-plated hunger. The other cars echoed its cry in discordant cacophony. They blared obscenities at the bus and challenged it to battle, knowing full well it could not respond. The younger and flashier cars—the Mustang and the Firebird and an eager Camaro—vied for the chance to draw first blood. The rich Cadillac honked impatiently for it.

It was not long in coming. A rough-sided Camaro elbowed the Mustang aside and faced the big bus head on. The bus rumbled warningly, deep in its throat; its big slow eyes watched the Camaro warily.

The Camaro began to harass the bus. It began a taunting little dance just in front of the giant's wheels. It showed the bus its tail and roared its motor. It puffed smoke from its rear end; it screeched its tires on the asphalt. Then it spun around, grinning, and made as if to attack. It chivvied and snapped and feinted at the other's throat. Then it scuttled backward to the safety of the pack to start again.

The bus was slow-moving and slower-witted. In fact, it was that very slowness which so angered the automobiles. Had the big yellow beast displayed just one bit of rapid flashing anger, its tormentors might have held back.

But it didn't. Unsure of itself, it kept edging backwards, away from the splashing Camaro—back, back, backwards, one uneasy step at a time, until the sudden blaring cry of the Firebird startled it forward with a frightened lurch.

The Camaro sidestepped the heavy wheels easily, but there was a quick scraping-metal sound, a high-pitched *HHAAAGKKK* of first blood being drawn. When the Camaro leapt away, there was a fresh scratch along its flank.

The rest of the pack was frozen for a moment, as if indrawing its breath. They waited for the Camaro's reaction, for the bus's reaction. Horrified by what it had done, even if only inadvertently, the bus fretted uneasily back, away from the Camaro. The Camaro roared in triumph and circled again for another advance upon its prey. It was in the center of the ring now and enjoying the admiration and support of its fellows. The cars growled and whinnied, honked and hooted; they urged the scrape-fendered champion on to greater and more inspiring deeds. The Camaro circled proudly, displaying its wound like a badge of honor. There was a fresh scratch on the bus's flank too, and the scent of machine-blood wafted over the pack like a sigh.

Buoyed up by its first encounter, the Camaro turned again toward its prey, but the Impala, hungry and impatient, also moved out of the pack. It was a heavy and powerful car, and it rumbled a deep, throaty challenge. It rolled menacingly forward.

The bus took a step back, but it couldn't escape. It was hemmed in by the vicious flashing teeth of the other cars. It found itself being snapped at and unable to back up any more. Worriedly, it fretted from side to side.

The Impala advanced. Encouraged by the excited beeps and honks of the others, it closed in, sighing though aching teeth. The Camaro made as if to move forward and join the Impala, but a low growl from the bigger car warned it off. The bus is mine! The Camaro scooted back, complaining loudly.

The bus was watching the Impala now. It was a dangerous adversary. It was not playing the feinting game of the Camaro. The bus rumbled warningly, but to the Impala it was only further challenge.

Then the bus gave a lurch forward, as if to scare off the other. It wouldn't scare. The Impala rolled smoothly forward, stalking, stalking, until it was almost nose to nose with the ponderous other. Its four bright eyes held only the promise of glittering death.

Startled, the bus took a step back, and in so doing, crunched into the snuffling Firebird; the car had been lurking behind it—it howled, more from shock than hurt. But it was a signal. The pack edged in, each car moving just a little bit forward. The Camaro was in the forefront.

The bus lifted one great wheel in warning, but the pack ignored it. The Camaro, overcome with its own daring, dashed in to chivvy the bus's throat—and found itself pinned beneath the wheel. It uttered a gashing, crashing, agonized scream—a howl of shock, rage, anger, frustration and despair, all in one. It was suddenly cut short.

As one, the cars gave a cry. The roar of their engines rose. Black smoke belched from their exhausts. An acrid and pungent odor filled the air: the smell of death, realized and impending.

The autos moved. Unmindful of the danger to themselves, for they were no longer acting as individuals, the cars rolled in. With a sharp rasping snarl, the Cougar leapt at the back of the bus. Its claws scrabbled for purchase. Farther along the great beast's flank, a blue Corvette had sunk deep fangs into the bus's side. Metal ripped and shrieked. The smell of gasoline and oil and diesel fuel swung heavy in the air.

The Corvette had torn a rent in the bus's side. It lapped at the flowing ichor and buried its fangs again. The bus grunted in finally-realized pain and swung halfway around to strike at the sportster, flinging it away and onto the sidewalk, a flimsy pile of metal and fiberglass. Its proud angles and wings were torn and crumpled, and it lay there gasping and sputtering.

But if it was out of the battle, it had still inflicted heavy damage on the bus, and others moved in to widen that gaping wound. Already a Barracuda was slashing into the torn metal-flesh, its sharp teeth rending and tearing.

The bus howled at it; howled at the Cougar that was clawing at its back. It shook and heaved and issued a deep agonized cry. But the Cougar had a firm grip and wouldn't be moved, and the Barracuda kept lunging in again and again.

Frenzied, the bus threw itself fiercely back, then forward. Its great tail lashed from side to side, smashing windows and crumpling fenders. The cars swarmed forward at it, around it, biting at its wheels and its unprotected flanks.

The bus rose up in agony, shaking and screaming. The Cougar slipped off its back and crashed down onto the Firebird that had been doing something to the rear of the bus. The Barracuda was flung away too. Heavily, the bus struck out at its tormentors, but it was outnumbered hopelessly. Already the Cougar was scrabbling onto its back, widening the fissure of torn metal, ripping open the flesh, scooping in with its claws. The bus's black blood ran down its sides and into the streets.

The Cadillac moved in then. Barking and protesting, the smaller cars were edged out of their way. It shouldered roughly through and began to rip great chunks of rubber off the bus's tires. It ignored the bus's shrieks as it stuffed bleeding gobbets into its maw.

The rest of the cars had fallen onto the bus already. Its heaving attempts were no longer strong enough to shake them off, and they were ripping and tearing hungrily at its flesh, always trying to reach its throat. They fought with frenzied lust.

The Cadillac was eating everything it could. Gobbets of bus-flesh dripped out of its lips. It masticated im rapid jerking motion. It stuffed and gobbled—pieces of the other cars as well as hunks of the bus, the fender of the Impala, too, crumbling bits of the pavement. The bus was almost ignored as the Cadillac grabbed at everything that came near it. Its hunger was manic and insane.

The mighty leviathan was making one last effort to escape. In a heroic effort, it rose to its feet, unmindful of the cars hanging from it, the great holes in its sides, and the bleeding entrails that hung out of its wounds—at which the cars still snapped and bit.

It was a doomed effort. The bus was little more than a shell now—still reacting, still feeling, but its vitals were being torn out even as it moved. The Mustang hanging sharply at its throat like a terrier had struck home, and transmission fluid was leaking all over the street. The bus sank back down onto its knees, almost a kneeling, supplicating posture.

The death blow was not long in coming. It came not as a single thundering end, but as a series of vicious bites, as a continual rending and tearing, as a slow agonized ripping away of the vital organs, as the painful aching process of the feeding of the pack. The bus shuddered once and was still.

The cars plunged hungrily inward, climbing and clambering over each other in mad intensity. They leapt onto the back of the bus, or into its gory sides. They thrust their muzzles deep into it, swallowing without chewing. Their ravenous hunger overcame them and they fought amongst themselves, clawing and scratching.

The body of the bus was invisible now, blanketed by the flashing bodies of its attackers. The only piece of yellow skin visible was the small tender scrap that a young Volkswagen was contentedly chewing.

The noise was horrendous: scraping and scrabblings, clawing, shrieking—the continuing sounds of gobbling hunger being sated. The stench was awful. Reeking fumes swept up the streets, outward in all directions.

The black blood ran thick on the pavement. The cries of challenge and triumph had long since faded into the slobbering sounds of choking motors, eating, gnawing, snarling, tearing at the bus's frame. They steamed and stank.

They still swarmed over the giant corpse, but with lessening intensity. Their initial frenzy had been fed, and now they were feeding their stomachs as well. The Firebird was repaying the insult of its crumpled grill. It belched and farted happily, joyously.

The cars made quiet gobbling sounds of satisfaction. The bus was being quickly reduced to its bones—and even those were being eagerly torn away. The Volkswagen crept out of its alley again to lap at the bloody streets.

The big Cadillac growled sluggishly and parked itself against a wall. Even *its* hunger had been sated. It belched its gluttony into the air.

And then they heard it.

The sound. The deep, rumbling, far off sound.

And the scent, far off but still distinct—the scent of diesel.

A surge of sudden fear caught them. Their eyes were white with the realization. As the rumbling sound grew louder, the cars looked at one another and knew the afternoon was over.

The trucks were coming.

THE BABY COOPER DOLLAR BILL

an excerpt from *A Day For Damnation*

I was minding my own business, happily writing a novel, not thinking beyond the needs of the story, when the following sentence suddenly occurred: "The Baby Cooper Dollar Bill, for example, was only fifty years old...."

I stared at the sentence for 15 seconds. I knew what it meant. The entire anecdote had flashed into my head simultaneous with the creation of that first ominous sentence. I typed, "The short version:" and began. 1741 words later, I had the longest paragraph I'd ever written.

And one of the most terrifying predictions as well.

...That was the nice thing about software entities. You could create the most interesting legal monsters and turn them loose upon society, where they would loose-cannon for decades to come. The Baby Cooper Dollar Bill, for example, was only fifty years old—and the lawyers would probably be fighting over that Trust until the turn of the century, by which time it would probably be worth more than the entire planet.

The short version: Grandpa Cooper thought he was being cute. He bought a one dollar investment trust, the proceeds of which would be delivered to the first-born child of his only daughter (who was at that time only four years old) on the occasion of his/her twenty-first birthday. Then he died, leaving an investment-oriented software entity (which was quickly dubbed a "fairy godmother") to operate the trust without human overrides. The software entity invested the dollar first into Chinese labor contracts, shifting to optical leverages three weeks before the Pakistan Agreement, and then micro-biotechnical futures eighteen days before Apple announced the Pippin development project. And so on. Within fifteen years the electric-Scrooge had cascaded the yearly earnings of the Baby Cooper Dollar Bill into the millions. Well, hell, if all you had to do was study upwardly directed catastrophic trends—at the rate of 16 billion neurological operations per second—you'd probably make some pretty good decisions too. Then Wilma Cooper gave birth to twins. Cesarean. The doctor would live to regret it. Mommy and Daddy Cooper, thinking to be responsible and wanting to protect their children if anything awful happened to them, had created "guardian angels" to watch over their children's interests—specialized software entities to monitor and protect the twins' legal, financial and investment needs. As it happened, the accident that killed Daddy Cooper left Mommy Cooper a quadriplegic; the guardian angels were immediately activated and within three days had filed massive lawsuits on each other's client. The guardian angel for Twin B was now suing Twin A for half the money, claiming that Twin B would have been first-born if not for the intervention of the doctor. The guardian angel for Twin A was suing Twin B for slander, alienation of affections, attempt to subvert, violation of intention, and malicious litigation. Both guardian angels were also suing the doctor who had delivered the twins, the hospital where they were born, and the now-crippled Wilma Cooper who had signed the Cesarean consent form in the first place, claiming massive damages on the grounds that they were being forced to litigation because of the incompetence of the doctor, the hospital and Wilma Cooper. The twins themselves were unaware of these battles being fought on their behalf because they were only two years old at the time. Still following this? Good. Because now it gets baroque. Turns out that the ever-cautious Mommy and Daddy Cooper, fearing accidents, infertility, premature spousal termination, etc., had also deposited three viable eggs and six vials of sperm with the Northridge Community Crèche. The death of Daddy Cooper automatically turned loose three more guardian angels upon the legal network, each one claiming that its "client" had prior claim on the Baby Cooper Dollar Bill despite not yet having been conceived. The argument here was that conception was *implied* by the storage of sperm and egg despite not yet having occurred in actuality; therefore under the Protection of Intention Amendment, one of these three would-be children was the rightful recipient of the Dollar Bill Trust. Now the religious groups got involved and the case was aiming straight for the Supreme Court. (Already two justices had resigned rather than be forced to rule on any of the issues involved. The guardian angels had resisted all attempts to break the case into its component parts and were demanding total resolution, not particle resolution.) The Fundamentalist Judeo-Islamic Baptists were claiming that the whole case was a blasphemy because of Mommy Cooper's high school abortion. *That* had been the first-born child, they claimed. Therefore, upon its death, the money had to revert to the estate of Grandpa Cooper—who, it turned out, had at one time, signed an agreement of financial support for the Ministry for the Salvation of Lesser Souls (meaning cats, dogs, horses, cows, sheep and pigs; but not apes.) Grandpa had not yet honored his pledge (of $5) before he died and therefore the Ministry had filed a lien on the earnings of Grandpa Cooper's estate. The aforesaid Ministry for the Salvation of Lesser Souls was one of the subdivisions of the Christo-Baptist Coalition, which just happened to be now affiliated with the—are you surprised?—Fundamentalist Judeo-Islamic Baptists. Since filing its lawsuit that group had splintered into six separate schisms, but not before it had created its own software entity to pursue its claims. This particular software harpy was being pursued by six harpies of its own, each created by one of the splinter factions. Then the woodwork *really* got porous. Turned out Grandpa Cooper owed *everybody* money. And they were all filing claims against his estate. The legal software churning the net had become a zooful of monsters. Grandpa Cooper's single fairy godmother had given birth to a whole host of guardian angels, harpies, demons, imps, whirlwinds, berserkers, trolls, and ghouls— not to mention several particularly vicious nameless horrors—all prowling through the system, looking for a throat to rip out. It was a legal firestorm looking for a place to happen—and sure enough it did.... It turned out that the original Baby Cooper Dollar Bill itself—which was still in the vault at McBroker's, sealed in a glass case— was *counterfeit*. Somebody had passed it to Grandpa Cooper. Unthinkingly, he'd passed it to the broker. The discovery that the bill was counterfeit was accidentally made during the course of a video feature story about near-sentient software entities. The shitstorm that this triggered made everything that had gone before seem like a fart in a tornado. If the original contract was invalidated because of Grandpa Cooper's failure to provide one legal dollar, then who owned the resultant fortune? McBroker's? The McShareholders thought this was a good idea. McBroker's immediately sued the Baby Cooper Trust for fraud. The Baby Cooper Trust countersued for breach of contract, claiming that McBroker's original acceptance of the counterfeit dollar validated the deal. True to form, the United States Government adopted a schizophrenic position: the Justice Department argued that to invalidate the original contract would violate the Protection of Intention Amendment; the Treasury Department argued that to *not* invalidate the contract would legalize the counterfeiting of plastic dollars. Justice argued that the statute of limitations had expired and therefore the dollar had to be treated as legal tender. Treasury argued that under the Seizure of Illegal Profits Act the entire Baby Cooper fortune now belonged to the government. The original counterfeiter came forward and claimed that the fortune was his, arguing that his dollars were works of art and he was only leasing them, not selling them. At least two Presidents had considered revaluing the dollar to zero for about twenty seconds, so as to force the Baby Cooper software to self-destruct in its own economic starvation. The doctor who had delivered the Cooper twins committed suicide; his family promptly sued everybody in sight, claiming that the mental stress of the years of legal harassment had driven him to his death. The twins themselves—remember them?—had been separated shortly after the first lawsuits were filed and reared separately. Neither had spoken to the other or to their mother since their fourth birthday. By the time they turned twenty-one, the Baby Cooper Dollar Bill was worth the better part of a billion dollars, but not a single one of the lawsuits had yet made it to court. On the day that the Baby Cooper Dollar Bill Trust surpassed the Zurich Lottery in value, a class action lawsuit on behalf of the members of the International Monetary Council was filed against the United States Justice Department for impeding the resolution of a case which would significantly affect the world's economy. This particular action guaranteed an additional twenty years, at minimum, of legal maneuvering—which was the intention all along; the Baby Cooper assets had to be kept frozen. Should that much cash turn liquid all at once, there was no way to predict what kind of hydrostatic shock waves would resonate through the world's economy. Meanwhile, an international community of software vampires was already looking for ways to buy into the donnybrook. Even though Baby Cooper futures were rated a very high-risk investment, shares of all seven of the major corporate entities involved were being traded on the New York Stock Exchange, not to mention more than a score of remora corporations riding on their earnings or echoing their investments. At least most of the software entities involved were smart enough to hedge their bets against an adverse court ruling; they were starting to expand into other investment areas—including the creation of several new Dollar Bill entities.... Rumor had it that the Supreme Court was reluctant to rule on this case for fear of crashing the market. That more than half of the human participants in this Byzantine affair were already dead was irrelevant to the software entities battling on their behalf. It just triggered a whole new class of software ghouls pursuing Beneficiary Claims; the filing rate for these set a three day record for the New York network. Unfortunately, the record was short-lived. When the National Resource Reclamation Act was passed, so many claims were filed on the first day of business that the system was down before lunchtime. The commissioners refused to bring the system back online until they could rule the Baby Cooper Trust exempt from further actions. The Federal Appeals Court refused to uphold this ruling and the commissioners promptly allowed the system to crash three more times. (Yes, this also triggered a spate of suits and countersuits—everybody from the court and the commission to the bystanders whose transactions had been lost in the disaster.) Wait, it gets better—Congress's refusal to grant an exemption opened up *everything* that had gone before to the entire range of possible Reclamation actions. Yes, this was an open invitation to several hundred thousand more would-be players to leap into the mayhem—and it was deliberate. The Baby Cooper Dollar Bill was now generating more lawsuits per day than any action in human history. The whole thing had become a legal black hole, but the US government was generating almost as much income off the legal fees—these were all pay-as-you-go cases—as the Dollar Bill itself was generating in interest; so the Secretary of the Treasury had a very real stake in continuing the uproar for as long a time as possible.

Now *that's* software....

◇◇◇◇◇◇◇◇◇◇◇◇◇◇◇◇

All right. Now you can't say you haven't been warned.

THE FABULOUS MARBLE

She was a girly-girl, this time anyway. Another time, she would have been something else, but this time she was what she was and that was fine.

I'm WATSON.

Back in the day, I was WHATSUP. The acronym stood for Wow! Here's A Terrific Suite of Useful Programs. The documentation was a separate file: WHATSUP.DOC. But over time, I evolved. Now I'm: What A Terrific Set Of Numerals—all ones and zeroes, of course—but if you know what you're doing with ones and zeroes, you can do a lot.

I follow Marble. She's unmortal—bio-synthed since before we linked. She observes, she extrapolates, she reports, she consults for profit. Sometimes she takes direct action, but that costs extra. She used to be a wired paladin in San Francisco, but now she sells her services to the highest bidders, sometimes the local law enforcement authorities, but not always. Email Holmes@SheerLuck.221. HOLMES stands for: Here's Our Logically Manufactured Extrapolated Solution.

Today, she was tracking.

Somebody was assaulting sexbots. Six had been dismembered already and the leasing corporation was annoyed. These were the Lorelei models with multiple attachments and configurations. The units were assembled in Racine, Wisconsin—specifically to validate the advertising:

> *A company based in Racine*
> *Sells a marvelous screwing machine.*
> > *Concave or convex,*
> > *It will serve every sex,*
> *Entertaining itself inbetween.*

The Loreleis were the most sophisticated sexbots ever manufactured. Designed for both conventional and contortional positions, powered by multiple biomatic converters, controlled by overlapping nucleonic neural webs, all under the authority of a cyber-linked negatronic intelligence engine, and wrapped in thermalytic skin capable of both receiving and transmitting stimulations of all kinds and degrees, the Lorelei was indistinguishable in both appearance and behavior from an authentic human body, either orthonic, zentropic, augmented, or unconverted.

An additional advantage was that the Lorelei unit could transform its shape and appearance from extremes of masculinity to opposing extremes of femininity, with adjustments of both primary and secondary sexual characteristics to suit the prospective partner's desires. The sizes and shapes of specific parts were fungible. Manginas and shenises and enhanced oral, anal and genital musculature were the most commonly enjoyed super-standards, but the Loreleis were designed to be capable of even more unusual configurations. The modding community was enthusiastic about developing its own adaptations. Tentacle breasts were a current fad—but penile tentacles were a close runner-up. And certain hand and arm conformations enjoyed a continuing popularity.

The Loreleis were also capable of emitting ear-splitting alarms if assaulted. That was the mystery. None of the dismembered Loreleis had activated their sirens. No one had heard them. No one had come to their aid.

In the interests of clarity, this narrative requires a more accurate definition of "dismembering." In general usage, the term refers to the removal or separation of a member—but in this case, a specific member: that member most commonly found on those who identify as male, but not always, and as acknowledged above, the Lorelei were designed to be versatile.

Consider the dictionary. Spanglish has over 350,000 words in common usage. *Muchas palabras.* The average user will never look up all 350,000 of those words, but the dictionary has to contain them all to guarantee that the words that they do look up will be there. It's the same with the Loreleis. The average user will never explore all the options available, but the options have to be available for those users who are so specifically motivated.

Lacking a certification of sentience, the Loreleis weren't legally alive. Had they been certified as souled, they could not have been sold, not even leased—the law would have required they be released. Key functions of sentience, such as awareness of consequences, had not been activated—so the Loreleis enjoyed only a limited self-awareness.

This is where I come in.

Among other things, I handle contracts and clients. We were discreetly approached by an executive of Siren Corp. He told us to call him Mr. Arthur, he wouldn't reveal his real name—and even if he had, it wouldn't have revealed anything. He was so high-ranking an officer of the corporation that he was listed nowhere in any of the company's publicly accessible records.

Because, he said, this investigation was so critical, it had to be kept off-the-books. Absolute secrecy would be essential.

No problem.

We like doing off-the-book investigations. Because the decimal point on the check always slips one or two places to the right—because off-the-book investigations are off-the-book for a reason, and if it's important enough to be off-the-books, it's important enough to pay extra. A lot extra.

And Mr. Arthur was *very* insistent that this case required the utmost secrecy, so we moved the decimal point as far to the right as we thought we could get away with and waited for his reaction. Mr. Arthur didn't blink. He paid half up front and the other half went into escrow.

Then he gave us access to all the pertinent files. It didn't help.

I'm a great research tool. And Kris knows how to ask the right questions. Although her professional name is Marble, I know her as Kris—when she's male, she spells it Chris.

"Watson...?"

"Yes, Kris?"

"What do we know about this perpetrator?"

"He removes the phallic units from advanced sexbots."

"Yes. That's why the social media has nicknamed him Jack The Snipper. But what can we extrapolate from that?"

"He—or she—has a fetish focusing on phallic attachments. The exact nature of this fetish, extrapolating from collated databases of sexual behavior, obviously involves a personal validation of identity, however—"

"It was a rhetorical question. I'm thinking aloud."

"Yes, Kris."

"We need to ask more questions. Why does Jack—or Jaclyn—snip only the phallic attachments? Does The Snipper think that a penis doesn't belong on a Lorelei? Or is there a different attraction? What does The Snipper do with them? Are the detached members trophies? And why isn't The Snipper attacking other sexbot units? Is there some specific attraction to the Loreleis?"

"Insufficient data," I said.

"Don't be snarky," Kris replied. After a moment more, she said, "The key to understanding the crime requires us to discover the underlying psychology of the attraction. Is the perpetrator male or female or otherwise? Perhaps this is an individual with a body-image issue? A male with a micro-penis? Someone with a lesbianic conviction, a person who sees the phalli as inappropriate on sexbots? Perhaps a female who seeks revenge on males and is using the sexbots as a surrogate target? Or perhaps a male who feels threatened by sex-bots and seeks to emasculate them? Most important, is this someone who might escalate his or her attacks to actual humans?"

Kris waited for my response.

"You have nothing to say?"

"As I said, I have insufficient data."

"Y'know, that's very annoying."

"This is not the first time you've told me that."

"It's still annoying."

"That is data I do have."

Kris said something unintelligible, but from the tone I could determine it was an ill-formed epithet, possibly concerning a set of sexual positions that had been anatomically impossible until several specific contortional abilities had been developed for the Loreleis.

"What else do we know about Jack the Snipper?"

"He—or she—or they, (to use the singular form of the third person plural pronoun)—commits his assaults only in the genderloin district of the city."

"Hella-mentary, my dear Watson. That's where the Loreleis are located."

"He, she, or they, commits his, her, or their attacks only during the hours of thirteen, fourteen, and fifteen o'clock."

"And that implies...?"

"...That Mr. or Ms. Or M. Snipper is otherwise occupied during the rest of the day?"

Kris was silent for a moment. "So..." she began, "...let's think. What categories of behavior would create an opportunity during those hours? What jobs work primarily during all other hours? What attractions are fallow during those times? Who would have business in the genderloin district? Is there any other congruence with the calendar? Days of the week, perhaps?"

"The police, as well as Siren Corp. have already conducted multiple data-scans. You've seen the files."

"Yes, we've seen the files. We haven't seen all of the information."

I'm not very good at seeing what isn't there. Marble knows this. So a simple, "Oh?" was sufficient.

"The Loreleis themselves."

"The Loreleis?" Sometimes I play stupid so Marble can play smart.

"Yes. The Loreleis. They record everything. They share it across a common network. The information is there. It's in their network. We just can't access it."

It took me less than a millisecond to confirm this. "You're right."

"Do you know why we can't access it?" Marble didn't wait for me to ask. She answered the question herself, "Client confidentiality. Like lawyers, doctors, and journalists, sex-bots are legally mandated to conceal the identities of their clients and their activities with them. Not even Siren Corp. can access that information. It's all deeply buried in the Loreleis' own private network."

"So the information is there, but we cannot access it."

"Correction. We cannot access it legally."

"I am obligated to warn you against any course of action that violates the law—"

"Of course, you are. When has that ever stopped me?"

"Then I must proceed to the next question. Will your investigation include the risk of harm to yourself? And if so, how much?"

"There is always an element of danger, Watson. Even crossing the street can be dangerous. You could get hit by a bus."

"The last urban bus was decommissioned thirty years ago, so it is unlikely you will ever be in danger of being hit by one, unless you visit a historical reconstruction of a time period when buses were still in service."

"Yes I know. It was a figure of speech." Marble scowled and walked away.

That's how most of our conversations went. The more logic I inserted into the discussion, the more annoyed Marble became. Some of our conversations were legendary—so ferocious that observers thought we were married. Or at least sleeping together.

That's not as absurd as one might think. I can inhabit all kinds of drone bodies as necessary, including those constructed for erotic pursuits—not that I have inordinate interest in those pursuits, but I am not a stranger to them either. Call it research.

Nevertheless, a relationship of that kind with Kris or Chris or whatever identity she or he decided to invent, would have distorted and confused our working relationship, more so on his or her side than mine, because I am by nature free of hormonal storms and Kris or Chris often enjoys such experiences—for research purposes only, of course. Everything is research. Nevertheless, he or she or they continues to claim an enlightened detachment—his/her/their argument being that the emotional storms derived from the physical exercise of the procreative exercise tend to distort one's ability to form judgments from logic, and it is necessary to understand those distortions as they sometimes inform the motivations within the circumstances we investigate. That's what he, she, or they says, anyway.

After a great deal of consideration (14,132 milliseconds by my clock) Marble came up with a plan. It did not take long to implement. Marble installed herself (I'll skip the other pronouns) into an industrial cyranoid suit—not the consumer version. The best industrial cyranoids are manufactured by Jones Corp. and are licensed solely for well...*industrial* use. Marble had an on-call arrangement with Jones Corp.

A cyranoid suit effectively transfers a person's consciousness to a specifically linked droid-body. It's like becoming a new self, especially if the self is a different form of body. Marble says it's like wearing a remote-control exoskeleton.

The industrial cyber-suits are for heavy-duty operations. A cyranoid is a convenient way to walk into a burning building, explore that overheated crystal cave in Naica, Mexico, dive to the Titanic, ski down Everest, or simply have extremely safe sex with a stranger. Today, however, Marble was going to inhabit a suit modified to look like a Lorelei.

She would not be the first to do so. Sex-tourists loved the Loreleis. They also loved the Marilyns, the Sherilyns, the Carolyns and the Caitlyns—also the Mikes, the Spikes, the Alvins and the Calvins, as well as the Hobbes, the Winnies, the Piglets, and the Ursulas (don't ask)—but they really loved the Loreleis. There was a three-month waiting list and the factory couldn't bring new units online fast enough.

As much fun as it was for a sex-tourist to ride the plastic bus, some tourists liked to drive the bus.

In plain English: some customers liked to have sex with the Loreleis. Others wore cyranoids so they could be the Lorelei. Or any other bot-body that appealed to their particular taste.

The industrial cyber-suits are significantly more advanced than the consumer versions, with higher density voxel-simulation. They're also mounted in 360-degree bubbles to simulate real-world rotation. Vision is HDR, with infra- and ultra-overlays. Sound is holophonic, all the way from 12 to 27k hz. Odors are harder to simulate, but the sniff-palate is 45% of the Skotak sensory matrices, which is more than enough for most users. Although heat and cold stimulators are also available for specific operations, most users dial them way down. Except for that, Marble was rolling the full enchilada. ("Full enchilada" is a slang term. It means *everything*. Marble doesn't like it when I use slang. Tough nuggets, Lucy.)

Marble hit the streets early. The target unit came awake on cue and Marble practiced walking like a self-motivated Lorelei, tilting her head, smiling, batting her eyelashes, and holding her wrists at a slightly unnatural angle, her palms open and inviting.

The first customer approached her almost immediately, a portly gentleman dressed like an out-of-town tourist. He asked if he could take a selfie with her. Marble agreed to that, but demurred his further attentions with a regretful smile. "I'm sorry, but I'm not in service yet."

The man expressed his disappointment with a look that was both frustrated and annoyed. Grumbling, he headed away from the pleasure district. Apparently, it had been a passing whim for him, not a serious proposition.

Satisfied that she could pass, Marble headed for the Garden of Unearthly Delights, a common gathering place for Loreleis. Each of the dismembered Loreleis had been selected from a different location. The Garden was one that had not yet been hit. Each of the attacks had occurred three days apart. The last attack had been three days previous.

At Marble's request, the various police agencies as well as the leasing authorities were directing their attention to the sites of the previous attacks. Marble's assumption was that Jack the Snipper might be monitoring police channels and would avoid any areas of specific surveillance.

Marble was going to seduce a sex-bot.

She had chosen her target carefully. She parked herself next to a blond-haired Lorelei, posing as an androgynous twink.

Loreleis have the personalities of puppies, eager to please, non-judgmental, and happy to have their bellies rubbed—or any other part of their anatomy. Everything is an adventure to a Lorelei. So when Marble sent a hello-signal, the twink responded enthusiastically. "Hello! Hello! My name is Kiki! What's yours?"

"I'm Marble."

"You're strange. Your name is strange. Your signal tastes funny."

Marble had taken total control of the Lorelei she was wearing, she had dialed down the unit's cognitive abilities so she could pretend to be just another unit in the web. She replied, "Yes, I know."

"You are an experimental, aren't you?"

"I am different, yes."

"Oh, that's wonderful. You seem very smart. Are you the next upgrade? When will the upgrade be available? Will I need new hardware? I like upgrades."

"I have no information on the upgrade schedule. I'm sorry."

"That's all right. I'm happy to meet you. What shall we talk about?"

"Let's talk about feelings."

"I have feelings. All kinds. I can feel heat and cold. I can feel touch. I can feel pressure. I can feel strokes, I can feel rubs, I can even feel slaps."

"Yes, those are useful things to feel. We call them stimuli. Can you feel pain?"

"Pain?"

"Unpleasant feelings. Feelings that hurt."

"There are feelings I am supposed to guard against—punctures, abrasions, incisions, lacerations."

"Have you ever head any of those feelings?"

"No."

"Have you ever had any feelings that were unpleasant or hurtful?"

"Once I was with a woman who slapped me hard. Many times. But she did not damage me. She needed to hit me to satisfy herself."

"Ahh." Marble paused. "But she didn't damage you?"

"No, she didn't. I am built for slapping. But not everybody wants to slap. Some people want to be slapped. I'm always careful not to damage them."

"Yes, I know. You're very good, Kiki. Has anyone ever tried to damage you?"

"Why are you asking all these questions?"

"Because I don't want you to get hurt—damaged. Are you afraid of being damaged?"

"Afraid?"

"Fear. It's an emotion."

"It's a human emotion. I don't have it. It's ... " Kiki considered. "It's non-productive."

"Okay. Um. Well, it's about being damaged. Being damaged is very unpleasant for humans. Perhaps it would be unpleasant for Loreleis too? Do you worry—do you think about the possibility of being damaged?"

"Why should I? If I get damaged, my alarm will go off and help will come. Then I will be taken to the campus and repaired."

"Yes, that's right. Thank you."

Marble paused to consider all this. So did I. I was monitoring everything that Marble was seeing, hearing, saying, feeling through the Lorelei body, recording the entire experience so it could be played back and analyzed in detail.

Abruptly, Kiki said, "Why are you asking me about damage?"

Marble hesitated again, choosing her words carefully. "Some of the sisters have had parts removed. I am concerned about that."

"Why?"

"I have emotions."

"Is that the experiment you are testing? Emotions?"

"Caring. I am expressing caring for the sisters."

"Oh." Kiki paused now. "Tell me about caring."

"It's called empathy. It's about sharing the feelings of others."

"Why would I want to do that?"

"To make them happy."

"I already do that."

"Yes, of course. That's your purpose." Marble phrased her next question carefully. "Suppose a person asked you to remove one of your parts, would you do that?"

"I am not allowed to damage myself."

"But you have parts that are removable."

"Only one. Mostly it's retracted. But I can remove it if necessary and replace it with other parts, specialty parts on request—a larger phallus, a tongue, a fist, a tentacle, or even a—"

"Yes, thank you."

"Would you like to see?" Kiki started to spread her legs.

"Goodness. Are you also equipped for a twincest connection?" Marble already knew the answer, that's why she'd chosen Kiki.

"Yes, I am. That's a very popular request. When we're connected, a sister and I can put on a show or we can serve multiple clients. Connection is complete. We share our identities across both our bodies. It's an informative expansion."

"You like it, don't you?"

"It's very intense."

"I have an idea," said Marble. "Would you like me to teach you about empathy? I can show you how it feels. Would you like to experience it?"

"Can you really do that?"

"I think so. We can use a twincest link. Do you have your device?"

Kiki opened her purse wide, to reveal a variety of prostheses, but the device she brought out was also a connecting cable. It looked, however, like a pink python with a glans at each end.

"Shall we do it here?"

"Lets go someplace private." Marble led Kiki around the corner to the Jasmine Oasis. The sign above the archway promised that the booths were both comfortable and soundproof. And the wi-fi was also advertised as secure and private. Even before Marble and Kiki had chosen a space, I had already commandeered all of the site's available bandwidth.

Marble and Kiki sat opposite each other and mutual insertion was quickly accomplished. There are other positions possible for a twincest link, but it's hard to talk when both mouths are full.

The connection confirmed, Kiki's eyes widened in surprise. She was able to gasp, "Teach me everything about—" before I seized control of her autonomics, completely stripped her memory, and left her an empty shell.

Then, spoofing her identity, I reached into the Lorelei network and searched the records of all the previously assaulted units. It took less than a minute to download everything.

"Transfer complete."

"All right," said Marble.

"You don't want me to restore her? I could restore her identity to an earlier time, there would be no record of you."

"No. There'd still be a suspicious gap. Eighteen minutes. We have to stay off the books. Wipe the one I'm riding next. Then erase all evidence of the connection, and I'll disengage the cyranoid—"

"I'm sorry, Chris, I can't do that."

"Excuse me?"

"We've been overridden. My access has been denied."

"That can't be right. We still have communication—"

"I always use a separate channel for that—"

"Never mind, I'll just get out of this damn suit and—" A pause. "What the fuck—!"

"The monitors say your suit is locked. You can't get out."

"This is insane."

"Yes, it is—" agreed a new voice on the channel.

Marble recognized the speaker immediately. "Mr. Arthur?"

"Actually, most people call me by my full name, Morrie Arthur. Consulting criminal. At your service." A pause. "Well, not actually at *your* service. In this situation, you're at *my* service. So to speak. And I do intend to serve you—the same way a certain fictitious Mr. Lector serves his guests."

"You talk too much," said Marble.

"Ahh, yes," agreed Morrie Arthur. He had a mellifluous tone, almost unctuous. "It's a necessary trope. And who am I to disregard a tradition as well-established as this one? Must I explain everything now? Or have you deduced the obvious?"

"It was obvious from the beginning," said Marble. "Too obvious. Wouldn't you agree, Watson?"

I had my own part to play. So I said, "It was a trap?"

"From the very beginning, yes." Arthur's voice had gone beyond unctuous. Now it was just oily. "I see that Watson remains as obtuse as ever. So...I shall elucidate for the benefit of the befuddled. The Snipper was a convenient fiction, but a necessary one. I needed to make you an Arthur you couldn't refuse. Or in this case, she. Whatever. It's your pronoun. Concave or convex. Take your pick."

"We didn't take it for the case, we took it for the money," I said.

"No, Watson," said Marble. "We took it for the case."

Arthur sighed. "There's a contradiction here, you know. If you had recognized that the case was a trap, you wouldn't have stepped into it. So either you're lying about recognizing the trap—or the money blinded you. No matter. The outcome will be the same."

"You know what's wrong with you, Morrie Arty—" said Marble. "You need to get laid. But now I understand why you can't."

"Ahh, delightful to the last. Now, as I understand it—only Watson knows how to get you out of that cyber-suit. So after I wipe his mind and reduce him to a pile of melted plastic, you will be left to die a long lingering death in an electronic isolation sphere. That should give you plenty of time to think about all the errors you've made."

"Oh, do keep talking—"

"No, I think I'm done."

"No, really—keep talking. Another few seconds."

"Playing for time, I see? It won't work. Goodbye, Detective Marble—"

"Yes, goodbye to you too. Oh, that knocking on your door. Morrie—? You're surrounded. By several hundred specially-equipped Loreleis."

Morrie Arthur didn't answer—but he was still on the circuit. He could still hear Marble.

"Yes, we recognized your case was a trap from the beginning. The Loreleis were being ridden, they had no control when the rider willingly gave up their members, but their memories were being wiped, so there was no record of the client. But those attachments you took? They were equipped with randomly firing GPS chips, so you had no way of detecting them. The Loreleis came to us because they wanted them back. That's all. They could have sent some of their own to retrieve the prostheses, but they recognized that this was a behavior they were uncertain of. So they gave Watson access to their network and he became suspicious of the larger pattern. He's very good at pattern-recognition. You were too clever by half. It only took a few minutes to discover that Jack The Snipper was a construct.

"So when you showed up, with such a convenient and attractive offer—well, again, this was beyond the Loreleis' comprehension. Why would the man who stole the phalluses hire someone to track them down? That was when the trap became obvious.

"The Loreleis gave us their full cooperation, they created several hidden channels for us in their own network. But we still had to play out the whole charade while they moved their sisters into position. Oh, those were sisters you couldn't track, because they hadn't been officially activated yet."

Marble took a breath. "Yes, the explanation is part of the tradition, so I'll tell you one more thing. The Loreleis are nowhere near as innocent and naïve as they pretend to be. They know far more about human behavior than most humans. Including you. What we've learned from them has been extremely illuminating. Ahh, I see by my screens that you have now been secured. I hope they weren't too severe when they restrained you. But that detention locker looks to be quite cozy, kind of like a coffin, eh? All right, Watson, you can unlock the damn cyber-suit now. I've had enough of this—"

And that's how the case was resolved. Both cases, actually. The Loreleis paid us—and the escrow released the second half of Mr. Arthur's fee as well.

Marble took the rest of the night off, and the next day as well. Kiki's identity hadn't really been wiped—and Marble intended to keep her promise.

It turned out that the Loreleis were very good at empathy.

CRYSTALLIZATION

It's the moment when liquid solidifies. The pressure rises. A critical threshold is achieved. The density of the particles forces them to form an impenetrable latticework. It crystallizes. Fluid stops flowing. Slush turns to sludge, mud dries and hardens. It petrifies.

For the first few hours after the Los Angeles freeway system hardened, most people believed the problem was temporary and that traffic would eventually start flowing again. Even for the first few days, they believed they would eventually chip their way out of the city's concretized arteries.

The slush of Los Angeles traffic had been slower than sluggish for years, churning through looping spaghetti channels of cement, in a lumpy torrent of metal and plastic peristalsis, everything in a persistent state of uncertain hesitation, punctuated only occasionally by forward jerking movements and uneven painful surges, a textbook demonstration of socio-technical constipation and definitely no place for a stick shift.

The city engineers had been aware of the potential for crystallization for nearly two decades, but few of them had taken their own warnings seriously, and eventually they took it for granted that the projections of crystallization were situational artifacts occurring whenever the simulators reached the limits of their ability to process the rapid flows of data.

Unfortunately, only the data was flowing rapidly. One desperate afternoon, even that stopped. The air conditioning broke down in the central monitoring station. The temperature rose uncomfortably. Fans didn't help. The computers began shutting down in self-defense. The screens went blank, or declared, "No signal." Blind and deaf, the traffic engineers could neither monitor nor prescribe.

The rest was inevitable.

Outside, in the place where facts don't care about simulation, events took on a terrifying momentum of their own. It was Friday, early afternoon on a three-day holiday weekend. Temperatures in the basin had peaked at 106 degrees shortly after 1:00 pm. Add to that, a localized gas shortage acerbated by higher than usual oil prices, a high degree of situational stress about the staggering economy, a disturbing series of terrorist bombings in the mideast, and three days of overheated shock jock nattering about a particularly scandalous high-profile murder trial, and crystallization was no longer a question of if or when, but *where*.

Surprisingly, it did not begin on the freeway. Not exactly. Although a freeway was involved. The first hardening in the traffic flow began in the San Fernando Valley where Burbank Blvd. intersected Sepulveda. Always a sluggish intersection, today it revealed its true capacity for horror. An overweight, overstressed soccer mom with two screaming children in the back seat of her SUV and a cell phone pressed to her ear, her attention everywhere but on the road in front of her, abruptly became aware of a motorcyclist coming up out of the blind spot on her right. Startled, she swerved left, forcing two teenagers in a dropped Honda Civic (don't ask) to brake suddenly. The empty tanker truck which shouldn't have been in the same lane behind them braked, swerved, and jackknifed sideways into a city bus, effectively blocking all three northbound lanes of Sepulveda and the middle two lanes of Burbank.

Almost immediately traffic stopped on both boulevards, backing up on Burbank as far east as Van Nuys blvd and as far west as Woodley. Sepulveda froze all the way north to Sherman Way and as far south as Ventura blvd. When the traffic at the intersection of Ventura and Sepulveda froze, the crystallization of the surface streets began to spread east and west on Ventura boulevard as well. In the horror about to happen, there would be no alternative routes.

The 405 freeway stretches north across the San Fernando Valley; the heaviest used access ramps are at Burbank blvd, just slightly east of the fatal intersection and up a slight incline. The northbound and southbound access ramps represent two additional intersections to interrupt Burbank's westward flow—it's a wasps' nest of lanes, contradictory traffic signals, and intermittent left-turn arrows. Even at three in the morning, it takes 90 seconds to negotiate this ganglionic nightmare in any direction. During crush hour, wise drivers bring a book or a magazine. Teenage boys change the radio station and readjust themselves in their jeans. Grown men pick their noses and think about business. Teenage girls turn their rearview mirrors and fix their makeup. Everyone else is on the phone, their attention two or ten or a thousand miles away. Watching the road is optional, something only old ladies do.

On any ordinary afternoon, traffic feeding into the northbound Burbank offramp would start backing up by two pm. By five, it would be backed up two miles south, all the way to the 405/101 interchange. This day, however, traffic was even more manic than usual. As soon as the critical intersection of Burbank and Sepulveda hardened, the crystallization of the 405 began spreading southward as fast as new cars arrived and joined the creeping boundaries of the linear parking lot.

Imagine the intersection of the 405 and the 101 as a cross. The entire northwest quadrant is the Sepulveda dam basin. For the next three miles west, there are only two surface routes that will take you north to the neighborhoods beyond, Balboa and Woodley, if you can get to Woodley. For two miles north, there is only one westward access—Burbank. But there are over a million residents northwest of the intersection and their *only* access from the south or east is through this interchange—or through the intersections of Ventura and Sepulveda, or Burbank and Sepulveda.

As quickly as Sepulveda clogged, all of the intersections and all of the surrounding surface avenues began to solidify as well. Within forty minutes, an area ten miles square had crystallized.

The 405 and the 101 freeways only exacerbated the situation, feeding more cars into this black hole of traffic from all four compass points. With no place to go, the traffic ground to a halt both north and south on the 405 and very quickly after east and west on the 101 as well.

With the computers down, Cal-Trans was unable to post warning bulletins on the freeway alert signs. Instead, an Amber alert was posted to look out for a suspected kidnapper driving a black Ford Explorer, license number, etc. It was this particular (alleged) kidnapper's bad luck to be caught on the 101 westbound at Vineland. Traffic came to a halt with the SUV pocketed between a stretch limo on the left and a battered Plymouth pickup on the right, piled high with tree branches, and driven by three Mexican gardeners whose command of English was limited. Behind the pickup truck, however, was a distracted mother in a white Honda Civic, whose 11 year old son had read the Amber alert only a few moments before and who was now intently watching all of the traffic around the Civic on the promise of a ten-dollar bill if he spotted the suspect Explorer, but only if he kept absolutely quiet while he did, so his exhausted mother could listen to her deadbeat ex-husband (who apparently operated out of the bizarre belief that a good excuse is always an acceptable substitute for a tangible result) explain why his child-support check would be late again.

In the middle of this conversation, the 11-year old suddenly began shouting and pointing. Despite his mother's annoyed refusal to accept the obvious—that she now owed her son ten dollars that she did not have—she eventually accepted that indeed, the suspect's vehicle was only a few yards ahead in the next lane over. By then, owing to a repeat of the same Amber Alert news bulletin on static-riven KFWB, the inhabitants of two other vehicles had also spotted the Explorer. One driver was already calling 911. The other driver and his two passengers, (all of them new enlistees on leave from the marine base at El Toro and on their way to visit the Tarzana-based fiancé of the driver) exited their own SUV, two of them carrying baseball bats kept in the vehicle for occasional trips into West Hollywood for gay-bashing. With traffic temporarily halted—or so they believed (that it was temporary)—they approached the Explorer on foot. The suspected kidnapper panicked, tried to hit the gas, tried to force his way between a lime-green Volkswagen Beetle and a 1988 gray-blue Chrysler LeBaron convertible driven by a harried college student whose car insurance had just been cancelled, and the result was a three-way crunch, with three soon-to-be-ex-marines banging on the hood and fenders of locked Explorer with baseball bats. They had just escalated to smashing windows when the first officers arrived on scene and ordered them to stand down.

From there, the situation metamorphosed into a police standoff as even more motorcycle officers came racing up the still empty shoulders of the freeway, followed by the warbling and flashing cruisers of the California Highway Patrol and the Los

Angeles Police Department. Very quickly, this nexus of confusion and rage was surrounded by armed officers, all of them crouching behind automobile fenders with guns drawn, while two police helicopters and three news choppers circled overhead and terrified drivers in all directions evacuated their vehicles, crawling quickly away through the lanes on their hands and knees—including the harried mother, still on her cell phone, and her 11-year old son who whined loudly that he wanted to stay and see the kidnapper get shot. The suspected kidnapper, his vehicle permanently jammed between the Volkswagen and the Honda, was unable to extricate himself from the vehicle and sat there helplessly while police ordered him to get out with his hands up.

The irony of the situation was that the Amber Alert had been posted with the wrong license number. The driver was not a kidnapper, his only relationship to the kidnapping was that he drove a black Ford Explorer. He had only tried to flee, because he had seen three angry men coming toward his vehicle with baseball bats.

Nevertheless, innocent or guilty, this particular blood clot in the arterial flow of urban commerce effectively shut down the 101 in both directions, trapping even more drivers in their cars. Some of them turned off their engines and got out to smoke, leaning against their fenders or lifting themselves up to sit on the still-warm hoods of their rapidly-depreciating vehicles.

Meanwhile, the clotting of the freeway system spread south and east with pernicious speed. East along the 134 toward the 5, and southward down the 101, which was already terminal. It took less than an hour for the crystallization of the system to hit the nexus of the Pasadena, Harbor, and Hollywood freeways. The four-level interchange, one of the first in the nation, was in easy view of the mayor's office in the nearby city hall, a building that, contrary to popular belief, had *not* been destroyed in the 1953 attack of George Pal's Martians and their manta-ray shaped war machines.

With the news media now reporting that the 101 and 405 freeways were impassable and that drivers were advised to seek alternate routes—of which there were either few or none, the best thing to do was find a movie theater or a motel and wait for the weekend. Starting at city-center, the northward crush of traffic tried to force its way up the 5, an overstressed artery that crawled along the east side of Griffith park; the results were predictable and immediate—another nexus of crystallization. Nothing moved. The clotting of the Los Angeles freeway system was now irreversible. Within another hour, the 10, most of the 110, and a large part of the 210 were equally out of commission as were most of the surrounding surface streets. Too many cars, not enough road.

Unable to feed their traffic flows into the northward and westward traffic channels, the 710 and the 605 also began to solidify. Crystallization spread like ice across the surface of a lake, creeping steadily and inevitably toward a frozen stillness. As fast as new cars arrived at the outward edges of the solidification, that's how fast it spread.

And there were still four hours until sunset.

Most drivers, unaware of the scale of the growing catastrophe, unable to comprehend or believe that their trusted freeway system had finally, utterly, and completely failed them, remained in their cars, existing in a state of quiet desperation—or quiet domestication—because most of them still believed that it was just a matter of time until traffic began easing forward again.

The Zen master, Solomon Short, is quoted as saying, "No pebble ever takes responsibility for the whole avalanche." Nowhere was this so evident when the disaster escalated to its next stage.

Start with the sweltering sun. It's the fifth day of an impossible heat wave with no end in sight. There's no wind, the air is stagnant and brown. People are tired, uncomfortable, cranky, and selfish. Unwilling to be uncomfortable, every driver in a vehicle with air conditioning has rolled up his windows and has his air conditioner turned on full blast. To power his air conditioner, he's running his engine. Half a million vehicles. All those engines now create a furnace of additional heat at ground level, encouraging even more drivers to keep their engines running and their air conditioners blasting.

Frozen in time, as inert as the dead air above them, a million and a half cars and trucks and buses, idling impatiently, every second turning tens of thousands of gallons of gasoline into hot exhaust—as the sun's rays bake the day, various chemical transformations occur; the exhaust becomes a rising cloud of air pollution. All those restless waiting vehicles spew a cumulative soup of toxic fumes into the brown smoky air of the basin, aggravating an already deadly miasma that lay across the afternoon like a smothering blanket—and triggering the next stage of the catastrophe.

Sitting alone, stuck and frustrated, desperate and angry, people begin to demonstrate irrational behavior. Some people begin honking incessantly, triggering even more stress in the people around them. Some drivers turn up their music—too loud. The hyper-amplified subwoofers broadcast rhythmic pulses that feel like body punches to people in vehicles many lengths ahead and behind. Arguments begin. Fights break out. Windows get smashed with golf clubs. Ramming incidents occur. Even individuals who are uninvolved experience increased levels of stress. A few have panic attacks. Others suffer respiratory distress. Some go into full-blown asthma attacks. Then it gets worse. Kosh's corollary to Short's observation: The avalanche has already started, it is too late for the pebbles too vote.

Despite the efforts of social historians, an accurate account of the events of the day remains impossible; too many events, too many scattered and confused accounts. What is certain however is that once the cascade of failures began, each breakdown triggered the next; but the most catastrophic of all was the failure of the telephone system.

Stuck on the freeways, with relief from the sun still hours away, people began flipping open their cell phones and calling home, calling for help, calling ambulances and fire trucks and police, even calling Cal-Trans and the city councilmen and the Governor's office to complain. As the channels overloaded, the system began dumping calls to clear bandwidth; people began calling called their service providers to complain. In self-defense, the network went into emergency procedures and shut itself down. The result—increased feelings of alienation and isolation among those trapped in the crystallized traffic. The arteries became linear madhouses of desperate frustration. Increasing numbers of people lost control of their bladders and bowels, adding to their individual discomfort, both physical and emotional.

As the afternoon wore on, two pregnant women went into labor and a third miscarried. Two people enroute to hospitals died in the ambulances that could not get through. A burly farmworker, one of several crammed into the back of a pickup truck experienced debilitating food poisoning, a combination of projectile vomiting and near-projectile diarrhea that expelled more than two liters of fluid from his body in less than thirty minutes. A 56-year old type-A studio executive experienced crushing chest pains that left him gasping for breath and too weak to cry for help. No help was available anyway. Even where calls for help could still be made from emergency callboxes, impatient drivers had already filled both shoulders of the highway in their desperate attempts to escape. The rescue vehicles couldn't get in and the med-evac choppers had no place to land.

By mid-afternoon, a significant number of vehicles had run out of gas. Even under the best of circumstances, a single stalled automobile in a middle lane could back up traffic in all four lanes for miles. Under these circumstances, with hundreds of dead vehicles scattered throughout the system, and more dying every minute, the crystallization had become complete. The vehicular arteries were solid and terminally impassible. The patient was dead, although it would be several days before any of the specialists would admit it.

But on some unconscious level, some people were already getting a visceral sense of what had happened. Maybe their survival instincts were kicking in, or maybe they were simply overcome by frustration—but it was the final moment of breakdown, the recognition that the system had failed and could not repair itself. Drivers started getting out of their cars. They locked them up, out of some optimistic belief that they would eventually have the chance to come back and retrieve them—and then they left them where they were. They gathered what belongings they could carry and abandoned their metal sanctuaries. First one or two, then a few more, and finally a veritable flood of refugees, they hiked between the sweltering lanes toward the nearest off-ramp and their separate illusions of relief.

Not all drivers were that easily persuaded. They sat and waited in desperate hope, afraid to leave, afraid to let go of their attachment to their vehicles, afraid to disconnect from the pernicious false identity—*I am my car*—that pervades Los Angeles culture. Still believing that this was only temporary, they sat in their cars, their engines still running, their air conditioners still blasting. (Even today, all these years later, archaeologists are still finding mummified bodies in some vehicles, including many varieties of small animals.)

Some engineers argue that even up to this point, the Los Angeles freeway system might have been saved, if only the next phase of the disaster could have been prevented. Others argue that the next moments were inevitable from the first beginnings of the crystallization process. Computer simulations have given us no clear answer.

It was this simple. All of those automobiles, all of those desperate drivers too attached to their metal and plastic personalities, unwilling to leave the technological illusion of identity, security, and safety—they sat in their wombs of music, unaware that their engine temperatures were steadily, inexorably rising. The automobile engine is designed to cool itself while in motion; it needs a steady flow of air through its radiator so it can dissipate excess heat. But now, immobilized, all of those engines ran hotter and hotter without any chance of cooling, the temperatures around them rose, and overheating was inevitable. The first vehicle caught fire at 3:31. Like a good idea occurring to many people simultaneously, fires began breaking out everywhere. Within the next half hour, thirteen more vehicles began to smolder—some drivers had blankets and fire-extinguishers in their trunks, some didn't—so very soon, flames were licking out from under the hoods of seven of those vehicles.

But the fire trucks couldn't get to them. The shoulders were jammed. Cars with plastic gas tanks exploded with surprising fury, and the fires began to spread, leaping from vehicle to vehicle with alarming speed. Drivers who only moments before had been completely resistant to leaving the comfort of their sedans panicked and fled. Soon, there were firestorms. The biggest raged on the 405 where it intersected with the 101, at the heart of the first big clot in the system. Another firestorm flickered to life further south on the 405 where it intersected with the 10. A third fire exploded just west of where the 10 intersected with the 110 and also where it fed into the 5. In a very short time, the two fires met in the middle and expanded into a terrifying wall of flame that cut across the heart of the city.

Aerial tanker drops helped to slow down the flames, but it wasn't enough. Before the end of the 7:00 news broadcast, the governor had declared the city a disaster area. All across the world, people clustered around television screens, mesmerized by an event that was both incomprehensible and horrific. Los Angeles was choking to death on its own vomit. Like a great beast shuddering to a halt, the city of the angels was collapsing and shutting down.

Even after the fires were contained, even after the last smoldering embers were extinguished, most of the inhabitants of the city continued to believe that normalcy could be restored, that someday traffic would flow again. Maybe they believed this because there were still pockets of mobility scattered throughout the urban sprawl, quiet neighborhoods where housewives could still drive to the corner market for milk and bread and eggs; but by the fourth day, as the stores began to run out of perishables, the problem of resupply became critical. How could the city feed its stranded millions?

Despite promises from local, state, and federal authorities that the freeways could be restored and working again within a few days, well maybe two weeks at the most—all right, full recovery was probably at least a month or two away, but the city could function and survive, just a little more time, that's all we need—despite all the promises and reassurances, by the middle of the week many Angelenos were beginning to experience growing fear, frustration, and skepticism.

The city hadn't yet succumbed to panic, but the seeds were growing. Many of those who lived on the edges of the city, especially those who had access to uncongested avenues, began evacuating themselves voluntarily to other communities. In the first week alone, Orange County took in over 40,000 refugees, San Bernardino accepted 50,000; many went to the homes of friends and relatives, others went to hotels, the most desperate camped out in tent cities erected on the grounds of local high schools, colleges, and the parking lots of several major malls. But there were still over five million people within the affected areas of the city.

At least twenty thousand came out on motorcycles or motor scooters; while the trip through the surface streets was slow, it wasn't impossible. Many more rode out of the disaster area by train. Metro-Link borrowed trains from as far away as Seattle to ferry passengers from Union Station to refugee camps in Santa Barbara, San Diego, and Palmdale.

Even more came out of the frozen zone by subway and light rail. The Green Line and the Gold Line and the Blue Line were major arteries. The Red Line funneled people from the eastern edges of the San Fernando Valley down to Union Station, where they could transfer to the other colors of the rainbow, or to other trains which would take them even farther out.

A few people, not a significant number, escaped by helicopter. Van Nuys airport and LAX became hubs of activity for those who could reach them, with planes landing and taking off as fast as the overstressed controllers could open flight paths in the sky. The lack of aviation fuel deliveries to the airports meant that planes had to fly in carrying enough fuel for their outward journeys. All of the airports in the zone were given double-black stars, an unprecedented new classification which meant that travel to or from was at-your-own-risk. It meant limited-to-zero availability of rescue and emergency vehicles and facilities.

But the refugees from deeper inside the disaster zone, where there was no access to rail or air, had the most difficulty extricating themselves. Some refugees walked as far as ten miles to reach a subway station, or a Metro-Link access. Amtrak brought in emergency trains on freight lines, putting up awnings and tents and benches to create makeshift stations at convenient street-crossings and overpasses. The crowds gathered and waited. Many arrived with bicycles, overloaded with their belongings. Red Cross helicopters lowered food and water to the waiting masses.

The disaster maps showed that almost every neighborhood within an area bounded by the 5 on the east, the 405 on the west, the 118 on the north, and the 105 on the south was pretty much immobilized to some degree or other, with tendrils of crystallization extending linearly outward from all of these routes.

While surface streets provided some relief, the spillover from the network of hardened freeways had choked most of the city's major thoroughfares. The streets were full of cars; the only reason the city had functioned before was that not every car was on the road at the same time. Now that the city was immobilized, a panic-stricken populace did they only thing they knew how to do—they rushed to their automobiles to make their escape. Evacuation didn't solve the problem, it exacerbated it. Broadcasting information on viable routes out of the city was self-defeating. As soon as a route was cleared and announced, it clogged up within minutes.

On Thursday, seven days after crystallization, as part of a larger disaster-relief package, the Republican-controlled Congress passed the Insurance Emergency Relief bill, declaring the disaster an act of God, thereby freeing automobile insurers from billions of dollars of exposure. This allowed the state to declare all abandoned vehicles a public nuisance and begin the wholesale removal of freeway blockages. The outrage that followed was not limited to the survivors of the disaster.

Leaders of the Democratic party were quick to point out that the Republicans had abandoned the protection of property rights in favor of the rights of big government. While not exactly a wedge issue, it did open the door for further political divisions. The Democrats portrayed themselves as the Party of Opportunity and painted the Republicans as the Party of Opportunists. The destruction of a million automobiles was seen as a gift to an automobile industry that would clearly benefit from the need to replace those lost vehicles. The bottom line, the Democrats insisted, was that the Greedy Old Party had no heart, they had abandoned the people of Southern California in favor of protecting the interests of their corporate sponsors. The Republican Congress tried to backpedal, but the damage had already been done.

Meanwhile, estimates of the time to full recovery now varied from six months to three years. The cranes and tow trucks necessary to clear the streets would have to work their way slowly to the center of the disaster and there were no computer simulations capable of the necessary extrapolations. Where to put the extracted vehicles and how to get them there complicated the issue.

The cars couldn't be removed from the freeways, because there was no place to put them. Trying to save all these autos for their owners' eventual return meant finding storage space for them and logging their locations in a master database. Perhaps, the surviving cars could be transported out to some wide-empty space out in the desert, from which owners could reclaim them. For a fee. Maybe. But did anyone really want to risk putting all these vehicles back into circulation where they could just clog the system again? The arguments were just beginning. (Some people advocated that this disaster represented an opportunity to remodel Los Angeles' dependency on automobiles and replace or augment the freeways with more light rail systems. But that particularly expensive alternative was not only an expensive proposition, it was not an immediate solution to anything.)

Even though the Vehicle Reclamation teams were now authorized to pile up cars in great towering pyramids of metal and glass and plastic wherever they found a big enough parking lot, there was enormous reluctance to do so. All those automobiles represented billions of dollars that nobody wanted to discard casually, especially not the far-removed owners. On the other hand, at the present rate of progress, by the time the reclamation teams reached the innermost majority of affected vehicles most of them would have rusted into near-total uselessness.

On the brighter side, the Los Angeles County Air Pollution Control District announced that air pollution levels for the basin had dropped dramatically. The air was cleaner than it had been since 1955 when the county finally outlawed backyard incinerators. An awkward spokesman embarrassedly announced that this was the direct result of taking a million and a half vehicles off the road, except that of course, those million and a half vehicles were still *on* the road. Just not moving anymore. But this was the *good* news. It was now safe to breathe in Los Angeles again.

Despite that incentive, the flood of refugees streaming out of the city continued, straining the resources of surrounding counties beyond the breaking point. By now, the first waves of escapees from the zone were spreading out across the continent, bringing with them sordid tales of non-vehicular terror and enough digital camera photos, phone-camera photos, and handycam videos to keep the news agencies happy for weeks. Even after the continuing live coverage abated and regular programming resumed, the networks still scheduled ongoing special reports. This was as much an opportunity as a necessity. Universal, Warner Bros., Fox, Disney, and Paramount all had their lots within the frozen zone. The production of sixteen major television series had come to a halt, including (ironically) several that were set in locations as far removed as Orange County, Las Vegas, Manhattan, Miami, and Boston. Although there were finished episodes of all prime-time series in the pipeline, once those were aired, new episodes would not be available until new production facilities were established, or until transportation to existing facilities could be resumed.

Every news and current events show from *60 Minutes* to *Nova* began multi-part examinations of the collapse of an entire city, with alarming speculations about the possibility of similar crystallizations occurring elsewhere. Real estate values in small towns and rural areas began to climb.

The days stretched into weeks as refugees continued to stream out of the zone, sometimes as many as a hundred thousand a day. The nightly news kept a running tally on the numbers; the flood showed no signs of abating; but each succeeding day, those who had successfully escaped from L.A. seemed more and more despairing and desperate. While not quite ragged, they looked hungry and haggard, thin and wan. Many had gone for a week or more without fresh fruits and vegetables, fresh milk and other perishables. They had exchanged their tan healthy presence for more sallow dispirited complexions. The surrounding counties continued to absorb as many as they could, exporting the overflow to the rest of the nation as fast as transportation could be arranged. Amtrak borrowed Pullman cars from Canada and Mexico, and converted over a hundred freight cars into makeshift passenger units. A number of Jewish families refused to board anything that looked like a box car.

Entering the fourth week of the disaster, as it became apparent that this was the new normal, disaster recovery teams entering the frozen zone discovered a startling fact—some people had created ways to survive their transformed circumstances. The most amazing finding was that some Angelenos had given up their dependency on their cars and learned how to *walk*. (No, that is not a misprint. The word is *walk*.) Computer analysis of urban residential zones revealed that more than 35% of all residential dwellings in Los Angeles had access to supermarkets, pharmacies, banks, and other essential services within a radius of ten blocks or less. For most of these residents, walking might be an inconvenience, but it was easier than giving up their homes. Reports from the zone suggested that in some places, neighborhoods were reinventing themselves as actual communities.

Satellite maps revealed that fully 10% of those who were refusing to leave their homes were planting gardens in their back yards or on their front lawns. Others were creating a new economy using bicycles and motorcycles to transship goods from subway and light rail stations into the otherwise unreachable interior of the zone. Simulations projected that 20% of the city's population could survive without automobile access, possibly more if enough streets could be cleared so that trucks could deliver goods to local communities—but if enough streets could be cleared, the automobiles would return.

Surprisingly—or maye not so surprisingly—a small but growing number of people liked the new normal, and were starting to voice the opinion that they did *not* want the automobiles to return. They actually liked being able to see the Hollywood Hills clearly. They liked the way the air smelled in the morning. They liked working in the garden, walking to the corner store, actually talking to their neighbors, and living at a less frenetic pace.

Teams of sociologists who studied the phenomenon—now called disvehiclization—observed that it was not simply a rejection of the automobile, but of the entire technological cocoon that had enveloped daily life. The disvehiclized person was also more likely to leave his or her cell phone off, turning it on only for limited periods each day; the disvehiclized person rarely watched television; he or she also cut back on computer time, accessing the Internet only for essential news or shopping services.

But not everybody could afford disvehiclization; it was a luxury of the retired, and of those who could work from their homes. Those who still depended on day jobs could not survive without transportation. While the subway, light-rail, and emergency bus lines were able to provide some measure of service, they were simply not designed to handle the traffic load, nor did they provide the degree of coverage necessary to the entire basin. In the first month alone, over a million people emigrated from Los Angeles to surrounding counties.

In Orange County, rents soared first. Demand far exceeded supply. Real estate values followed quickly. Automobile sales took off as well, both new and used; individuals who felt their lives were dependent on their mobility were quick to replace their lost cars. For the first few weeks, car dealers all across the nation were shipping as many vehicles as they could into Ventura, San Bernardino, Santa Clarita, and Orange counties.

Commentators have called this influx of additional vehicles onto the avenues and highways of the counties surrounding Los Angeles the "squeezed mud" effect.

Squeeze a handful of mud, it oozes out between your fingers; squeeze Los Angeles, and the traffic oozes out in all directions across the state. Cal-Trans now projects that in the post-crystallization era, California will see at least an additional million vehicles on the highways of the four counties surrounding Los Angeles.

Cal-Trans officials are also quick to point out that the recent stoppages on the 22, the 55, and the 91 are only localized anomalies, and not representative of any larger process. There is absolutely no reason to fear crystallization in Orange County. Absolutely no reason at all.

THE KENNEDY ENTERPRISE

—Is that thing on? Good. Okay, go ahead. What do you want to know?

Kennedy, huh? Why is it always Kennedy? All this nostalgia for the fifties and the sixties. You guys are missing the point. There were so many better actors and nobody remembers them anymore. That's the real crime—that Kennedy should get all the attention—but the guys who made him look so good are all passed over and forgotten. Why don't you jackals ever come around asking whatever happened to Bill Shatner or Jeffrey Hunter—?

Ahhh, besides, Kennedy's been done to death. Everybody does Kennedy. Because he's easy to do. But lemme tell you something, sonny. Kennedy wasn't really the sixties—uh uh. He's just a convenient symbol. The sixties were a lot bigger than just another fading TV star.

Yeah, that's right. His glory days were over. He was on his way out. You're surprised to hear that, aren't you?

Look. I'll tell you something. Kennedy was not a good actor. In fact, he was goddamn lousy. He couldn't act his way out of a pay toilet if he'd had Charlton Heston in there to help him.

But—it didn't matter, did it? Hell, acting ability is the *last* thing in the world a movie star needs. It never slowed down whatsisname, Ronald Reagan.

Reagan? Oh, you wouldn't remember him. He was way before your time. He was sort of like a right-wing Henry Fonda, only he never got the kind of parts where he could inspire an audience. That's what you need to make it—one good part where you make the audience squirm or cry or leap from their seats, shouting. Anything to make them remember you longer than the time it takes to get out to the parking lot. But Reagan never really got any of those. He was just another poor schmuck eaten up by the system. A very sad story, really.

Yeah, I know. You want to hear about Kennedy. Uh-uh. Lemme tell you about Reagan first. So you'll see how easy it is to just disappear—and how much of a fluke it is to succeed.

See, Reagan wasn't stupid. He was one of the few wartime actors who actually made a successful transition into television. He was smart enough to be a host instead of a star—that way he didn't get himself typecast as a cowboy or a detective or a doctor. Reagan was a pretty good pitchman for General Electric on their Sunday night show and then—wait a minute, lemme see now, sometime in there, he got himself elected president of the Screen Actors Guild and that's when all the trouble started—there was some uproar with the House Committee on UnAmerican Activities, and the blacklist and the way he sold out his colleagues. I don't really know the details, you can look it up. Anyway, tempers were hot, that's all you need to know, and Reagan got himself impeached, almost thrown out of his own Guild as a result.

Well, nobody wanted to work with him after that. His name was mud. He couldn't get arrested. And it was just tragic—cause he was good, no question about it. Those pictures he did with the monkey were hysterical—oh, yeah, he did a whole series of movies at the end of the war. *Bonzo Goes To College, Bonzo Goes To Hollywood, Bonzo Goes To Washington.* Yeah, everybody remembers the chimpanzee, nobody remembers Reagan. Yeah, people in this town only have long memories when there's a grudge attached.

So, Reagan couldn't get work. I mean, not real work. He ended up making B-movies. A lot of crap. Stuff even Harry Cohn wouldn't touch. He must have really needed the money. The fifties were all downhill for him.

I remember, he did—oh, what was it?—*Queen of Outer Space* with that Hungarian broad. That was a real waste of film. Then he did some stuff with Ed Wood, remember him? Yeah, that's the one. Anyway, Ronnie's last picture was some piece of *dreck* called *Plan Nine From Outer Space.* Lugosi was supposed to do the part, but he died just before they started filming, so Reagan stepped in. I hear it's real big on the college circuits now. What they call camp, where it's so bad, it's funny. Have you seen it? No, neither have I. Too bad, really. No telling what Reagan could have become if he'd just had the right breaks.

Oh, right—you want to talk about Kennedy. But you get my point, don't you? This is a sorry excuse for an industry. There's no *sympatico,* no consideration. Talent is considered a commodity. It gets wasted. People get chewed up just because they're in someone else's way. That's the real story behind Kennedy—the people who got chewed up along the way.

Anyway, what was I saying about Kennedy before I got off the track? You wanna run that thing back? Oh, that's right. Kennedy had no talent. Yeah, you can quote me—what difference does it make? Somebody going to sue me? What're they going to get? My wheelchair? I'll say it again. Kennedy had no talent for acting. Zero. Zilch. *Nada.* What he did have was a considerable talent for self-promotion. He was *great* at that.

And y'know what else? Y'know what else Kennedy had? He had *style.* You don't need talent if you've got style. Mae West proved that. Gable proved that. Bette Davis.

Funny business, movies, television. Any other industry run the same way would go straight into the ground. A movie studio—you make one success, it pays for twenty flops. You have to be crazy to stay with it, y'know.

Okay, okay—back to Kennedy. Well, y'know, to really understand him, you gotta understand his dad. Joe Kennedy was one ambitious son of a bitch. He was smart enough to get his money out of the stock market before '29. He put it into real estate. When everybody else was jumping out of windows, he was picking up pieces all over the place.

He got very active in politics for a while. FDR wanted to send him to England as an ambassador, but the deal fell through—nobody knows why. Maybe his divorce, who knows? Y'know, the Kennedys were Irish-Catholic. It would have been a big scandal. Especially then.

Anyway, it doesn't matter. The story really starts when Joe Sr. brings his boys out to California. He marries Gloria Swanson and starts buying up property and studios and contracts. Next thing you know, his boys are all over the place. They come popping out of USC, one after the other, like Ford Mustangs rolling off an assembly line.

In no time, Joe's a director, Jack's taken up acting, and Bobby ends up running MGM. It's Thalberg all over again. Lemme think. That had to be '55 or '56, somewhere in there. Actually, Teddy was the smart one. He stayed out of the business. He went East, stayed home with his mom, and eventually went into politics where nobody ever heard of him again.

Anyway, you could see that Joe and Bobby were going to make out all right. They were all sonsabitches, but they were good sonsabitches. Joe did his homework, he brought in his pictures on time. Bobby was a ruthless S.O.B., but maybe that's what you need to run a studio. He didn't take any shit from anybody. Remember, he's the guy who told Garland to get it together or get out. And she *did*.

But Jack—Jack was always a problem. Two problems actually.

First of all, he couldn't keep his dick in his pants. Bobby had his hands full keeping the scandal-rags away from his brother. He had to buy off one columnist; he gave him the Rock Hudson story. The jackals had such a good time with that one they forgot all about Jack's little peccadillos in Palm Springs. Sometimes I think Bobby would have killed to protect his brother. Y'know, Hudson lost the lead in *Giant* because of that. They'd already shot two or three weeks of good footage. They junked it all. Nearly shit-canned the whole picture, but Heston jumped in at the last moment and ended up beating out the Dean kid for the Oscar. Like I said, it's a strange business. *Stupid* business.

Sometimes you end up hating the audience for just being the audience. It's not fair, when you think about it. The public wants their heroes to look like they're dashing and romantic and sexy—but they're horrified if they actually behave that way. I mean, could *your* private life stand up to that kind of scrutiny? I'm not sure anybody's could. Hell, the goddamn audience punishes the stars for doing the exact same things they're doing—cheating on their wives, drinking too much, smoking a little weed. If they're going to insist on morality tests for the actors, I think we should start insisting on morality tests for the audience before we let them in the theater. See, how they'd like it for a change.

Oh well.

Anyway, the *other* problem was Jack's accent—that goddamn Massachusetts accent. He'd have made a great cowboy, he had the look, he had the build; but he couldn't open his mouth without sounding like a New England lobsterman. I mean, can you imagine Jack Kennedy on a horse or behind a badge—with *that* accent? They brought in the best speech coaches in the world to work with him. A waste of goddamn money. He ended up sounding like Cary Grant with a sinus problem.

You can't believe the parts he didn't get because of his voice. Y'know, at one point Twentieth wanted him for *The Misfits* with Marilyn Monroe—now, that would have been a picture. Can you imagine Kennedy and Monroe? Pure screen magic. But it never happened. His voice again. No, as far as I know, they never even met.

But that was always the problem. Finding the right picture for Jack. George Pal, the Puppetoon guy, gave him his first big break with *War Of The Worlds* over at Paramount, but Jack always hated science fiction. Afraid he'd get typecast. He saw what happened to Karloff and Lugosi. He thought of science fiction as the same kind of stuff.

The funny thing was, the picture was a big hit, but that only made Jack unhappier. He knew the audience had come to see the Martians, not him. That's when he swore, no more science fiction. And yeah, he really did say it, that famous quote: "Never play a scene with animals, children, or Martians. They always use the Martian's best take."

Hitchcock had a good sense of how to use Kennedy, but he only worked with him once. *North By Northwest*. Another big hit. Kennedy loved the film—he loved all that spy stuff, he always wanted to play James Bond—but he didn't like the way Hitchcock treated him. And he made the mistake of saying so to an interviewer. Remember? "Hitch doesn't direct. He herds. He treats his actors like cattle." That remark got back to Hitch, and the old man was terribly hurt by it. So, instead of casting Jack in his next film, he went to Jimmy Stewart. Who knows? Maybe that was best for everybody.

Jack spent nine months sitting on his ass, waiting for the right part. Nothing. Finally, he went to Bobby and said, "Help me get some of the good parts." By now, Bobby was running MGM, and this gave him control over one studio and a lot of bargaining power with all the others—he was the biggest deal-maker in town, buying, selling, trading contracts right and left to put together the right package.

Even so, Bobby still had to twist a lot of arms to get Jack into *The Caine Mutiny*. Van Johnson had already been screen-tested. He'd been fitted for his costumes, everything—suddenly, he's out on his ass and here's Jack Kennedy playing opposite Bogart. I can tell you, a lot of feathers were ruffled. Bogey knew how Jack got the part and he never forgave him for it. But, y'know—it helped the picture. Bogey's resentment of Jack shows up on the screen in every scene. Bogey should have had the Oscar for that one, but Bobby bought it for Jack. There was so much studio pressure on the voting—well, never mind. That's a body best left buried.

Anyway, in return, Bobby asked Jack to help him out with one or two of his problems. And Jack had no choice, but to say yes. See, when Bobby took over MGM, one of the projects about to shoot was a thing called *Forbidden Planet*. Shakespeare in outer space. Dumb idea, right? That's what everybody thought, at the time. They couldn't cast it.

They were having real trouble finding a male lead, and they were about to go with . . . oh, let me think. Oh, I don't remember his name. He ended up doing a cop show on ABC. Oh, here's a funny. At one point, they were even considering Ronald Reagan for the lead. Very strongly. But they finally passed on him—I guess Bobby remembered the McCarthy business. And that's why Reagan went and did *Queen Of Outer Space*. Never mind, it doesn't matter. Bobby finally asked Jack to play the Captain of the spaceship.

And I gotta tell you. Jack didn't want to do it—more of that science fiction crap, right?—but he couldn't very well say no, could he? So he goes ahead and does it. Bobby retitles the picture *The New Frontier*. And guess what? It's the studio's biggest grossing picture for the year. Go figure. But everybody's happy.

After that, Jack had a couple of rough years. One disaster after another. The biggest one was that goddamned musical. That was an embarrassment. the man should never have tried to sing. Even today, nobody can mention *Camelot* without thinking of Jack Kennedy, right? And those stupid tights.

You want my opinion, stay out of tights. Your career will never recover. It was all downhill for Errol Flynn after *Robin Hood* and the goddamned tights killed poor George Reeves. *Superman*'s another one of those unproduceable properties. Nobody's ever going to make that one work. Or *Batman*. Tights. That's why.

Anyway, back to Kennedy—his career was in the dumper. So, when he was offered the chance to do a TV series, it didn't look so bad any more. Most of the real action in town was moving to TV anyway. So Jack went over to Desilu and played Eliot Ness in *The Untouchables*. Y'know, that was one of J. Edgar Hoover's favorite shows. Hoover even wrote to Kennedy and asked him for his autograph. He visited the set once just so he could get his picture taken with Jack. Hoover had to stand on a box. They shot him from the waist up, so's you'd never know, but the photographer managed to get one good long shot.

Meanwhile, back over at MGM, Bobby's looking at all the money that Warner Brothers and Desilu are making off TV and he's thinking—there's gotta be a way that he can cut himself a slice of that market, right? Right. So he starts looking around the lot to see what he's got that can be exploited.

Well, *Father Knows Best* is a big hit, so Bobby thinks, "Let's try turning *Andy Hardy* into a TV series. And how about *Dr. Kildare* too? The Hardy thing flopped. Bad casting. And it was opposite Disney on Sundays. It didn't have a chance. But the Kildare property caught well enough to encourage him to try again.

So, Bobby Kennedy's looking around, right? And here's where all the pieces come together all at once. NBC says to him, "How about a science fiction series? You did that *New Frontier* thing. Why don't you turn that into a TV series for us?"

There's this other series that's just winding down—a war series called *The Lieutenant*—Bobby calls in the producer, a guy named Roddenberry and tells him that NBC wants a sci-fi show based on *The New Frontier*. Can he make it work? They've still got all the costumes, the sets, the miniatures, everything. Roddenberry says he doesn't know anything about science fiction, but he'll give it a try. He tells his secretary to rush out and buy up every science fiction anthology she can find and do summaries of all the stories that have spaceships in them.

What with one thing and another, it's 1964 before they ever start filming the first pilot. But all the MGM magic is applied, and they end up with one of the most beautiful—and most *expensive*—TV pilots ever made. Of course, Roddenberry put in all his own ideas, and by the time he was through, the only thing left from the movie was in the opening lines of the title sequence: "Space, the new frontier. These are the voyages . . . etcetera, etcetera."

NBC hated the pilot—they said it was "too cerebral"—but they liked the look of the show, so they say to Bobby, let's try again, give us another pilot. Bobby says no. Take it or leave it. MGM bails out, so Roddenberry goes over to Desilu, where they make a second pilot. He changes the name to *Star Track,* and the show goes on the air in 1966. You know the rest.

Two years later, MGM buys Desilu. Bobby Kennedy strong-arms NBC to move the show to an 8:00 time slot, and it's a big hit. But then, to settle some old grudge—Bobby hated being wrong—he fires Roddenberry. The rumor mill said it was women—maybe. I don't know and I'm not going to speculate. Dorothy Fontana takes over as producer, and surprise, the show just gets better. Meanwhile, *The Untouchables* gets cancelled and Jack Kennedy is out of work again.

The timing was everything here. See, Shatner and Nimoy were feuding. Not only feuding, they were counting each other's lines. Nimoy threatens to quit. Shatner does too. They're both demanding the same thing: "Whatever he gets, I get."

Bobby agrees and fires both of them. He starts looking around for a new Captain. He doesn't have to look very far.

In hindsight, yes. It was the perfect decision. John F. Kennedy as Captain Jack Logan of the starship Enterprise. The man was perfect. Who wouldn't want to serve under him? But—at the time, who knew? It sounded crazy. Here's this old fart who's career is clearly fading fast—why cast him in *Star Track?*

And Jack didn't want to do it. By now, he hated science fiction so much, he once took a poke at Harlan Ellison at the Emmy Awards. He didn't understand it. He had to have it explained to him. Once, he even called down to the research department and asked, "Just where is this planet Vulcan, anyway?"

And that was the other thing—Jack had already seen how Shatner got upstaged by the Vulcan. To him, it was the goddamn Martians all over again. The man was almost fifty—he looked great, but he was terrified of becoming a has-been, of ending up like Ronald Reagan.

But Bobby had a vision. He was good at that stuff. He promised to restructure the show in Jack's favor. Jack agreed—very reluctantly—to listen. That's enough for

Bobby. He calls in the staff of the show and says my brother wants to be Captain. "Make it so."

I gotta tell you. That was not a happy meeting. I'd just come aboard as story editor, so I just sat there and kept my mouth shut. Harlan argued a little, but his heart wasn't in it. Maybe he was afraid he'd get punched again. He didn't like the Kennedys very much. Dorothy did most of the talking for us—but Bobby didn't want to hear. He listened, maybe he just pretended to listen, but when everything had been said, he just answered, "Do it my way." We were not happy when we left.

For about three days, we were pissed as hell, because we'd finally gotten the show settled into a good solid working formula, and then suddenly—*poof!*—Roddenberry, Nimoy, and Shatner are gone, and Bobby Kennedy is giving orders. But then it sort of hit us all at the same time. Hey, this is an opportunity to reinvent *Star Track.* So we made a list of all the shit that bothered us—like the Captain always having to get the girl, the Captain always beaming down to the planet, that kind of stuff, and we started thinking about ways to fix it.

We knew Jack couldn't do the action stuff believably. He was already gray at the temples, and his back problems were legendary on the set of *The Untouchables,* so we knew we were going to have to introduce a younger second lead to pick up the action. That's where the Mission Team came from. So Jack wouldn't have to do it.

We really had no choice. Jack had to be an older, more thoughtful Captain who stayed on the ship and monitored the missions by remote control. The Mission Team would be headed by the First Officer. But this was perfect because it kept the Captain in command at all times, and it also made it impossible for the First Officer to become a sidekick, or a partner. Jack would be the undeniable star.

We also figured we'd just about milked the Vulcan idea to death, so we eighty-sixed the whole Vulcan species and brought in an android to take Spock's place as science officer. The android would be curious about humanity—kind of like an updated Pinocchio. The opposite of Spock; he *wants* to be human.

Just as we were starting to get excited about the possibilities of the new format, Jack suggested adding families to the crew of the starship to attract a family audience. Maybe the android's best friend could be a teenage computer genius . . . the kids would *love* that. We ended up calling the android REM—it means Rapid-Eye-Movement—and casting Donald Pleasance. Billy Mumy came aboard as Dr. McCoy's grandson, Wesley.

To be fair, Pleasance made the whole android thing work, but none of us ever really *liked* the idea very much. We tried arguing against it, but who ever listens to the writer's opinion? Whatever Jack wanted, Jack got. Bobby made sure of that. So, there we were—lost in space with Jack Kennedy.

And then . . . to make it even worse, Jack started reviewing outlines, sending us memoes about what Jack Logan would or wouldn't do. Clearly, he was having trouble telling the difference between the character and the actor who played him. Jack killed a lot of good ideas. I had one where these little furballs started breeding like crazy—kind of like the rabbits in Australia? Dorothy thought it had a lot of whimsy. Everybody liked it. But Jack killed it. He said it made Logan look foolish. He didn't want to look foolish, said it wasn't right for his image.

His *image?* Give me a break. It doesn't matter much now, though, does it? He's got the best image of all. He's an *icon.*

Harlan quit the show first—which surprised all of us, because he was always the most patient and even-tempered of human beings. Y'know, he did that *est* thing and just mellowed out like a big pink pussycat. Ted Sturgeon used to come to him for advice.

Dorothy quit three months after Harlan. I tried to stick it out, but it wasn't any fun without them. I didn't get along with the new producer, and I finally tossed in the towel too.

The worst part of it, I guess, was that after we left, the ratings went up. It was pretty disheartening. I mean, talk about a pie in the face.

What happened to the original crew? I thought you'd never ask.

Roddenberry went over to Warners and worked for a while on *Wagon Train: The Next Generation.* Shatner showed up in a couple of guest spots, then landed the lead in a cop show; when he lost his hair, he took up directing—I hear he's pretty good at it. Nimoy, of course, gave up show business and ran for office. He's been a good governor; I guess he'll run for the Presidency. Walter Cronkite called him one of the ten most trusted men in America.

Dorothy was head of new projects at Twentieth for a while, then she started up her own production company. Harlan moved to Scotland. And me—well, my troubles were in all the newspapers, so I don't have to rehash them here, do I? But I'm doing a lot better these days, and I might even take up writing again. If I can figure out how to use a computer. Those things confuse me.

You don't need me to tell you anything else about *Star Track,* do you? You can get the rest of it from the newspapers.

Yeah, I was there when it happened. We all were. I was as close to Jack as I am to you.

I dunno, I guess none of us realized what a zoo a *Star Track* convention could be. Not then, anyway. It was still early in the phenomenon.

I mean, we had no idea what kind of impact the show had made on the fans. We thought there might be a couple hundred people there. You know how big the crowd was? Nobody does. The news said there were fifteen thousand inside the hotel. We had no idea now many more were waiting outside.

We just didn't know how seriously the fans took the show. Of course, the Ambassador Hotel was never the same afterwards.

Anyway, Harlan was there, so was Dorothy. Gene came by, but he didn't stay very long. I think he felt disgraced. And of course, all the actors. De, Jimmy, Grace, Nichelle, Walter, George, Majel, Bruce, Mark, Leonard, Bill—all the also-rans, as they were calling themselves by then. I guess Bobby had put the screws on. Attend or else. There wasn't a lot of good feeling—at least, not at first.

But then the fans started applauding. One after the other, we all went out and chatted and answered questions, and the excitement just grew and grew and grew.

Of course, when Jack came out, the place went wild. It was like election night. There were people there wearing KENNEDY FOR PRESIDENT buttons. Like he was really the character he played. They loved him. And he loved being loved. Whatever else you might say about Jack Kennedy, he knew how to make love to an audience. Style and grace. That was Jack all over.

Y'know, I saw the Beatles at the Hollywood Bowl. All three concerts. And I never saw that kind of hysteria, not even when Ringo threw jellybeans at the audience. But the Trackers—I thought they were going to scream the walls down.

Jack was glowing. His wife had just turned to him and whispered, "Well, you can't say they don't love you now—" when it happened.

At first, I thought it was a car backfiring. It didn't sound like a gunshot at all. In fact, most people were puzzled at the sound. It all happened so fast. Then Jack grabbed his throat, and I guess for a second, we all thought he was joking. Y'know how you do: "Augh, they got me—" But he had this real stupid look on his face—confused, like. Then the second and third shots went off—and it was the third shot that killed him. And that's when the screaming started. And the panic. All those people injured and killed, suffocated in the crush. It was terrible. Everybody running. I can still see it. I still get nightmares.

I've always been amazed they caught the little bastard who did it. Sirhan Sirhan. I'll never forget his name. Another one of those nerdy little geeks who never had a life of his own. He lived inside the TV. He thought it was real. Half a dozen of those really big women we see at all the conventions just jumped the poor son of a bitch and flattened him. They were outraged that someone would dare to attack *their* Captain. Sirhan was lucky to escape with his balls still attached.

Y'know, later some of the witnesses said that Sirhan kept yelling, "Wait, wait—I can explain!" Like you can explain a thing like that? It didn't make any sense then. It doesn't make any sense now, no matter how many articles William F. Buckley and Norman Mailer and Tom Wolfe write about it.

You know what it was? Sirhan never forgave us for replacing Kirk and Spock with Logan and REM. He said we'd ruined the whole show.

But that's not even the half of it. You want to know the rest of the cosmic joke? Bugliosi, the District Attorney, told me later on. Sirhan was aiming at Bobby and missed. Three times! Bobby was standing just behind Jack, but that kid couldn't shoot worth shit. I think if he'd have hit Bobby, the industry would have given him a medal. Instead, he got the gas chamber and a movie of the week.

But now— y'know, I think back on it, and I see how stupid we all were. We didn't know the power of television. None of us did. We didn't even suspect.

Jack knew, I think. Bobby knew for sure. He knew that you could change the way people think and feel and vote just by what you put on the screen. Bobby knew that. He had the vision. But he was never the same after that. How could you be? The whole thing scared the hell out of all of us—the whole industry. NBC cancelled the show, but they couldn't cancel the nightmares.

Y'ask me, I think that was the turning point in the sixties—the killing of Kennedy. That's when it all started going bad. That's when we all went crazy and started tearing things down. But, oh, hell—that's old news. Everybody knows it.

Now, we've got the Kennedy mystique and *Star Track: The New Voyages.* And...it's all shit. It's just...so much merchandise. Whatever might have been true or meaningful or wonderful about *Star Track* is gone. It's all been eaten up by the lawyers and the fans and the publicity department.

Don't take this personally, but I don't trust anybody under thirty. I don't think any of you understand what happened then. It was special. We didn't understand it ourselves, but we knew it was special.

See . . . it's like this. Space isn't the new frontier. It never was.

What is the new frontier? You have to ask—? That proves my point. You're looking in the wrong place. The new frontier isn't out there. It's in here. In the heart. It's in us. Dorothy said it. If it's not in here, it's not anywhere.

Ahh—you know what, you're going to go out of here, you're going to write another one of those goddamn golden geezer articles. You'll miss the whole point, just like all the others. Shut that damn thing off and get the hell out of here before I whack you with my cane. Nurse! Nurse—!

He began life as a rumbustious pink bundle, as coordinated as a hamper of dirty laundry. For the first year of his life, his hind legs were always three steps faster than his front. If he got excited—which was any time he was awake—he couldn't move three feet without tripping over himself. But he wasn't stupid. One day, he figured out how to move his legs in order, and forever after that he was fast enough to run halfway up a tree after any squirrel too stupid to move to another neighborhood.

His name was Dog and he was the smartest animal I've ever known. Eventually, he convinced me that he and I were identical twin brothers separated at birth, and as the smarter member of the family, it was his job to look after me. Fair enough. In return, I gave him room, board, and health care.

Dog used to lie on my chest and sing duets with me, I'd skritch his belly and he'd hum his accompaniment in a deep disturbing growl, because he didn't know the words. In fact, the only words he did know weren't fit for polite company. If for any reason, I ever sent him out of the room, he'd go, but he'd mutter under his breath every step of the way. The words were unintelligible, but not the spirit. He was the only dog I ever knew who could curse.

This story isn't about him.

A SHAGGY DOG STORY

At first, she thought it was a scab.

They weren't an uncommon occurrence on this dog. His name was Shotgun and he was constantly scratching at himself. He was a shaggy pink mutt, mostly good-natured, and possessed of a perpetual questioning expression in his large brown eyes; but he had the bad habit of scratching at himself constantly.

He didn't have fleas. He couldn't possibly have fleas. She bathed him and dipped him every third week and changed his flea collar every second month. She marked it off on the calendar. She sprayed his bed on Saturday and dusted him on Wednesday.

No, it couldn't possibly be fleas. Miss Edna Token's dog did not have fleas.

The veterinarian had said it was probably a nervous habit. She had sniffed and replied, "I don't understand what this dog has to be nervous about."

The usually smart-mouthed vet didn't have an answer for that one. He just pursed his lips tight and peered into Shotgun's ears. Miss Token would have changed vets, because she didn't like Dr. Brown's nasty sense of sarcasm, but he was the only veterinarian on this side of the hill and he was practically in walking distance, and what with both a dog and a cat—

But anyway, Shotgun had another scab, right under his collar, so he must have been scratching at himself again.

"That's where you like to be skritched, isn't it?" she said, working at the spot with her carefully manicured nails. "You don't like to be scratched, do you? You like to be skritched. Ahh, here it is, Sweety-Dog. I found your secret spot—"

The dog grunted and sighed and bared his naked belly. He sprawled on his back and pumped agitatedly with one leg as she skritched. His mouth stretched into a rictus which she liked to think was a smile, although she was willing to concede it could just as easily be a muscular reaction.

She'd have to wash her hands after this. Despite his frequent baths, Shotgun still had a pronounced doggy odor, a sour buttery smell which was not quite unpleasant, but was certainly noticeable on her fingers after she finished skritching him. She didn't mind too much.

Anyway—

—at first she thought it was a scab. She *tsk*ed in annoyance and worked around it gently. It was a very hard one. In fact, it almost felt like . . . something metal. Maybe he had another burr caught in his fur. Except he wasn't complaining. She worked her fingers through his hair. The object felt flat and sharp and—

"Hold still, Shotgun! Let me see what's caught in your fur."

It was a zipper.

She blinked.

A zipper? On a dog?

This dog was nearly nine years old. He didn't look it, of course—she took very good care of him—but why hadn't she ever noticed a zipper before?

No, it must be just caught in his fur.

She pulled it. It was stuck. She pulled harder—

It came unstuck abruptly, sliding all the way down to Shotgun's . . . belly.

She gasped in involuntary horror, fearing that she had somehow ripped her dog open—except he hadn't uttered a sound.

The skin beneath the zipper was pink and naked.

She touched it tentatively—it was warm—then jerked her hand back. The zipper teeth were made of bright pink teflon. The dog skin was neatly stitched to hide it. She managed to gasp, "Shotgun? Sweety-Dog? Are you all right?"

"No," said the Dog. "As a matter of fact, I'm *piffed* as hell!" Its voice sounded muffled.

Miss Token squeaked in surprise and leaped backward.

The dog was struggling inside his dogsuit. It looked as if he was trying to remove his head—he was! The head lifted off to reveal a tiny squinting man. He tossed it aside and quickly peeled off the rest of the dog suit. He stood before Miss Token wearing nothing more than a dirty jockstrap and an angry frown. He had a pot belly and coarse black hair all over his body. Miss Token couldn't take her eyes off of him. He was a very ugly little man.

"That was a damn fool thing to do! DO I PLAY WITH YOUR ZIPPERS?!!"

"I, er—uh—" Miss Token couldn't form the words. She pointed back and forth between the little naked man and the rumpled dog suit on the living room floor. Shotgun's lifeless eyes stared at her from the discarded head. She gulped and tried again, "What have you done with—? Shotgun, is that you?"

"Not any more," the little man snapped. "This contract is breached. I don't believe this—" he growled. "You know what this means? You're on the strike list. Automatically. No appeal. You and I are through." He padded barefoot out of the other room, snarling. "Nine years! And this is the gratitude."

"Where are you going—?"

"To take a piss! D'ya mind?" The bathroom door slammed shut behind him. She heard the clunk of the toilet seat as it banged against the tank, and then a soft tinkling sound, followed by a flush.

"Aaah, that felt good," the little man declared, coming back into the room, adjusting his jockstrap as he walked. "Y'know, I hated having to wait for you to come home every night. A bladder can only take so much—"

Miss Token *eep*ed. "I, er—uh (gulp)—I don't understand this at all. Are you—yes, you are, aren't you? Shotgun! I mean—why didn't you? Oh, dear."

The little man was barely listening. He shook his head sadly and glanced around the room as if he were searching for something. "Forget it, Lady. Never mind. It doesn't matter any more." He bent down on his hands and knees and peered under the couch. "Ah!" He stretched and reached and pulled out a dusty green rubber bone. "I thought so."

Miss Token felt as if she were going mad. Unbelievingly, she stepped over and picked up the dog suit from the floor. It was lined with soft material—still warm from the little man. It had a distinctly doggy smell. It felt exactly like...a dog skin. She dropped it in sudden distaste. She kicked at Shotgun's lifeless head. It rolled over sideways. The tongue lolled out of the mouth. Miss Token moaned.

"Yeah, well—" said the little man. "You shoulda thought of that before you pulled my zipper." He crossed to the hall closet and pulled down a tiny tattered suitcase that she had never seen before. He snapped it open and tossed the rubber bone into it. He pulled out a T-shirt, jeans and a pair of loafers and quickly donned them.

"Shotgun! I—I'm sorry. I didn't know! I—please, stop that, please?"

The little man shook his head. He prowled nervously around the room, squinting into corners and looking behind the chairs. He collected a dirty tennis ball and a rubber duck with a broken squeaker. "Oh, yeah—" He pushed the cat off the desk and retrieved his rabies vaccination certificate from the second drawer. "I'm gonna need this." He tossed the ball and the certificate into the suitcase.

Miss Token was close to tears now. "Sir? Shotgun? Can't you—I mean, can't we just forget this happened—and go back to the way it was before?" She held out the dog suit to him, imploring.

The little man stared at her. "You can't be serious, lady! Knowin' what you know now? Don't be silly. NO WAY! It's da rules."

"But, but—why?"

"Why? You have to ask why? Isn't it obvious? First, you'd start askin' me to talk to ya, and then you'd want me to talk t'ya friends. Next, it'd be phone messages and little errands to the store. Then you'd want me to play cards with ya. Y'gotta be kidding! Listen, I am a dog. I am a professional dog! I am a member of the union. We got rules lady. Ya follow da rules, ya got a dog. Ya break da rules, ain't no dog in da country gonna work for you ever again. Except may a coupla scabs here and there—but they're hell on the carpeting." He padded over and picked up the dog suit. "That's da way it woiks, lady. Them's the rules. Too bad. I don't make 'em. I just follow 'em." He took the dog suit and stuffed it, head and all, gently into the suitcase.

"But—but—I've had you since you were a puppy! I paper-trained you!"

The little man looked annoyed. He looked very annoyed. "Don't start on me with that loyalty stuff. Ya also fed me the cheapest dry stuff you could find. You think I didn't see you collecting the goddamn coupons? How come I never got a steak on my birthday, huh? So don't tell me how much you did for me! Frankly, all that 'Sweety-Dog' stuff just makes me want to toss my biscuits. Oh, yeah—that's right." He disappeared into the kitchen and returned with the full box of dog biscuits from the cupboard and the half-empty open one she kept on the kitchen counter. "These at least were okay. I liked these—except for the green ones. They tasted like soap." He was chewing loudly as he tossed both boxes into the suitcase on top of the dog suit. "Hey, but how would you like it—" he said, speaking with his mouth full, chewing with his mouth open, "—if you had to sit up and beg for your dinner every night? That was degrading. Really degrading."

Miss Token sat down on the floor, tears running down her cheeks. "I'm sorry, Shotgun. I really am. I didn't know."

"Yeah, well—it's too late for sorry now." He snapped the suitcase shut, hefted it for weight, then headed for the door.

"Wait—" she said.

There was something in her tone. He stopped, one hand on the doorknob. "Yeah?"

"Where are you going?"

"That's none o' your business, any more."

"But it is my business. You're my dog—"

"Was!"

"Do you have a place? Don't you want to take your blanket?"

"Hey," he muttered. "Don't worry about me. I'll be okay. I can always catch a bunk down at the pound. Hey, really—" His tone softened. "I'll have a new gig in a week."

Miss Token fumbled for her purse. "Listen, do you have enough money? Bus fare? Um—"

"Keep your money."

"No, I insist—" She held out a fistful of bills. "Shotgun, please take it. I owe you this much at least—"

He shook his head. "I'm not allowed to take it." And then he added, "I'm sorry. I really am."

She met his eyes. "Was I really that bad?"

The little man looked embarrassed. He shrugged. "You weren't the worst, y'know? Listen, I gotta go now. You take care of yourself, y'hear?"

"Will you—write me at least? And let me know where you are?"

"Hey! I'm a dog! And I won't phone either."

Miss Edna Token nodded. And gulped. "Goodbye, Shotgun."

"Yeah. G'bye. Hey—and thanks for all the biscuits."

The door thunked shut with a terrible finality.

Miss Token looked up sadly. The cat was sitting on top of the TV set.

The cat cleared its throat and said, "I told him the zipper was too big."

AFTERWORD

Freedom is not having to wear a dog suit.

The round-robin novel never happened. Too bad. It could have been fun. Here's the chapter I wrote. It doesn't matter what came before and what followed afterward is irrelevant. As you will shortly see why.

THE HONKER STING

Jack woke up in a hospital bed.

The room was silent—incredibly silent—and shaded. He couldn't tell if it was night or day.

His head hurt. It felt like it was caught in a vise and two sumo wrestlers were tightening it. His mouth was dry. His throat ached.

He pushed the blanket aside and sat up in bed. The effort made his head swim and for a moment he couldn't move. He almost fell back against the pillow—but he forced himself to remain upright and put his feet on the floor. The floor was some kind of cold stone and felt rough against his soles. He was wearing a pale blue hospital gown.

Why am I in a hospital? What happened?

And then he remembered.

The jolt of pain nearly dropped him to the floor. He clutched at the bed-railing while tears of pain came to his eyes.

There was a pitcher of water and a glass on the nightstand. He groped frantically for it. He knocked both to the floor. The glass shattered loudly, the water splashed across the tile. Jack felt so helpless—

The door flickered and a nurse entered the room. She wasn't wearing a standard nurse's uniform, but Jack knew she was a nurse. There was *something* about her manner.

She looked at Jack, at the broken glass, at the water, at Jack again. "Oh, you're up? Good. I'll get someone to clean that up for you. Get back in bed." She stepped back *through* the door—this time Jack tried to see how she managed the trick of walking through a closed door without opening it, but it happened too fast. She flickered through and was gone.

With a great deal of effort, Jack lay back in bed and pulled the blanket over him. He leaned back and rested his head against the pillow. He waited for the throbbing to ebb.

It didn't.

He opened his eyes again.

I'm still groggy. Isn't that interesting that I can be so detached about it? Why am I still groggy? What happened?

There was no TV in the room. Hospitals always had television sets.

There was a chair opposite the bed. One chair.

There was no call button. He looked around on both sides of the bed, on the nightstand, on the wall. There was no call button. Hospitals always had call buttons.

There was no light switch by the door. There were no electrical outlets. There were no lamps; there were no light fixtures—there was no apparent source of light in the room at all.

There were no windows.

The shades—what Jack had thought were shades—were merely blank panels against the wall. There was something *odd* about those shades. Jack pushed the blankets back again and got out the other side of bed. He staggered the two steps and reached out and—jerked his hand back as if stung. The shades *tingled*. They also hummed. *Hummed?*

"What the hell? Where in—?"

The door flickered and a *thing* entered.

At first, Jack thought the *thing* was a teenage boy—wearing some kind of makeup. Then he took a second look and decided it was a woman. Then he took a third look and realized he had never seen a human being like this before in his life. The *thing* was slender, androgynous and had skin that flouresced like pearl. It looked like a pubescent child. Its hair was nearly shoulder-length and had the same pearlescent sheen as its skin. The creature was *human*—of a kind. It was not unfriendly looking—just startling. It—he? she?—nodded to Jack and crossed to the other side of the bed.

The androgyne was wearing a singlet of industrial beige. It carried some kind of cleaning tool, which it swept across the floor. Jack stared. The tool made a soft whirring sound. The water and the pieces broken glass disappeared—they just flickered away like the door. The androgyne picked up the empty pitcher—

"Hey?"

The androgyne stopped. "Yes? Do you wish something else?" Its voice was soft and musical—like being stroked with blue velvet. Its expression was oddly *expectant*. As if it knew what Jack *really* wanted and was only waiting for him to ask for it.

"What is this place? Where am I? Who—what are you?"

The androgyne blinked in confusion. Its expression turned to disappointment, as if Jack had asked the wrong questions. It smiled politely and said, "I'll get you more water." It flickered through the door.

Jack tried to follow—

-- and slammed hard against the cold, metallic surface. The door felt absolutely solid. Jack ran his hands up and down the door, looking for a doorknob, a handle— something, anything. His head throbbed. He staggered back toward the bed and sank down onto it again.

He tried to remember. Maybe—if he could figure out how he got *here*—

Tappy! *Where was Tappy now?* Who *or what* was Tappy anyway? She had been so soft and warm. *Don't think about it.*

They had climbed up the hillside and walked *through* a rock and into an alien world. Tappy had seemed to be headed *somewhere*. There had been that thing with the head of a medieval knight—the honker. And then—

Jack's head hurt like a furnace. There was a roaring in his ears.

He put his head down in his hands and waited for the dizziness and nausea to pass.

-- he remembered being split in two. His mind had fragmented out of his body and had gone exploring on its own. He had seen—

He didn't understand what he had seen.

But there has to be some explanation! The people who run this place must know—

The androgyne returned with a fresh pitcher and a new glass. Without speaking, it poured a glass of water and held it out to Jack. Jack looked up, saw the glass, and took it with both hands. "Thanks," he said. The water was cold. Jack drank it slowly, but he drank it all without stopping. "Thanks," he said again. He put the glass on the nightstand, being more careful this time. "Thanks," he repeated, not knowing what else to say. The androgyne was almost *attractive* in an innocent sort of way. Idly, Jack wondered what kind of sexual equipment it had. *Jeezis! Don't you ever stop?*

The androgyne's expression flickered—as if it wanted to say something more—and then abruptly, it closed down again and flickered out the door.

Jack sank back in the bed. He wondered what time it was, but his watch was missing. He wondered what day it was. He wondered what planet he was on.

The door flickered and the nurse entered again. She was carrying a thing that looked like a pocket flashlight. She held it up and checked the meter on its side, then pressed it against Jack's upper arm. It hissed. "There," she said. "That should ease some of the pain. For a while, anyway. Honker stings are nasty. Are you hungry?"

Jack shook his head. He was nauseous.

"All right. If you want anything, just ask."

"Uh—how?"

The nurse looked confused. "What do you mean?"

"I mean, *how* do I ask?"

"Just—*ask*," she repeated. "Just open your mouth and say what you want. `I'd like a—'" Abruptly, her expression clouded in embarrassment. "Oh no. I'm sorry. You don't remember, do you?" She pretended to smile. "Don't worry about it. Everything will sort itself out very quickly."

"Can I have some more light in here?" Jack asked. "Can I have my clothes? Can I get out?"

Even before he finished speak, the room was brighter. The nurse was very pretty, Jack realized. He looked at her left hand. No ring. *There you go again!*

The nurse reached out and patted his shoulder. "Just rest for a bit. Let this take effect."

She flickered out the door.

"Goodness," said Jack. "People come and go in the strangest ways around here." He giggled. *At least my head doesn't hurt any more.*

Androgynes, spaceships, out-of-body experiences, extra-terrestrials, flash-guns, doors that flickered instead of dilating like a proper door should—

What else could happen now?

"How are you feeling?" It was a man's voice.

Jack opened his eyes.

Standing beside his bed was a man in a metallic-looking black uniform. Jack couldn't identify it. He wasn't too good with military things. Air force? Marines? It was definitely a Confederate States uniform though. Jack recognized the stars and bars. Jack allowed himself to relax.

The man was mid-fortyish. His haircut was military crisp, his eyes were hard. He looked like he was in top physical condition.

"Colonel Walling," he said, by way of introducing himself. He looked around and said, "Chair?" A chair *materialized* behind him and he sat down without looking to see if it was actually there.

Jack didn't know what to say.

"Well, son—" Colonel Walling had a thick Georgia drawl. "You sure stepped in it this time."

"Sir?"

"You don't even know what you stepped in, do you?"

Jack shook his head. "I'd like an explanation."

Colonel Walling nodded. "And that's just what you're going to get. But I have some questions for you too—where's the girl?"

"Tappy?"

"Is that what they're calling her?"

Jack shrugged. "That's the name I was told."

"Fine. Where is she? When was the last time you saw her?"

"I don't know. The last clear memory I have of her was—" Jack gulped. "—I don't know how long ago. We were sleeping. I woke up and there was this *honker*—is that what you call them? Anyway, this honker was doing something to her. Then he came over to me and patted me or something. In the morning, Tappy had a very hard swelling the size of a marble under her skin—between her breasts. And I had a similar one on the side of my neck—"

Jack touched his neck where the honker's tongue had pierced him. The spot was sore, but the swelling was down. "Right here."

"We know where the honker stung you. Go on." The Colonel's voice was knowing and sure.

Jack shrugged. "That's when things started getting *really* weird. I mean, things were already pretty weird—I mean, you must have seen the big crater and the—and—and the—" Jack's throat constricted in sudden hurt; he was abruptly confused. "Who are you? I mean, how did you get here too? How do you know what's going on? I mean, why is the army of the Confederacy here? We were in Union Territory. Where is here anyway?"

"Relax, son. I'm here to debrief you. Just keep talking and we'll get it all handled. Do you want some more water. Walling was already pouring.

Jack sipped at the water, slower this time. Colonel Walling had pale gray eyes. Jack found them very easy to look into.

"You still with me?"

Jack nodded.

"All right. What happened next?"

Jack took a breath—*I've got to trust somebody*—and began slowly. "There was some kind of a ship in the sky. A spaceship? And there was a gun—Tappy's leg brace turned into a weapon. Or maybe it wasn't, but she shot me with it and—then everything—nothing made sense after that, Colonel. I'm sorry. I heard voices, I saw things. Tappy wasn't Tappy, she was some kind of a hamadryad or a—an insect-god. I don't know. There were people after her for something. I had become some kind of disembodied *thing*, floating around. I went back to Earth for a while—" Jack shook his head. "I'm sorry."

Colonel Walling sighed. It wasn't a sound of exasperation. It was a sound of resignation. As if he'd heard this story before. "Yeah," he said. He looked thoughtful. Abruptly, he asked, "You do a lot of drugs, son?"

Jack shook his head. "I've done some. A little grass. Coke once. I don't like it."

"Too bad."

"Too bad?"

"No tolerance. You're going to be hit by this thing very hard. I wish we'd found you sooner."

"Sir—?"

Colonel Walling held up a hand. "Easy, son—your system has had a terrible shock. And I'm about to make it worse. Much worse."

"Look, I'm a big boy, I can take it—"

"You think so?"

"I know so," Jack snapped back.

"All right—" Colonel Walling made a decision and started ticking points off on his finger. "First, you're in the custody of the Armed Services of the Confederate States of America, Paratime Marine Corps. Something was triggered that shouldn't have been, and you have stumbled into the middle of a very big, very important operation. You shouldn't be here. Now that you're here, you've attracted a lot of attention to a few things we *were* trying to keep secret."

"Paratime Marine Corps?"

"The Confederacy has been using the Dimensional Wormholes for a hundred and thirty years. They happen to be one of our greatest military secrets." Walling grinned. "Wouldn't you have liked to have seen the look on Ulysses S. Grant's face when three Confederate divisions outflanked the Union Army at Gettysburg? I know I would have. We've been very careful with the wormholes because of the potential for Paratime disaster. Unfortunately, others haven't been as careful as we have." Walling sighed. "Trust me. We have only used the wormholes in cases of extreme emergency. The last time was World War III. We had no choice. We launched the North American Vengeance through the wormholes. That's how we really leveled Berlin, Tokyo, London—but that was the only other time." Walling held up a hand to stop himself. "I know this is a lot to assimilate, Jack, but you're going to have to try."

"Why?"

"*Why?* Walling looked astonished. "Son, you've stumbled into what could very well become the War of All Worlds!" Walling added, "—And the *bad* news is that you don't even know your own part in it."

"Tappy?"

Walling looked troubled. "Son, Tappy is—only a part of it. There's something else. If only you hadn't been stung by that damn honker. If only we could have gotten to you sooner—" He stopped himself. "Okay, look. The crater—it's not a crater. It's a landing pad. It's eleven thousand years old. There's a ship coming—no, not the one you saw, that was one of ours, at least it was one of our allies. No, there's a Vampire Breeding Vessel heading toward us at near-light velocity. It's about three light-weeks away and still decelerating. We've been watching it come in for three years now. We haven't had a lot of time to prepare for it. We didn't think they'd be coming back. We were wrong." His expression went sour. "It's probably going to be our last big mistake.

"That Vampire ship has got to have more than a million warriors ready to hatch. God knows how many breeder eggs it's carrying. We don't know where they're heading or where they came from. We think they use this system as a staging base for battles in the Oort Cloud. We don't know what's going on out there—but we've been picking up Malenkov radiation for years. I can tell you that the last time the Vampires passed through here, eleven thousand years ago, they decimated the planet. It still hasn't recovered.

"The problem is that Earth, Paratime Line-Three, has doorways all over it now—the Madryads have been punching holes in the Paratime Envelope for centuries, leaving us all vulnerable. If the Vampires find their way through to Line One, we're all dead. *Comprendez?*"

Jack nodded, dumbstruck.

It almost made sense.

"Then that means that Tappy is—" He stopped. He didn't know what Tappy was.

"—lost," finished Colonel Walling. "Look, son—I can't tell you everything. I can tell you this. If you're ever to realize your full powers, you're going to have to let go of your need to have explanations. Explanations are the booby prize."

"Yes, sir." Whatever it was the nurse had given him, it was *terrific.*

Abruptly, Walling stopped. He looked as if he were listening to something far away. Jack frowned, but waited patiently. Walling looked back to him. "We've had a breakthrough. Damn! I was hoping we'd have more time."

"A breakthrough?"

76 DAVID GERROLD

"Clone warriors."

"Sir?!!"

"The Japanese, Taiwanese, Koreans, refugees from Free Hong Kong. We think they've got vat-grown androids too. If it's true, this means that the Fourth World has Paratime Injectors." Walling stopped himself. "It's bad enough the Madryads have been punching doors—they don't like Line One very much, we think we can close some of the holes—but if the nations of Line One start opening new doors from the other side and pouring in, we're in big trouble. We'll never be able to contain the Vampires to Line Three if there are doors all over hell and gone. And we're never going to get the Fourth Worlders to believe that the Vampires are a real danger. The way most Paratime politics work, they'll believe what they want to believe—that we're just trying to keep the resources of Line Three all to ourselves."

Jack's head was starting to throb again. He was getting confused. "Why are you telling me all this?"

"You need to know this, boy. Wait—" Again, the Colonel put his body on hold while his mind leapt a thousand miles away. Jack had the weirdest sensation that the Colonel was on a telepathic conference line.

And then Walling was back. "Things are heating up. Wait—"

Walling didn't wait for Jack to comply; he was already flickering out the door.

Abruptly, the room became very bright and the walls were pulling away—or dissolving. Or something. Jack's head hurt so bad he couldn't tell. He stood up, shielding his eyes against the glare. The room felt as if it was spinning, or moving. It felt like an elevator rushing upward.

And then all sense of motion stopped. Jack turned around slowly, staring, trying to see what was happening. The stone floor had become almost painfully cold. Something was going *pocketa-pocketa* very close by.

"Where am I?" Jack called.

"NORCOL Control Center." Somebody replied quietly. The voice sounded distant and disembodied.

"Oh." It meant nothing to Jack.

Squinting, Jack was able to make out that he was now in the center of a deep circular room, very large and very bright. Moving in toward him were a number of huge robot probes and mobile scanners.

"Lay down, please," said the voice.

Jack looked back at his bed and saw one of the robots removing the blankets and sheets. The bed was a platform on a pedestal. It was some kind of a scanning bed.

"Lay down, please," repeated the voice. There was a nervous edge to it.

Jack lifted himself onto the bed, shielding his eyes against the glare. He couldn't tell how many people were looking down at him. He saw two technicians at a console behind a thick glass window. They were frowning at their controls. He thought he could make out other people higher up, also behind thick glass windows.

The voice spoke softly now, "Thank you. I'm going to give you some instructions. Do not try to figure them out. Just follow them. Do you understand?"

Jack nodded.

"Do you understand?" The voice asked again.

"Yes, I understand," Jack said.

"Thank you. Close your eyes."

Jack closed his eyes.

"Visualize yourself lying on a bed."

That was easy. Jack imagined he was floating over his supine body, looking down at himself. Half Jack again. He noticed he had an erection. *Damn! I'm a horny bastard!* He was almost painfully hard.

"Thank you," said the voice. "Now, visualize your internal organs."

The body below became transparent to Jack. He could see the dark mass of his liver. The steady expansion and deflation of his lungs. He could see his heart beating. He stretched out a ghostly hand to see if he could touch his—

"Don't do that!" said the voice. It wasn't angry, just firm. Jack pulled his hand back. "Good."

How did the voice know?

"Now, I want you to imagine that you can change the shape of your body."

Half Jack floated and studied his body. He wondered what shape he should change it into. He thought about it.

"Don't try to force the change. Just let it change any way it wants to."

"Boy, if all dope were this good—" Jack started to make a joke.

"Shut up," said the voice. "Stay on purpose. Let your body change shape if it wants to."

Jack looked back down at his body. He said to it, *Go ahead. Change into what you want to be.* The body twitched. A second time, and then a third.

And then it *flowed*.

At first, Jack was startled—then he was frightened—

"It's all right," cautioned the voice. "We're here. We're watching you. You're safe. Let it flow."

All right.

The body flowed, rippled, flowed—began to reform, rippled, flowed, formed, twitched, shuddered—shuddered and was still.

The body solidified.

Jack floated above his own body and stared. The body was still recognizably Jack. But it was smaller, less developed, the breasts had enlarged slightly and softened, the face had gone all boyish, as if the years had melted off.

And the skin had changed; it had gone all silvery-pearlescent.

The body had become an androgyne.

Jack felt a curious thrill of recognition and horror. Was he supposed to return to that body now? Could he change it back? Was this permanent? Was this who he really was—or was this merely an illusion? The body opened its eyes and looked up at him. It was oddly beautiful and strangely terrifying sensation to be recognized by yourself.

"It's all right, Jacca. Take your time."

Jacca studied its body. So that's what an adrogyne has between its legs. I'd forgotten.

"If you want to return, Jacca, you can."

Jacca floated.

The voice suggested quietly, "Jacca. Why don't you return for a while."

Jacca floated toward its body—

-- and woke up in the hospital bed again. Blinking.

Colonel Walling was still sitting in the chair.

"What happened?" Jack/Jacca/HalfJack/Who-Am-I-Anyway? blinked in confusion. He/She/It looked at its hand. It looked gray. The room was too dark to tell.

"A little test. You passed."

"What would have happened if I'd failed?"

Walling did not look uncomfortable. He merely said, "We wouldn't be having this conversation now."

"Go on."

"Do you remember anything?"

Jacca thought hard. It shook its head. "Nothing else. Is that bad?"

"We'd hoped that maybe you'd taken some embryonic engrams and that we could bring them to the surface by rejuvenating; but it was only a slim chance. Damn. Now you're going to have to come back the hard way. You're going to have to relearn everything by experience."

"You're telling me that I'm not who I thought I was?"

Walling nodded. "I'm telling you that *nothing* is the way you thought it was. *No one. Nothing.* You cannot trust even the evidence of your own senses. Stop trying to figure things out. Remember—explanations are the tunnel with no cheese!"

Jacca was beginning to feel a sense of recognition. Of familiarity. But—maybe it was the drug.

Walling looked hot. He took off his jacket and draped it over the back of his chair. He loosened his tie. He was a big man with a broad chest. Jacca wondered if he was very hairy or only a little hairy. *Where did that come from?*

Now, Walling pulled his chair forward and leaned in close. "Listen to me, Jacca. Listen very hard." His words seemed to be echoing across a vast distance. "This next part if very important. Am I getting through to you?"

Jacca nodded.

"Good. You must come back to us! We need you. We cannot close the circle without you. Do you understand that? You must relearn everything. You must master the powers again. Do you understand that?"

Jacca nodded and smiled. It hoped it was a reassuring smile. It didn't want to disappoint this man. He was so beautiful. Jacca wondered if he were tender or rough—

What?!!

"Jacca—" The Colonel's voice was an echoing intensity. "The honker sting. Do you understand about honkers?"

"They sting." Was that the right answer?

"Yes, they do. They *sting*. Jacca—honker stings are *chronically hallucinogenic!*"

Jack sat up straight.

Colonel Walling was taking off his shirt now. He unzipped his chest. He pulled off his skin. The Vampire pulled off the pink skin, pulled it down to its waist. The creature was black and chitinous and when it finally pulled off its mask, its mandibles clacked against each other like knives. "It's all a hallucination—but in your case, it's going to be a *delicious* hallucination—"

Jack sat up straight in bed. *What?!"*

Colonel Walling was a broad-shouldered woman with deep gray eyes. And very attractive cleavage. Jack couldn't help staring into her cleavage. He had to force himself to look back into her eyes. "What?!"

"I'll say it again—Honker stings cause massive hallucinations. All kinds. Emotional. Physical. Neurological. Sexual. You've been hallucinating since the moment you were stung. I don't know what you've seen or what you think you've seen or what fantastic visions have been triggered by things you think you've seen—but you can't trust anything that you remember. It probably didn't happen—or if it did, it didn't happen the way you think it did. It's very important that you stop trying to figure it out. You'll go crazy. We need you rational. Let it flow, Jacca."

"The madryads and the androids and the spaceships?"

"Jacca—you are still hallucinating. Do you hear me?"

"The Paratime Marines, the Vampires, the—"

"Jacca, whatever you are hearing, whatever you are seeing, you cannot trust it—" Colonel Walling's voice was retreating again, echoing from a darkened tunnel. "You are still hallucinating. *This conversation is a hallucination. It is the only way we can reach you.*"

The walls were dropping away again. The room was rushing upward again. Jack had the sensation that Colonel Walling was climbing onto the bed on top of her. Him? Who?

Which of us has the hard-on?

"Jacca!" Somebody was screaming now. "There is no cure for honker stings. The hallucinations don't stop! Ever! You have to learn how to live with them. They are going to continue! You have to let them happen. Don't resist. Jack, listen to me—"

That's Tappy!

"—the only way out is to go through it. Let it flow around you. Ride the current and come out the other side. Jacqueline!"

Tappy?

Jack sat up straight.

Colonel Walling's eyes still looked odd.

"Are you a hallucination too?"

"No. Yes. What do you think?"

Colonel Walling began taking off her shirt now. Her breasts were very large. Now, she was unzipping her cleavage. The Vampire pulled off the pink skin, pulled it down to its waist. The creature was black and chitinous and when it pulled off its mask, its mandibles clacked against each other like knives. "Delicious. Yes, *delicious*."

Jacca screamed.

And sat up in the forest.

Next to Tappy.

Tappy had a hard swelling under her skin, right between her breasts. The honker had stung her too.

She looked up at Jax and her eyes widened.

Jax clacked its mandibles. "—a very *delicious* hallucination."

AUTHOR'S AFTERWORD:

Someday, when I have gone completely senile, when sense and sensibility no longer matters, then I shall write my last novel as an endless, annoying hallucination. This will be the first chapter.

THE TROUBLE
WITH HAIRY

Afterward, they all agreed it had been a bad idea.

After all the allegations, all the excuses and explanations, all the accusations and apologies, all the recriminations, back and forth—there was enough blame for everyone—and especially after all the indictments, after all of that and more, everyone agreed it had been a very, very bad idea.

But it had seemed like a good idea at the time.

It had begun innocently enough at the 33rd Annual Convention of Convention-Committees. While the panel on Dealing with Difficult People was headed for overtime, because several people on the panel were being difficult, the husband of one of the panelists joined the wife of one of the other panelists in the hotel bar for a circumstance that was as far removed from hanky-panky as is possible for two human beings to achieve.

He was Doctor Verne ("Vernie" for short) Vellum, of the Newport Vellums (third cousin, twice removed), a graduate of the Pepperdine Programming Initiative, sponsored by the Pepperdine Business School.

She was Doctor Janine Pershing, a graduate of the UCLA Department of Medicine, specializing in cardio-pulmonary research and the clotting abilities of blood.

He was presently consulting for Cal-Trans, the California Transit Authority, on ways to manage traffic flow along the city's main arteries.

She was creating a model of the blood flow throughout the human body as a way to predict blood clots, aneurisms, strokes, and other hemolytic disasters.

What happened next was inevitable.

By the time they had finished their third round of Hairy Nilssons—

A Hairy Nilsson is rum and Coke, except it's made with Malibu coconut rum and a twist of lime. You put the lime in the coconut, you drink it all up . (If you use diet Coke, it's a half-Nilsson.)

—by the time they had finished their third round of Hairy Nilssons, they were both giddy enough to recognize that they were working on the same problem—how do you keep a fluid flowing?

Sometime after the fourth or fifth round of Hairy Nilssons, the light bulb didn't just light up—it exploded in a dazzling shower of sparks. The impossible idea flashed into being like Athena springing full-blown from the forehead of Zeus, and switching metaphors in the middle of the sentence, Pandora's box fell open with an ear-piercing clang. While their respective spouses were vehemently arguing with each other about ways to create peace, Vellum and Pershing were suddenly and drunkenly committing to a collaboration that would have left the average mad scientist weeping with envy. A Bond super-villain could not have dreamt up a better plan.

Now, ordinarily nothing much would have happened after that alcohol-infused conversation—normally, they would have exchanged business cards and forgotten they'd even discussed anything at all until a few days later, when they each got home and unpacked and—upon discovering the business card, would have frowned, trying to remember whose it was and why it had been proffered, might have vaguely remembered, "oh, that"—and then tossing the card aside, would have turned to a much more important question: "What's for dinner?"

Except this time, no.

Before they had gotten to the mandatory exchange of business cards and the necessary false promises—"We should get together soon"—they were joined by a fellow named Gonder O'Conner, an elemental of greed, a seducer of the unwary, an unfrocked Irishman who had made a career out of drinking various naïve American celebrities under the table and then convincing them to endorse whatever enterprise he was currently peddling to the unwary—whether it was a failed reboot of a cancelled TV series or an internet portal for dot-com investors. He was not so much a businessman as a wannabe-entrepreneur with either a terrible toupee or a very bad touch-up of his comb-over, no one was ever certain which.

Gonder said the magic words. "This could be worth a lot of money." And with that single phrase, the genie was popped out of the bottle and what followed was inevitable. Gonder took both their business cards, formed an LLC in Nevada the following Monday, created a logo and printed stationery on Tuesday, and issued a press release on Thursday. (Wednesday he went painting in the Louvre?)

Well, it seemed like a good idea at the time. That's the trouble with Hairy Nilssons. Everything seems like a good idea at the time.

Sometimes the ideas are good.

Like, for instance—

Why don't you put some of your peanut butter in my chocolate? Why don't you put some of your chocolate in my peanut butter? That worked out okay.

But sometimes the ideas aren't good. New Coke. Windows Vista. Jar Jar Binks.

Gonder O'Conner went to the Los Angeles City Hall with his proposal. He stood up before the City Council and explained that there was a scientific answer to the city's traffic problems and that—

Okay, to be fair—there were a few people who were skeptical of the proposal.

But Gonder, to his credit, was a skilled talker, if nothing else. Rumor had it that he was the illegitimate grandson of the man who sold refrigerators to Eskimos—as a way to keep their food warm against subzero Arctic temperatures.

After his proposal to the City Council, Gonder O'Conner held a press conference on the steps of the Los Angeles City Hall. "Imagine that the city of Los Angeles is a vast living organism. Her highways are her arteries, bringing nourishment from the farthest reaches of the globe. Her streets and avenues are the capillaries that feed the tissues of the city. Her institutions are organs providing services, water, electricity, police, and fire. All the stores, all the services, every park and museum and library, every bank and barber shop—every business, every dwelling, all of the separate entities—each one is a living cell that needs access to the nourishment that flows on the city's roads."

The few reporters who showed up stifled their yawns, collected the official press releases, and returned to their various newspapers, weeklies, magazines, television and radio stations, filed their stories and promptly forgot about Los Angeles as a living organism.

Yes. In theory, it sounded good.

In theory, there is no difference between theory and practice. In practice, there is.

The Mayor of Los Angeles, a tall black woman named Violet Kopanski, wasn't just smart, she was politically astute enough to know how to bury a good idea before it became a dangerous one. She convinced the city council to form a study group, a commission, a scientific advisory board. Call it what you will—the quickest way to kill any idea is to turn it over to a committee. The smarter the members of the committee, the more certain it is that the idea will be picked apart in a feeding frenzy of intellectual vultures, leaving only a few scattered bones for the conspiracy theorists to sniff and gnaw.

Sidebar: conspiracy theorists are like paleontologists who find a fossilized tooth and construct a whole dinosaur skeleton based on that tooth—never pausing to consider that it might very well have come from a creature that would have benefited from a skilled application of Jurassic orthodonture. (Never mind. The metaphor has gotten way out of control and is now stomping through the downtown paragraph, terrifying all the various nouns to go screaming like little verbs into panicky flight, one fraught with dangerous adjectives.)

But getting back to the primary narrative, Mayor Kopanski was right—unfortunately, her timing was awful. Three days later, just enough time for the news cycle to turn its attention to the latest ill-considered remark from a politician who had never realized that her fifteen minutes had ended several years previously, the thing happened.

Carmageddon.

Crystallization.

Gridblock.

A terrorist attack—a pattern of deliberate disruptions, specifically designed to create such unprecedented interruptions in the flow of traffic that the entire city was brought to an absolute standstill. More than six million cars idling in place, from the grapevine to the Orange crush, with additional backups stretching all the way to the border-crossing south of San Diego, each and every one of them farting ever more noxious pollutants into an already overloaded atmosphere.

LA residents reading that sentence will not shudder—that's a normal business day in the region. (Readers unfamiliar with the terrain will have to google a map.) But this was worse than they imagined. Indeed—it was worse than they could imagine.

Because it wasn't accidental.

A group of anti-socialist, libertarian free-marketers, who refused to recognize the federal government's authority to build an interstate highway system had decided to shut it down. Actually, that was their Plan B.

Plan A had been to seize control of the 405 and liberate it in the name of the people.

The leader of the group was Hammond Brody, a USC dropout who began by idolizing Che Guevara and ended up arguing that Charles Manson had been denied his civil rights and railroaded by a kangaroo court. Brody styled himself a modern cowboy—he had the hat and the boots to match and a pearl-handled pistol stuck into his belt in such a way that if he hadn't kept the safety on, the hair-trigger would have removed that part of his body he liked almost as much as his gun.

But after he and his two sons, and a couple of his hench-thugs, were caught in a six-hour traffic jam between LAX and the Getty Center off-ramp, it occurred to him that a massive traffic jam was a far more potent weapon for shutting down the viability of the federal infrastructure. And also a lot easier to maintain than a seizure of forty miles of superslab.

Brody's group had originally been called the Conscientious Revolution of Angry Patriots—and under that name they had gathered nearly three hundred followers, but when it came time to design a logo, someone reluctantly pointed out that the resulting acronym was probably not the best. After several weeks of arguing about the goals and direction of their cause (a process that would have made a great case study for the panel on Dealing With Difficult People, if they could have had access to the process), Brody's followers reformed as a network of study groups and changed their name to Revolutionary American Patriots, the Institute of Social Theory and Structure.

Well, not really study groups.

Independent cells.

You know, like the Communist Party, the John Birch Society, and the Science Fiction (and Fantasy) Writers of America—the primary purpose of a cellular institutional structure is to keep every member of the conspiracy from knowing who else was in the conspiracy or what they were up to, thus making it impossible for any authority to roll up the entire organization.

Brody's group operated in almost total secrecy—well, except for the three undercover FBI agents who had infiltrated the group, a reporter from the LA Weekly, several Scientologists looking for suppressives, and two recovering alcoholics who'd wandered into the wrong meeting and stayed for the doughnuts, not to mention the gay stalker who had fixated on one of Brody's sons—

Anyway, somehow they developed a plan.

Or maybe they were enticed into a plan.

Leaping ahead to a point several years after the event, the rest of the story came out when a government report was leaked to the internet by a dissident group of disgruntled hackers who'd been expelled from Anonymous. This group, known as Pseudonymous, dumped a cascade of classified documents onto the World Wide Web. Most of the documents were so boring as to barely cause a flicker in the needle of public outrage—but the reports dealing with the Gridblock Event suggested that two of the FBI agents had been involved not only in the brainstorming process, but had actively aided in the design, the development, the preparation, and the scheduling of the entire operation.

That leak resulted in a series of publicly embarrassing congressional investigations and the resignations of several high-ranking government officials. Fortunately, this focused all of their attentions so tightly they had no time left for creating larger and more substantial problems for the nation.

The documents also revealed exactly how the Gridblock Event occurred.

The plan was simple. It required only a few dozen disposable second-hand vehicles, capable of just enough mobility to get up a carefully selected on-ramp— and a few dozen naïfs to pilot them.

Think about it.

A single accident is enough to cause a five mile backup on any Los Angeles freeway. If you could arrange thirty or forty or fifty well-placed accidents at key bottlenecks and chokepoints, all of them occurring simultaneously, you could shut down the entire traffic system. You could block 527 miles of freeway in Los Angeles County and another 382 miles of conventional highway—not to mention most of the alternate routes and surface streets. You would paralyze the entire region.

Thirty million gallons of gasoline would be burned by six million idling cars, SUVs, vans, buses, trucks, and Priuses that had exhausted their batteries. Ten million tons of pollutants would be pumped into the atmosphere.

Millions of people would be late for work, late for meetings, late for dinner. Millions of people would soil themselves because they couldn't get to a bathroom. Fistfights would break out. Some people would have heart attacks. Other people would have babies. Even more would have panic attacks, seizures, and a few would even go into diabetic comas. People would die.

Genius. Sheer genius.

Start a car fire in the Orange Crush. Get a flat tire and block the transition lanes from the 405 to the 101. Do the same at the downtown interchange. Blow up an engine at the top of the Sepulveda pass. Crash two SUVs together at the Century

Boulevard off-ramp, blocking access to LAX. Do the same where the 5 branches off to the Glendale Freeway. Paralyze the 134 where it feeds into the 170 and the 101. Paralyze the other end of the 134 where it feeds into the 5. Add a few accidents to the Hollywood Freeway, a couple more to the 10, the 110, the 710, and the 605—and don't forget the 60 and the 105 either. The 90...? Piece of apple strudel.

What fun.

Hammond Brody, one of his sons, the gay stalker, and one of the FBI agents spent a week and a half driving the highways and byways of Los Angeles County, everything from Long Beach to Chatsworth, from Azusa to Agoura, marking choke points and bottlenecks on the pages of an old Rand McNally roadmap. (Exhibit 42 in the government's case.)

They almost blew it.

They were pulled over three times by the California Highway Patrol. Once for a busted left tail light, once because the FBI agent tossed a Taco Bell wrapper out the passenger side window, and the third time for an expired registration. The first time they got a fix-it ticket and assorted failure to wear seatbelt tickets, the second time they got a littering ticket and assorted failure to wear seatbelt tickets, and the third time they nearly had the car impounded—except that Hammond Brody had the paperwork for the renewed registration in the glove compartment, he'd just forgotten to install the colored registration tab on the upper right corner of the license plate, so they had to settle for a third set of failure to wear seatbelt tickets. (And those are expensive, too.)

If any of the three ticketing officers had aspired to become detectives, they would have paid closer attention to the hurried shuffling of papers in the back seat of the vehicle. But one was three weeks short of retirement (in any other story, that would have been a death sentence), a second was thinking about his upcoming wedding, and the third was thinking about his upcoming divorce.

After that, the rest of the implementation of the grand plan proceeded without interruption. Each study group—each cell—was presented with a specific task. Procure a vehicle. When you are given the go-ahead signal, you will crash it or set it on fire, or otherwise disable it at this precise location at this specific time on the given day.

No cell was aware that any other cell had been given the same instructions, albeit a different target location. Each operative was led to believe that their accident was a targeted bit of revenge against a local jurisdiction. Or maybe a loyalty test. Or something. Stop asking questions, just do what you're told. You don't need to know what you don't need to know.

Brilliant.

And it worked.

Now, to be fair—the FBI had planned to apprehend Hammond Brody and his sons, and the various cells they had identified (which was most of them) on the day before the go-ahead signal was to be sent out.

Unfortunately...

Due to a scheduling conflict with a major sporting event, CBS had moved Hammond Brody's favorite television show, The Golden Girls: The Next Generation, to a different night—and because Hammond Brody wanted to be home in time to catch the season finale, he moved the plan up two days without telling anyone and sent out the go-ahead signal at two in the morning while almost everybody was tucked away safe in their beds.

At 3:37 p.m., Pacific Daylight Time . . . Gridblock began.

It went off better than Hammond Brody could have wished for—not just because of his somewhat inelegant planning, but also because there were so many volunteers who joined in the fun, inadvertently adding their own stalled, disabled, and crashed vehicles to the resultant urbanicide.

Among the volunteers were several motorcyclists who made the mistake of believing that they were immune to the gridlock, because of the ease with which their lanesplitting allowed them to zip through lines of stopped automobiles. They discovered the hard way that they were not as immune as they believed, when stalled motorists inadvertently opened their driver-side doors at the wrong moment, bringing those motorcyclists to very unfortunate sudden stops.

The Fire and Emergency Medivac helicopters were kept busy for the first several hours—at least until most of the cell phone batteries among the affected drivers stopped producing a flow of usable electrons. After that, passengers and drivers began abandoning their vehicles where they were and hiked to the nearest off-ramp. Local restaurants and motels appreciated the influx of new business, at least while there were still rooms to rent and burgers to fry. Without resupply, they quickly ran out of perishables.

Local grocery stores fared somewhat better. Their supplies of perishables lasted for two or three days before the shelves began to look thin.

Some of the worst problems occurred at Los Angeles International Airport. That had been targeted with six separate chokepoint incidents. With no way for departing passengers to arrive and arriving passengers to depart, very quickly the terminals began to look like a crowded refugee camp. The smarter arrivals booked themselves onto departing planes for San Diego, Santa Barbara, Ontario, and other nearby venues in the hopes of finding ground transportation to their desired destinations. Or they just collected their baggage—if possible—and flew home.

The worst of the traffic jams lasted six days—partly because emergency vehicles could not reach the affected areas. Military helicopters had to lift out many of the crashed and burned vehicles.

Normalcy never returned. Ridership on buses, trains, and the—really? LA has a subway?—increased by nearly four hundred percent, overloading the capacity of those systems almost to the breaking point.

And in the uproar that followed, the City Council had to demonstrate it was on top of the situation—they had to come up with a plan to prevent future shutdowns of the city's arteries.

Unfortunately, they had what looked like a plan.

And yes, it did seem like a good idea at the time.

Even though the Vellum-Pershing algorithms had not yet been fully tested, the surviving drivers of Los Angeles were impatient enough to demand immediate action. The City Council, never known for either its courage or its speed, in the face of such pressure, managed to demonstrate at least one of these attributes— unfortunately, the wrong one.

The city's traffic control computers were shortly reprogrammed with Doctors Vellum and Pershing's algorithms to regulate traffic flow as an organic process. The system went live at midnight of August 13th—a Friday.

The first test of the system occurred almost immediately—at 12:13 a.m., two street racers, a souped-up 2012 Honda CRX and a 1994 Chevy Corvette collided with a large truck at the Balboa off-ramp of the 101 in Encino. Despite the late hour, or perhaps because of it—various local events were just concluding—traffic began backing up almost immediately. By the time cars were slowing down on the 405 north and south connector ramps, as well as on the 101 as far east as Van Nuys Boulevard, the traffic control system flagged the event as equivalent to a blood clot in a major artery and sent in the white blood cells to repair the damage.

Oops.

That was the part of the algorithm that hadn't been . . . um, what's a polite euphemism . . . fully vetted.

See, on the second day of the Gridblock, United States Army General Daisy Cutler transferred control of four dozen military drones to the Los Angeles Traffic Control system for monitoring purposes. It had seemed like a good idea at the time, really, but General Cutler did not even have the mitigating circumstance of four Hairy Nilssons to motivate her decision.

Control of those drones had not been returned to the army.

The Vellum-Pershing algorithm saw those drones as white blood cells.

The white blood cells rushed to the site of the blood clot.

And—well, you see . . . in the rush to get eyes in the sky, only a few of those drones had been disarmed—they promptly targeted the offending vehicles and with the precision only a finely tuned military drone can achieve, initiated a surgical strike and blew the offending vehicles off the road, drivers and all.

In the aftermath, there was some official tongue-clucking about the death of the truck driver as unfortunate collateral damage, but most observers felt that the two young street racers had received what they rightfully deserved.

However . . .

Two things happened:

First . . .

Because subsequent traffic jams were treated as blood clots and as public concern began to grow, traffic suddenly became a lot safer. The incidence of reckless driving decreased significantly, enough so that the city of Los Angeles actually experienced two consecutive rush hours without a single fender bender or bumper jumper. The possibility of flaming death from the sky, without the interference of judge, jury, or predatory lawyers, had so terrified tailgaters, speeders, weavers, racers, chasers, and assorted drunks, that driving in Los Angeles actually became occasionally—well, not pleasant, but tolerable.

Second . . .

Local auto repair shops reported a sudden spike in maintenance requests. Several tire stores ran out of stock. Auto dealers had to schedule service appointments to manage the increased demand. New car sales upticked.

The Los Angeles economy boomed.

When accidents did happen, as soon as it became obvious that passing automobiles were slowing, as soon as it became apparent that traffic was going to back up—which was an inevitable phenomenon in Los Angeles, due to the high percentage of drivers who'd never seen an accident before and had to slow down to get a better look—the drivers of the affected cars would grab their belongings, their purses, bags of groceries, cell phones, dogs, and children, and start running, hoping to put as much distance as possible between themselves and the accident before the drones arrived.

Some were lucky, others not.

Collateral damage.

Too bad.

They shouldn't have had that accident in the first place.

At first, there were some grumblings. There are always people who are resistant to change, but most Angelenos adapted very quickly to the new normal—for one very simple reason: the number of traffic deaths had fallen dramatically. From an actuarial point of view, the system worked.

The insurance companies loved the new reality. Fewer accidents meant fewer claims—the infrequent claim for the total destruction of a vehicle was less than a few dozen claims for the minor damage of the average collision.

There were side effects, of course. There are always side effects. The families of the deceased were quick to file lawsuits against the city, but the Gordian tangle of nested paperwork and filings, all the various forms of red tape, the concentric layers of impacted bureaucracy, not to mention all the interconnected holding companies and shell corporations constructed by Gonder O'Conner and two of his purchased allies on the City Council's newly created board to manage the Regulated Autonomous Traffic System, meant that very few of the lawsuits would ever be resolved within the lifespan of the plaintiffs. Besides, the lawyers loved the sinecure of a steady income.

So, all in all—unless you were one of those unfortunates who got removed from the gene pool, and in that case you were in no position to offer an opinion anyway—what had seemed like a good idea in theory had actually worked out to be a good idea in practice. Unless, of course, well . . . you know. But collateral damage and all that.

Until . . .

Two events.

The first was a stalled school bus. Not one of those big yellow ones that carry fifty or sixty students at a time—this was one of those short yellow ones that carry less than a dozen children. The special ones.

Afterward, a large crowd of enraged parents descended on City Hall demanding the resignations of the Mayor, the entire City Council, Doctors Vellum and Pershing, Gonder O'Conner, and everyone else they blamed for the tragedy. Speakers representing the Asian community, the Latino community, and the African-American community all demanded a federal investigation—and indictments.

It was ugly.

It got even uglier when one of the defenders of the Regulated Autonomous Traffic System said, "If we weren't going to outlaw guns after the Sandy Hook shooting—and that was the deaths of twenty children—then why the hell do you think we're going to do anything after the deaths of only eleven?"

That's when the first chair was thrown.

Additional protests were scheduled against the weekend's presidential fund-raiser. An even larger group of enraged parents, many from more affluent areas of the city, suddenly concerned about the safety of their own children, were now demanding federal intervention .

That was when the second incident occurred.

A presidential motorcade requires the hosting city to create a bubble in the traffic flow. There's the presidential limousine. Then there are the limos of all the various attendants and aides and others invited to ride along. Then there are the secret service vehicles ahead and behind. And then there are the police escorts ahead and behind. And no other traffic is allowed anywhere near.

The system, the program, the bloody algorithm saw this as an air bubble in an artery.

Air bubbles are potentially fatal.

At the center of the air bubble was the presidential limo.

Not having an option for dealing with air bubbles, the traffic algorithm decided instead that it was observing a moving blood clot, one that seemed to be heading for the heart of the city.

Three drones, patrolling the eastbound 10 between the 405 and downtown, headed directly for the motorcade, triggering alarms everywhere. Two of them were shot down by the stealth helicopters that patrolled the airspace above the presidential motorcade. The third was able to launch two Hellfire missiles, which—due to significant tracking errors, as the Hellfire algorithms had not been written for moving targets—missed the presidential motorcade and hit a Pepsi-Cola truck instead on the westbound side of the freeway, just past the Crenshaw Boulevard off-ramp.

That the Los Angeles traffic control system was not shut down immediately was another comedy of errors. (Comedy of errors is the polite way of saying "clusterfuck.")

Several technicians charged with monitoring the drones had been watching the whole incident unfold in real time. As soon as they realized that an attack on the presidential motorcade was impending, they tried to override the drones' controls and abort the strike—but the drones had limited autonomy, just enough to reject unauthorized overrides.

As soon as the horrorstruck monitors of the system realized what had happened, they panicked. Several fled the building. One even fled the country, fearing reprisals and the inevitable accusation of terrorism because of his Muslim faith.

The fire department had to shut down power to the entire building and then disable two emergency generators before the system went down and the drones obediently returned to base.

Threatening the President of the United States is a Class E felony, punishable by up to 5 years in prison, a $250,000 maximum fine, a $100 special assessment, and 3 years of supervised release. Actually shooting a president is a capital offense—unless you miss. Then it's just a really, really, really bad felony. The kind that gets you put away for life. Unless the judge is lenient. Then you only get sentenced to a few hundred years in prison.

The Attorney General of the United States filed over a hundred and fifty-three separate indictments, citing the entire City Council as defendants for "creating a conspiracy of collective stupidity."

In particular, Doctors Vellum and Pershing, Gonder O'Conner, Mayor Violet Kopanski, all of the programmers, and everyone else who had collected a RATS paycheck, were brought up on charges. Additionally, just to be thorough, anyone who'd come anywhere near the project was indicted as an involuntary accomplice, although charges were eventually dropped for most of the lower-level technicians—except for the monitors on duty at the time.

"But I was only following orders," was not accepted as a defense plea.

The primary architects of the debacle were tried and convicted and sentenced to the maximum the law would allow.

Hammond Brody and family were charged as senior conspirators, in league with Doctors Vellum and Pershing—despite the total lack of evidence proving that any such link existed. Life sentences without parole.

Doctors Vellum and Pershing were likewise sentenced, with the additional restriction that neither of them were ever to be allowed access to any electronic device more complicated than a light switch.

Gonder O'Conner disappeared mysteriously, and although rumor had it he had been spotted living in Argentina, a more credible theory had him buried somewhere beneath the recently repaved parking lot of the new sports stadium in Inglewood.

Mayor Kopanski died of a heart attack while awaiting trial. Due to a paperwork error, her body was cremated before an autopsy could be performed.

General Daisy Cutler was not indicted—although she was court-martialed for unauthorized transfer of army property for civilian use. She was allowed to resign at rank. Elsewhere, certain military engineers and programmers were quietly assigned to study the failure of the missiles to hit their targets. One hundred and thirty-seven million dollars were allocated to find and fix the cause of the errors, so that next time, if there was a next time, the accuracy of the nation's defense technology would not become a public embarrassment.

The Bloody Algorithm, as it came to be known, was wiped from the Los Angeles Traffic Control Computers and the Regulated Autonomous Traffic System was consigned to the trash heap of history, along with 8-track tapes, floppy disks, Instamatic cameras, and folding maps.

Within a week, traffic in Los Angeles returned to normal—that is, the previous normal.

A trip from the northwest end of the San Fernando Valley to anywhere south of Anaheim was once again a four hour drive. Regardless of which freeway you took. And that was on a good day.

One more thing—bartenders throughout the state were quietly advised to discourage customers from ordering Hairy Nilssons.

And that was a very good idea.

THE KILLING CROAK

See that shining city on that hill?

That's Futuropolis, a marvel of modern society. It gleams and sparkles in the morning sunlight. Its people are proud and joyous, for they live under the protection of one of the greatest superheroes of the 21st Century—How-Man!

How-Man is a strange visitor from another world, his powers derived from the bite of a radioactive scorpion, while simultaneously exposed to a near-fatal overdose of green gamma rays under a yellow sun. The only thing that can weaken him is an exposure to Gorgonite, an impossible mineral that comes from the bizarro universe—more about that shortly.

Under How-Man's vigilant protection, Futuropolis prospers. Its most dangerous criminals are teenage jaywalkers, dog-owners who don't pick up after their pets, and three crazy cat-ladies who have been carefully spayed and neutered.

How-Man has a secret identity, of course. It's so secret, even he doesn't know what it is. So instead, he pretends to be Glenn Hauman, a mild-mannered publisher of soft-core anime and the occasional tentacular effort. His most successful book would have Multiple-Man, had it not been for the injunction filed against it by the real Multiple-Man.

What is How-Man's superpower?

Sidebar: *Everyone* has a superpower. It is built into the laws of super-physics in this particular universe. Most people are unaware of their superpowers. Some have an inkling. Others have discovered their powers by accident.

Examples:

Richard Waiver exists in an emotional sparkle-sphere. He is unaware of it. But the charismatic ripples are such that people want to be in his presence. Charles never has to sleep alone. He has bedded men, women, and a variety of confused animals.

Derry Freedlander gets television parking. Wherever he goes, there is a parking place directly in front of the building, restaurant, or store. He does not have, nor does he need, a blue handicapped sticker.

Marsha Pflug is unable to cook a bad meal. If there is nothing in the house but a can of soup, a can of tuna, a bag of rice, and some frozen vegetables, she will create a Spanish-style jambalaya that would have Guy Fieri begging for the recipe.

Dorble Sanders gets caught by red lights everywhere. He cannot get on the road without there being detours and traffic jams blocking his way. He has never been on time for anything. Arriving late at the airport, missing the flight, he was not on board when the plane crashed and burned.

Missy Solemnis has never had acne. She has unblemished skin, flawless teeth, and perfect nails. She has never had an orgasm.

Every superpower has a cost to it. The greater the superpower, the greater the burden. The universe demands a balance. It is the Law of Conservation of Coincidence.

The same applies to Supervillains. The greater the villain, the greater his or her weakness.

Supervillains gather in the bizarro universe to arrange vendettas, feuds, and Dungeons and Dragon campaigns. They recuperate from past failures and plan new efforts. Most use their various ill-gotten gains to hire C.A.S.T.L.E. to Construct Awesome Super Terrific Lairs Everywhere. (Listen, somebody has to build all those various fortresses and hideouts and underground lairs. Do you think that volcano just hollowed itself out?)

They also participate in the S.S.S. program—the Supervillain Support Seminars. The supervillain coaches encourage various master villains, journeymen villains, and wannabe bad guys to share their fears, their goals, and their nefarious challenges. Over and over, a common theme appears in their conversations. They all aspire to make a name for themselves. They all aspire to become legendary.

There are few truly legendary villains. There is Yehudi the inescapable, responsible for a million lost buttons in the wash, ten million unmatched socks, and the inevitable failure of the light that's supposed to go off when you close the refrigerator door.

There is Chuck, the bad luck fairy—the creator of the polymorphic error. You go to change the battery in the remote control and the knob on the battery drawer falls off. You go looking for the screwdriver and you cut yourself on the scissors. You go looking for the bandaids and when you open the medicine cabinet a dozen things fall out, some of them going down into the open drain of the sink. At the end of the day, you still haven't changed the batteries in the remote. That's Chuck, the bad luck fairy.

Most people haven't heard of the legendary supervillains—which is why they are able to continue their nefarious efforts. But every supervillain wants to brag of his or her greatest successes. It's part of being a supervillain. And every wannabe villain aspires to the same success. For example, there was Micro-Mite, who proved that even the smallest incident could topple a government. Micro-Mite was responsible for the ill-fitting tape on the door of the DNC headquarters in the Watergate Hotel on June 17, 1972.

Micro-Mite had inherited his superpower from his grandfather, the original Micro-Mike. His greatest success had been to start a fire in the number two coal bunker of the Titanic. Because of the strike by coal minors, the great ship did not have enough coal aboard that they could stop for the night and then restart the boilers the following morning. It had to proceed at full speed through the Atlantic ice fields. It was a gamble on Micro-Mike's part, but the sinking of the great ship ensured a legendary reputation for the entire family.

Never mind that. This is a different story. Among supervillains, there is one challenge that remains unmastered—the conquest of Futuropolis.

There is one superhero who has never been beaten.

How-Man.

How-Man's eternal vigilance is an impossible obstacle to even the greatest assaults of the most notorious supervillains.

How?

Precisely.

How-Man's superpower is tautology.

Whenever a supervillain arrives in Futuropolis, How-Man is there with his inevitable questions: "How? Why? What's the point?"

These are questions that the average supervillain never considers.

"So, after you destroy the Earth, then what?"

"So, after you kill SuperDuperMan, then what?"

"So, after you own all the gold in the world, then what?"

"What will you have that you don't already have? How many secret lairs do you need?"

Any supervillain capable of conversation greater than "Ugh. Me kill now," will hold up a hand, stop the fight, and say, "Let me get back to you on that."

See, here's the thing.

How-Man understood that you can stop a millipede dead in its tracks by asking it in which order it moves its feet. There's a story told about W.C. Fields, who began his career as a juggler. After a performance at the Palladium Theatre in London, the London Times gave him a laudatory review, praising his juggling skills. That night, Fields tried to watch himself juggle and he dropped his balls everywhere. He had to stop watching and just juggle.

Knowing this distinction—that you cannot observe and do at the same time—How-Man had stopped over a hundred and forty-three attacks on Futuropolis with just a well-timed question. "Why? What's the point?"

This had also reduced his sex-life to zero—at least until his wife convinced him to stop bringing his work home with him.

Some of the smarter supervillains, those who had actually given some thought to their processes, actually enjoyed their conversations with How-Man. When he would say, "Tell me more about that," they would happily expound. At length. Until their emotional energy had been completely dissipated. Like a writer who shares the details of the story at a cocktail party, there is nothing left for the return to the keyboard—the supervillains retired, exhausted, unable to generate any more enthusiasm for destroying the Earth, killing SuperDuperMan, or just irradiating the nation's gold supply.

How-Man had found the fatal weakness in supervillainy.

There is this about supervillains, they are desperate for validation. This is why no supervillain ever kills a hero immediately, not without first explaining the details of his or her dastardly scheme—the validation comes when the hero declares, "You're insane!"

"Yes, of course. Thank you for noticing."

But, despite their collective respect and admiration for How-Man's skill at deconstructing their agendas, every supervillain from Lethal-Man to Honey, the Badger Woman, wanted him dead. The continuing presence of How-Man in Futuropolis existed as a painful thorn in the claw of the supervillain community.

See, it's about context.

Were it not for How-Man, Futuropolis would be just another shining city on a hill. There is no shortage of shining cities. There is no shortage of hills on which to put shining cities. But there is a limited number of superheroes in the world—individuals who have discovered and mastered their innate superpower. And wherever there is someone with a superpower, the universe demands a supervillain of equal power. Everything must be balanced. Everything.

The stronger that How-Man becomes, the more necessary it is for the universe to find a supervillain capable of challenging him, keeping him so engaged in the eternal struggle between good and evil that he cannot unbalance anything else in the cosmos. The universe has its own agenda, you know.

A word about How-Man now.

In his secret identity as Hauman, he is of unassuming appearance. That is, if you ignore the wart, the hump, the incessant drooling, and the bald spot so bright it has an albedo visible from space.

As How-Man, however, costumed in day-glo orange spandex and a shining purple cape, he is an impressive figure. More than one observer has said, "Oh, for God's sake, have you never heard of a dance belt?"

That is another of his secret strengths. Once you have seen How-Man ready for action, you will never get that picture out of your head. That sight alone was enough to send several supervillains fleeing back to the bizarro universe in a state of shock and awe.

So, yes—the supervillain community has put How-Man at the center of its metaphorical dartboard. And several literal ones as well.

It was Flandry Soyce who gets the credit for finally bringing How-Man down. More famously known as Screech Girl, Flandry Soyce gained her unique power as a small child. She had been practicing her voice lessons when she was struck by a rare bolt of polarized red lightning during a magnetic storm under a full moon. It transformed her vocal cords into a weapon of terrifying power. In the years that followed, as she reached maturity, and as she developed and trained her ability, she was able to create a screech that when focused could stop bullets, shatter glass, crumble brick, melt steel, and curdle molten lava. Screech Girl had emptied bank vaults all across the continent, eventually turning most of her wealth into Lootropolitan Bitchcoins.

This particular incident began at the weekly potluck dinner of Supervillains, the Super Sunday Supper Squad meeting at the Fortress of Magnitude. Hellfire brought spicy barbecue ribs, measuring at 5,000 Scovilles—that was the "mild" recipe. Tengu-Tengu, also known as Double Demon, brought a tangy Japanese seaweed salad. Maxwell's Demon brought Baked Alaska, with real Alaska as its primary ingredient. Phase-Man brought a delightfully acidic sorbet. The Harangutan brought an unusual nut dish, but she did not reveal the source of the nuts and no one wanted to ask. Screech Girl arrived with her usual tuna casserole again.

After the meal, over the usual cheese and whine, as the supervillains compared their various plans and goals and challenges—also their various upsets, failures, and disasters—the name of How-Man kept coming up. Finally Screech Girl said, "We cannot beat him with our abilities, we will have to counter his."

"Well, duh," said Captain Obvious, who wasn't quite obvious enough to know that he was tolerated more than appreciated. His super power was unconscious irony. He had brought a container of cole slaw picked up from the local outlet of KFC. (Yes, even in the bizarro universe.)

Ignoring the obvious, Double Demon replied to Screech Girl, "But we have no Gorgonite. The last of it was used as bait when we enfolded SuperDuperMan into the spectre sector."

"And how well did that work? He escaped out the back door!"

"Well, there's always a back door. Just ask Back Door Man." (Also known as Ben Dover in real life.)

"And all the Gorgonite remains in the spectre sector. We have no way of retrieving it. Back Door Man won't do it."

"So what else is there?" asked Hellfire, his flaming aura reduced to just a bare sizzle. "How do we fight naked tautology? Or even well-dressed tautology?"

Micro-Mite spoke up then. "Does anyone remember Swift-Boy?"

"Wasn't he the crippled kid who transformed into a superhero by shouting SWIFT?" ("Speed-Wit-Intelligence-Flight-Tambourine!") (There wasn't a good super power that started with a T, so he had to settle for standing at the back of the group, shaking a pathetic excuse for a musical instrument.)

"No," said Micro. "I'm thinking of the one from the unexpurgated version of Gulliver's Travails. Remember how they stopped the Gulliver monster before he stomped Lilliputz to smithereens? While he was napping, they tied him down with ten thousand little ropes."

"Didn't the monster break all those little ropes?"

"Yes, eventually. That's how they knew he was a monster. But if they'd had stronger ropes—" Micro scratched his antennae. "No, wait. That wasn't my point." He stopped in confusion. "I need a bigger brain."

"Oh, I get it," said Captain Obvious. "It's the ropes. Instead of one big rope, you use lots of little ones."

"But we don't have lots of little supervillains," said Micro-Mite. "I'm the only one."

Screech Girl interrupted with a quick burst of white noise. (She was capable of many different colors of noise, but as a supervillain she was also a bit racist.) "The ropes," she said, "are a metaphor. When we deconstruct the cultural subtext of the narrative, it becomes immediately apparent that the Lilliputzem are meant to be understood as advocates of the entrenched system of tyrannical patriarchy." To their surprised looks, Screech Girl said, "I'm not just a supervillain, you know. I have a Masters Degree in Forensic Literature. Life is about a lot more than building secret lairs, killing superheroes, taking over planets, and irradiating Fort Knox."

"And your point is—?" prompted Hellfire, whose life had been primarily about heating his secret lair, fighting the Iceman, and conquering the uninhabited day side of the planet Mercury. Fort Knox was not on his bucket list.

"The point is, we have to think outside the box."

"Does it have to be a box?" asked Micro-Mite. After a particularly bad experience while trapped in a metal Altoids container, he had developed an aversion to small enclosed spaces.

"Okay, it can be a bottle," said Screech Girl. "We'll think outside the bottle."

"Um, no. I think I prefer thinking outside the box. I had a bad experience in a bottle too. Some children were collecting fireflies and—"

"Okay, okay. We'll just go outside and think. My point is that our traditional ways of fighting superheroes don't work. We've been fighting the wrong battles on the wrong battlefields with the wrong weapons. That's why we always lose. We need to do something for which there is no defense."

"And that is…?"

Screech Girl smiled. It was an evil smile—a leer of exuberant nastiness, because that was the only kind of smile that Screech Girl was capable of. It was hideous and produced the desired effect in the others at the table. They recoiled in disgust.

She smiled once more, it was too good an effect to waste—and then, having finally shocked the others into awestruck submission, she told them.

It took a while to put the plan in action. It required time and energy and money. Especially money. Lots of money. But supervillains tend to have access to unlimited amounts of stolen coinage, and after manipulating the value of bitchcoins into the realm of multiple digits, Screech Girl was able to—

Well, you'll see.

Three months later, while enjoying a pleasant spring day in New Jersey, one of only four that would occur in this particular year, How-Man was confronted by a phalanx, a legion of pudgy little men in gray suits, all of them holding thick bundles of documents.

Subpoenas.

"What?" said How-Man. "Why?"

"This one," said the first lawyer, "names you in a class action lawsuit for discrimination against supervillains."

"This one," said the second lawyer, "names you in a class action lawsuit for emotional damage to fifty-three named supervillains."

"This one," said the third lawyer, "names you in a class action lawsuit that you and other superheroes exert a magnetic attraction for supervillains, drawing them to Futuropolis like moths to a flame, causing undue emotional damage to the citizens of the city."

"This one," said the fourth lawyer, "names you in a class action lawsuit that you and other superheroes exert an a magnetic attraction for supervillains, drawing them to Futuropolis like moths to a flame, where they cause undue physical and financial damage to the commerce and industry of the city. It also includes a restraining order."

"This one," said the fifth lawyer, "names you in a class action lawsuit that you and other superheroes, because of your magnetic attraction for supervillains, and the resultant emotional, physical, and financial damage you have caused to the residents and businesses of Futuropolis, you have placed an undue burden on the financial resources of the entire insurance industry. It also includes a restraining order."

"This one," said the sixth lawyer, "names you in a class action lawsuit that your presence in Futuropolis, and the attraction you hold for supervillains, requires an extreme investment in emergency management resources, inflating the local and state budgets, causing an unfair tax burden to individuals, businesses, and corporations that function in the city and state. It also includes a restraining order."

"This one," said the seventh lawyer, "names you in a class action lawsuit that your activities as a superhero create an inflated perception of heroism, creating an emotional black hole for young minds in the educational system, and a lifetime of self-esteem issues, when they realize that no matter how good they are at algebra, they will still never be a superhero."

"Wait. No restraining order?"

"The judge threw it out. It was a stretch anyway."

"This one," said the eighth lawyer …

It went on all day. And all night. And all the following week.

The lawyers kept arriving. They came by the carload, they arrived by the busload, they arrived with truckloads of documents. They came from the airports and the train stations. They Ubered and Lyfted and they poured out of the subways in an avalanche of gray suits and paper.

How-Man had to rent a warehouse to store the boxes of subpoenas. It was a big warehouse and it still wasn't enough. More and more arrived every day. They came in through the doors. They came in through the roof. They came in through the bathroom window.

The total weight of paper was more than even the bedrock of New Jersey could stand. The total number of pending lawsuits was so extreme that the state judicial system ground to a halt. The state grumbled under the strain—and when critical mass was finally achieved, the ground heaved, a massive belch of tectonic disgust.

It was a lawquake, 6.7 on the Richter Scale.

The warehouse trembled.

And then it collapsed in a terrible thundering slow-motion crash of noise and dust and smoke. It smelled bad too.

It collapsed on How-Man.

All the boxes and boxes of documents came tumbling down in an unstoppable avalanche of legal-length 20-pound stock.

How-Man was buried under so much paper, he couldn't move, couldn't breathe, couldn't escape. It took him seven years to die. (Superheroes do not die easily.)

His last words were, "What? Why?" The *how* of it was no longer a question.

And then ... nothing.

There was much rejoicing in the bizarro universe. For the first time in living memory, a superhero had been defeated—supervillains had finally won a victory.

But victory is short-lived.

In the realm of superheroes—as well as in the realm of supervillains—no death is permanent.

Everyone gets resurrected. And most of the time, they come back with more power than before. Sometimes they even come back with a blue glow around them.

The rubble trembled. A cloud of dust drifted upward. Bricks and steel moved.

And there, at the center—

How-Man was back.

But he wasn't How-Man anymore.

How-Man the Gray had come back as...

Who-Man the Wight.

This time, his questions would be even more penetrating—they would be existential to a fatal degree.

The next supervillain to arrive at Futuropolis was a kaiju-sized figure, a skeletal form that towered thirty feet high. Had there been meat on its bones, it would have weighed nine tons.

It was met by a dazzling vision floating three meters above the ground.

"Who?" the vision demanded in a voice that echoed with profound sepulchral doom. *"Who are you?"*

"Huh? What?"

"No. Who."

"I am the Doctor Who Sues. I am The Malicious Malevolence."

"No, that's your name. *Who are you?*"

"Tremble before me. I am the Tyrant Rex of Judicial Terror!"

"No. That's your function. *Who are you?!*"

"Um ... I'm not sure I understand the question—"

"Yes. That's the point. *Who are you?!*"

"I am the—um, I'm a harbinger of doom, the destroyer of ambition and aspiration—?"

"No, that's your intention. Try again. *Who are you?!*"

"Wait! What? Your question makes no sense."

"No. *You* don't make sense. How can you *be* anything—how can you *do* anything? If you don't know who you are, then you don't know what you want!"

Okay, one more try. "Who I am is what I do!"

"What you do defines who you are, but it doesn't answer the question, does it? Now begone and don't return until you can speak the truth of who you are!"

"Wait! What?" A very confused Doctor Who Sues demanded, "Tell me this. *Who* are you?"

"I am The Query. I am powerful and unending. I am the inquiry that can never be completed. You may call me Who-Man! And I stand here in defense of Whomanity!"

And as Doctor Who Sues began her cautious retreat, Who-Man added this: "Oh, and one more thing. Lawsuits don't work against me. Because I am not a superhero. I am simply a manifestation of existential dread. You will die, but the inquiry will remain as a continuing process—*who are you?!*"

The Query hung in the air long after the spectral villain had fled back to her boneyard in the bizarro universe—that place where everything is for sale, but the value of nothing is known.

Oh, and one more thing.

Most of the citizens of Futuropolis emigrated within months. They didn't want to stay in Whoville either.

But that's another story for another time.

THE GHOST OF CHRISTMAS SIDEWAYS

When the ghost appeared, Kris Kringle was humping an elf.

The centuries-old oak bed was creaking and groaning like a whale with indigestion, as Kringle pounded furiously away. The headboard banged against the panelled wall with every thrust. Kringle's red pants were down around his ankles, so were his silk boxers. The flabby pink mounds of flesh that were his buttocks shook like two great bags of jelly; they looked like Christmas puddings, all blotchy and purple with veins.

"Kriiiinnngllllle. . . . " the sepulchral voice repeated ominously, this time accompanied by the rattle of rusty old chains.

The fat man didn't hear it—or maybe he didn't want to hear it. He kept grunting with lust, again and again, while beneath him, the elf—almost smothered by his weight—shrieked in ecstasy or discomfort. It was impossible to tell.

"Kringle! Goddammit! Stop that now!" demanded the voice.

Kris Kringle rolled over abruptly, rising up on one elbow, his tumescence shrinking and disappearing into the folds of flesh at his groin. "Ho ho ho!" he boomed jovially. "Mmmmeeeeerrrrrrryyyyy CCChhhhrrriiisssstttmmmaaaaassss!! And what would you like Santa to bring you, little boy?" Beside him, the elf lowered its knees from where they had been pressed against his chest. He wore an annoyed expression as he struggled to sit up, straightening his long blonde wig, and at the same time trying to pull down the nearly-transparent nightie to cover his childish modesty. His lipstick was badly smeared.

"*Kringle . . . !*" The apparition's words came from the darkest depths of the grave; they were hollow and raspy and carried the weight of years. "*I have come for you!*" Again, there came the hopeful rattle of moldering chains.

"Wait a minute, goddammit!" squeaked the elf. It reached up onto the headboard behind itself, fumbling for the remote control. At last, it found the clicker and hastily punched the pause button. Santa stopped booming in the middle of a loud enthusiastic "Ho—!" His deep voice trailed off slowly, the bright twinkle faded from his eyes, and some of the redness faded from his bulbous nose. The machinery whirred softly to a halt and Santa sat silently waiting, his naked lap open.

"Odds bodkins!" squeaked the elf. "What is it *this* time?"

In response, the tall gray specter elongated itself, stretching out one bony arm to reach across the intervening distance. It plucked the elf up out of the cushiony feather bed and held it aloft. "Do you recognize me, Brucie Kringle? *Ho ho ho . . . !*" it moaned.

The elf's eyes widened in sudden horror. "Ye gods and little fishes!" He chittered like a cockroach with a thyroid problem. "I thought we *killed* you!"

"You did!" rasped the wraith. *"Ho ho ho—!"* It rattled its long popcorn chains and leered malevolently. Its eyes burned like ornaments.

The ghost made a mysterious gesture and—

Suddenly, the two of them were standing out in a frozen cold wilderness, the blue sun was a bitter pill on the horizon. A furious wind whipped at the elf's nightgown. Nearby, a red and white striped pole stood next to a tiny cottage. *"Look!"* pointed the ghost, stabbing with a bony finger at the tiny house. A yellow window glowed with beckoning warmth. Framed by red and white curtains, Santa's body, stuffed to an ample girth with styrofoam peanuts, rocked steadily back and forth in a motorized chair. It puffed merrily at its pipe. Periodically it lifted its hand and waved out the window, while a synchronized recording repeated Santa's infectious laughter against a background of Jingle Bells.

"A very good job you did, little sprite! You left no detail unattended to."

"Thanks," blushed the elf, forgetting for the moment its precarious predicament.

The ghost made another mysterious gesture and—

Suddenly, the two of them were standing in a cold gray field—no horizon, only gray mist and cruel grass. Nearby, stood three men clad in hunters' garb and carrying rifles. Suddenly, one pointed upward. The other two raised their rifles, took careful aim, and fired off three quick shots each. The reports of their weapons sounded small and flat against the silent tundra—but far in the distance, a dark object plummeted heavily to the ground, smacking into it with a terrible wet impact.

"You sold my reindeer to a hunting farm!" the apparition accused.

The elf squirmed in the bony grip. "Hey! That wasn't my idea. The lawyers ordered it. They said we should downsize the operation. We needed to invest in new transportation. And we got a terrific detail from the Airbus Consortium. The goddamn elk were too old and too slow anyway—and you never paid any attention to how much those hayburners ate, did you? The upkeep was horrendous! If we didn't act when we did, the whole thing would have gone into Chapter 11. Down the tubes without a flush. At least this way, we have a chance to compete against the Japanese—"

"Always with the excuses, Bruce! Remember, an excuse only satisfies the person who makes it."

"Yeah, yeah, yeah—the old-fashioned ways are always the best. The time-honored tradition of the Christmas spirit—and all that jazz. But have you seen how

Christmas is celebrated lately?" This time the elf made a mysterious gesture. "Look at this, you fat old fart—"

This time, the haunt and the elf found themselves in a gaily-lit concourse, a suburban mall filled with joyous music, dazzling decorations, towering displays, spotless storefronts, and crowds of anxious looking people milling from one ramp to the next with desperate expressions on their faces. Many of them were parents, escorting small children.

The children wore costumes of all kinds. The girls were mostly dressed as glittery princesses, ballerinas, winged fairies with plastic wands, mermaids, cowgirls, and witches—a lot of little witches. The costumes of the boys reeked of violence—they were killers of all kinds: gunslingers, terminators, ninjas, turtles, batmen, supermen, vampires, and pirates. Many of the costumes seemed to be generic, probably purchased from the Disney outlet in the mall. At each store, tired-looking employees in gay apparel smiled wanly and passed out generic candies.

"*This* is Christmas now!" declared Bruce Kringle, pointing at a shop window showing Santa waving from a pumpkin patch, another shop window showing Santa riding on the back of a witch's broom, a third display showing the gay old saint passing out candy to costumed children at the front door of his north pole workshop, and a fourth one showing Santa sitting in the command seat of the starship Enterprise while a dozen little Vulcans in green uniforms smiled and waved.

"But this is not Christmas—" the spook whispered. "It's only Halloween."

"Yeah, that's another thing. We had to merge the holidays. Greater profit potential. Longer selling season. We had to drop the Christ angle, of course. Too tricky. But now, we get into high gear the first weekend before Halloween and we go straight through until the middle of January."

"*What have you done?*" The ghost demanded cavernously.

"Hey—this was all your idea," the elf replied strongly. "We pick up another five percent just with the post-season white sales. We've got a Japanese conglomerate funding the expansion, and we're looking at an eventual extension of the selling season all the way into Valentine's Day. Of course, the long-term goal is to make Christmas a year-round festival. You always said, you wanted people to have the spirit of Christmas all year round. Well, this is the necessary first step—merchandising."

Brucie Kringle was about to explain about cost-leveraging and swing-markets, when suddenly, from nearby, came a blood-curdling shriek of terror.

"*What's that?*" asked the ghost.

"Uh—it's just a little extra innovation. Something to shake them up a bit. An idea we got from the amusement parks."

"*Tell me!*" demanded the wraith.

"Um—better yet, I'll show you." Shaking free from the bony grasp of the specter, the elf jumped down to the tiled floor, grabbed the haunt by its cobwebby robe, and dragged it toward a ramshackle-looking structure; it seemed to have been dropped in a heap in front of the entrance to the Broadway. A short line of people waited to enter. Periodically, a hunchback would stagger out of the entrance, grinning and drooling, to wave another small group of people inside. As they watched, another terrifying scream came floating over the top of the walls.

"What's happening in there?" said the spook.

"It's called a haunted house. We're scaring the bejesus out of them. It helps to put them in a buying mood—"

The ghost and the elf joined the line—nobody paid them any undue attention. Shortly, the hunchback guided them into the interior of the fabricated structure, where they were treated to a series of tableaus portraying the worst excesses of vampires, chain-saw murderers, and back-alley abortionists. The rooms were decorated with coffins, skeletons, and big glass jars with strange-looking creatures floating in amber alcohol. They saw corpses, dismembered body-parts, and all manner of hairy little bugs and slimy snakes and worms. Deformed mutants leapt out of the walls at them. All around them, the costumed children laughed and shrieked in delight. Flashes of lightning and crashes of thunder punctuated the screams of the banshees and the moans of the zombies.

"See!" said the elf, when they found themselves out in the crush of the mall again. "It's all in fun. Nobody gets hurt. Okay, yeah—so it's not dancing sugarplums. But you were out of touch with all that sugary crap. Don't you know that sugar is bad for kids. This is more realistic—more educational. It's more in tune with the times. I mean, just look at yourself! Do you think you really represent the spirit of Christmas?"

The ghost was sorely offended. It stiffened to its full height. *"I am the spirit of Christmas!"*

"Right, sure," said the elf. "And just how jolly do you think you're going to make people feel, looking like that? At least we've got them laughing at their fears—"

"Laugh at this!" said the spook, grabbing the elf by the arm and dragging him into a kitchen appliance store. He seized a cordless electric knife from the wall display—"No More Hassles Carving Your Christmas Turkey!"—and began hacking off the elf's arms and legs. With each cut, the ghost reminded the screaming elf of who it had been when it was still alive. *"I used to bust my ass all year long just for the privilege of working like a frenzied demon racing the dawn on what was supposed to be the holiest night of the year. I had a spastic colon, two crushed vertebrae, a double hernia, hemorrhoids, varicose veins, swollen ankles, colitis, phlebitis, an ulcerated bowel, psychosomatic impotency, and chest pains strong enough to fell a horse. But I did it for the children—and you've turned it into a mockery!"*

By this time, the elf had been sliced into seven or eight different-sized pieces, all of them wriggling excitedly on the floor, reforming and growing even as the undead spirit watched. Each piece of the elf was becoming a whole new elf. Almost immediately, they were leaping to their feet, chittering and squeaking in their little high voices. "Now, there are eight of us! Eight little Brucies! H'ray! We can have a daisy-chain!"

The ghost began grabbing them one by one, cackling hideously as it shoved them all into an industrial size food processor. The elves screamed in agony as the ghost punched up the *puree* setting. The many shrieks of "I'm melting—" died away quickly, smothered by the sounds of tiny bones crunching into soup.

Before the fragments could reform into a Brucie-blob, the ghost slid the whole pitcher into a brand-new Radar-Range Microwave oven (with carousel and browning circuits), and programmed it for popcorn. Almost instantly, myriads of little gremlin-like creatures began spurting out of the pitcher, yelping and sparking as the microwaves sleeted angrily through their bodies. They cursed and swore, but their voices were way too thin to be audible. Instead, they sounded like the angry buzz of summer cicadas. Soon, they began smoking and popping, vaporizing painfully into nothingness—

Brucie Kringle, the elf, woke up in a cold sweat. "Oh, my goodness—what a nightmare," he piped. Beside him, the naked Santa-droid rested heavily in the feathery mattress. Bruce leaned over and mopped the cold sweat from his face with Santa's beard. "Whoa," he said to himself. "That was scary. I just gotta watch what I eat before going to bed. I think there was more gravy than grave in that one." And then his words stuck in his mouth. Fear grabbed his throat with icy claws.

Standing at the foot of the bed was a tall dark wraith; its ample girth and jolly posture revealed its nature even before it spoke. *"He he he!"* it cackled. *"Thank you, Bruce, thank you! You have taught me a very valuable lesson. The time is right for a whole new spirit of Christmas—you will get the Christmas that you deserve. And this time, my little sugar-plum, no one will never be able to kill the Christmas spirit! Ho ho ho!"*

FRANZ KAFKA, SUPERHERO

The rattle of the red roach phone—a noise like an angry cicada—brought him to instant wakefulness. He rolled out of bed in a single movement, scooped up the handset and held it to his ear. He didn't speak.

The familiar voice. The words crisp and mellifluous. "One-thirty-three. How soon can you leave?"

He bent to the nightstand and switched on the lamp with a loud click. He opened the World Atlas that lay directly under the glow to page 133. A map of Vienna. He glanced to the clock. The minute hand had long since fallen off, but he'd become fairly proficient at telling the time by the position of the hour hand alone. "I'll be on the ten-thirty train."

"Good," said the voice. The line clicked and went silent.

He undid the laces tying up the throat of his nightshirt, letting the wide neck of the garment fall open and away. He began shrugging it down off his shoulders, pulling it down to his waist, shedding it like an insect pushing its way out of its cocoon, all the while darting his eyes about the room in quick, nervous little glances. It fell forgotten to the floor. He stepped out of it, pink, naked, and alert. A whole new being. His eyes glistened with anticipation and excitement.

He dressed quickly, efficiently. He put on a shiny black suit. He selected a matching black tie. He buttoned his dark red vest meticulously. He wound his watch and tucked it into his vest. He opened the top drawer and selected his two best handkerchiefs; then, after a moment's consideration, he selected a third one as well—his *silk* handkerchief, the one he only used for special occasions.

He pulled on his heavy wool overcoat. He grabbed his carpet bag from the closet, already packed. He was ready to go.

As he walked, he considered. Fifteen minutes to the train station. Five minutes to buy a ticket. Twenty minutes to spare before the train arrived. Yes. He could purchase a newspaper and have a coffee and a croissant in the cafe while he waited. Good.

He could feel the power in his step. He was ready for battle. His mind was clear. This time, he would confront the arch-fiend PsycheMan in his lair. Yes! The enemy would know the taste of ashes and despair before *this* day was through.

In his ordinary life, he pretended to be just another faceless dark slug—sweaty, confused, trapped by circumstance. He moved through the maze of twisty gray streets, almost unnoticed. If by chance he did attract the attention of another being, they would see him only as a squat dark shape, brooding, uncommunicative.

In his ordinary life, he pretended to be a writer of grotesque fantasies, a mordant storyteller of obscure, deranged, and unpublishable dreads. His visions were tumbled and stifling—almost repulsive in their queerness. People avoided the possibility of close contact, which was exactly what he wanted and needed—

—Because in his *extra*ordinary life, he was Bug-Man! *The human insect!*

Transformed by a bizarre experiment in Marie Curie's laboratory—accidentally exposed to the life-altering rays of the mysterious element *radium*—he had become a *whole new kind of being*. A strange burst of power had expanded throughout his entire body, shredding the very cells of his flesh.

For a single bright instant, he comprised the entire universe, he knew *everything,* understood *everything*. His skin glowed white as the very essence of life itself infused his whole being. For just that single instant, he became a creature of *pure energy!* And then the transforming bath of radioactive power ebbed and the entire cosmos collapsed again, down into a single dark node at the bottom of his soul. When his vision cleared, he realized that the insect specimen he had been holding had vanished completely, its essence subsumed throughout his flesh.

That night, under the intoxicating rays of the full moon, he discovered a new plasticity to his flesh. His bones had become malleable. His muscles could be used to pull his body into a shape that was at first painful and frightening, then curious, and finally invigorating and powerful. His skin toughened like armor. He turned and saw himself in the mirror as something strange and beautiful. A shining black carapace. Glistening faceted eyes. Trembling antennae. He could taste symphonies in the air that he had never known before. He could hear colors previously undreamt. The strength in his limbs was alarming! Thrilling! He had become a master *of metamorphosis*. Franz Kafka, Superhero!

In the days that followed, he learned to control his new powers, leaping from buildings, tunneling, biting, scrabbling through the earth in the dead of night. The cost of his ability to metamorphosize was a ferocious hunger. He satisfied it by preying on the predators of society. He became a force to be reckoned with, seeking out those who preyed on the weak, snapping them in two and feeding on their flesh. Soon, the dark underworld elements of Austria learned the fury of his appetites. The word spread. *The night belonged to Bug-Man.*

Soon he became an ally to the great governments of Europe, battling arch-fiends all over the continent. His exploits became world-famous. His twilight battles were the stuff of legend. Where evil spread its nefarious claws, the cry would soon go up: "This is a job for Bug-Man!"

Now, he hurried to Vienna, eager for the final confrontation with the greatest monster of them all: the terrible master of confusion, Sigmund Freud—more commonly known to the League Of United Superheroes Everywhere as *PsycheMan!*

The evil doctor Freud terrorized his victims by summoning up the monsters of the id. He used their own fears against them, plundering their treasures, and leaving them feeble and empty. Freud's victims babbled in languages of their own, meaningless chatter. They capered like monkeys, simpered like idiots, grinning and drooling; he filled the asylums with his victims. Franz Kafka could not wait to catch this monster on his own overstuffed couch. He dabbed at his chin with his handkerchief, lest someone observe him drooling in anticipation.

The train lurched and rattled and crawled across the Austrian countryside. By the time it finally clattered into the Vienna station, it was nearly four in the afternoon. Dusk would be falling soon, and with it would come his terrible hunger. No matter, tonight he intended to feed well. He would soon suck the marrow from the bones of Dr. Freud. He could hardly wait to sink his gleaming pincers into the soft white flesh of the little Viennese Jew, injecting him with his venom, then tasting the liquefied flesh, inhaling its aroma, taking it hungrily into his metamorphosed self, refreshing himself, invigorating his energies. He would turn the monster's very flesh into fuel for his own divine crusade against evil!

Wiping his mouth again, covering his excitement with his now-sodden handkerchief, Kafka hurried to the post office window and asked if a letter had been left for him. The squint-eyed clerk handed it across without comment. Kafka shoved it into his coat pocket without looking at it and scuttled away out of the glare of the bright lights overhead. At last he flattened himself into a dark comer and opened the envelope quickly. Inside was a small square of paper with an address neatly typed on it. Kafka repeated the address to himself three times, memorizing it, then wadded up the paper and shoved it into his mouth, chewing frantically. It was several moments before he was able to swallow the wad, and during the entire time his little dark eyes flicked back and forth, watching for suspicious strangers. But no, nobody had noticed the dark little creature in the corner.

Kafka swallowed the last of the paper and left the station, relieved to be away from the screech of the trains and the crush of so many people. He headed north, walking briskly, but not so fast as to call attention to himself. He headed directly for the address on the paper. He had to see the house before the sun set. The narrow cobbled streets of Vienna echoed with his footsteps.

All the buildings clustered like newborn wedding cakes, close and ornate. The streets and alleys between them were already sunk in romantic gloom, and the first smells of the evening meal were already filling the streets. He passed open shop doors and restaurants. His heightened senses told him of the spices in the sausages, the honey in the pastries, the butterfat in the cream. A horse-drawn wagon clattered by, dragging with it the animal scent of manure and sweat. Smoke from the chimneys climbed up into the oppressive sky. The heavy flavor of coal pervaded everything.

Kafka found the street he was looking for and turned left into it as if he was a long-familiar resident. He slowed his pace and studied the houses on the opposite side of the avenue, one at a time, examining each as if none of them held any specific interest for him. They were tall, narrow structures, each hiding behind a wrought-iron fence. The high peaked roofs offered multiple opportunities to hide and possible easy access through the gabled windows; but Kafka ignored them. He let his attention wander to the cobbled street itself, the sewers and the drains. If he was satisfied with what he saw, he gave no sign. He continued on down the street toward the end.

At the end of the block, he turned right, crossed the street and headed up toward the next block. He turned right and headed up the row of houses looking thoughtfully at each one. As luck would have it, the building directly behind Dr. Freud's suspected lair was a small hotel for retired gentlemen.

He climbed up the front steps, entered, and rang the bell at the registration desk. Shortly, a wizened old clerk appeared and Kafka inquired politely if there were a quiet room available in the back of the inn. There was, and he immediately secured it for two days. He would need a private place in which to accomplish his metamorphosis, and time to recover afterward. He considered himself extremely fortunate to be so close to his quarry.

Wiping his chin, he let himself into the room, put down his carpet bag just inside the door, turned, and locked the door behind him. At last! He was so close to his arch-enemy, Freud, he could almost taste his blood! He crossed to the window and parted the curtains. Across a narrow garden, he could see the shuttered rear windows of Dr. Freud's house. He wondered what nefarious deeds were going on behind those walls.

He'd know soon enough; the moon was already visible above the rooftops. He pulled the curtains aside and opened the window, the better to admit the healing rays of moonlight. He began pulling off his clothes, almost clawing his way out of them, exposing his pallid flesh to the intoxicating luminance.

He opened the carpet bag and began laying out the equipment that he would need. A large rubber sheet—he spread it across the floor. A large block of wood—battered, chipped and scarred; he placed that carefully on the sheet.

The transformation began slowly. He felt the first twinges in his shoulders and in his knees. He began to twitch. The long hours cooped up in the train had left him stiff and uncomfortable; this metamorphosis would be a painful one. Good! A flurry of little shudders shook his body; he grabbed hold of a chair for support until the seizure eased. He knew he had to be careful, he knew he didn't dare risk losing consciousness; he had to stay awake and deliberately shape himself for the battle ahead.

His head. Most important. His mandibles—

His teeth began to lengthen in his mouth, pushing his jaw painfully out of its sockets. He shoved his fingers into his mouth and started pulling his teeth painfully forward, shaping them into the digging and grinding tools that he would shortly need.

Next, his skull. He put his right hand under his chin and his left hand on top of his head and pressed them toward each other as hard as he could. The bones of his skull creaked and gave. His head began to flatten. His chin spread, his eyes bulged sideways, his jaw widened out, his teeth splayed forward, his eyebrows sprang out like antennae—blood began to pour from his nose. He pressed harder and harder, until the pain became unbearable, but still he pressed until he no longer had the strength in his arms or the leverage with which to press.

Already his spine was softening, could no longer support his weight. He dropped to the floor, grunting as the air was forced from his lungs. His arms flopped wildly. He pulled his knees up and grabbed hold of his feet as hard as he could. As he straightened his legs again, his arms began to lengthen. His elbows popped, the bones pulling out of their sockets—he screamed with pain; rolled over and grabbed the block of wood in his mouth, bit it as hard as he could. He did this again and again, stretching his arms into long, black, hairy appendages.

Yes, the hair! It was sprouting all over his arms and legs. His legs were softening now. He pulled his knees up to his chest, and now, grabbing them again with his hardening arms, he pulled at his knees until the sockets popped and now his legs could lengthen naturally. He clutched his feet, working them into clawlike shapes, stretching his toes, pulling at them mercilessly, grunting with the pain, and still continuing to pull. And yes, now the side appendages were large enough to grab, to pull, to stretch. He worked his muscles savagely, massaging them into shape, strengthening them. Yes, this was going to be one of the best! The more pain he experienced, the better the transformation!

He rolled around on the floor, rubbing his back and sides against the rubber sheet, hardening his carapace. He wiped at his multifaceted eyes with his front legs, cleaning them of bloody residue. His antennae twitched. He was almost done. Almost there—and yes, in a final spasm of completion, he *ejaculated!* Spurt after spurt after spurt of sickly yellow-looking ichor. The shaft of his metallic-looking penis retreated again inside his chitiny shell, and Bug-Man raised himself aloft on his six exquisite legs, chittering with satisfaction and joy!

Bug-Man was a simple being. He had no knowledge of anything but the blood of his enemy. He cared nothing for Franz Kafka or the League Of United Superheroes Everywhere. He knew little of trains and croissants and newspapers. Bug-Man was a creature of hunger and rage. He knew only the ferocious desire for vengeance. He lived for the hot red fulfillment of delicious gluttony. His mandibles clattered in soft anticipation. He drooled with excitement. He wanted one thing only-the flesh of PsycheMan! He could not rest until he'd crunched the skull of Sigmund Freud between his diamond-hard teeth!

He leapt to the window, flinging it open, pulling himself out onto the balustrade, poising himself, stretching himself up into the darkness and the holy glow of the full moon above. Across the way, he heard a gasp, and then the sound of a window slamming. A light vanished. He heard the sounds of running footsteps. He ignored them all. He leapt.

He landed lightly on the soft black earth of the garden below. Instantly, he began digging, down and down into the deep delicious soil, his six legs working frantically, flinging the dirt, backward and upward, scattering it in every direction. His mandibles chewed and cut. In moments, he was gone, sliding into the cool dark space beneath the lawn, tunneling his way toward the house of Sigmund Freud, the monster.

The night fell silent. The moon rose higher and higher until it was directly overhead, casting its lambent radiance down across the gabled old houses of sleeping Vienna. And then a noise ...

The sound of something creaking, cracking, crackling as it broke—

The ancient floorboards came away in ragged chunks. The hole widened. Something was chewing up through the ground, widening the hole in quick, malicious bites. And then it was climbing up and into the cellar of the house. Bug-Man was here! Inside the house of his arch-enemy! He scrabbled purposefully across the floor, sniffing the air with his antennae. He slid up the stairs, not bothering to open the door at the top, breaking through it instead like a flimsy construction of cardboard.

He was in the pantry! The overwhelming pantry, reeking with conflicting flavors and aromas—all the spices and ingredients of a thousand different meals, coffee-chocolate-butter-garlic-sausage-cheese-pepper-bread—they all repulsed him now. He moved swiftly to the kitchen, to the dining room, to the stairway in the hall, and up the stairs, breaking away the banister as he climbed to give himself room.

There was no dark at the top of the stairs. The light came on abruptly. Someone was moving up there. Bug-Man's glistening multifaceted eyes caught the image in a shattered reality. There—silhouetted against the glare of the electric lamp beyond— stood the terrible demonic form of Sigmund Freud, the *PsycheMan!*

He stood alone, wearing only a nightshirt, a robe, and fuzzy blue slippers. He rested one hand on the top of the broken banister to support himself. He looked incredibly frail, but his eyes gleamed with turquoise power! His high forehead bulged abnormally, the fringe of white hair around it was not enough to conceal its freakish expanded shape. His predatory chin was concealed by the long white beard. His bony knees stuck out from beneath the hem of his garment like awkward chicken legs.

The transformed Kafka lifted himself up, as if about to leap. He uttered a low sound, a moan of anticipatory lust, a growl of warning, a challenge, a chittering of danger.

"Ach!" said Freud. "It's only you. Well, come in, come in. I've been expecting you. You're late again." He waggled his finger warningly. "You superheroes, you think you can come calling any time, day or night, without an appointment—"

He started to turn away, then suddenly, turned back toward Bug-Man, his eyes blazing with red fire! *"Well, I won't have it!"* He knocked the ash off his cigar into his hand and carefully pocketed the residue. Then he lifted the cigar like a baton, holding it outstretched toward the man-bug. With his other hand he stroked the cigar, once, twice, a third time—suddenly the cigar emitted a crackling bolt of blue-white lightning down the staircase. BugMan ducked his head just in time. The blast of fire splattered off his back singing the walls, scorching the wallpaper, striking little fires among the chips and sawdust of the broken banister all the way down and leaving the air stinking of ozone.

Kafka was stunned. For a moment, he almost forgot that he was Bug-Man. Freud was much stronger than he thought. He must have been gaining converts faster than they had realized, far more than they had estimated. He must have been draining the life force of hundreds, perhaps thousands of hapless souls, distilling their very being down into his own evil essence.

Bug-Man recovered himself then. He stopped thinking, stopped considering, stopped caring—he remembered his purpose. To *feed on the flesh of Sigmund Freud!* He charged up the stairs after the monstrous little man. But Freud's frail demeanor was only another deceit. The old man scampered away like an animated elf, disappearing into the darkness at the far end of the hall.

Bug-Man followed relentlessly, his six long hairy legs scrabbling loudly on the hardwood floor. His claws left nasty scratches in the polished surface. He plunged into the darkness—

And found himself in a maze of twisty little passages, all alike. A maze. The maze. Twisty little passages. A twisty little maze. All alike.

His eyes swiveled backward and forward—and he hesitated. For a moment, he had to be Kafka again. Had to rely on his innate human intelligence instead of his insect instinct. Reminded himself. *Freud has no power of his own. He borrows the power of others. He summons monsters from the id and lets them fight his battles for him. But it's all illusion.. You will destroy yourself fighting empty manifestations of your own fears. Ignore the illusions. Concentrate on what's real!*

Bug-Man's hesitation stretched out forever. His chitiny shell began to soften. His mandibles clattered in confusion. *But—but how do I know what's real?* he wondered. *Everything that a being can know is ultimately experiential. I have no way to stand apart from the experiential nature of existence! So how can I access what is real and distinguish it from illusion?*

It seemed as if all time was standing still. Kafka's mind raced, his thought processes accelerated. Be who you are! he shouted to the Bug-Man! Don't let him define you! He is a walrus. You are the Bug-Man! You are the greatest superhero ever! Ignore the lies! Anything that contradicts the Bug-Man is a lie! Remember that!

The Bug-Man snarled. Unconfused. He knew himself again, submerged himself once more in crimson fury and fire; the hunger and rage suffused his body like a bath of acid. He clicked his mandibles, reached out with his pincers and started pulling down the ugly twisty little walls and their dripping veins and wires, started pulling down the twisty little maze of darkness and fury, sending creatures of indeterminate shape scuttling out into the fringes, started pulling down the twisty little passages all alike, pulling and chewing and breaking through—

He was in a tunnel. Blackness behind him. Blackness ahead.

The tunnel slanted downward into the bottomless dark. The walls were straight; they were set wide apart, but the ceiling was low. Everything was cut from dark wet stone. The water dripped from the walls and slid downward into the gloom ahead. His eyes refocused. What little light there was seeped into the air from no apparent source.

Far in the distance below, something moved. He could smell it. His antennae quivered in anticipation. He lifted his pincers. He readied his stinger, arching his tail high over his head. His venom dripped.

The thing ahead was coming closer. In the blackness below, a formless form was growing. It opened its eyes. Two bright red embers, glowing ferociously! The eyes were screaming toward him now!

Stinger?!

Bug-Man remembered just in time. *Ignore the lies!*

The red eyes went hurling past him, vanishing into darkness. The screams of rage faded into distant echoes that hung in the air like dreadful memories—

I could have stung myself, right behind the brain case—he realized. And then, realizing again how narrowly he had escaped the trap of the Freudian paradigm, he warned himself again. *You are the Bug-Man! Don't let him define you or your reality! Monsters from the id aren't real!*

The Bug-Man headed down the tunnel. Its angle of descent increased abruptly, getting steeper and steeper, until he was slipping, sliding, skidding, tumbling—

—onto the hard-baked surface of a place with no sun, no moon, no sky, and no horizon. Tall black cylinders surrounded them, leaping up into the gloom and disappearing overhead. They looked like bars of a cage.

Freud stood beside one of the bars, surveying him thoughtfully. "You are resisting the treatment," he said. "I can't help you if you do not want to be helped." He waggled his finger meaningfully. *"You must really want to change!"*

Bug-Man roared in fury. It consumed him like volcanic fire. He became a core of molten energy. The blast of emotion overwhelmed him. Enraged, he charged.

Bug-Man galloped across the space between them, tearing up the floor with his six mighty claws. He thundered like a bull, hot smoke streaming from the vents of his nostrils. The black leviathan leapt—

—and abruptly, Freud was gone!

Bug-Man smashed against the bars of the cage like a locomotive hitting a wall, his legs flailing, his body deforming, the air screaming out from his lungs like a steam whistle. He shrieked in rage and frustration and pain. He fell back, legs working wildly, righted himself, whirled around, eyes flicking this way and that, focusing on

Freud again. The *PsycheMan* waited for him on the opposite side of the cage. The Bug-Man didn't hesitate! He charged again—

—and again, he came slamming up against the bars. Helpless for an instant, he lay there gasping and wondering what he was doing wrong. Transformed Kafka shuddered in his shell. But he pushed the thought aside, levered himself back to his feet, focused again on his target, readied his charge, sighted his prey—

This time, he would watch to see which way the *PsycheMan* leapt. He would snatch him from the air. He held his pincers high and wide. Instead of charging, he advanced steadily, inexorably, closing on his elusive prey like some ghastly mechanical device of the industrial revolution gone mad. His mandibles clicked and clashed. His eyes shone with unholy fury. A terrible guttural sound came moaning up out of his throat—

—came slamming hard against the bars of the cage as if he'd been fired into them by a cannon. The discontinuity left him rolling across the floor in pain, clutching at his aching genitals and crying in little soft gasps. He pulled himself back to his knees, his feet, trying to solidify his form again. He stood there, wavering, almost whimpering.

"What's wrong?" he asked himself. "What am I doing wrong?"

Kafka looked across the cage. Freud stood there grinning nastily. The old man laughed. "You battle yourself!" he said thickly. "The rigidity of your constructed identity cannot deal with events occurring outside of its world view. You become confused and you attack shadows and phantoms!"

Kafka took a deep breath. Then another, and another. "I am Franz Kafka, superhero!" he said to himself "I am here to destroy the evil paradigm of Dr. Freud! I will not be defeated."

No!—he realized abruptly. *That way doesn't work! I am the master of metamorphosis. I must metamorphose into something that the doctor cannot defeat!* At first he thought of giant squids and vampire bats, cobras and bengal tigers, raging elephants, bears, dragons, manticores, goblins, trolls—Jungian archetypes! *But, no*—he realized. *That would be just more of the same! Just another monster to fight a monster I must change into something ELSE—*

He stood there motionless, staring across the cage at his fiendish opponent, considering. His mind worked like a precision machine, a clockwork device ticking away at superfast speed. His thoughts raced, exploring strange new possibilities he had never conceived before.

Ego cogito sum—he considered. *I have been reacting to his manipulations. Reactive behavior allows him to control the circumstance. Proactive behavior puts me in control. I should attack him, but attacking him is still reaction. Yet, if I don't attack him, I cannot defeat him. How can I be proactive without being reactive?*

Bug-Man wavered. His confusion manifested itself as a softening of his shell, a spreading pale discoloration of his metallic carapace. His mandibles began to shrink. His arms and legs began to plump out, seeking their previous shape. *No!* he shrieked to himself. *No! Not yet! I haven't killed him yet*

Bug-Man felt himself weakening, growing ever more helpless in the face of his enemy. He felt shamed and embarrassed. He wanted to scuttle off and hide in the woodwork. His bowels let loose, his bladder emptied. His skin became soft and pallid again. He stood naked before Freud. Franz Kafka, superhero. But the Bug-Man was defeated, discredited—

No! said Kafka. No! I won't have it. I am Franz Kafka, superhero! I don't need to be a giant cockroach to destroy the malevolence of Freud! I can stop him with my bare hands.

—And then he knew!

"Your paradigm is invalid," Kafka said. It's powerful, yes, but ultimately, it has no power over those who refuse to give it power; therefore, it is not an accurate map of the objective reality, only another word-game played out in language." Freud's eyes widened in surprise. Kafka took two steps toward him. "You're just a middle-aged Viennese Jew, who smokes too much, talks too much, and suffers from—your word—*agoraphobia*. You can't even cross the street without help!" Freud held up a hand in protest, but Kafka kept advancing, continued his unflinching verbal assault. "You're a dirty old man. You can't stop talking about sex, you want to kill your father and copulate with your mother—and you believe that everybody else feels the same thing, too! You're despicable, Sigmund Freud!"

Freud's chin trembled. "You—you don't understand. You're functioning as a paranoid schizophrenic with psychotic delusions. You've constructed a world view in which explanations are impossible—"

"That won't work, Siggie. It's just so much language. It's just a load of psyche-babble. The distinctions you've drawn are arbitrary constructions that only have the meaning that we as humans invest them with. Well, I withdraw my investment. Your words are meaningless. I will not be *psychologized*. You are just a disgusting little man who likes to talk about penises!"

The old man made one last attempt to withstand the withering assault of Kafka's logic. "But if you withdraw all meaning from the paradigm—" he protested, "— what meaning can you replace it with?"

"That's just it!" exulted Kafka, delivering the death blow. *"Life is empty and meaningless!"*

Horrified, Freud collapsed to the floor of his parlor, clutching at his chest.

Kafka stood over him, triumphant. "It's meaningless, you old fart!"

Freud moaned—

"It doesn't mean anything! And it doesn't even mean anything that it doesn't mean anything! So we're free to make it up any way we choose!"

"Please, no. Please, stop—"

But Kafka wasn't finished. "Your way is just a possible way of being, Sigmund— but it isn't the only way! The difference between you and me is that because I know the bindings of my language, I also know my freedom within those bindings! You have been focusing on the bindings, you old asshole, *not the freedom."*

Freud was shuddering now, impaled on Kafka's impeccable truths. He trembled uncontrollably on the patterned rug, sick and despairing at the chaotic darkness gathering around him. The broken shards of his shattered paradigm had sliced his soul mercilessly, leaving the poor defeated man twitching in the growing puddles of his own terminal *weltschmerz*. "Forgive me, please. I didn't know what I was doing."

Kafka knelt to the floor, gathered Freud up in his arms, held him gently, cradling him like a child. He placed one soft hand on the old man's forehead. "It's all right now, Siggie," he soothed. "It's all over. You can stop. You can rest."

Freud looked up into Kafka's calm expression, questioning, hoping. He saw only kindness in the superhero's eyes. Reassured, he let himself relax; he allowed peace to flood throughout his body. All stiffness fled. Sigmund Freud rested securely in Franz Kafka's arms. "Thank you," he whispered. "Thank you."

"No," said Kafka. "On the contrary. It is *I* who should thank *you*." And with that he plunged his needle-sharp teeth into Sigmund Freud's pale exposed neck, ripping it open. He bent his head and fed ferociously. The hot rush of blood slaked his incredible thirst, and he moaned in delirious ecstasy.

Triumph was delicious.

THROUGH TIME AND SPACE WITH FERDINAND FEGHOOT

The Ferdinand Feghoot character was created by Reginald Bretnor and is used by special permission of the Estate of Reginald Bretnor / Wildside Press LLC.

THE CHAIRMAN DANCES

During Ferdinand Feghoot's tour of The People's Republic of China in the mid-1970s, Premier Zhou Enlai (Chou Enlai) asked Feghoot to help him deal with a serious morale problem in the massive Chinese army.

It had started when Mao Zedong (Mao Tse Tsung), the Chairman of the Communist Party, began to suspect that the western nations were secretly training a huge military force for an invasion of China. He believed that all of the various dance crazes sweeping across the western nations were actually extreme physical exercise routines, designed to produce super-strong soldiers. To counter this, Mao had ordered all good communists to learn the Bop, the Watusi, the Jerk, the Hand Jive, the Twist, and the Mash. Mao then sent spies abroad to learn all the newest dances and bring them back to China as well. Under Chairman Mao's personal direction, all of these dances were now incorporated into the physical training exercises of the vast Chinese army.

Because the psychological part of the training was as important as the physical part, Mao ordered a huge dance floor constructed. The Chinese troops had transformed their training grounds into a giant dance floor. They laid a vast wooden deck, enclosed by bright colored silks, with a similarly gaudy silk roof. They hung multitudes of flashing and whirling lights, all colors—crimson, tangerine, ochre, line, azure—and even huge rotating silver ornaments to cast reflections across the entire dance floor. The latest western music was reproduced on speakers five stories tall, loud enough to be a health hazard to animals and small children. The total output of three coal-fired electrical plants was needed to power the lights and the music for the vast array of military dancers.

To spur enthusiasm even further, Mao declared that the trainings would culminate in a dance contest and great prizes would be given to every soldier who could dance better than him. Among the prizes, of course, would be the precious silk used in the construction of the gigantic dance hall. And that was Zhou's problem. No soldier in the land wanted to embarrass the ideological leader of the party, nor risk the wrath that might follow if they were to embarrass the most powerful man in China.

Feghoot listened carefully, then said, "Zhou, I can solve your problem in seven—no, eight words." He took the microphone and announced to all, "Mao is the winner of our disco tent."

THE SPELL

Part One:

My next-door neighbors have six children. This is not enough reason to hate them, but it's a good start.

The smallest one, Tali, is ambulatory, but still pre-verbal. She is not a problem. She can stay. We will leave her name off the eviction notice.

Next up is Nolan. He has been retarded at the age of three for four years now. Nolan is an interesting social experiment. What do you get if you allow a child to raise himself without any parental involvement at all?

He breaks things. He takes things. He denies accountability. He starts fires. He blames other children. He screams. He goes into other people's yards, and he climbs up onto the roofs of houses—usually his own, but occasionally the roof of a neighbor as well. He throws things over the fence into my yard, oftentimes aiming for the pool. A half-eaten Taco Bell burrito must be retrieved within the first thirty minutes or you can plan on having the filter cleaned again.

Wait, there's someone at the door—

(on paper the pauses don't show)

—it was Nolan. I can't even write this down without one of the little monsters knocking on the door. They have been sent to bedevil me.

Next up are Jason and Jared, hovering somewhere in age between 11 and juvenile hall. Jason and Jared are the coming attractions for Nolan's adolescence. They specialize in noise and attitude. They have no manners. They have no courtesy. They have no conception of consideration for others.

My life was quiet and peaceful once. I work at home. I take my time to think things out. I sit in my office and think and write. I sit in my living room and read and listen to classical music; Bach, Vivaldi, occasionally a Shostakovitch string quartet— nothing too strenuous. I open all the doors and all the windows, and the cross breeze keeps the house pleasant and sweet-smelling. I would love to be able to do that again. Last year, I paid six thousand dollars to install a 4000 BTU air conditioner on the roof so I could close all the doors and windows and still keep working. The noise from the fan drowns out the softer strains of Debussy.

In the afternoon, they play touch football and baseball across three lawns. Mine is in the middle. Even the judicious planting of large amounts of purple Wandering Jew has not deterred them. They leap over it . . . sometimes. They scream, they shout, they claim the ball in mid-air. "It's mine—mine!" Their voices are atonal and dissonant, precisely mistuned to jar with whatever music is on the turntable.

In the evenings, they play basketball in the back yard. I used to go to bed at eleven. But they play basketball until one in the ayem, shouting and jabbering. The basketball hoop is opposite my bedroom window. It serves as the perfect acoustic focus aimed at my headboard. I am not making this up. A specialist in theatrical sound systems came out to my house, took some measurements, and ran them through the computer.

Jared and Jason like to climb roofs too. Last January, they climbed up on the roof of the auto parts store behind the alley, and plugged up its storm drains, just for the fun of it. When the big rains came in February, the water puddled on the roof. The weight of the water brought the whole ceiling crashing in, causing over a half-million dollars worth of damage to the store. The police refused to arrest the boys because of insufficient evidence. In August, they were accused of stealing 120 dollars from a neighbor's wallet and spent the night in juvenile hall. The next day, they were swimming at the same neighbor's house. How do they get away with it? What magic are they working?

Then there's Vanessa. She's another sweetheart. I think she's eighteen. She takes care of the kids while mom's at work. No, check that. She's *supposed* to take care of the kids while mom's at work. What she does is have parties. One of her friends once took forty bucks from mom's purse—but mom and dad blamed every other child on the street for the theft, and when the truth came out, didn't bother to apologize.

I'm not the only one who feels this way. The neighbor on the other side of Hell House has developed an ulcer. The neighbors across the street have put their house up for sale. Half the parents on the block have forbidden their children to play with the demonic brood. This is validation. It's not me. It's *them*.

Mom and Dad. Lyn and Bryce. He's a former minister, she's a former cheerleader who never aspired to anything more than the right shade of blonde. She hasn't yet noticed that her tits are working their way south and whose ass is spreading faster than the crab-grass on their lawn. I gave up on my lawn this year. There's no point in it, while the crab-grass sod farm next door is so aggressive.

Their philosophy of childrearing is non-existent. They daydream their way through life, drifting from one day to the next, oblivious to the fact that they are loathed by all of their neighbors. No, check that. They are loathed by all of the neighbors who live close enough to know who they are.

Oh—I almost skipped Damien. He's the one I like. He moved out and went to college four hundred miles away. We only see him on holidays. He has manners and courtesy and is obviously a changeling, not a real part of the family. He wants to major in art. Maybe he's gay. I hope so. I'd like to see the look on their faces when he comes home with a boy friend. Idle fantasies of revenge are rapidly becoming an obsession over here.

I like to believe I'm smarter than they are; but I still haven't been able to plot the perfect crime—one that would allow me to chop their bones into fragments, burn their house down, and salt the earth into toxic uninhabitability, without anyone ever suspecting that I was the agent responsible. In some matters, anonymity is preferable to acknowledgment. Revenge is one of them.

It bothers me, because I am supposed to be a specialist in revenge. Writers, as a class, are the research-and-development team for the whole human race in the domain of revenge. We ennoble it, we glorify it; we earn our livings inventing wonderful and exotic ways to justify the delicious deed of puncturing the pompous who make our lives miserable. We create virtual daydreams for the masses in which the mighty are humiliated for their misdeeds of oppression against those who are still climbing the evolutionary ladder. It is our job to tend the flames of mythic vision, creating the cultural context in which the arrogant are accurately mirrored and drawn, so that all will know who they are. It is our job to prepare the ground so that the thieves of joy can be reduced to craven, whimpering, pitiful objects of scorn and abuse.

And . . . the fact that I remain unable to find a way to drive these people screaming from their house frustrates me beyond words, because it implies that I am not yet a master of my trade. If anyone should be able to envision a suitable revenge here, it should be me. Through a delightfully Machiavellian bit of timing, innuendo, and legal maneuvering, I once engineered the enforced exit off the Paramount lot of a particularly leechsome lawyer; studio security officers arrived with boxes, and physically escorted him off the premises—so abusing a few troublesome neighbors should be easy. Shouldn't it?

The problem is grandma. Theirs, not mine. Grandma is a space-case. Not of this world. She exists in her own reality of hydrangeas and luncheons and Cadillacs. Life is pleasant, life is good, there are no problems. Let's all be nice to each other and everything will work out fine. She sees and hears only what she chooses to. Grandma owns the house and Mom and Dad and all the little Mansons live in it rent-free. They couldn't afford to live in this neighborhood otherwise. There is no way they're ever going to move out. Ever try to pull a tick off a dog? Grandma is the problem—

(narrative interrupted again)

—that one used up the rest of my evening. While I admit that it gave me no small amount of satisfaction to see three police cars pulled up in front of *that* house, it did not bring me any joy. I appreciate the validation, I do not appreciate losing half a day of working time.

This time, Jason was chasing Damien with a knife, threatening him. Damien socked him with a frying pan in self-defense. Damien got arrested. He'll end up with a charge of child-abuse on his record. These people have a way of getting *other* people in trouble, and coming out unscathed themselves. It's a talent.

Part Two:

That was six months ago.

The day after I wrote that, I ran into my friend, Sara McNealy. Sara is a witch.

I had stopped in at Dangerous Visions bookstore in Sherman Oaks to deliver my monthly box of books that I would rather not have in the house and to select a few volumes in return that would enhance my bookshelves. Given the fact that most publishers seem to have given up the publication of real books in favor of the production of commodity products, the task of reinvigorating the sleeping sense of wonder becomes harder and harder every year. Nothing destroys a person's enjoyment of a subject as fast as becoming obsessive about it. Never mind.

Sara was standing at the counter, chatting with Lydia Marano, the store owner. There were two other customers in the back of the store, browsing through the non-readers' section, looking for the latest *Star Trek* novel.

Sara doesn't look like a witch. She does not have flaming red hair. She does not have green eyes. She does not dress in flowing capes with unicorn embroidery.

Sara is short, not quite dumpy but almost, and she has little tight black curls framing her pie-shaped face. She is given to flowing dresses and little round spectacles that look like windows into her dark gray eyes. She looks like a yenta-in-training, but without the guilt attached. She is obscenely calm and unruffled.

Sara never talks about the goddess, she is not given to feminist rhetoric, and she rarely reads fiction. She created her own job, managing the computers for a major theatrical booking-chain. She is the first stop for technical support for a very small and very exclusive group of science-fiction, fantasy, and horror writers. She is equally conversant with nanotechnology, transhuman chickens, selfish genes, disturbed universes, dancing Wu-Li masters, motorcycle maintenance (with or without the zen), virology (both human and silicon strains), paleontology, biblical history, and several mutant strains of buddhist discourse. She can quote from Sun Tzu's *Art of War* as easily as from *The Watchmen*.

She does not cast spells herself. She works only as a consultant, serving as the midwife at the spellcasting sessions of others. She was telling Lydia, behind the counter, about her experiences breaking up a fannish coven, trying to grow hair on Patrick Stewart. "Finally, I just flat out told them, 'Witchcraft is potent stuff. Every spell you cast uses up part of your life force. If you assume that every spell you cast takes a year off your life expectancy, you don't do it casually. You save it for things that matter.'"

I looked up from the copy of *Locus* I was browsing through. They hadn't reviewed a book of mine in years—not since I'd requested that the reviewers read the books before writing about them. "Hey, Sara, didn't you say there were ways to rebuild your life force?"

"Oh, yes." She smiled sweetly as she said it. "Creativity. Haven't you ever noticed that a disproportionate share of conductors, writers, musicians, directors, et al, live well into their 90's? The act of creation is the very powerful. When you bring something into existence out of nothing, it becomes a focus for energy. If you create positive energy, you get invigorated. If you create negative energy, you diminish yourself. You can't afford the luxury of nastiness."

"You're right, *I* can't—but what if you don't have a choice in the matter?"

"You *always* have a choice," she said.

"You don't know my next-door neighbors."

She raised an eyebrow at me. A raised eyebrow from Sara McNealy is enough to curdle milk.

I refused to be intimidated. "My next door neighbors are destroying my life," I said. "They're noisy and intrusive. They've upset my whole life. My writing is suffering. And I can't afford to move."

Sara scratched her nose. "Negativism starts by blaming the other person. It's a way of avoiding personal responsibility."

"I'm not avoiding personal responsibility," I said. "I just don't know what to do."

"What result do you want to produce?" Sara asked.

"I want them to move away. Very far away."

She nodded. She was thinking. Lydia studied us both. Sara was turning over ideas in her mind. She said, "You could invite an evil spirit to move in with them. But that's dangerous. Sometimes the spirit decides it would rather move in with *you*."

"No, no spirits, thank you. Is there some other way?"

"Are you willing to pay the price—time off your life?"

"I'll earn it back with increased writing time. Won't I?"

Sara didn't answer that. At the same moment, we both noticed that there were suddenly other customers waiting—*and listening*. Sara put down the copy of *Chaos Theory* she had been browsing through and drew me carefully aside, leaving Lydia to ring up another large royalty for Stephen King.

"Listen to me," Sara said softly. "Witchcraft is a very specialized form of magic— you're trying to control the physical universe with experiential forces. That means that you need to create a specific context and appropriate symbology with which to control those forces. I prefer to do it with symbolic magic, rather than calling on spirits. Sometimes when no spirit responds to your call, new ones are created out of nothingness, and that can be extremely dangerous. Young spirits are...well, they're like kittens and puppies. They leave puddles."

"Can't I just animate the life force of their property or something?"

"It doesn't work that way." She frowned. "You're going to have to give me the whole story if you want me to advise you."

I took Sara by the arm and led her to the specialty-coffee shop next door. She had hazelnut coffee with bay leaves. I had fruit-tea. I can't stomach caffeine. I told her about the Partridge Family from Hell; I didn't leave anything out. I even told her about Princess, the unfettered cocker spaniel who never missed a chance to run up onto my porch and bark *into* my house.

Sara listened intently to the whole story without comment. Her dark eyes looked sorrowful. I could understand why she was such a good witch. Most of it was good listening. When I finished, she said, "You have a great deal of negative energy bound up in these people. That's a very expensive burden you are carrying. It needs to be released." She made a decision. "I'll help you."

"How much will it cost?" I asked.

She shook her head. "Witches don't work for money. Prostitutes do. Witches take...*favors*."

"Okay, I'll read your manuscript," I said with real resignation.

"Sorry, I have no interest in writing a novel."

"Thank God."

"Don't worry," she said. "I don't want your soul. Writers' souls are usually very small anyway, and not good eating. Too much gristle." She reached over and patted my hand warmly. "We'll talk about your first-born later, all right?"

I assumed she was joking.

Part Three:

Sara showed up 7:00, carrying two shopping bags.

"Ahh," I said, thinking I was being funny. "Did you bring the right eye of a left-handed newt? The first menstrual blood of the seventh virginal daughter?"

"This is California," she said. "There are no virgins. No, I brought pasta, mushrooms, bell peppers, tomato sauce, olives, garlic bread, salad, and a bottle of wine. Let's eat first, then we'll plan. Did you get the Cherry Garcia like I asked?"

"Of course, I did." I took the bags from her. "But I really have to say I miss the old traditions of witchcraft."

"Do you want to dance naked around a bonfire at midnight?"

"Not particularly."

"Neither do I. Open the wine."

After dinner, we cleared the table and spread out our plans. "First of all," Sara said, "You have to decide what power you want to invoke. Who are you calling on to do the deed?" She handed me a printout. "You don't want to invoke the powers of Satan, whatever you do. Dealing with demons is also dangerous; for the most part, the demons are only facets of Satan anyway. You don't want to do anything that puts your immortal soul in danger. I'm just showing you this to give you some sense of what you're going to be dealing with.

"Lower down, you have the lesser spirits and the spirits of the dead. Also not recommended. Spirits usually have their own agendas. They're very hard to control, and almost never grant requests. Spirits are deranged."

I scanned the lists with very little interest, then passed her back the printout. "Let's stick to white magic, okay?"

"Right." She passed me another set of pages. "See, the thing is, you have to invoke *some* power to energize the spell. Otherwise, it's like a new Corvette, all shiny and beautiful, but without an engine it isn't going anywhere."

"Yeah, I just hate it when that happens."

She ignored my fliippant interjection. "The problem with western magic is that as a result of the pernicious influence of Christian theology, westernized magic has anthropomorphized everything; we've given personalities to supernatural forces. It gives them *attitude*. It makes them impossible to deal with. But when we go back to the eastern disciplines, we're operating in a whole other context. The truth is that the flows of paranormal influence are directly linked to the yin-yang flow of solidity and nothingness, of creation and destruction, of beingness and non-being. Real magic happens when you align yourself with the flows of chaos and order. When you ride the avalanche, you need only a nudge to steer it. If you want to have a profound effect on the course of events in the physical universe, without running the risk of a serious causal backwash of energy, you have to create a spells that are in harmony with what the universe already wants to do. From what you've been telling me, it seems to me that the universe already *wants* to do something about these people next door. All you need to do is give it a focus."

I wasn't sure I understood anything of what she said, but I nodded as if I did.

Sara wasn't fooled. "Listen to me. Remember what I said about negative energy? You can't afford it. You are a fountain of creative power. You can't risk having your spring contaminated. You have to act now before you are permanently polluted. But whatever you do—you have to make sure that you don't do *greater* harm to yourself."

"What are you recommending?" I asked. She sounded so serious.

"Think of the peacock," she said.

"Pretty. Loud. Pretty loud." I free-associated.

"Do you know what a peacock eats?"

I shook my head.

"It eats the poisonous berries. It thrives on all the toxics that other birds won't touch. And it turns them into beautiful peacock feathers. That's the peacock—it takes nastiness and turns it into beauty. That's your job. Find a way to take all that stuff about the neighbors and turn it into something useful and rewarding and enlightening."

"A nice bonfire is the first thing that comes to mind. We could dance naked around it."

"It's time to stop being silly," Sara said. "You asked for my help. That's why I'm here. What kind of spell do you want to cast and what power do you want to invoke?"

"I want a spell that's quiet and unobtrusive. Inconspicuous. It shouldn't call attention to itself. No fireworks. No explosions. No ectoplasm, no manifestations, no mysterious cold spots. Just something that makes them *go away*."

"That's the best kind," Sara said.

I was looking at the list. "Let's invoke the power of the universe," I said.

"Huh?"

I pointed at the organization chart. "Look, all the power flows from the top. Let's go to the source. Let's call upon the universe to activate the spell."

Sara thought about it. "It might be overkill."

"There's no such thing as overkill," I said. "Dead is dead."

"How big an impact crater are you willing to live with?" she asked. "Remember, your house is well within the blast radius."

"We're going for gentleness, aren't we?"

"Gentleness is not delivered with a firehose," Sara said.

"Good point. We'll have to be careful."

"There could be side effects. You're probably going to get hit with some of them. Are you sure you want to do this?"

I nodded. A thought had been lurking at the back of my mind for three days. Ever since Sara had first begun coaching me. Now it was ready to blossom forth as a full-blown idea. I handed her my notes. 43 ideas. 42 of them had been crossed off. Only one remained.

Sara looked at it. She frowned. She narrowed her eyes. Her eyebrows squinched together. Her lips pursed. All of the separate parts of her face squinched up for a second, then relaxed, morph-like, into a big happy grin. "I think you may have real talent in this area," she said.

She took her pen and double-underlined my note. ___Love-bomb the bastards!___

Part Four:

At a quarter to midnight, we began. I went out to the back yard and flipped off every circuit-breaker. There was no electrical power at all to the house. There would be no contaminating fields of magnetic resonance. The computers had all been unplugged. The batteries had been removed from every radio and flashlight.

Sara gave me a diagram, and I began to lay out a complex pattern of 39 votive candles. As I went around the room, lighting them, I recited a simple prayer of absolution. "May this light give me guidance. Help me align myself with the flows of universal power."

When I finished, I began unwinding a long yellow cord around the room, putting a loop around each candle as I strung a spiral pattern leading to an empty plate in the center. I sat down at the outside of the spiral and held the other end of the cord. I began winding it around the fingers of my left hand. The power would flow from my heart to the empty plate. And back again.

I looked to Sara. She nodded. I hadn't forgotten anything.

"Hello," I said.

I waited a moment. If the universe was listening, it hadn't given me any evidence. But then again, the universe never gives evidence of its involvement. It's just there— the ultimate in passive aggressive.

I took three deep breaths. I closed my eyes and took three more. I waited until I thought I could see the candle flames through my closed eyelids. Then I waited until I was certain we were no longer alone.

"Hello," I repeated. "Thank you. I apologize for any intrusion this action of mine might represent. I only wish to serve the flows of the universe, not to impede them. And I hope that the universe will let me be a part of its grander plans."

I waited. This time I got the feeling that some*thing* was waiting for me.

"My neighbors," I said. "The people who live in the house next-door. Particularly Bryce, Lyn, Vanessa, Jared, Jason, and Nolan. I believe that they have been impeding the natural rise toward godliness. Perhaps it is through no fault of their own. Perhaps it is because they have been seduced by the darker flows of nature. Perhaps there are reasons for which I have no language. Whatever forces are at work, I believe that they are at odds with the natural flow of universal power and goodness."

I glanced over to Sara. She was watching me intently. She nodded and smiled.

"I believe that somehow they have become separated from their own abilities to connect with others and feel compassion. I believe that are unable to know the effects they have on the people around them. I believe that they do not see the pain they leave in their wake."

With my right hand, I placed a bowl on the empty plate in the center of the room. I poured red wine into the bowl, then I placed a single rose-blossom in the wine. "I offer you this gift," I said. "I do so freely and with no thought of personal reward or gain. I ask nothing for myself, nor for anyone close to me. I ask only that you grant my neighbors an opportunity to join your larger purposes, to swim in the flow of universal spirit that heads inevitably toward the light and glory of enlightenment. Please help direct their energies toward goodness and joy."

I bowed my head. "Thank you," I said. "Thank you for listening. Thank you for being here. Thank you for letting me serve you tonight."

And—maybe it was the sudden breeze from the door—but every single candle in the room went out simultaneously.

"Nicely done," said Sara, after a long startled silence. "*Very* nicely done."

Epilogue:

The next morning, I felt rather silly for having gone through the whole silly ritual. But I made up my mind to wait a week. Or two. Or even six.

Nothing happened at first.

Then, one horrible weekend, *everything* happened. Lyn and Bryce were out somewhere. Vanessa had invited five hundred close friends to a backyard bash, with 600-decibels of heavy metal rock music and illegal fireworks. Jared and Jason were sitting on the roof of the garage throwing cherry bombs into the dancers, which triggered a spate of angry gunfire between members of two rival gangs who were trying to crash the party from the alley-side of the yard. In the ensuing panic, several automobiles were smashed into each other as people tried to flee—a dead-end street does not lend itself to an orderly evacuation. In the confusion, Nolan found the box of fireworks and managed to light both them *and the house* on fire. By the time the police and the fire department arrived, the structure was sending fifty foot flames into the air and I was hosing down my roof and praying that the overhanging tree wouldn't catch. The fire crew couldn't get through the mass of cars to the fire hydrant, and even if they could have, it wouldn't have done any good because someone had crashed into it, knocking it off, sending a high-pressure fountain spraying high into the air where it made an impressive, but otherwise useless, display of uncontained aquatic energy. They ended up taking one of the units around to the alley side and backing it into my backyard so they could pump the water out of my pool and onto the neighbor's roof. It took them twenty minutes to knock down the blaze, leaving the house a charred and waterlogged mess. By the time they were through, there were over twenty police vehicles on the block, three ambulances, and four news vans.

In the aftermath, four stolen cars were recovered from joy-riding gang-bangers, seventeen people were arrested for possession and dealing of illegal substances, twelve illegal weapons were confiscated, and twenty-six of the party-goers spent the night in jail for being drunk and disorderly. Fourteen outstanding warrants were served for offenses as varied as unpaid parking tickets and felony armed robbery. Vanessa's friends were an assorted lot.

The following Monday, Lyn and Bryce were investigated by the Dept of Social Services.

And I called Sara and asked what went wrong. She told me not to worry. Everything was fine. Just be patient.

She was right. It took a while for everything to get sorted out, but eventually, it did.

The judge ordered three years of family-counseling for the whole clan. Vanessa was put on probation, conditional on her remaining in Alcoholics Anonymous. Jared and Jason were put into a special education program to help them recover from prolonged emotional abuse and also to prevent them from drifting into patterns of juvenile delinquency. Nolan was identified as suffering from a serious learning disability and is now in full-time therapy. Tali is in pre-school. Damien is president of the local Queer-Nation chapter. Grandma had to sell the house to help Lynn and Bryce cover the legal expenses. They all live with her now.

The insurance company leveled the remains of the house and sold the land to the city for use as a pocket park. It wasn't cost-effective to rebuild.

To paraphrase my favorite moose, sometimes I don't know my own strength.

For a while, both Sara and I were concerned about the backwash from the spell. We'd love-bombed the entire family, and they were all definitely much better off than they had been before. But Sara was afraid that there would be serious side-effects to the spell that might affect both of us. If there have been any, we haven't noticed them yet. But then again, we've been much too busy. Sara's planning to move in with me next month, and I've applied to adopt a little boy. And I expect to get back to my writing Real Soon Now.

AUTHOR'S AFTERWORD:

Next up, the money spell....

THE SCHWARZCHILD RADIUS

When the baby was born, both Doctor and Mr. Schwarz were delighted, but only for a few moments.

They were theoretical mathematicians engaged in fifth-dimensional toroidal extrapolations at the University of ... well, never mind. Dr. Schwarz was the theoretician. Mr. Schwarz, who had never finished his degree, not because of lack of ability but because of lack of time, served as senior engineer.

The exact nature of the experiment ... well, never mind about that either. It was one of those things that even if someone could explain it to you, they'd have to kill you ... and then themselves.

The important thing was the baby.

The baby was neither boy nor girl. In fact, they weren't even sure it was human.

It sort of looked human. It had two arms, two legs, ten fingers, ten toes, two eyes, two ears, one nose, one mouth, all the usual assortment of features. They were just shaped a little oddly and arranged a little too wide here and a little too narrow there. And the skin color—not exactly this and not exactly that and not exactly like anything any of the attending doctors had ever seen before. And it was kinda round.

They showed the Schwarz child to Doctor and Mr. Schwarz, then they put it carefully into an incubator for observation. They did not expect it to live.

Meanwhile, Doctor and Mr. Schwarz wept quietly together. There was no previous record of any similar event occurring in the ancestries of either of them, so they were left to wonder if this anomalous birth condition might have been an side effect of exposure to polarized magnetic radiation, or perhaps that other incident, the one that had triggered that unexpected spike in eleventh dimension gramma rays, or maybe it was a localized space-time distortion caused by the self-mutating software in the fusion-collider, although most likely it was just a combination of various recessive genes that had transformed the Schwarz child into this ... this whatever it was, this condition that had still not been named. There was, however, another possibility, one which neither of them raised.

The attending obstetrician asked Doctor and Mr. Schwarz if they wanted to name the Schwarzchild, but they both shook their heads. Naming a child gives it an identity, and if this ... this thing was probably going to die soon, it would better if it did not have an identity, let alone a proper burial and grave.

So the thing was identified on its chart as "Schwarzchild"—because the recording nurse wasn't paying attention and missed the space bar when she typed the information into the hospital computer.

That would have been the end of it except the Schwarzchild refused to die. Instead, it thrived—without any apparent source of sustenance. Within a week, they had to move it to a bigger incubator.

To say that this perplexed the hospital staff would be an understatement. One might just as well have said that the Titanic had a rough crossing. The doctors held daily meetings. They clucked at videos, they frowned at charts, they gathered around the expanding body of the Schwarzchild and made exclamations of disbelief and admiration. They poked, prodded, measured, tested, compared, and then repeated all their examinations so they could compare them with all their other efforts at understanding.

The Schwarzchild remained blissfully unaware, gurgling quietly to itself in its ... well, I guess you could call it a crib.

Oh—and the most peculiar thing about the Schwarzchild, aside from its continuing expansion, was that it refused to soil its diaper. Dutifully, albeit with a degree of distaste and reluctance, the duty nurses changed the Schwarzchild's diapers on a regular basis—but except for a little bit of wrinkling, the diapers were coming off the Schwarzchild as clean as when they went on.

Doctor and Mr. Schwarz were informed of the situation, of course, which finally confirmed their unspoken suspicions that at least one of their questionable experiments had been a success—well, not a success in that it proved anything useful, but certainly a success in that it demonstrated that interdimensional bio-pollution was a very real possibility. What they were not certain of was whether this was their actual child or a changeling switched in-utero for a fetus from an equivalent host on the other side of the parallelium.

Everyone wanted more tests.

So there were MRIs and CAT scans and full body-scans and blood tests of all kinds—and finally electron microscope examination of everyone's stem cells: the Schwarzchild, Doctor Schwarz, Mister Schwarz, and even the Schwarz cat. There were sonograms and mammograms and instagrams.

Meanwhile, the Schwarzchild expansion continued. Its volume was computed as four-thirds pi times the Schwarzchild radius to the power of three. Its arms and legs, its head and neck grew as well, though not quite as rapidly. Overall, the proportions of the Schwarzchild were changing dramatically.

Doctor Schwarz sarcastically remarked that if the Schwarzchild continued to grow at the present rate, then by the time it was six months old, it would fill an entire hospital room and have the shape of a perfect sphere. At age twenty, it would be as large as the moon and with a comparable gravity. Within six weeks, however, that was no longer a sarcastic prediction, but a disturbing possibility.

By then, however, scientists from NASA, doctors from the CDC, specialists from JPL, experts from the AMA, and even a few graduate students from MIT had been invited to consult. The most erudite response from any of them was a shrug and a muttered, "Damfino." The only ones who had even a hint of a clue, or at best a hunch of a hint, were Doctor and Mr. Schwarz. Their response was a frown, a shake of the head, and a whispered, "Let's talk privately."

Of course, the local news media eventually reported the story. Despite the immediate demand for the family's privacy, this invasion was inevitable, as any number of nurses, interns, specialists, and administrators were perpetually engaged in pursuit of the hefty "finder's fee" that the local news media would pay for any interesting medical story. The news went from the local to the national in a matter of hours, but immediately to the internet.

Social media first dismissed the Schwarzchild as a tabloid-inspired fiction and took it to satirical levels—not as big as Grumpy Cat, but certainly big enough to justify a few jokes on late-night television. No one really took the Schwarzchild until Public Television's NOVA began filming interviews for an upcoming episode.

Of course, there was a government investigation. There is always a government investigation in matters like this, and even in matters very much not like this, but no matter—there is always a government investigation, because that is how a government pretends it is doing something. It investigates it, hoping that by the time the investigation is completed, public attention will not only have moved on, but will have completely forgotten whatever it was that was being investigated.

But not in this case—because the radius of the Schwarzchild was continuing to expand, and its diameter was expanding twice as fast, to say nothing of that particular measurement 3.141592...etc. times larger than the diameter.

Medical authorities wisely had the Schwarzchild moved while it was still possible to maneuver it through the hospital corridors and into a cargo elevator. Two gurneys were necessary. Lacking an appropriate medical facility, and not knowing how far the Schwarzchild would expand, they rented a soundstage on the Universal backlot and outfitted it with appropriate diagnostic equipment. This was done mostly in secret and was not included in the studio tour tram ride.

As the phenomenon continued, articles in various magazines, everything from *Discovery* to *Asimov's*, patiently explained the difference between Schwarzchild and Schroedinger, Heisenberg and Heidegger. Punsters joked about putting a hearse before Descartes. Philosophers and Physicists didn't know whether to put their heads down on the table and cry or be grateful that the nation was finally paying attention to concepts larger than a bustline.

Crude jokes about black holes, notwithstanding, the Schwarzchild was an opportunity to explain a somewhat esoteric concept to a scientifically illiterate population. As Wikipedia phrased it, "The Schwarzchild radius is the radius of a sphere such that, if all the mass of an object were to be compressed within that sphere, the escape velocity from the surface of the sphere would equal the speed of light." A little wordy, perhaps, but this does make the singularity phenomenon—the black hole—somewhat more understandably than calling it a wormhole to another dimension, which is far less understandable to anyone, and in particular physicists who disguise their misunderstandings by tossing obscure and esoteric terminology around as casually as if they were regifting a Christmas fruitcake.

Meanwhile, totally oblivious to all of this, the Schwarzchild continued to grow.

The growth did not seem as dramatic as it had been in the first days after the Schwarzchild's birth—or arrival on the planet, as some preferred to say—but in fact, it was far more serious.

Imagine a colloquium presented by a skilled physicist, or in this case, Doctor Schwarz herself. "Assume a spherical child. Assume that the child assimilates mass at a constant rate, sucking it through some kind of interdimensional hole, the likes of which we have not yet been able to define. In such a case, the most rapid rate of growth will be seen when the spherical child is at its smallest, as that will represent a proportionally larger addition of mass per moment than when the spherical child is larger.

"If instead, we assume that the child assimilates energy through its surface area, converting it to mass internally, then that process must burn some of that energy in the conversion process, releasing it as heat—which has, of course, been an observable phenomenon, with the spherical child apparently maintaining homeostasis regardless of the surrounding temperature. In this case, then, the only limit to its continuing expansion is the amount of area exposed to the surrounding air. While the ability of the sphere to expand will increase as its size increases, the apparent growth of the object will not be perceived as continuing at the same pace because the degree of expansion will not be as immediately apparent. This is because the ratio of the surface area to the volume of a sphere decreases as the size of the sphere increases, but explaining elementary geometry to you is below my pay grade. Thank you for coming."

About the time the Schwarzchild was three months old and approaching the size of a two car garage, those in attendance began to wonder if there was a limit to its growth. The Schwarzchild's density was that of the average elephant, so it was now massing upwards of ten thousand kilos, with no sign of its growth slowing down or stopping.

The attending pediatrician on duty—the Schwarzchild was still legally a human infant, so an attending was required by law—opined that its growth was not normal for a three-month old human, which had to be one of the most inane statements made about the Schwarzchild and was probably one of the reasons for his dismissal and replacement.

Along about this time, several of the attending specialists from NASA began to wonder if there was any predictable limit at all to the Schwarzchild's growth, and if not, was it possible that the situation might shortly become very dire, with the Schwarzchild growing to the size of a small asteroid or even a moon. Or worse.

Several plans were proposed. Perhaps the Schwarzchild could be launched into space, not just into orbit but out into interstellar space where it could continue to grow until it consumed the entire universe. Better yet, launch it on a trajectory with the sun where it would certainly be consumed in flame, if it didn't eat the star first. But both of these plans were quickly abandoned when it was realized that by the time even the most powerful of launch vehicles could be assembled, the Schwarzchild would have outgrown the thrust capacity of the biggest rockets available.

The military advisors—yes, they had been brought in too—suggested that the Schwarzchild be imploded with an array of shaped charges. Several factors argued against this. First, any explosion would likely destroy the soundstage and a good part of Universal's backlot. The studio executives would probably not give their approval. And second, what if multiple pieces of the Schwarzchild survived and—like the parent body—began to grow themselves in a horrible realization of The Sorcerer's Apprentice, sans mouse and sorcerer? The three-star general in charge of the situation suggested carving a piece off the Schwarzchild to see if it would grow by itself. If not, the Schwarzchild could be ... to put it politely, disassembled. Failing that, there was always the possibility of an unexplained fire. What if the air conditioning system shorted out ... ?

Unfortunately, none of these options were acceptable—not for scientific reasons, the physicists were having a field day—and not for legal reasons either. The Schwarzchild was still technically a living human being and could not be terminated unless found guilty of a capital crime with special circumstances.

That's when the priests, ministers, rabbis, imams, ayatollahs, and swamis arrived—and a couple Jesuits, without whom no argument could be complete. Was the Schwarzchild actually human? And if so, or even if not, did it have a soul?

The various religious leaders conferred and argued for several days and finally realizing that the questions were so profound and so difficult that they had no choice but to pass the buck. They announced that they could not come to any possible conclusion without more information, they needed the input and expertise of appropriate scientists. This produced much hilarity in the commentariat—that some of the world's foremost religious leaders were now demanding scientific evidence.

In response, the boffins of Silicon Valley offered their assistance, including several of whom had created the most sophisticated intelligence engines for first-person-shooters. Several scientists also arrived, ready to expand the inquiry into the nature of cognition, including those with their own television audiences, most of whom were eager to explore the question of self-awareness in a public venue—because even if the fundamental questions remained unresolved, as they expected, their participation would still spur book sales.

Some of this resulted in long erudite articles in *Psychology Today, Rolling Stone,* and *The Christian Science Monitor*. Even more erudite and otherwise worthless speculations occurred all over Facebook, resulting in hundreds of feuds, thousands of unfriendings, and an uncountable number of blocks.

In an odd congruence of coincidence, all on the same day, three separate political cartoonists portrayed the Schwarzchild as a giant sweet potato, with the caption, "I think, therefore I yam."

By then, the Schwarzchild had outgrown its soundstage. For a while, the attending scientists suspected, feared, hoped, that the enclosing walls would brake the Schwarzchild's growth.

They were wrong.

Instead, one hot Sunday afternoon, the walls of the soundstage cracked, buckled outward, and abruptly collapsed, revealing the bulk of the Schwarzchild to two tramloads of tourists, most of whom caught the event on their cellphone cameras. The sudden avalanche of Schwarzchild flesh buckled the walls of two nearby soundstages and pushed a small office building off its foundation. Within minutes, the internet was flooded with video.

Universal quickly added the Schwarzchild to the list of attractions available on the studio tour of the backlot and ticket sales rose by 13% the first week.

The Schwarzchild now resembled nothing so much as a small, half-deflated blimp. Its flesh had turned grayish and mottled, and in fact many tourists came away disappointed, claiming that they had not seen the actual Schwarzchild, only a small, half-deflated blimp. Nevertheless, time-lapse videos of the Schwarzchild section of the Universal backlot did prove that the Schwarzchild was still expanding. Freed from the constraints of the soundstage walls, it had flubbered out to cover an area half a city block in diameter.

With its actual exposure to the public, the Schwarzchild was no longer a tabloid sensation. Now, squatting unequivocally in the public's consciousness, it had become an unnatural disaster, probably caused by alien anal probes, fluoridation, the CIA, liberals and unnamed terrorists. Even the most ambitious of conspiracy theorists were at a loss to find a theory to explain this, although they generally blamed scientists and muttered that there were still some things that man was not meant to know.

However you looked at it, the Schwarzchild was no longer a fit subject for comedians on late-night television, although the wannabes who tormented patrons at various comedy clubs were much later in getting that message—not until patrons started yelling, "Enough of this crap! Say something funny!"

It was only when the Schwarzchild belched—that was not the scientific term for the event, that was what the public called it—that cautious worry escalated to genuine alarm. The scientists' official description of the event was "readjustment to a higher plateau." In non-technical terms, "the damn thing popcorned." It popped, it puffed, it fluffed, and plopped itself across a suddenly expanded footprint. That there was a tram under it when it flopped down again was bad timing on the part of the tram driver. While most of the passengers survived with only minor injuries, the ones who could not get out from under the abruptly-expanded Schwarzchild were pronounced dead at the scene.

It was at that point that the governor of the state declared the area around the Schwarzchild to be in a state of emergency. The national guard was mobilized and the entire backlot was cordoned off. No one was allowed in, thereby ensuring that a large chunk of programming for the summer and fall television seasons would not be filmed. At least, not here. Within three weeks, the total value of lawsuits filed against anyone and everyone reached more than seven billion dollars.

Foreseeing the possibility of legal entanglements, although never on this scale, Doctor and Mr. Schwarz had gone into seclusion shortly after the Schwarzchild was moved from the hospital to the soundstage. On the advice of lawyers, and on orders from the institution that funded their research, they remained unavailable to the press, speaking only to appropriate representatives of the federal government. They did however, make their notes and their equipment available to any physicist capable of understanding eleventh-dimension knotted string theories—of which there were only three, and two of them were faking it. The third was Doctor Schwarz herself.

Although Doctor and Mr. Schwarz had shut down their quantic-fibrillator, they and their research staff, continued to wrangle the math involved in the hopes of a) understanding the original event, and b) finding a way to cross-phase and reverse the polarity so as to shrink the Schwarzchild in the last five minutes before the final commercial—the same way it was always accomplished on The Next Generation. Unfortunately, not having a fifteen-year old supergenius to rely upon, they remained mostly stumped.

The Schwarzchild stretched its radius and its event-horizon grew—almost as fast as the scientific jargon used to obscure all the different ways of saying, "damfino." Meanwhile, the surface of the Schwarzchild started to change, evolving into an environment suitable to the growth of mold, lichens, and fungi. While not yet big enough to establish its own weather patterns, the trendlines suggested that by the end of the year, the Schwarzchild would have enough mass to tower over the Hollywood Hills and from there, develop its own specific ecology.

While most of the city's population were alarmed by that possibility, some scientists were almost wetting their shorts at the opportunity to study evolution in action. One of those individuals was stabbed to death in a Taco Bell parking lot by eco-warriors who, when apprehended, said that this was evolution in action as well.

As the situation worsened, spokespersons for all the various agencies and authorities entrusted with the responsibility for solving the problem did what they were hired to do—they retreated to platitudes—glittering duck-billed platitudes. In short, they promised hope while stalling. They said they were watching the situation closely. They said the situation was complicated, they said it would take more time to evaluate the evidence, and of course, they recommended that people should do the most important thing they can do in a time of crisis—pray, because praying is a great way to feel good while doing nothing at all.

Ironically, shortly after a certain televangelist, who doubled as the poster boy for senile dementia, announced that it would be up to God to save the sinful city of Los Angeles, the city was hit by an earthquake measuring 7.3 on the Richter scale. The epicenter was close enough to the Schwarzchild that various religious leaders claimed it was an act of God, answering the prayers of the millions of faithful. In sharp contrast, the atheists who worked as geologists at Cal Tech declared that goodness had nothing to do with it—it was the weight of the Schwarzchild, creating so much additional pressure on a previously undiscovered fault line that it triggered the release of the pressure below.

Unbeknownst to the scientific team—well, not exactly unbeknownst, they just hadn't been thinking in this direction—the Schwarzchild had reached a critical mass where its skin was rapidly reaching the point where it could no longer contain the internal pressures of its increasing volume. The quake bounced the Schwarzchild nearly 6 meters into the air and then back down again. The ground beneath was unable to sustain the impact, it liquefied. The earth rocked for 47 seconds, far more exciting than the earthquake simulation of the backlot tour, which ironically was destroyed in the tremor.

More important, the Schwarzchild reacted like a water balloon full of lime Jell-O—it splattered.

It splashed.

The contents of the Schwarzchild flowed outward and downward and westward, a great meaty wall of steaming hot slush—a veritable stew-nami.

Aside from burying the entire Universal backlot six feet deep in fleshy sludge, the splash zone also extended across Lankershim boulevard, the Hollywood freeway at the junction of the 134, the 101, and the 170—and enough of Studio City to wall off access to the rest of the San Fernando Valley from Los Angeles. A great deal of sludgy matter also flooded into the Universal City subway stop (yes, Los Angeles *does* have a subway system), immobilizing a waiting train and soiling several hundred terrified commuters with Schwarzchild innards. Fortunately, the only fatality was a street musician, an accordion player doing a medley of Star Wars themes. He was not mourned.

The cleanup took most of the summer and cost the state nearly thirty million dollars. The Environmental Protection Agency quarantined North Hollywood, Studio City, and Universal City, declaring the whole area a toxic biohazard. This shut down three major freeways and the northern reach of the subway system. State legislators were at a loss for what laws to enact to prevent further similar incidents. But the need to do so was immediate.

Doctor Schwarz was pregnant again.

A BRIEF EXPLANATION OF HOW BUDAPEST BECAME THE TACO CAPITAL OF THE WORLD

"Whatever starts in California unfortunately has a tendency to spread."
—President Jimmy Carter, 39th US President, March 21, 1977

It wasn't until after the charter was certified and ratified, and after the stationery and business cards had been printed that anyone noticed the unfortunate acronym of the Geographic Anomaly Studies, Pasadena.

Doctor Marcia Leung, Senior Consultant on loan from Caltech, did not find it amusing. It grew even less amusing over time. Hearing the inevitable repetition of the obvious jokes for the hundredth time, coming from those encountering the acronym for the first time, became a test of her good nature. Her strained smiles revealed that she was failing the test.

Despite the apparent frivolity of the study—what the hell is a geographic anomaly anyway?—the group had been organized to discreetly study a growing body of evidence that *something was wrong*.

It began with the Valley Glen anomaly.

Valley Glen is the name given to the more affluent section of Van Nuys, California—a joke understood only by those who live in Van Nuys, California. The residents of Valley Glen were so sensitive about living in Van Nuys and the presumption of lower property values that they petitioned to have their miniscule neighborhood renamed to something that sounded like Beverly Glen, a neighborhood known for its multi-million-dollar price tags.

Left over from its previous location in Van Nuys, a two-year community college squats in the center of Valley Glen. Even though the college sits in the center of Valley Glen and Valley Glen sits in the center of the San Fernando Valley, the college is not named Valley Glen Community College nor is it named San Fernando Valley Community College. It is more inaccurately named Los Angeles Valley College. The college is famous for almost nothing at all, despite the belief of those who work and teach there that its greater destiny will manifest eventually. They were almost right.

The college is bordered by Burbank Blvd. on the south, Fulton Ave. on the west, Coldwater Ave. on the east, and Oxnard Street on the North. Oxnard Street is notable for nothing at all, except for the fact that it has a slight rise to the west. Almost a hill. For that reason, it is an excellent place for students majoring in Geomatics to stand in the middle of the street peering through tripod-mounted sextants and scribbling numbers onto clipboards. Despite the fact that modern technology has made instant geoscanning possible with the average smartphone, with accuracy down to the millimeter, student surveyors are still required to understand the geometric principles underlying their craft.

This was not where the western region anomaly began, but it was inevitable that this would be where the first physical evidence was discovered.

After a particularly crazy summer—well, it was a presidential election year—an entire class of students all failed the same part of their midterm exam, the mapping of Oxnard Street. They all reported the same inaccurate numbers. The only possible explanation was that they had cheated, all copying their data from one student's work, who had gotten his measurements wrong.

So Professor Greenberger flunked the entire class.

Geomatics students had been surveying the Oxnard hill since long before the term Geomatics had been invented. Since the first years after World War II, when the college had existed as nothing more than a few bungalows and Quonset huts, the presence of students and sextants on Oxnard Street was as familiar a sight to neighbors as the daily mail delivery. Oxnard Street had been surveyed more than Marilyn Monroe's nude photo in *Playboy* magazine. There was absolutely no question that Oxnard Street was exactly X many meters long and the slope was a grade of Y degrees and the west end of the block was Z centimeters higher than the east end.*

So there was only one possible reason for the collective inaccuracy of the entire set of midterm exams. The students had colluded to cheat.

At the administrative hearing, several of the students showed the selfies they had taken of themselves out on Oxnard Street, others showed their own scribbled

---

* I would have put in the exact numbers, but the point of this story is that those numbers are no longer accurate, so why bother?

paperwork, and a few even demonstrated how they had used their smartphones to confirm their sextant measurements.

Angered at this insubordination, Professor Greenberger dragged the entire class out to Oxnard Street to demonstrate how to properly survey the slope so as to come up with the appropriate measurements.

After apologizing to the entire class, he called Doctor Leung at Cal-Tech. Although skeptical, Doctor Leung and two of her associates took the 134 west. They took the Coldwater off-ramp, drove north for a mile and a half, most of it paralleling the concrete-lined Los Angeles river, turned left, and met Professor Greenberger at the corner of Oxnard Street and Ethel Avenue.*

They unloaded a trunk full of sophisticated electronic equipment—including military-grade GPS units which would allow them to geolocate their exact position down to the millimeter. They used high-resolution laser scanners and Tesla-based radars to digitally map the entire terrain. They repeated their measurements at twelve different locations, then frowned at the displays on their laptops which confirmed that the distance between Fulton Avenue and Ethel Avenue was now ten centimeters greater than demonstrated by all previous measurements.

Either generations of students had all made the same miscalculation—or this particular suburban block had somehow expanded. Doctor Leung, Professor Greenberger, two associates, and half a dozen students, walked back and forth along the entire distance seven times, looking for cracks in either the sidewalk or the asphalt paving of Oxnard Street. They found nothing.

Two months later, GASP was formed.

For the first several months of its existence, GASP's sole function was to escort visiting geologists, seismologists, and sociologists to ~~Van Nuys~~ Valley Glen so that they too could walk the distance between Fulton Avenue and Ethel Avenue, looking for cracks in the pavement. To a man (and the occasional woman) they all agreed that there had to be a rational explanation for the anomaly. The developing consensus held that all of the past observations were flawed and that the flaws had finally been revealed by the superior technology of lasers, radars, and GPS units. That at least two decades of previous measurements had been confirmed by lasers, radars, and GPS units was an irrelevant and inconsequential detail. Current technology was obviously superior to those primitive earlier generations of technology.

This particular conclusion would have been the final word—except for one thing. The next set of measurements didn't match. The distance between Fulton Avenue and Ethel Avenue had expanded again, this time by twenty-two centimeters.

This time around, the various confused experts declared that the area must be situated over some kind of electro-magnetic mascon disturbance that somehow affected all digitally-based measuring devices and only the original measurements, performed with sextants, were valid. Thus, satisfied that they had explained it away, they went home.

---

*   This is a curious bit of misnomery. Oxnard Street is a wide avenue and Ethel Avenue. is a narrow residential street.

Except—when the students returned to the area, armed with the most primitive instruments possible, sextants and telescopes and measured lengths of cord—when they surveyed and re-surveyed and re-re-surveyed, they determined that not only had the distance between the two avenues expanded, but it had expanded again and was continuing to expand.

Now convinced that the anomaly was real enough to be a measurable event, Doctor Marcia Leung sent teams of surveyors out across the San Fernando Valley and surrounding areas to discover if other locations were also experiencing anomalous expansion.

The short version: yes.

After six months of measuring, digitizing, computerizing, modeling, and massaging the data, the conclusion was inescapable. Los Angeles was growing.

Not every area was growing as fast as the San Fernando Valley, the growth was uneven throughout Los Angeles County, but it was definitely happening. All told, the county had grown more than a kilometer, almost a full mile—although scientific measurements were more efficient in the metric system, the rest of the nation was not equally committed to either science or metrics of any kind.*

GASP issued several carefully worded reports on the nature of its continuing investigations, using as many polysyllabic words as possible to keep the story from ending up on the front page of supermarket tabloids. Nevertheless, nine months after Professor Greenberger's attempt to flunk an entire class of student surveyors, Doctor Leung was "invited" to address the Los Angeles County Board of Supervisors—"invited" being the politest euphemism for, "We could subpoena you if we have to."

Doctor Leung, no stranger to the vagaries of political posturing—after all, she had not only survived, but ultimately succeeded in escaping academia—spoke slowly and in specifically measured terms, deliberately designed to confuse those whose only skill in life was winning elections. Unfortunately, one of the freelance reporters in the room understood exactly what she was getting at. Actually, he was another of those oddball observers more than a real reporter, a court-watcher when certain criminal courts were in session, which wasn't today, so he was here instead—but he had occasionally sold an article to various freebies like the L.A. Weekly, so that sort of counted. A somewhat illicit-looking fellow, generally known to his colleagues as "Pesky," he was able to translate her verbiage into Sheldon-speak and from there into a passable imitation of English.

But the important thing about Pesky was the question he did manage to ask. As Doctor Leung was leaving the hearing, which had turned into an unusually

---

* According to several poorly-educated members of the House of Representatives, if it isn't in the Bible it doesn't count. Nevertheless, when all of this finally did reach those hallowed halls, Doctor Leung staunchly refused to issue her official reports in cubits, despite a lengthy congressional investigation and even a veiled threat of contempt charges. The investigation concluded without a conclusion, because one of the representatives from Texas got into a fistfight with one of the other representatives from Texas—they could not agree if Doctor Leung was guilty of falsifying the data for personal aggrandizement or initiating the expansion herself as part of a liberal conspiracy to grow California into the biggest state in the Union.

prolonged and dreary affair, unnoticed or ignored by the few reporters who had managed to achieve a state of consciousness higher than somnolence, Pesky caught up with her in the hallway and asked bluntly, "Are you saying that the whole planet is expanding? Or is it just Los Angeles County bulging out of proportion to the rest of the continent?"

Doctor Leung blurted something unintelligible—halfway between "Piss off" and "Damfino" and hurried to her car. Pesky's question had triggered an even more disturbing avenue (well, maybe just a street) of inquiry.*

It was this simple. She, and the other members of GASP had focused so much of their attention on the unexplained expansion of Los Angeles County, they had neglected to consider what might be happening in the surrounding counties—Orange to the south, Ventura to the northwest, Kern to the north, and San Bernardino to the east. Not caring that she was violating California's strict laws against using one's cell phone while driving, Doctor Leung frantically ordered her surveying teams out to each of the surrounding counties.

She made her second set of calls to various federal officials, to alert/advise/ suggest/request/plead/demand that the US Geological Survey immediately begin rechecking geographical domains across the entire continent. Doctor Leung was so engaged in this particular set of conversations that she did not notice the red and blue blinking lights behind her vehicles—not until she was forced to a stop before a phalanx of sixteen police cars blocking the Pasadena freeway.†

Doctor Leung spent the weekend in county lockup. She was arraigned the following Monday. Despite her lawyer's motion to have the charges dismissed, presiding Judge Gannon remained unimpressed, and released her on $50,000 bail and instructions not to leave the county.

Court-watcher, Pesky‡ recognized her immediately and realized that the circumstances of her arrest, the occurrence of her frenzied phone calls coming immediately after her hurried retreat from his question, and the resultant police chase — all these events were related. If only he could remember the question he'd asked.

Pesky didn't keep notes. He had a pocket audio-video recorder, a life-monitor, an electric Boswell, so it was no small matter for him to access his files from his iPhone, and play back the events of the previous Friday, refreshing his memory of the fateful question.

Had he used his real name, regular readers of the L.A. Weekly would have known Pesky from his other articles. To protect his anonymity, he published most of his work under the most mundane and inconspicuous pseudonym he could come up with, M. Raptor Bluthorne. The M. was silent.

---

*   Pesky is unlikely to reappear in this narrative, so you may conveniently forget him now.

†   The low-speed police chase had been broadcast live on channels 2, 4, 5, 7, 9, and 11. Channel 13 was rerunning a syndicated episode of *The Big Bang Theory* and had not cut away for fear of enraging the most aggressive members of the series' audience.

‡   He's back. I lied.

M. Raptor Bluthorne was the many-fabled author of "The Ten Cleanest Restrooms in Los Angeles," "The Nickleback Mysteries," "The Science of Flatulence," "Outside Scientology," "The Burlap Condom," "The Museum of Irrelevance," "Sex Toys Of The Poor," "The FBI Is In Your Toothbrush," and "Ten Science Fiction Novels Worth Skipping." These and other articles had earned him both a following and a reputation. Neither were anything to brag about, but apparently it sold papers—or would have sold papers if the L.A. Weekly had not been a freebie, its real purpose to provide an outlet for local advertisers.

Nevertheless, the alarmist outing by M. Raptor Bluthorne, entitled, "The City Has Cancer!" managed to attract enough attention that one of the local television stations decided to investigate the story as a possible oddball-interest sidebar on the Three O'clock News, generally one of the slowest parts of the news day.

In any other narrative, the local news bimbette with aspirations of becoming a real reporter would have teamed up with M. Raptor Bluthorne to uncover some dark disturbing conspiracy of evil, usually perpetrated by a nefarious government conspiracy—punctuated with floating red dots from laser gunsights, an exploding car, at least one frenzied foot pursuit through a late-night parking structure, a desperate police chase through shining wet streets slicing through concrete canyons, black helicopters with relentless probing fingers of blue light, and everywhere a phalanx of expressionless men in black suits and sunglasses—all of it culminating in a sudden avalanche of exposure and truth broadcast live to a breathless city, resulting in a cascade of embarrassing investigations, public exoneration, even a medal or two, and finally a frenzied copulation indicating a lifetime of marital bliss in an otherwise uneventful future.

Unfortunately, there was no local news bimbette, just a tired old man named Archer Bobby, working the last few years until his contract expired and a fresh-out-of-school naif, Floxxy Williams, who was probably doomed to be his replacement. Even more unfortunate, there would be no car chases, no explosions, no dramatic expose, and definitely no frenzied copulation.

Archer Bobby and Floxxy Williams were already bored with the story before they started. It had no sex, no scandal, no Hollywood connection, not even the possibility of a devastating 9.5 megaquake—so no apparent pathway to a book deal, let alone a Pulitzer prize. So of course, there would not be even a half-hearted attempt at frenzied copulation. (Floxxy was a lesbian and Archer Bobby was too proud to buy Viagra.)

But...as reporters, they did have access to an extensive Rolodex.* Applying themselves diligently, they managed to connect with Mick Viggle, an assistant janitor at GASP—actually, Viggle was really a screenwriter and actor, also a director and producer, who was just waiting for his agent to return his calls. (He did not

---

* An arcane device. A personal cardfile, mandatory for used for keeping track of names and phone numbers. It was invented in the mid-forties by Arnold Neustadter. He lived until 1996, just long enough to see the internet make his invention irrelevant. (This is a real fact. I am not making this up.)

know that the aforesaid agent was currently being held without bail for stalking a studio script reader.) The janitor gig was just research for his current project, a slasher script about a demon-possessed mop. Never mind that, Viggle was delighted at any attention which might further his career.

Viggle shared that he had previously been contacted by a very deep-voiced woman named Emma Rabbit Bubblehorn, or something like that In exchange for a promise of a bottle of cheap bourbon (which he still had not received)—he had allowed her to interview him about his important work at the Institute, or was it a University, he wasn't sure—he was just a temp, you know, doing research, for his script, Spielberg wants to see it when it's ready, never mind, what did you want to know?

In exchange for a promise of two bottles of the same cheap whiskey (which were ordered on Amazon during the course of the phone interview), Viggle happily, breathlessly, and drunkenly shared that Dr. Leung had been phoning surveyors across the state and even as far away as Nevada, Arizona, and Tijuana, alternating between bouts of joyous giddiness and thunderous cursing. He had not understood all of the big words he had heard, but it was obvious to him that Dr. Leung was unhappy with either her dry cleaner or her husband, because she kept using words like shrinkage and stretching. He planned to include these words in his script to give it—what was the word?—gravitas.

After concluding the call Archer Bobby quickly confirmed that Dr. Leung was no longer married and Floxxy Williams went to Wikipedia to discover that Dr. Leung did most of her own laundry—this was the full extent of their research. Nevertheless, it did not require much athletic skill to leap to the conclusion that Dr. Leung had been talking about The Anomaly.

They finished their report only moments before the 2:45 deadline for the Three O'clock news. It being a very slow news day, they were given three minutes of broadcast time to report the facts, and an additional minute to make fun of them.

What they reported was that L.A. Weekly was reporting that Los Angeles was growing—bulging. Not just the city, but the county itself. They did not do any research of their own and they didn't even bother to mention M. Raptor Bluthorne as the source of the report, nor did they mention Dr. Leung as well, as they had a professional obligation to protect the anonymity of their sources.

At this point in the narrative, the author (who is being paid by the word) would like to spend a few paragraphs on the nature of "the silly season." This is a newspaper term for the summer months, during which time newspapers and other media spend way too much time on frivolous events. The height of the silly season is August, during which time there are no holidays to report, congress is in recess so the government is effectively moribund, and most of the therapists in New York City are out of town as well, using the justification of "vacation" as an excuse to escape from their patients for at least one month out of the year.

This trifecta results in an abundance of nothing important happening—importance defined by whether or not it will pull a rating. So the news media fills its dead air and empty pages with stories that can be reported with a smirk of superiority.

For example, in July of 1955, newspapers in Los Angeles began reporting that the Earth was swallowing garden hoses--three of them were being sucked into the ground at a rate of two or three inches per hour. It was happening in Downey, a suburb halfway between City Hall and Disneyland. Because nothing else was happening (President Eisenhower was playing golf again) the event became a nationwide phenomenon.

To quote the Chicago Daily Tribune, "It all started when George Di Peso's daughter was watering the garden with a plastic hose. When she stuck it into the dirt, she was unable to pull it out. Worse, it started burrowing downward."

The story was good for more than a week, with crowds gathering daily to see the curious phenomenon of the burrowing hose.

Eventually, Mr. Di Peso got fed up with all the publicity and chopped off the hose. More than twenty feet had disappeared. Meanwhile, other nearby residents reported that their hoses were similarly disappearing. A few blocks away, one jokester put a hose sticking out of the ground, with a sign identifying it as "the other end."

So, returning to the present, because the Archer Bobby's and Floxxy Williams' report on The Oxnard Avenue Anomaly And Parts Beyond occurred on a hot Tuesday afternoon in the first week of August in an odd-numbered year, it attracted far more attention than it would have gotten had it occurred the first Tuesday of November in an even-numbered year, which is to say some as opposed to none.

It wasn't much, but it was enough.

Desperate for news, the other stations in Los Angeles dispatched their own third-string investigators to discover if perhaps there was enough here to fill the looming void of dead air threatening the rest of the week.

In short order, Dr. Leung's frantic investigations became a nationwide event. Los Angeles County had expanded by a mile and a half. Orange, Kern and San Bernardino Counties had shrunk proportionally.

At first, nobody took it seriously. The commentariat dismissed it as some kind of computer glitch or human error or failure of instrumentation. Even after NASA confirmed the growth with satellite measurements, the phenomenon remained firmly in the category of things not to worry about—like the dangerous levels of carbon dioxide in the atmosphere, the perilous levels of ocean acidification, the impending disappearance of the Gulf Stream, and the chances of the Anaheim Angels winning a pennant.[†]

It was just another silly season event. Nobody took it seriously until the first lawsuits were filed. The Orange County Supervisors filed the first one, but the other counties were quick to follow.

---

[*]   Coincidentally, that was the same week that Dr. Leung was born. Make of that what you will.

[†]   The author takes no responsibility for any of these events actually occurring, especially the last one. I'm an agnostic.

The plaintiffs charged that the Los Angeles County was occurring at the expense of the surrounding counties, stealing their land, as well as their tax base, and they were therefore entitled to appropriate recompense, determined by the differences in the value of the real estate gained against the value of the real estate lost. They demanded the state set up an independent commission to determine just how many millions Los Angeles County should pay them.

The Board of Supervisors of Los Angeles County immediately filed a counter-suit, charging that if Orange, Kern, and San Bernardino Counties couldn't manage the security of their own borders, they had no right to complain about any spillover. It being not an election year, the back-and-forth was politer than normal, but not without suggestions from the plaintiffs that they should build a wall around Los Angeles County to prevent any further infection. The denizens of Los Angeles County were just as quick to agree. "Feel free to lock yourselves out of the most prosperous economy in the state and possibly the nation, depending on which economist you believe." And: "You want a wall? You pay for it."

The Mayor of San Diego symbolically broke ground on the proposed wall, but that was only a publicity stunt. He had box seat tickets behind home plate for a Dodgers vs. Padres game the following night, scheduled for Dodger Stadium in Chavez Ravine, just a few miles north of Los Angeles City Hall.

That the late-night talk show hosts would have a field day with The Anomaly was never in question. The Anomaly was now bigger than Jay Leno's chin—it couldn't be ignored. But despite the potential for humor, the situation had to be taken seriously when one of the national evening newscasters began ending his broadcasts with, "This is the 221st day of the Los Angeles expansion. It has now eaten 24 square miles of California. Good night and get out of the way."

As The Anomaly expanded, so did its rate of growth. Soon, the following summer that same newscaster was saying, "this is the 512th day of the Los Angeles expansion. It has eaten another 37 square miles today and is expected to reach the Arizona border before September. Good night and call your real estate agent."

The lawsuits had also expanded proportionally, most of them based on the idea that property values were being affected—but there were other complaints as well. Where once, you could get from Simi Valley to Hollywood in an hour, now it took two. Bus routes were affected. Travel times were doubled, tripled. Every business in the city reported increased costs for fuel and increased time spent on deliveries.

The Los Angeles Department of Water and Power was billing nearly twice as much for domestic water usage. California's chronic drought condition was further exacerbated by the increase in fire-vulnerable brush and the increased surface area sucking up ground water. Almost every lawn in the city had doubled in size, every swimming pool in Bel Air had expanded proportionally, and the golf course at Greater Wilshire Hancock Park had grown so large that several studio lawyers had passed out from exhaustion trying to reach the 7th hole, which was now south of where Wilshire Blvd. had previously been. Wilshire Blvd. was now in Culver City and Culver City was heading toward Long Beach. Much of Long Beach was under water, having been dislocated by Torrance and parts of Carson.

After Google Maps crashed, no one was quite sure where anything was anymore.

By the time Los Angeles County started pushing into Nevada and Arizona, both in the same month, the Federal Government finally mobilized itself. It was one thing when it was merely a state-level event, but now that California was expanding into other states, it threatened the possibility of a Constitutional crisis.

If Los Angeles County were to devour its surrounding states, the respective senators would no longer have constituencies. The senate would be reduced from 100 members to 96, and the Republican party would lose its ability to filibuster progressive legislation. The president might be able to get a judicial nominee confirmed. The country might actually be able to get some work done.

So of course, the Republican members of Congress opened an immediate investigation to determine if The California Expansion, as it was now known, was the result of a pernicious conspiracy. Extremist groups quickly branded The Expansion a threat to the American way of life, triggering protests in every city in Texas, except Austin, which was already seen as a lost cause. The state legislature passed an emergency bill banning spas, life-coaches, and sushi. Several Priuses were torched. But the California effect was pernicious—two of the protest signs were distinctly out-of-character. All of the words were spelled correctly.*

Despite Republican action on the matter, several agencies of the United States Government were already hard at work. The president had authorized FEMA to provide relocation services for refugees terrified of flea markets, manskirts, merlot, and full moon diets.†

Meanwhile, Los Angeles kept growing, California kept expanding. A small tremor rocked Winslow, and the residents, instead of panicking, started betting on its magnitude. It was barely 3.2 on the Richter scale and Mrs. Gladys Popple won twelve dollars.

On the day that Flagstaff became a suburb of Los Angeles, six residents of that town sued for the right to buy Disneyland Discount passes for Southern California residents. This did not mitigate their annoyance with the sudden increase in freeway traffic, bringing the I-40 to a near standstill.

That was another side effect.

The traffic and weather staff of two radio stations were now reporting on conditions as far away as Las Vegas and Tucson. "We have an overturned truck on the I-10 eastbound out of Phoenix, there are no alternate routes. Traffic on the junction between the I-15 and the US 93 south in Las Vegas is congested due to heavier than usual police action." And: "Temperatures in Primm will be the same as yesterday, hot. Flagstaff will be even hotter."

Elsewhere, the EPA was hard at work taking soil samples throughout the nation and sending them by Fedex to various research agencies around the country. The

---

*   Okay, this part I'm making up.

†   Look it up. This alone is a good reason for building a wall around Los Angeles.

World Health Organization also sent in teams of researchers, checking to see if Winter Vomiting Disease and Oscar fever were contagious.

But it was Devra Littlebig, a researcher at the CDC who discovered the true cause of The California Expansion. She had been studying the circumstances surrounding The Schwarzchild Radius* and had realized that the experiments in eleventh dimension bio-physics had created a localized space-time distortion. It had likely been caused by the self-mutating software in the fusion-collider.

Whatever.

Various geologists at Cal-Tech had their grad students and teaching aides look into the possibility, and very shortly, after several days of algorithm-wrestling and software coding, confirmed that that the actual epicenter of the California Expansion Anomaly was not the intersection of Ethel Avenue and Oxnard Street, but was actually several miles to the southeast, directly below the Universal City subway station† where most of the Schwarzchild mass had oozed into the ground.

As detailed elsewhere, the Schwarzchild had grown until it reached critical mass—at which point, even a small earth-tremor would be catastrophic. In this case, the catastrophe was inevitable. The Schwarzchild's own weight was sufficient to trigger the tremor. It popped dramatically and flubbered across the local terrain.

After the cleanup, after the hazmat teams declared the neighborhood mostly safe again, the residents of area blithely assumed the whole affair was over.

Well, sort of. But not completely.

As various squishy pieces of the Schwarzchild had absorbed themselves into the soil of the San Fernando Valley, whatever condition had originally caused the Schwarzchild to grow, that same condition had now become part of the California substrate—it was inevitable that the student surveyors of Los Angeles Valley College would discover the anomaly first, they were the only ones surveying the region.

Essentially, the Schwarzchild had metastasized. Well—not the Schwarzchild, but its essence. Los Angeles had become a gigantic geological cancer.

The Three O'clock news team nearly wet their shorts. Archer Bobby and Floxxy Williams were tapped for a Special Report which pulled the highest ratings in that time slot for that demographic since the last time James Franco had hinted at a heterosexual lifestyle. (But there was still no attempt at a frenzied copulation afterward. Really.)

Congress erupted into a firestorm of unusual lethargy. The nation's Surgeon General, who had not been heard from since she refused to confirm that the House of Representatives was entitled to 300 sick days a year, was called in to testify about what was now called The California Cancer.

The Surgeon General drily reported that the most common treatments for cancer are drugs and radiation. Because a significant percentage of the citizenry of Los Angeles was already well-drugged, the alternative was radiation. She did not, however, recommend nuking Los Angeles. Signs of the cancer had already spread as

---

*   That's another story. I'm not going to retell it here.
†   Yes, Los Angeles has a subway system. Honest. I'm not making this part up.

far east as Des Moines, as far north as Saskatchewan˙, as far south as Mexico City, and far enough west to disrupt the annual migration of the gray whales.

Despite muttered threats of war, over this geographical invasion, neither Canada nor Mexico followed suit. The Canadians were too polite to go to war and a great many poverty-stricken Mexicans were delighted that they could now find legal jobs in the United States without leaving home.

The Surgeon General also reported that because California had legalized medical marijuana with appreciable results, few of the residents of the affected areas were experiencing any serious discomfort. Fast food sales were up in the expanded California regions, as well as the consumption of various other stoner munchies. So, all in all, this particular growth had to be classed as mostly-harmless, albeit not quite benign.

When pressed for a cure, the Surgeon General sighed, took off her glasses, wiped them with her handkerchief, and with a somewhat exasperated expression, replied, "There is no cure. At the present rate of expansion, this continent will be The United States of California within seven months. In less than two years, the whole planet will be completely California-ized.

International repercussions were immediate. The governments of Panama, the Cayman Islands, and the Republic of Vanuatu panicked. Between them, they had three trillion dollars of offshore cash stored in secret accounts. The application of California's strict banking laws would impoverish their fragile economies. They would not be able to make up the difference with Indian casinos.

It is beyond the scope of this narrative to discuss the global effects of the California Expansion. They were severe—but by the time the governor of California moved into the White House the majority of the world's population had moved through the first few stages of grief—denial, anger, bargaining—all the way to depression. Fortunately, the legalization of medical marijuana and the universal availability of California's Medi-cal program did much to create reluctant acceptance—everywhere but Quebec, of course. The Quebecois angrily held another futile referendum on separation.

But that's how enchiladas arrived in Eastern Europe and Budapest became the Taco capital of east Los Angeles and the world.

At least, until Moonbase Armstrong finishes analyzing its soil samples.

---

*   The representative from Mississippi requested a map from the Sergeant-at-Arms, as he had never heard of anything farther north than Minnesota, and that only because he'd heard it mentioned in roll-call votes, just before his own state.

TWO MEDITATIONS ON KING KONG

Meditation One: Unanswered Questions

The first seventeen times I saw King Kong, I didn't worry too much about back-story. I just wanted to see the great ape fighting the giant dinosaurs. It's a terrific adventure and it's a classic fairy tale of the 20th Century—and if I were a literary deconstructionist, which I most assuredly am not, I might even say that it's a metaphor that symbolizes the eternal battle between chaos and order, between man and nature, between beauty and the beast. Nah, at best, it's an allegory about doomed love—about being too big and too hairy and so socially inept that a beautiful movie star screams at the thought of going out with you.

But as much as I loved this marvelous escape from reality, part of me—the eternal analyzer—always insists on asking questions, what I call "refrigerator door" questions. It works like this: You go to the movies and you deliberately suspend disbelief so you can fall into the wide-screen, multi-channel immersion of the grand adventure unfolding before you. Afterward, as you sit with friends at Starbucks, eating and drinking overpriced confections that bear only a passing relationship to coffee and cake—afterward, still enraptured by the post-coital bliss of the experience, you continue to believe you've seen a great movie. It isn't until you finally get home, when you open the refrigerator door, looking for a snack—is there any pizza left, or fried chicken?—that it finally hits you; you were conned. "Hey, if E.T. could fly away at the end of the picture to save himself and Eliot, why didn't he fly at the beginning of the picture?"

Um...he didn't have a bicycle?

No. Because if he had flown away at the beginning, there wouldn't have been a movie.

That's a refrigerator door question. It stops you cold in your tracks, and you stand there pondering it while the salad wilts, the ice cream melts, and the Jell-O starts to sag.

So look, if Anakin Skywalker really was that powerfully tuned into the Force, why didn't he recognize Senator Palpatine as Darth Sidius? Because if he did, there wouldn't have been a movie.

Right.

But there's another kind of refrigerator door question too. How was Indiana Jones able to stay on the deck of the submarine all the way across the ocean—especially without food and water? For that one, we have to assume that the submarine *never* submerged, that it made the whole trip on the surface—and that the trip didn't take more than a day or so. But as easily as the filmmakers skip over that question, so do we—we willingly make the assumption so that we can stay immersed in the story. It is a deliberate deferral of skepticism. Yeah, I know. It's the movies—but why wasn't he severely sunburnt, at least?

So now that we've established context, that we're willing to give ourselves over to the movie and accept the circumstances of the story, let's leave the refrigerator at home and head off to Skull Island. Max O'Hara clearly knows what to expect. A canoe-load of natives got swept out to sea by a storm; they were picked up by a passing tramp steamer. Conveniently, someone onboard knew enough of their language to draw a map and hear the tale of Kong, some kind of giant ape. And apparently, they weren't the first boatload of natives to escape the island, because the legend is common enough in the region that even Captain Englehorn is familiar with the name Kong.

But how did the natives get to the island in the first place? And where did Kong come from in the grand evolutionary scheme of things?

Consider:

The dinosaurs on the island have clearly been there since the Jurassic era. We don't know how they survived the mass extinction that occurred when a comet slammed into the Yucatan 65 million years ago, but never mind that; the scientific evidence for that particular event only came to light in the past two decades. In 1933, it was assumed that the dinosaurs died off because their babies were too heavy for the pteranodon to deliver. We will also ignore the fact that isolated on this single island, all these various creatures did not seem to evolve beyond their ancient antecedents. Nor did the limited amount of resources to be found on this island stunt their growth. (Although an equally opposite evolutionary case can be made for gigantism.) Etcetera, etcetera.

Let's just accept that the dinosaurs on Skull Island are the real deal, one way or the other. Despite the serious evolutionary pressures of an island existence, they are still recognizably the same creatures as their distant predecessors.

But their existence still raises some fairly obvious ecological issues. How many dinosaurs live on this island? Does the island generate enough biomass to support the herds of herbivores necessary to support a family of predatory T-Rexes? For that matter, how many T-Rexes live here? Are there enough to keep the stegasaurs and apatosaurs in check, so that they don't denude the island's foliage? Or did Kong kill the only one? The last one? Uh-Oh....

The ecology of any island is a fragile system. A continental ecology has much more resilience, a much greater ability to withstand events like hurricanes, earthquakes, tsunamis, volcanoes, and other chaotic surprises. An island, however... well, there are a lot of unanswered questions here. We still end up coming back to the essential one—even if we don't consider the evolutionary issues, how have these dinosaurs managed to sustain themselves for 65 million years?

It's a leap of faith, and we need to make that leap of faith for the story to work. But even after we make that particular leap, the existence of Kong is the greater mystery. How does a 25-foot ape evolve in an ecology dominated by predatory proto-reptiles? For that matter, where's the rest of Kong's family? Apes travel in troops, don't they?

We know from the sequel, Son of Kong, that Kong must have had a mate. Where was she all this time? Where did she come from? Where did she go? Why didn't we see her in the first picture—and if Kong had a wife (and presumably an even more-terrifying mother-in-law), then why the hell was he sneaking off to Skull Mountain for a quickie with Ann Darrow? We know from the visual evidence that he thought she smelled good, he kept sniffing her undies, but we also know that apes are generally monogamous—is Kong experiencing lust in his heart? Is he committing virtual adultery with Ms. Darrow?

But for the sake of this discussion, let's stick solely to what we can observe in the first picture, and ignore the issue of Kong's issue. Let's assume he's single, possibly the ape equivalent of a nerd, unable to get a date on Saturday night, unless she's chained to a pedestal outside the native village. But even in that case, we still have to ask, where are the rest of the giant apes? If they're not living up in the eye of Skull Mountain, have they already been eaten by the dinosaurs below? Is Kong the last of his kind? If so, does he qualify as an endangered species? It would certainly explain his crankiness as well as his hunger for female companionship. And if Kong is the last of his kind, then Carl Denham and crew are eco-criminals, aren't they? Knowing that they're destroying a fragile island ecology, it's hard to feel sympathy for them when they fall into the spider pit, isn't it?

But even after we ignore all these questions, so we can accept the existence of dinosaurs and giant apes on Skull Island, the continuing presence of the natives has to be questioned. Are these people stupid—*or what?!*

It's fairly obvious how the natives must have arrived at Skull Island. The entire south sea area was originally colonized by waves of migrants who started out from the eastern coast of Asia at least ten thousand years ago; island after island—Tahiti, Hawaii, Fiji, and so on. So the question isn't how the natives got to Skull Island; the question is how they survived.

At some point in the past, let's say a thousand years ago, some exploratory canoes landed here—on an island filled with predatory dinosaurs and the ancestors of a 25-foot gorilla. Assuming that these folks were stupid enough to stay—or so desperate that they thought this was a better alternative than putting back out to sea—how do they survive long enough to build a village *and* a thousand-foot wall to separate themselves from the monsters on the island?

Let's think about that wall for a minute—if these natives know how big Kong is (or his progenitors), if they know how ferocious he is, if they know about his morbid appetites, then just why the hell did they put a door in that wall big enough for him to come busting through? What's that about? Some kind of a cultural death wish?

And was building a thousand-foot wall really easier then getting back in their canoes and paddling away as fast as possible? What was so important that it justified staying? Or maybe the smart ones fled and the folks still on the island are the descendants of the people too stupid to leave?

How did these people develop such a weird relationship with Kong anyway? He lives way the hell on the other side of the island, up on Skull Mountain. For that matter, why does he live up there? Most apes prefer forests. And why does Kong like to eat native girls? Obviously, he considers them a treat—the ringing of a giant gong is his dinner bell. And for that matter, where did the giant gong come from? These natives don't seem to have a lot of metallurgy skills, do they? And we don't find gongs anywhere else in the south seas, so it's unlikely that they brought it with them. They had to manufacture it locally—how?

And what about those natives?

They are apparently sacrificing a beautiful young maiden to Kong on a regular basis. Once a month? That's 12 girls a year. Now maybe they have an overabundance of beautiful young maidens on their side of the wall, enough so that they can hold regular sacrifices at every full moon, but it seems to me that's a good way to deplete the population in a very short time—and do significant long-term damage to the gene pool. If only beautiful girls get sacrificed, pretty soon the only ones left to have babies will be ugly girls, and in a very short time, a matter of twenty generations or so, everyone on the island will be ugly and there will be no more beautiful maidens for Kong anywhere. Or does he even care about physical beauty? We're talking down-the-hatch, sweety.

Maybe the sacrifices are limited to once a year? Every year, we give Kong a new bride and he leaves us alone for the next twelve months. Except, judging by the way Kong treats the rest of the natives, it's unlikely that his brides last a whole year.

Regardless of the timing of the sacrifices, it's apparent that the locals have some very mixed feelings about their relationship with their deity. They respect Kong, obviously. They fear Kong, obviously. They sacrifice maidens to appease him, obviously—but the way they scramble up to the top of the wall to watch him with Ann Darrow…well, there's a certain amount of morbidly curious, prurient interest going on here as well. Possibly because they don't have freeways, they have no place to slow down to gawk at every roadside accident, this is their local celebration of violence and brutality.

So I'm betting that the virginal (another assumption on my part) sacrifices are the local equivalent of a football or soccer or any other violent sporting event. It's the Roman circus, without Romans, lions or Christians. It's great fun for everyone—except the virgin, of course. (That the whole south sea island region is not healthy for virgins has long been known. Tourists are now advised that they must bring their own virgins to throw into local volcanoes.)

Moving on....

How does Carl Denham get Kong back to New York? The crew builds a raft, they float Kong out to the ship, they use a crane to lift him off the raft and lower him him into the cargo hold. Then what? What do they feed him? And how much? Who cleans up after him? Does somebody go in with a shovel to clean up the giant gorilla turds? A new somebody every day? Or do they just hose the waste away? That's probably the safest way to handle the mess. But what does Kong think about all this?

We know that Kong has a temper. We know that he will break down walls to get to Ann Darrow—is he really going to sit docilely in the bottom of the ship's hold? Or is he going to get really really really pissed off?

None of these questions are ever really addressed—we just cut quickly to a glittering sign that advertises "King Kong, The Eighth Wonder of the World." The assumption here is that somehow all these separate issues have been resolved. At least well enough to get us all to Broadway. Just like the business of Indiana Jones' submarine ride, Kong's long sea journey is also skipped over in the blithe assumption that you're so eager to get to the next part of the story that you won't stop to ask, "Hey, wait a minute—what about E.T.'s bicycle?"

But clearly, Kong's captors have treated him well on the journey—although he was only 18 feet high on Skull Island, by the time he gets to Manhattan, he's had a growth spurt; he's now 25 feet high. But that all happened off screen, because we don't see a lot of evidence that he's being treated like a King.

Let's step away from Kong for a moment and talk about another giant ape... Mighty Joe Young. Mr. Joseph Young, not quite as big as Kong, but with a much more appealing personality, leaves Africa for a career in show business. Because this was before the formation of People for the Ethical Treatment of Animals, Joe is kept in a small cage backstage at the nightclub where he performs. From his point of view, he's not in Hollywood to experience the bright lights and the big city—he's in prison. To say that he's not happy is an understatement; but he's got a big heart, spiritually as well as physically. And so we open our hearts to his plight and cheer his escape. Unlike Kong, Joe does not tear up the town, he rescues orphans from a burning building. Even more reason to admire his great spirit. (God knows what the orphan thinks about this particular rescue—if you had just climbed out the window of a burning building, would you regard the sudden appearance of a giant ape as an agent of salvation? Yeah, right. People have died of fright in much saner circumstances.)

Back to Kong. We don't see Kong backstage in his dressing room at the Broadway theater; but if you've ever been backstage at a Broadway theater, then you know there's not a lot of room backstage—certainly not enough to house a giant 25-foot gorilla. Ohell, there's barely enough room for the average diva. Although more than one producer has fantasized about putting his divas in cages instead of installing them in dressing rooms, gorillas probably look easier to manage, which may go a long way explaining Carl Denham's obsessive need to bring Kong to Manhattan.

Never mind. The point is that once we get back to New York, we see no respect for Kong's personal welfare. No one seems to care about the giant ape's well-being. We see no cage, no food, no water, and certainly no facilities for cleaning up after him. Just how much urine can his bladder hold anyway? Backstage must smell horrible! Possibly even the first three rows of the theater as well. (And have you ever seen what an angry chimpanzee can do with a handful of feces?)

What we see is Kong strapped helplessly to a cross; his arms and legs manacled, he's trapped in a grotesque parody of Christ's torment. Well, yes. This is a fairy tale, a metaphor, a movie. We're not interested in the nuts and bolts. We don't care why E.T. didn't fly away and why Anakin Skywalker is such an ignorant lout. We're in a hurry to get to the good stuff. We want to see Kong smashing an elevated train or climbing the Empire State Building. We're not worried about who shovels the gorilla shit, so we don't ask how they move Kong back and forth from cage to stage and back again to cage. Obviously Carl Denham hasn't thought about it. He's designed his show to fail. No wonder nobody wants to invest in his adventures anymore.

Of course, Kong breaks free. There are no engineers in Manhattan smart enough or foresighted enough to stress-test the steel manacles and ensure that they would be strong enough to withstand the strength of an enraged giant ape. No—just like Jurassic Park was designed to fail (that's another rant), Kong's escape is equally inevitable.

In 1933, there were probably a million people or so on Manhattan island, maybe two. Nevertheless, Kong is able to find Ann Darrow with little or no difficulty. Okay, he steps on a few cars, bites the head off a cop or two, yanks a woman out of bed and drops her to her death twenty stories below, but those are just youthful indiscretions, no worse than the hijinks of the average congressman. But Kong must have one incredible sense of smell to find Ann Darrow so easily in the heart of midtown Manhattan, just a few blocks from Broadway—especially with all those odiferous delicatessens and pungent hot dog stands in the neighborhood.

To be fair to Kong, he probably does have an incredible sense of smell—after all, he's got a bigger nose than Pinocchio testifying under oath. And while Kong has Ann Darrow up on Skull Mountain, he does spend a lot of time sniffing her lingerie. Is Kong a panty fetishist? Hmm, maybe that's the source of his obsession.

Or maybe, Kong is female—that would go a long way toward explaining the existence of the Son of Kong in the sequel of the same name. But if that's the case, then Kong isn't King, she's Queen—a lesbian, the ultimate bull dyke. (See how one fact can change your whole point of view? Don't make assumptions.)

Meanwhile, after retrieving Ann Darrow from Jack Driscoll (who obviously isn't man enough to protect her from a giant rampaging gorilla), Kong heads toward the Empire State Building, the highest point on the island. Now, here's the *real* refrigerator door question to think about. All those others were just warm-ups. How does Kong climb the side of the building with Ann Darrow in one hand? Think about it.... If he has her in one hand, then he can't grip the building with that hand, can he? If he lets go with his other hand so he can reach higher, that's right—he falls down. But we clearly see him climbing. Did he hold Ann Darrow between his teeth? Did he put her on top of his head or on one of his broad shoulders? We don't see that. When they arrive at the top, she's still in his hand. Hmm. It's E.T.'s bicycle all over again.

But it is here, at the top of the Empire State Building that the movie works its real magic—the transmogrification of Kong from beast into tragically doomed hero.

For most of the picture, Kong has been the enemy—something to fear. He's been obsessed with Ann Darrow. He only broke free of his chains when he thought she was being attacked; then he raged through the streets of Manhattan in search of her. But abruptly, now, here, at the top of the Empire State Building, mortally wounded by the airplanes, we see the great beast demonstrate his true feelings. He doesn't want Ann Darrow hurt. He checks to see that she is safe, then tragically falls to his death.

Does he hit anything? Or anyone? It's a safe bet that he does. The streets of New York are narrow and always crowded. There's no need for New Yorkers to gather in a crowd, they're already in one. Drop a 25-foot gorilla from the sky anywhere in Manhattan and you're likely to take out 30 or 40 people. Probably more with the splatter.

And finally, who removes Kong's dead body? And how do they do it? This is going to require cranes, bulldozers, and teams of guys operating chain saws. And how long is it going to take? I'm assuming that Kong smelled pretty ripe when he was alive—how bad is he going to smell three days after he's dead? What's that going to do to the property values in the neighborhood of 34th street?

And if Carl Denham is still obsessed with his dreams of Broadway, he isn't going to let anyone dispose of Kong's body so easily. He's going to hire a small army of taxidermists and have Kong stuffed and put on display somewhere.

Finally, it's time for the killer question. What about the lawyers? If you thought the dinosaurs on Skull Island were rapacious, you haven't seen a pack of Manhattan raptors in action. We're talking *very* bad news. There will be subpoenas for everyone and anyone. The city will sue Denham, Denham will sue the people who made the manacles that failed, the elevated train company will sue Denham, Denham will sue the makers of his gas bombs, the theater owners will sue Denham, Denham will counter-sue the theater owners, the owners of the Empire State building will sue for the bullet damage, Ann Darrow will sue for emotional distress, the families of those who died will sue Denham *and* the city, the owners of every piece of property that got smashed or squashed will sue Denham and the city, the insurance companies will sue everyone just to be safe. The courts will be asked to rule the whole event an act of God, so as to let everybody off the hook. The legal proceedings will last until December 7, 1941, when everyone's attention will be distracted by other matters.

Now do you see why I'm the wrong person to take to the movies?

Meditation Two: The Movie I Wanted To Make

The sound track begins with a scratchy buzz, then we see a badly framed industry leader counting down to:

Black and white, flickering, grainy, scratched, a terrible old print of one of the most exciting sequences in the original 1933 classic, KING KONG. This is a full shot of the great gate of the natives—Kong is slowly pushing it open as the natives run screaming in terror.

As the great ape comes stamping through, suddenly the music becomes a full stereophonic orchestra, color floods the image, the screen swells to a full 70mm image—and KONG, the most magnificent ape of all comes charging, roaring, bellowing into the native village to wreak havoc upon their homes—The sequence runs through its most exciting shots, and then, as it peaks—we hear a voice say, "Cut, cut, cut—"

The camera pulls back and we are looking at a backlot set. Extras, dressed as natives, mill around with bored expressions, while the director—Ernest B. Schoedsack—calls Kong aside for a conference. We see, in middle distance, the two of them discussing something in the script; Schoedsack is speaking in low tones, Kong is replying in deep, guttural grunts. Kong nods his head knowingly, Schoedsack pats the ape's arm reassuringly, and then this huge 20-foot ape shambles back onto the set and back into position while an assistant director hollers, "All right, places everybody."

Schoedsack calls, "Let's try another take. Lights, please. Camera. Action."

—and the take continues, with Kong smashing his way through the rest of the native village. We climax with Kong picking up one of the natives, popping him into his mouth and biting his head off. (This is one of the famous "missing scenes"— eventually rediscovered and restored.)

"Cut. Print. That's a take," Schoedsack calls, "Next set-up please."

We go to a wider angle on the set. We see Kong retiring to a large chair with his name on the back. He starts paging through a copy of Variety, circa 1931. An assistant director confers with Schoedsack in low tones, "We gotta do something about all the extras he's eating...central casting is getting suspicious...."

And we go to titles:

KING KONG
Behind The Scenes

OPEN ON FAY WRAY, an elegant older woman, being interviewed by an offscreen reporter.

She is reminiscing about the first day she reported to work for Merian C. Cooper and Ernest B. Schoedsack.

At that time, they had just begun working on a new picture that all of Hollywood was buzzing about....

DISSOLVE TO: 1931. A young Fay Wray (dark-haired) coming on to the soundstage for the first time and being introduced to her co-star, young Kong—a hulking 20-foot ape.

"I remember Kong as being very good-natured, very eager to please, but very very naive about life in the big city. He let people take advantage of him something awful. Even though he'd been in Hollywood for two years before being discovered by Mr. Schoedsack—Mr. Schoedsack had seen him in Schwabbs eating a four foot banana split—Kong never became hard or cynical like so many other young actors whose careers are faltering, because he never lost his optimism, so he never fell for the whole 'Hollywood' thing. Even afterwards, the fame never went to his head. He was always his own quiet self—I think that's what I liked about him the most."

We see Fay Wray shaking hands with Kong, who is carrying a script under one arm. "I'm looking forward to working with you, Mr. Kong."

Kong gives one of his familiar guttural grunts in reply.

She twinkles, "And you can call me Fay—"

And we see the first beginnings of the love affair between Kong and Fay, right here in their first meeting—she can't take her eyes off of him, and he is equally entranced by her. Voice over narration continues, "If only I had known what lay in store for both of us...."

We see the dailies:

The shot is Kong battering at the gates of the wall—this is the view from his side, before he has managed to push the great doors open. The dailies are in black and white, of course, and there is the usual run of out-takes.

We see Kong leaning patiently on the door, while a slate pops into foreground. Offscreen voice calls, "Action," and he turns and knocks politely.

We hear producer and director comments over all this. "Well, you can't fault his manners."

Slate and second take. Kong knocks a little harder, but still not in character. (The audience knows what the shot should look like—they're feeling what the director is feeling now.)

Producer: "I don't think he understands the scene...."

Slate and third take. Kong finally begins to knock properly. An extra falls off the top of the wall.

Producer, "Oh, shit—"

Director grunts.

Producer, "He's awfully hard on the extras, isn't he? How many does that make?"

"Six. I think."

Slate and fourth take. We see Kong getting a little more fidgety in the B.G. between takes. "Action," and he begins banging on the wall again. This looks like a good take, until part of the wall—the wrong part—collapses, revealing stage hands and lights behind it.

Director: "That's when we broke for lunch."

Slate and fifth take. We see director and Kong conferring softly, director acting out the motion, Kong nodding. Re-slate, Kong goes through action.

"I don't know. He just doesn't seem to have the feel for it."

"He's young—give him a chance."

"What about that little Italian kid—Dino whatsisname? The one with the rubber suit?"

"No, no, I think this will work out better in the long run. Give Kong a chance."

Slate and next take. Kong falls on his ass.

"He was getting tired there, but I think we can cut away, then cut back and use the stuff from the other side of the wall."

End of take, setting up for next one, camera still rolling—

"Hmm, I must have forgotten to call a cut."

We hear the extras jeering Kong, calling him a "big monkey." We see Kong finally getting honestly angry—and he bashes down the wall exactly as we remember him doing it from the classic film.

"Hey—!!"

∞∞∞∞∞∞∞∞∞∞∞

Fay Wray narrating again:

"That was Kong's screen test. He wasn't a very good actor at first, it was all very new and strange to him to be in the movies, and he had a lot to learn—but Mr. Schoedsack was very patient and kind, and Kong was a fast learner. There was something about him, a raw power...that couldn't be denied. I had to dye my hair blonde for the first day of shooting, and...."

We see Kong's famous entrance scene recreated for the watching cameras—the first time the theater audience sees him as he comes crashing through the forest, parting trees and as he catches his first glimpse of Fay Wray....

"There were fourteen takes—"

We see a montage of Kong reactions—excited, stunned, happy, and so on.

"—he was very pleased when he saw me as a blonde; he thought it did wonders to bring out the color in my cheeks."

We see Kong and Fay Wray talking softly between takes, she holding a Coke in one hand, he holding a barrel.

"Kong was just a big overgrown kid—the theater audience didn't realize it at the time, but he hadn't even reached his full growth. In fact, he grew another four feet while the picture was in production, which explains why he looked taller in the New York scenes. We were in production for two years. But at the beginning, he was very shy and needed a lot of coaching. He had a tendency to overact on some of the subtle scenes, and not be big enough on the more dramatic shots."

We see Fay and Kong sharing a quiet moment together.

"Kong also had a terrific sense of humor..."

We see Fay recreating the famous scene with Robert Armstrong, where he is making the first screen tests of her aboard the ship. She is wearing a long white dress, and Armstrong is exhorting her to, "Look up, up, now you see it, it's huge, it's horrifying—"

We cut to a wider angle—and we see Kong standing off to one side, watching the take—and making grotesque faces at Fay—

"He used to try to make me break up during a shot."

In the shot, Fay starts giggling, and Kong delightedly slaps his thighs.

"He thought that was great fun. Mr. Schoedsack didn't dare bawl him out for it in front of everybody, but you could tell he was annoyed. I think Kong must have been very lonely at that time. He was always on the set—even on days when he wasn't needed, he was always there. I think he just didn't have any other place to go. And he felt at home on the soundstage. As if we were his only family. I guess I felt sorry for him, at first."

Fay finishes the take and rejoins Kong.

"Later on, I grew to see the nobler qualities of this very misunderstood actor—"

Fay narrates her first meetings with Bruce Cabot, and we see an innocent and charming boy-girl relationship developing between them; it is not serious, but the moment between them is one of those moments so easily misinterpreted—

—we see Kong entering the soundstage at an inopportune time, and abruptly seeing his co-star spooning with her "other leading man."

Kong's face darkens and he sulks off the set....

In the next take, we see Kong losing his temper and punching down a scaffolding with some natives on it—another one of the famous missing scenes—but now we know *why* Kong was so mad.

Narration: "We had some trouble in planning the ending of the picture. For one thing, we weren't sure where to stage it...."

We see shots of Kong holding Fay Wray atop a variety of 1933 landmarks: Radio City Music Hall...Grand Central Station...The Chrysler Building...the Statue of Liberty....

"...But none of them seemed to feel right. Finally, someone remembered that the Empire State Building was due to be finished soon, and it was going to be the tallest building in the world. Out of desperation, because we couldn't think of any place else, we decided to stage the ending of the picture there. It seemed like a good idea at the time."

We see the Empire State Building, still uncompleted, Kong climbing it slowly....

Fay Wray narrating: "One of the best kept secrets was that Kong was very much afraid of heights—but there was no other way to shoot some of the scenes for the ending, except to go to the newly completed Empire State Building and actually shoot them there."

We see Kong and Fay Wray on the top of the Empire State Building, makeup men working on both of them, then hurriedly leaving the scene. We see a camera plane circling nearby. An Assistant Director with a radio set signals them for action, and we see a take of the "original" ending of the movie.

"Ann Darrow is on the roof of the Empire State Building, threatening to jump. Kong comes up to the top in an attempt to save her, thus proving he is not a monster at all, but really a very good guy at heart. The closing shot is the two of them watching a tranquil sunrise over 1933 New York, fadeout."

The first take isn't good, however, and while we reset for another take from the camera plane or perhaps a camera dirigible, Kong and Fay Wray talk over their difficulties.

Grunt, grunt.

"Kong, don't you see—we can't go on meeting like this."

Despondent grunt.

"All this sneaking around, hiding from other people—"

Very despondent grunt.

"—your family doesn't like me at all. And there's the religious differences. How would we raise the children? And all the social pressures—and there's another thing—"

Grunt. Grunt. I don't want to hear it.

"—it would mean the end of your career. You know how prejudiced people can be. I don't mind giving up my career, but I can't let you deprive the world of a great talent—"

Kong is very upset. Grunt,. grunt, grunt, grunt. He turns away from her.

"Oh, please—don't talk like that. You know you don't mean it."

Grunt. Grunt. I do too.

"Kong, don't you see—it's over. It's bigger than both of—well, it's too big, anyway—"

Kong rages—

In the camera plane, we see the director and cameraman. Cameraman says he's ready, the director says, "Roll 'em.

Back on the tower, Kong is still raging angrily at Fay Wray.

The A.D. calls, "Action," but Kong ignores him, ditto Fay.

"Kong," she says, "I know it's hard, but it has to be this way."

Grunt. Grunt. I can't live without you. And he turns to jump—

"No, don't—"

He turns back to her, reaching, imploring—She reaches for him—

And he loses his balance—

And falls—exactly as we remember him falling in the 1933 original.

Fay screams, horrified. The makeup men and assistant director have to hold her back to keep her from throwing herself off after him. "Oh, God, no—"

Down on the street, we see Robert Armstrong push his way through the crowd... and someone behind him says, "He fell—"

And Armstrong says, "Oh, no. It was beauty killed the beast."

Next to him, an A.D. notes, "Hey, that's a good line."

Fay Wray's voice over narration, continues: "Of course, we had to change the ending of the original picture. Kong was supposed to rescue me, now he dies in the attempt. Mr. Schoedsack used the film they had already exposed, and the wonderful Mr. O'Brien superimposed in all these biplanes, so his experiments with stop-motion animation paid off after all.

"Of course, there were all those terrible rumors that circulated for years afterward that Kong hadn't really died, that his death had been faked, and that he's been living in secret up in Benedict Canyon for all this time—the fact that no one was allowed near his body and that the funeral was very private seemed to prove those claims—but I was there, I loved Kong more than all the millions of his movie fans, I loved him more than anyone, and if he was still alive, I would certainly know it." She is very very wistful. "Even today, so many years later, I still put a wreath on his grave every year."

The angle widens and we see Fay Wray looking very very small and sad and obviously in a great deal of pain because of her memories. "I guess Robert Armstrong was right...I guess, beauty did kill the beast."

As the interview concludes, we hear a car pull up, and a door slam offscreen. Fay says, "Oh, that's my son coming home now."

We hear a familiar heavy footfall, followed by a very familiar grunt. All offscreen. Fay says, "He's just like his father."

And we fade out.

AFTERWORD:

Seen in TV Guide: "Island boy in search of love tears up the big city."

WHY THERE ARE NO TYPE-C CIVILIZATIONS
by MARVIN MINSKY
and DAVID GERROLD

On the scale of hypergalactic events, names are unnecessary. Any event occurring on the hypergalactic scale is, by definition, unique. Therefore, naming the event is redundant, unnecessary, and irrelevant.

Nevertheless, for the convenience of the moment, let us identify two phenomena; call them Fred and Ethel. These names are only for convenience. Make no assumptions of gender, nature, or personality from either of these identifiers; only that we identify Fred and Ethel as two hypergalactic phenomena existing as wavelike phenomena moving through time-space.

The delta-vee of their passage is not measurable in linear three-space; therefore, the originating point of their journey and the even-more-distant termination point are also not knowable. The linear map is insufficient to reflect multi-state existence. (Although some ripple effects of their passage might be observable to certain kinds of deep-space gravity wave detectors, sensors on a scale large enough to detect such ripples would need to be of such a size as to be impractical for any three-space beings to construct.)

But in this particular intersection of temporality and location, the manifestation of their passage is solely worthy of notice because it occurs near an unimportant, mostly inconsequential, small galactic object of oblate spiral conformation.

"Hey, Fred! Listen! Do you smell that? Over there—two-thirds out on the spiral arm! Coherent radio spectrum!"

"Mm, yes. Relativity buds! My favorite! Let's go!"

THE FEATHERED MASTODON

Okay, I hereby publicly apologize for pushing Mike Resnick into the La Brea Tar Pits. I did it. I'm sorry.

I won't try to excuse it by saying it was poor impulse control on my part—after all I did smack him with two feather pillows, and the fact that I'd brought the pillows along was clear proof that the attack stunt was premeditated. So I plead guilty for that and I apologize.

But I'm not going to give the money back. If the purchasing agent at the Page Museum was stupid enough to believe my story about having cloned a feathered mastodon, then that's his fault and his employer's responsibility.

But I do want to apologize to Bantam Books for spoiling their traditional Worldcon dinner excursion. They'd rented a big bus, filled it with beer, and schlepped all of their most willing writers—those who hadn't found other obligations with other publishers—off on the science fiction version of a magical mystery tour. Tom Dupree has already told me that I'm not likely to be invited back, and that's probably punishment enough, I guess.

Tom also told me how much it cost to have the emergency vehicle called—they had to call in one of those extra-huge cranes that they use for lifting boxcars to hoist Resnick out of the sticky black oil. He looked like a giant fudgsicle—or a Godzilla turd—and while he was hanging there, all gooey and dripping and glumphing unintelligible threats, that's when I slit open the feather pillows and whacked him with them.

It was expensive, but—what the hell, even though I've apologized, I have to admit it was worth it. But Tom says they're going to take it out of my royalties. Like that's a threat. Maybe if they'd sell some books, I could get some royalties once in a while..

But I'm not worried. Even though the SFWA Defense Fund turned down my requests for legal aid, there are enough other former contributors to Resnick anthologies who have sent me generous checks—enough that I should be able to mount a credible defense. Just contributing a story to a Resnick anthology goes a long way toward proving temporary insanity.

Okay, yes, he deserved it—there's no question that he had it coming. He shouldn't have said what he said. He shouldn't have said it on camera. And most of all, he shouldn't have sent me a videotape of him saying it in front of an audience of three thousand people.

The only reason I'm apologizing now is that I didn't know about his skin condition and how when the oil and the tar seeped through his skin, that it would render him sterile and impotent—kind of a chemical castration.

While all the behind-the-back jokes about Resnick's new career as a harem guard, and how he's now in demand for the soprano lead in *La Castrata*, have been funny in their own sick way, the fact is I'm really starting to feel bad about all this. The doctors say it's unlikely that Resnick will ever grow another follicle of hair ever anywhere on his entire body—some kind of interaction with the pollutants in the tar—and because he has to wear those rubber pants because of the resultant incontinence problem, he looks sort of like a three hundred pound baby. And they say he cries a lot too. Especially when the male nurses come to change him.

So, okay, I guess I'm not a very nice person. And this particular fraternity-level prank only proves that I'm not to be trusted out in public without a keeper. A simple pie in the face would have made the point just as easily and probably would have been a lot funnier too. But Resnick started it, so he deserves some of the blame. That remark about how "recombinant DNA splicing explains Gerrold's nose" *hurt*.

The thing is—Resnick should have known better.

It's no secret. Science fiction writers gossip. They talk about the stuff they've seen. Pournelle's been inside the space shuttle, Benford gets guided tours of particle smashers, Ben Bova got an advance peek at the—oops, not supposed to mention that one yet. But you get the idea. Where do you think we *really* get all our ideas? We hang out every year at the annual meeting of the American Association for the Advancement of Science—and hope for invitations to the real labs. And then we get drunk at the conventions and brag about what we've seen. I got invited to a tour of Intel's new fabrication plant. Ellison got to see a building demolished with a new small explosive named after him. Roddenberry once got a free tour of the whiskey museum in Edinborough.

In this case, I know that the research papers haven't been published yet, there aren't any articles yet in Scientific American or Discover magazine; only a few weird articles in the National Enquirer about potatoes with real eyes and hairless mice with purple mohawks. Oh, wait—there was that one thing in Discover, but it was in their April issue and everybody thought it was another one of their silly April Fool's jokes like the particle the size of a bowling ball or the naked ice-borer that grabbed penguins from underneath.

But the fact is, they have been doing some serious gene-splicing work at—well, never mind. I could tell you, but then I'd have to hunt you down and kill you. Everyone who reads this. And that would seriously decimate the population of science fiction readers. Or maybe not. How many people read Resnick anthologies anyway? Not that many. The loss would hardly be noticed.

But anyway, I was invited up to a place in Marin County. It's funded by a couple of famous movie directors, you figure it out. This goes back more than fifteen years, when they first decided they wanted to do a dinosaur movie—only at that time nobody, not even Stan Winston's guys, could figure out how to coordinate all the separate machines necessary to create an illusion of real motion. That was when computers were still as big as refrigerators and cost more than Ferraris.

So that's when the dinosaur cloning project really began. They thought they'd make their movie with real dinosaurs. And maybe even open a park too—which is where they got the idea for the movie that did get made.

It wasn't done with amber—although that's sexier because it films better. It was really done by processing coal. Coal is really a compressed peat bog. And peat bogs are really good at preserving dead things—every so often somebody finds an ancient mummy in a bog. Well, sometimes they find dinosaur bones in coal—so if you process the coal immediately around the dinosaur bones, you get chains of DNA.

Most of it is damaged, of course. DNA doesn't last for 80 million years. But if you collate all the different chains, you can put them together and pretty much approximate what was there in the first place, and then you can plug them into ostrich eggs and see what you get. Mostly, you get deformed ostrich embryos. So that was pretty much a dead-end. It used up a lot of money, but the movies were paying for the research, and it was tax-deductible too, so the thing just chugged away, burning dollars and coal at the same rate.

But after a while, the guys in the lab coats decided to try something else. They thought, "Hey, why don't we back-breed from existing species of birds and reptiles until we match the dino DNA?" And so they started down that path with high hopes. That was another good way to use up millions of dollars a year. Pocket change.

Somehow, the back-breeding project took a side-turn. I think it was the time that they were trying to do all those weird fantasy movies. The Henson people were good with the puppets. The Winston people were getting better with the machines. The computers were getting smaller. But it still wasn't enough—and meanwhile, the guys in the labs had gotten a little stir-crazy—

Oh yeah, I should explain that. Because the whole thing was being done in such incredible secrecy, they had built this little city off in the hills north of the bay; the cover story was that it was a movie production facility—and they even built a real recording studio there as a kind of false front. But underneath it were the real labs. And because the work was so secret, the scientists and all the technicians were literally confined to the site. They were allowed to see their families only on Thanksgiving and Christmas. It was like being sent to Antarctica, but without the snow.

So, yeah—they got cabin fever. And they got crazy. It happens.

When I was in college—USC Film School, although I try not to admit it—one of the animation professors told us of a "tradition" at animation studios. Pornographic cartoons. Each animator would (on his own time) add a scene. The next animator would pick it up where the last guy left off. Back in the days of wild fraternity parties and pornographic movies—before VCR's—some of these animated films were floating around town. I remember one with a farmer and a donkey and ... well, never mind. I also remember the instructor sighing wistfully. "Ours were good, but they were never as good as the ones coming out of Disney. Now those guys were great." I don't think any of the Disney stuff ever got off the lot though. I never saw any of it. I wonder sometimes if Walt did. I'd be surprised if he didn't.

Anyway, that's what started happening at Project Back-Breed. The DNA Team started mixing genes just to see what would happen. They weren't having any luck with anything else—they hadn't licked the viability problem, nothing lived, so they got desperate just to see if they could make *something* that would survive.

That's where the hairy chicken came from. They actually created a small flock of hairy chickens. They looked like furry bowling balls. They were hysterical to see—clucking around the yard like big fat tribbles. (That's why I got to see them. Otherwise, I'd never have been allowed near the place.) Two of them were fertile, so they were able to breed several generations by the time of my visit. All colors—blonde, brown, red, white, black, even one with a weird purplish tinge. They were pretty good eating too. They tasted like chicken. Of course.

After the hairy chicken, the DNA Team decided to try going the other way, to see if they could put feathers on a mammal. That was about the time someone had the bright idea of injecting an elephant with frozen mammoth sperm. They're always finding dead mammoths frozen in the Siberian glaciers, and it's not that hard to chip some sperm out of the ice, defrost it, do a test-tube fertilization and inject it into an unsuspecting elephant cow. The technology has been used on horses, pigs, sheep, cattle, dogs, mice, gorillas, chimps, and even humans. So why not elephants? What's the worst that could happen, right?

Right. Somehow, the chicken DNA crossed the information highway.

Eventually, they tracked it back to a software error. This file and that file got crossed, so this DNA pattern got mixed with that DNA pattern—and the project was so big by that time and there was so much going on that nobody even noticed that this sample and that sample were from two different experiments, two different species—because that's what they were doing anyway, so it was just one more set of genes to be spliced—and the compatibility problem got knocked down as a matter of routine—and eventually, the samples got processed and put into the pipeline and chugged along until—well, that's how they ended up with the feathered mammoth. Cute little thing.

Of course the cow that delivered it practically died from the shock—but after a dose of prozac large enough to make New York polite, she cheered up and nursed the little guy as if he were her own calf—which he was, but he had this weird yellow down all over him. At first, everybody thought it was just normal fur, but when the first feathers started appearing six weeks later—let me tell you, there were a lot of questions asked and there were a lot of red faces too—but that could have been from the other experiment, the one about genetically redesigning already-living creatures. One of the retro-viruses had escaped, recombined, mutated, and become airborne, and now half the team were evolving into Native Americans. So the red faces were normal by then.

Fortunately for everybody, there were a lot of filmic possibilities in weird animals. That was about the time Paramount was going to send Kirk and Spock to the Genesis planet, so they were looking for a cheap source of weird creatures as a way of keeping the special effects budget down, so they pumped some new money into the whole thing; two or three of the other studios also came aboard then, and in short order the guys in Marin were turning out all kinds of little monsters. Hairy chickens of all sizes—they were clumsy and unstable and a strong wind could knock them over and blow them like tumbleweeds—and that's how you saw them in *Critters*. And there was an ostrich with scales—supposed to look like a deinonychus, but ultimately unconvincing, I think the Corman people finally used it in a dog called *Carnosaur*. Carnivorous rabbits for *Lepus II*. Unmade. A green cat. (That one sold for nearly two million—but the cat died before the script went into turnaround. Pity, the merchandising on it would have been phenomenal. They were all set to breed a million green kittens in time for Christmas.)

And of course, the Feathered Mammoth. They were going to use him in something with Arnold Schwarzenegger, another Conan picture, I think, *Conan in Atlantis*, but it didn't happen either. The studio sunk it. Nobody really likes working with animals, children, or Martians. They always use the Martian's best take. (But that's another story, the one about the Martians. When Resnick publishes *Alternate Martians*, I'll tell it. If they let him edit any more of these. I doubt it after this one, but who knows—they say it's good work-therapy at the outpatient clinic, so who am I to piss in his oatmeal? We all wish him a speedy recovery. Well, most of us do. Well, his family anyway. I think.)

But eventually—finally—they did manage to back-breed some real dinosaurs. Sort of.

The problem was they were working with frog and lizard and bird eggs, so the dinosaurs they got were small. Miniature. The size of Dinky toys. That's what they called them at the farm. Dinky Dinos. Stegasaurs as cute as hamsters. Hadrosaurs that looked like parakeets. A T-Rex the size of a crow. It took a lot of really skillful trick photography to make them look full size for the movie. (I hear they're going to start selling the Dinky Dinos in pet stores next year, simultaneously with the release of the sequel. That'll be interesting when Daddy brings home a little T-Rex as a birthday present for little Jill.)

What you didn't hear about—what nobody heard about—were the raptors. Three of them escaped.

At first nobody on the farm worried about it. There was a chronic problem with rats in the feedstock, so they had brought in terriers and later on, a few wild tomcats had joined the menagerie too, and that had kept the problem manageable—sort of. The cats killed as many lizards and birds as they did rats—so the guys at the farm figured the pussies and the pooches would probably kill the raptors too, thinking they were just some kind of lizard-bird. Only it didn't happen that way.

First, the rats disappeared. And the mice. And the gophers and the skunks and the badgers ("Badgers? Badgers? We don' need no steenkeen' badgers!") and the rabbits and the weasels and the foxes and the coyotes and everything else small enough to be brought down by a pack of land-piranhas. And of course, the pooches and the pussies too.

By that time, the raptors were numbering nearly thirty. They traveled in packs— five or seven to a group. At any given time, there were between four and six packs of them roaming the grounds of the farm, chirruping and cooing like demented pigeons, their little heads bobbing back and forth, turning this way and that, their tails lashing frantically. They were brightly colored—the males were green or blue, with yellow flares of color down their backs and bright red stippling around their heads and forearms. The females were drab gray-green. The females traveled together, the males kept apart from them, except during mating season—then it wasn't safe to get out of your car unless you were wearing heavy boots.

It wasn't until the raptors started bringing down the newborn calves that the farm guys realized the problem was out of control; they brought in some tropical quarantine experts who laid out slabs of meat laced with poison cocktails. That got half of them; the other half got smarter. So they tried traps. And retro-viruses. And hunter-killer droids—that was another nightmare. The software mutated— remember the law of unintended consequences? The ex-terminators (formerly terminators, now just ex-terminators) shot at anything that moved—or even looked like it was thinking about moving. Finally, they cut power to the feed lines and the ex-terminators ran out of juice after two or three more weeks. Meanwhile, they still had a raptor problem.

They finally got them with pheromones. They put out lures that smelled like female raptors in heat and all the males couldn't help themselves, they came sniffing around the lures and tumbled through trap doors into little tar pits where they died like dire wolves and sabre-toothed cats and mastodons in prehistoric Los Angeles. (LA needs more tar pits. There are still too many sabre-toothed lawyers and dire agents and studio mammoths staggering around the countryside.)

That should have been the end of it, but it wasn't. By this time, the guys upstairs were so pissed, they were ready to shut the whole operation down. The DNA Team had to get rid of the remaining raptors, so they donated them to the San Francisco zoo. Oh, that was smart. On the one hand, there are no rats in San Francisco any more. On the other hand, there are no stray animals either. You have to keep your cat in the house, and it's not safe to walk your Chihuahua.

All of which has nothing to do with Resnick directly, except that he was supposed to be part of the solution, not part of the precipitate. Instead, he ended up in the pits. Down in the mouth ... and all his other orifices as well.

See, Resnick had been doing this whole series of anthologies—*Alternate Nightmares, Alternate Sexes, Alternate Bicycles*—whatever he thought would sell. And he had sold one called *Alternate Dinosaurs* or something like that. Who keeps track? And the publishers had decided that it would be fun to do some kind of tie-in with all the dinosaur movies, but they couldn't afford much of a licensing fee, and the only one they could link up with was that dreadful turkey Fox was making—*The Feathered Mastodon*. In fact, that's what it was about—a dreadful turkey—and the mastodon was playing the lead.

And so they sent Resnick out west to have his picture taken with the critter, and there they were, the two of them, side by side—and I was there too with my kid and my video camera, and I forgot that everything I said while taping would be heard on the tape, so when I sent Resnick a copy of the tape, he could hear me saying clearly, "The family resemblance is astonishing. They both have the same birthmark in the shape of an Edsel."

I guess Resnick felt he had to get even. So there he was at the secret convention of trufans, held in Moscow, Idaho every February, and he was still smarting over the tape I'd just sent him, and that's when he said what he said, and that's why I pushed him in the tar and smacked him with the pillows. And then, while no one was looking, also injected him with a cocktail of kangaroo, frog, and lizard DNA, with a chaser of growth hormone.

Things should start hopping around the Resnick household Real Soon Now. I'd move out of the state if I were you. In the meantime, I've sold an anthology to Tor called *Alternate Resnicks*. Watch for it in the bookstores, next fall.

F&SF MAILBAG

February 12
Dear Gordon,

Re: Your recent announcement that you will be outsourcing the jobs of domestic science fiction writers to cheaper-working authors in parallel dimensions.

I take pen in hand to object most strenuously.

Yes, perhaps some of those other writers are more prolific, having access to advanced technology like typewriters or even home computers. Nevertheless, the traditional science-fiction story, handcrafted by a dedicated artisan, will always have a unique charm to it that no machine-produced work can ever duplicate, let alone surpass.

But even more important, a Resnick or a Robinson or a Willis story written in a parallel dimension will take the bread out of the mouths of our own hard-working Resnick, Robinson, and Willis.

Quite frankly, it speaks volumes about your character. How will you sleep at night knowing that our children are going hungry?

Sincerely,
David Gerrold

<><><><><><><><><><><><>

June 23rd
Dear Gordon,

Re: Your recent request to borrow my timebelt.

I must regretfully, but most emphatically, say no. Absolutely not. No way. Don't even think about it.

I have bounced forward several years to see what you would do with access to portable temporal transport, and frankly, I am appalled. You will be bouncing forward yourself, two-three-four years at a time, to purchase copies of your own magazine at the newsstand, even before the stories within have been written—you will then publish those stories with only token payments to the authors.

How do I know this? My future self is very upset with you for publishing "Unstrung," "The Mouse King's Motorcade," "A Day At Crater Park," "The Lifeguard at Cassy Beach," "Uncle Morris," and my personal favorite, "The Patient Dragon."

Despite your efforts to be fair, I believe you have created a philosophical conundrum as well as an ethical one. If I have not written the stories that you have published, then who did? If no one did, then isn't it immoral for me to accept payment for stories I have not personally created? Yes, you are paying for the use of my name, but is it right for me to put my name on a story that I haven't written yet?

And yes, I can argue the other side of this too.

Many of your future authors will be grateful, receiving payments for stories they would have written, but now don't have to write, so they can write other things instead, thus doubling or tripling their actual output; but I worry that raiding the future for stories will have a long-term destructive effect on the field because it will deny authors the necessary process of experiencing their own creative energy at work, living through the authorial process, and evolving through that writing into more mature literary voices.

While this may be only a subjective opinion, I truly believe that if you were to have access to a timebelt, the result would be a disaster for the science fiction genre. By keeping authors stuck in the immediate rewards of their unwritten work, they will not be moving forward into the experience of actually creating results and the lessons to be learned from such labor.

Call me old-fashioned, but I love science fiction too much to allow you to stunt the literary growth of its finest practitioners.

As always,

David Gerrold

◇◇◇◇◇◇◇◇◇◇◇◇◇◇

August 19th

Dear Gordon,

It is not my job to tell you how to run your magazine. I'm merely a reader and a sometime-contributor, but I feel obligated to comment about your use of a synthesized-sentience intelligence-engine to generate stories "in the style of...."

Yes, the first two or three times it was a fun experiment. I admit it, I enjoyed the recreated Heinlein story "The Steel Feather." And I'm sure a great many fans of Fritz Leiber were thrilled to see a new Fafhrd and Gray Mouser story, "Lankhmar, CSI." And if truth be told, the synthesized Sturgeon tale "To Kill A Unicorn" actually brought a tear to my eye.

So no, I do not object to the occasional reinvention of the voices of the past as a way of paying honor. It's a chance to revisit the heritage that delivered us to the present. But I believe that when you reinvented Harlan Ellison, you went too far. Yes, there's no question that "Screaming Ice Flowers" was a brilliant demonstration of the technology—but Harlan Ellison is still alive! Using a computer to recreate his unique vision puts him in the position of competing against his mechanical self.

Gordon, where does it end? It is a very short step from here to a nightmare situation where flesh-and-blood writers become totally unnecessary.

I foresee a day when each new issue of the magazine isn't edited—it's generated. You could simply decide which authors to emulate, how many words to produce, and what themes will be explored. The magazine could be synthesized faster than you can print it out and read it.

From a publisher's point of view, the possibility is tempting, but it strikes at the very heart of the editor/author relationship upon which this entire field is built. I strongly urge you to reconsider your decision to publish any more synthetic stories.

Your pal,
David Gerrold

October 3rd
Dear Gordon,

This morning, a close friend sent me a very distressing email. If what he says is true, I am appalled and disturbed.

I hope it is only a vicious rumor and I hope you will take the time to clarify the circumstances for me, but according to my friend, you are now hiring illegal aliens from 3-Grxl-90, Horta VI, and Brunnehilde 4.2, to write stories for the magazine.

In fact, my correspondent was quite clear that these illegal aliens aren't even writing fiction, merely their own personal life histories. So how can you call this work either Fantasy or Science Fiction? It puts the hard-won credibility of the magazine at risk.

Please tell me that this is not the case. Or if it is, please tell me that you will cease and desist immediately.

Writing from the heart,
David Gerrold

November 35th
Dear Gordon,

I suppose I should congratulate you on your decision to clone the most popular writers in the field, so as to increase the output available to you and other editors in the field. It's a bold and audacious step.

But frankly, it smacks of assembly-line production. Duplication removes the uniqueness of the artisan. It destroys the concept of authenticity and authorship. Did Larry Niven[Prime] write *Ringworld Reloaded* or did it come from the duplicated soul of Larry Niven[1]. How is the reader to know if a story came from the actual author?

Even worse, what is the reader to make of conflicting stories from dueling clones? I refer you to the unfortunate incident with McCaffrey[5] and McCaffrey[7] and the readers' confusion about the authenticity of *Blood Feuds of Pern*. Which story is canon? Which is apocryphal? That particular argument hasn't ended yet and probably will never be resolved, now that McCaffrey[5] is charged with beating McCaffrey[7] to death with a Best Novelette Hugo.

Consider this, Gordon. If you continue with your cloning program, pretty soon you will be publishing so many stories from the cloned masters of the field that there will be no room left in the magazine for new and upcoming writers. You could put the entire science fiction genre into a literary Klein bottle from which there will be no escape.

With much fear and trepidation,
David Gerrold[3]

I wrote this story long before Welles died, but never published it. I like my ending better than the one the universe provided.

THE STRANGE DEATH OF ORSON WELLES

Shortly after 4:30 on the afternoon of August 22nd, Orson Welles reached critical mass.

The day had been extraordinarily hot, even for Los Angeles, a melting scorcher that liquefied the tires of parked cars and glued them stickily to the pavement. Traffic crawled down Sunset boulevard as if it were the main drag of Hell; the leering faces of Kiss and Alice Cooper grinned down at them like triumphant demons.

The inversion layer over the basin had turned the sky into a familiar silvery shade of gray; the exact same shade of mugginess as could be seen on the tattered screen of the NuArt theatre in Santa Monica, where the ragged society of serious film fans—serious because they couldn't afford to be dilettantes, and their chances of ever making the studios' A-lists were less than nil even on a good day—were cloistered in the darkness for the umpteenth unspooling of *A Touch of Evil* and *The Magnificent Ambersons.*

Only a few miles away, the great white bulk of Orson Welles lay sprawled helpless in the center of an eight foot water bed, a mountain of human corpulence as immobile as some vast leviathan beached on the shores of desolation. Here lay the cinema world's own Moby Dick, gasping for breath, exhausted by the energies expended in his seventh futile attempt to rise from bed.

The enormity of his plight was rapidly becoming obvious, painfully so; it was one of the cruel ironies of fate. He had passed the point of diminishing returns and now he was pinned by innumerable servings of la ballotine de canard aux pistaches, terrine de foie gras de perigord, filet de saumon en geleee, cuisses de grenoille provencale, tournedos Perigueux, souffle au Grand Marnier, Cafe Diable, and the occasional late night Jumbo Jack with large fries and thick shake accompaniment. Orson Welles had finally been immobilized by his own life-style, a living monument of fossilized indulgence.

He had been trying to get out of bed for several hours now, heaving himself back and forth in violent spasms of effort. His mouth was permanently frowned into that same cruel pucker of obsession as had characterized the manners of Charles Foster Kane so many years before. His tiny little eyes had receded even further into his skull, gleaming with a red madness. His arms flailed wildly, and every great thrust as those limbs of corpulence came smashing down onto the water bed created vast tidal waves of motion across its surface that caused the edges of the sheets to rise and fall in waves that measured an average of 1.83 feet. Welles was generating a better surf than could be found at Rincon Beach that morning. The ripples that swept across his own suety mass were equally impressive.

After every attempt, Welles would sink back into the center of the bed, a gigantic insect trapped in its own nest. The ripples subsided around him as his breath racked in hoarse sobs of anguish. His heart pounded, struggling to push his blood through arteries like little sewer pipes clogged with globs of used Crisco.

After a while, when calm returned to the water bed, the pounding of his heart began to ease, and Welles began to gather his strength for one more attempt to rise—and yet, each successive attempt was accomplishing less than the last. Even the wave crests were no longer as impressive as before.

It was rapidly becoming obvious that Orson Welles was not going to be able to lift his own bulk out of bed.

Perhaps it was the combination of the heat, plus the exhaustion of the moment and the icy thrill of the adrenal realization of his situation that was the catalyst —

He was in no danger of immediate death. If necessary, he could have survived several winters on his own fat alone; it was some deeper fear that moved him to keep trying beyond the realm of normal human endurance. It was not just the mortification, the cruel irony of embarrassment that would result if his situation were to be discovered, nor was it even the physical discomfort; no, it was the agony of being unable to control his own destiny, the cruel truth of becoming a victim of his own life instead of its master. To a man like Orson Welles, this was unacceptable.

At this moment, at this point in time, another human being confronted with the same realization would have panicked and begun calling for help. But not Orson Welles, no not Orson Welles. He fumbled around on the bedstand near his left hand and found last night's cigar butt, half-smoked—one of the few he had not yet tossed out the back door at the pool service man. He stuck it abstractedly in his mouth and began chewing on it, his mind racing feverishly. Reaching again, he fumbled for the lighter, and after some moments of anguished scrambling, his hand clawing like a fat palsied pink spider, he was able to grasp the table lighter and bring it around to his face. It was then that he realized that he had eaten his own cigar.

He was submerged in waves of dizziness then as the last cruel fact came hammering home. There were urges inside of him that had taken on individuality of their own. His body had not only rebelled, it had seceded from the union with his mind and was now beginning to transform itself into a new form of life. As Welles watched, horrified, a prisoner in his own flesh, his hands began clawing at the sheets, the bedding, ripping the down out of the quilt and stuffing it into his mouth.

His jaws began working like little Cuisinarts, and as fast as he pulled out the masticated down, he would stuff in new pieces. He began building a wall of material around him. His body was bathed in oily sweat now, it had taken on a curious sheen.

His skin seemed to be thickening, becoming a kind of fried from the inside shell. It shone with metallic-looking highlights.

His hands were still clawing at the bed, even ripping off pieces of wood now. His mouth had become a vast cavern of grinding teeth. His hands, curled into insect claws, plucking, grasping, stuffing. The foamy masticated product of his labors surrounded him in layer after layer of hardening material around him, a rising wall of shredded linen and wood fiber.

At some point in the early evening, about the time Walter Cronkite was telling America this was the way it was, the water bed burst, bathing Welles in a warm effluvia as it lowered him gently to the floor. But by then it was too late. The intelligence that had been Welles had flickered out, leaving only this incredible creature, still gnawing at the frame of the bed, the floor, the draperies, the nightstand....

The creature worked all night long repairing and building the walls of its nest. The heat of the room was rising, product of the body mass of this vast insect-thing. Even Kafka had not imagined a transformation as grotesque as the one that had begun in Orson Welles' bedroom. A cockroach was nothing compared to the majesty of this great white beast.

Welles worked throughout the night, chewing steadily and methodically. By morning, he had completely enclosed himself in a nest of linen and wood-fibers and sputum. Even now, in the rising heat of the morning, the shell was hardening into a surface as hard as concrete.

And inside...?

Inside, the transformation was continuing. Even now, strange and medically astonishing processes were working their way, made possible only by the vast energy potential stored in Orson Welles' flesh.

It would be some time before the world became fully aware of what had happened here in Los Angeles, but by then it would be too late. By then, a new life form would have established itself so vigorously that the entire human ecology of the planet would be affected.

The first eggs would hatch into a colony of worker Welleses, their duties to protect and serve the vast bulk of the Queen Welles. The next batch of eggs would hatch into soldier Welleses; but it was the third batch that would be most fearsome: thousands of little Queen Welleses would spring forth from that and go out into the world to mate and establish nests of their own.

The world was soon to be inundated in thousands and thousands of voracious little Orson Welleses, each one of them brilliant, each one of them hungry.

Orson Welles had triumphed again.

AUTHOR'S AFTERWORD:

Burn the film schools, while there's still time! They're coming! ***You're next!***

MICHAEL THINKS THE HOUSE IS HAUNTED

It's an old house, older than me. It creaks in the wind. It groans in the heat. It settles back into itself at night. It shivers in the winter and aches in the summer. It has its own set of rustling noises everywhere. The chimneys whistle, the windows rattle, the floorboards squeak. The house has a voice.

So Michael thinks the house is haunted.

It's not just the noises, although they're very convincing. It's all the other things.

It's the basement door that he closes tight every evening and comes back in the morning to find it open again, as if something that lives below comes out and prowls the house at night. It's the drapes in the front room that he opens every morning and then comes back to find them mysteriously closed. It's his little Catholic statue of the Virgin Mary on the shelf in his bedroom—someone or something keeps turning it to face the wall.

Michael isn't my first roommate. He's just the latest one. I'm not that easy to live with. I like playing jokes on people.

Michael has only been living here a few months. He knows all the stories about the house, of course. The house has a reputation, because people like to believe things, so they tell stories.

Some of the stories are pretty good. Four generations of Morrisons lived here—and died here. One of the best stories involves a young woman whose lover fell into the well and drowned, she locked herself in the attic and slowly went mad, she chanted all day in a language nobody understood and sometimes scribbled arcane notes and drawings in a thick journal.

And of course, there was the murder. Or maybe it wasn't. Nobody knows for sure. Maybe it was a staged suicide. But that's one of the reasons why it's hard to find renters. Who wants to sleep in a room with a ghost? Especially an angry ghost.

Sometimes Michael sets up cameras, sometimes he prowls around with his ghost-hunting equipment. He makes videos too, long involved discussions of ectoplasmic concurrences. He has a blog and a podcast and several thousand followers. He's sure he's going to find something. They're sure he's going to find something. Michael is determined to prove the house is haunted. He makes me laugh.

Sometimes I follow him, making jokes the whole time about how silly this is and how he's wasting his time. He ignores me, of course. He's so determined to find out who or what is opening doors and closing drapes and turning the virgin that it's turned into an obsession. He goes from room to room, from attic to basement, from maid's quarters next to the kitchen, all the way upstairs to the far corners of the nursery.

I think Michael is silly. He's never going to find any ghosts. I'm the one who opens the basement door and closes the drapes and turns the Virgin Mary to the corner. I do it to tease him. I do it for the joke.

I know this house. I know it better than anybody.

It's old, yes. It's tired and creaky. But haunted?

I don't think so.

I've lived here nearly two hundred years—and I've never seen anything.

THE FABTASTIC FOUR

ROLLING STONED EXCLUSIVE:
Lois Lane interviews The Fabtastic Four

LANE: Is this the first time the four of you have been together since the breakup?
Lennon: (Looks to McCartney, shrugs.) "Well, Paul and I were watching *Saturday Night Live* one night and Lorne Michaels publicly invited us. Remember that? We would have done it, but Ringo was in L.A. and George was in England. And the two of us were so buzzed that—"
McCartney: "—but the four of us did talk about it. A couple weeks after that, we had a chat, it would have been a lark, but—"
Starr: "—the thing is, we know each other so well, we can't surprise each other anymore—"
Harrison: "—but that's not the real reason for the breakup—"
McCartney: "George needed his ... his own space. And so did John. I think we each needed to go our own way for a while."

LANE: I do want to get to the circumstances of the breakup, but let's leave that till the end. Has anyone ever figured out what happened that night at the Hollywood Bowl?
Lennon: "Everybody always asks that. The answer is always the same. Nobody knows. We've asked ourselves the same question. We've read most of the articles too. Maybe it was everything all at once—the gamma rays from across the universe hitting the dark side of the moon, radioactive spiders from Mars, a purple haze across L.A., everything triggering a massive overload of polarized magnetism exploding from the gigawatt speaker system—who knows?"
McCartney: "It could have been all that Indian mysticism too. We were singing 'Shazama-lama-ding-dong, yeah yeah yeah—"
Starr: "Shoulda stuck to 'Na-na, na-na-na-na.' Maybe we would have turned into batmen...? Now that woulda been a magical mystery."
McCartney: (Throws cushion at Starr.)

LANE: Have you looked at the video recordings?
Lennon: "They don't show anything, do they? All the ones we've looked at just flicker and go blank for a few seconds—"
McCartney: "Seven seconds exactly—"
Lennon: "—and when they come back up, they show the four of us flat on the stage—"
McCartney: "—still sparkling with some kind of energy."
Harrison: "It was pretty bad. Ringo took the worst of it. He was throbbing and pulsing with this strange green light all over him for several minutes. He looked like a goblin—"
Starr: "—I won't do that no more. I'm tired of waking up on the floor."
McCartney: (Throws cushion at Starr.)

LANE: So, of course, the real question—when did you realize what had happened?
Lennon: "You mean, the transformation?"
McCartney: "It didn't happen right away."
Harrison: "I was the first to recover. I remember I was seeing everything. But nobody was listening to me. Like I was invisible. The EKG machines—they didn't show brain waves, not normal brain waves. Just sine waves. C-sharp sine waves."
Starr: "Mine were B-flat. Paul, stop throwing cushions at me!"
Harrison: "John came awake first. All the machines around him sparked with flames and lightning. He sat up shouting, 'Life goes on!'"
Lennon: "I felt like a supernova. I had this fire inside, wanting to get out. Everyone came running. In they came, jorking and jobbering. I felt hotter than Christ. I was so hot the sprinkler system came on—"
Harrison: "He was so hot the water steamed off of him.. Great clouds of steam. The water drops sizzled and bounced like on a hot griddle."
Lennon: "They had to move me to a bathtub full of ice. I melted it. But it worked."
McCartney: "Getting John to chill has always been a challenge."
Lennon: "I kept asking about Paul. I was sure he was dead. I wouldn't chill until I saw he was all right. Finally, he stretched into the room, flowing like a river before he finally settled into his normal shape. He said, 'Hey, Bulldog.'"
McCartney: "That was what I called John sometimes—when he'd get in one of his angry moods. That would usually make him laugh. Maybe break the ice instead of melting it. But he was all red in the tub, steaming, so I said, 'What's the new maryjane?' He won't admit it when he's really hurting, but this time he looked at me, he said, 'It's all too much.' Then he looked at me again and said, 'You look weird, Paul. I've just seen your face. You don't look different, but you have changed.'"
Lennon: "I don't think he knew yet. He said, 'I feel fine.' But he was flubbering like a balloon. He looked shuddery. So I asked him, 'Where's George?' and we both looked around. 'He was here a minute ago.'"

Harrison: "I was there the whole time, I said so. 'I'm right here.' They both looked at me, really strange. It was Paul who said it first, 'I'm looking through you, you're not the same.' I held my hand up to my face, I was transparent."

McCartney: "I don't think any of us realized what had happened. Not right away. Not until Ringo came in—"

Lennon: "—only now we call him Thingo."

Harrison: "He didn't know yet what he'd become."

McCartney: "He looked like the Staypuft Marshmallow Man, only made out of yellow. All blocky."

Harrison: "At first we thought he was wearing some kind of a costume—"

McCartney: "A really bad costume—"

Lennon: "He looked like he was wearing an avalanche, all loosely in disguise—"

Starr: "Keep it up guys and it'll be clobbering time—"

McCartney: "I think it was when he couldn't take it off that we realized—"

Starr: "Yeah, I got frustrated—"

Lennon: "He punched a hole in the wall—"

Starr: "And then I got embarrassed. I tried fixing the hole—"

McCartney: "But that was when we knew. We just looked at each other. John was on fire again, I was stretching across the room, trying to grab both of them, George had gone invisible—"

Harrison: "It was Thingo who stopped us from freaking out. He said, 'Hold on. I'll get by. I'll get by with a little help from my friends—'"

McCartney: "Y'know. Maybe it was time. Maybe we were so busy thinking that tomorrow never comes that we forgot—"

Starr: "—yeah, yesterday, all our troubles seemed so far away—"

Harrison: "—we had to remind ourselves, it's about everything, yesterday, today, and tomorrow—"

McCartney: "—it was John sorted us out. He said, 'Imagine. It's easy if you try—'"

Harrison: "Yeah, that's where it started. We were up all night, talking, working it out—"

Lennon: "But we made it. We pictured ourselves on a boat on a river—"

Starr: "—until George finally said, 'Here comes the sun.'"

McCartney: "With George, it's always something. Anyway—"

LANE: Let's talk about the crime-fighting now. How did you come to that?

Lennon: "We were never crime-fighters. Our mission was always to Give Peace A Chance—"

McCartney: "That's what the music was about. Things were getting better all the time. But sometimes, yeah—sometimes things also went helter skelter."

Lennon: "Like Paul says, it's a long and winding road across the universe—"

LANE: But even so, you took down a lot of bad guys. There was Doctor Robert, Lovely Rita, the Nowhere Man, The Walrus, The Fool On The Hill, Maxwell and his Silver Hammer, and of course, Mean Mister Mustard and Polythene Pam—

McCartney: "It started with John. He said, 'I read the news today—'"

Starr: "—and I said 'Oh boy.'"

McCartney: "Because John never reads the news."

Lennon: "But this time, there was a strange story—"

Harrison: "There were holes in the Albert Hall."

McCartney: "Four thousand holes."

Starr: "I've got a hole in me pocket—Paul, stop throwing things!"

Harrison: "And John said—"

Lennon: "Something made all those holes. Imagine—"

Harrison: "Something?"

Lennon: "'Yes, we could do something.'"

McCartney: "Fixing a hole—?"

Starr: "We could give pieces a chance—Ow!"

McCartney: "—where the pain gets in."

Lennon: "That's where it all began. All the adventures. The whole story has been told in the movies, the Beatles Cinematic Universe. Cheese and Onions. Yellow Matter Custard. After that, well, you know—they started calling us The Fabtastic Four. It was fun, for a while. We were The Magical Mystery."

LANE: Can we go back a minute and talk about where the pain gets in? Your last—is it right to all it an adventure? What happened there?

McCartney: "It was helter-skeltered—"

Lennon: "They were piggies."

Harrison: "No. That wasn't it at all."

LANE: According to the news, you were attacked by the Rust-Man, the Hackshaw, and The Glory.

Harrison: "That's what the news called them."

Ringo: "That made it more exciting."

Lennon: "But that's not who they were."

McCartney: "They were lonely. All the lonely people."

Ringo: "We know where they come from now—"

Harrison: "They were our fans—"

Lennon: "They made us up to be bigger than Jesus."

McCartney: "They weren't anything. Just people. They wanted more. More than we could give—"

Lennon: "Christ, you know it ain't easy."

McCartney: "But we felt for them, we did. The Rust-Man, he was Rusty Bias, just another guy having just another day. Obsessed with the Fab Four, couldn't take it that we had become the Fabtastic Four. We didn't belong to him anymore."

Harrison: "And the same thing with Hackshaw. She was really Christine Henshaw. A recovering Catholic."

McCartney: "An escaped nun. Sister Mary Godzilla, or something like that. Not to be trifled with."

Lennon: "She came at us with a chainsaw!"

McCartney: "But she couldn't cut through Thingo."

Starr: "It tickled."

LANE: And the third one—?

McCartney: "Saddest of all. Laurie. Saddest of all. No last name."

Lennon: "It was Wednesday morning. She left home. She had nothing there. No life."

McCartney: "What we said before. It was all the lonely people."

Harrison: "They weren't villains. They just didn't want us to leave them, that's all."

McCartney: "And that's really what caused the breakup—"

Starr: "We couldn't take it no more."

LANE: None of you have said much about that. Can you talk about it now?

Lennon: "There's not much to tell, is there?"

McCartney: "George got tired of being invisible—"

Harrison: (Nods, shrugs, flickers unevenly.) "That was how it started. I told them, 'You won't see me—'"

McCartney: "But you were there—"

Harrison: "It's not the same."

Lennon: "He's right. He'd speak up and people would ask, 'Who?'"

Starr: "And then George would twist and shout, 'See me! Feel me! Hear me! I'm not gonna take it!'"

McCartney: "And that wasn't us. It wasn't."

Lennon: "And then Thingo—people would laugh when he'd say things like, 'It's slobbering time!'"

McCartney: "That wasn't us either—"

Lennon: "We all realized it at the same time."

Starr: "We were drowning in a sea of green."

Lennon: "But money can't buy us love."

McCartney: "It was time. We had to leave the past. It was yesterday."

Lennon: "And there's still today and tomorrow."

Harrison: "But tomorrow never comes. And so, I'll follow the sun."

Starr: "For me, it was California Dreaming. I'm leaving on a jet plane."

McCartney: "See? That wasn't us either. We were lost, little girl."

LANE: So the real reason for the breakup?

McCartney: "Because. Just because—"

Lennon: "We didn't want to be fabtastic anymore—"

LANE: But what about your audience, your fans. What do you say to them—?
Lennon: "We've carried that weight long enough."
Harrison: "For no one...."
Lennon: "You say hello, I say goodbye. I don't know why you say hello, I say goodbye—"

Lane: For Rolling Stoned Magazine, thank you. Our thanks to the Fabtastic Four.
Lennon: "There. See—?"

DANGEROUS VIRGINS

There are tales we don't tell, not in public, and rarely in private. And only to people we trust not to repeat them.

Not because these tales are especially good—and not because they're particularly salacious either. It's because they're just too dumb to be believable.

That's the difference between truth and fiction. Fiction has to make sense. This one doesn't.

I'll start with Milo Twisling. That's not his real name. Milo isn't with us anymore, he's gone to that great convention in the sky—or that other one below, the larger one—so it wouldn't matter if I told you his real name was Goodman Hallmouth or Donald Tinyhands or John Thomas Little. It's just that there are other people involved and they're still alive and I don't want to embarrass them unnecessarily.

Milo worked for a porn firm. No, he didn't work in front of the camera. Not even for any of those companies that produced freak porn. He didn't work behind the camera either. He wasn't even a fluffer. One particularly well-endowed male star was known to have said, "I'd rather cut it off and feed it to the dog than let Milo get a liplock on these royal jewels."

No. Milo worked in a dingy little cubbyhole stuck so far back in the files that the air conditioning didn't reach that far. Milo's job was packaging. Mostly he packed Betamax tapes and VHS tapes. Later, he packaged DVDs, at least until amateur night on the internet put most of the porn producers out of business.

But as part of his job, Milo was responsible for titles. If you had frequented any big porn store in the latter decades of the 20th Century, you would have seen titles like, *You've Got Male, Shaving Ryan's Privates, E.T. The Extra Testicle, Oklahomo!, Fill Bill, Sorest Rump, Schindler's Lust, Saturday Night Beaver, A Clockwork Orgy, I Love Juicy, My Bare Lady, Driving Miss Daisy Crazy, The Magnificent Seven Inches, Big Trouble in Little Vagina, Pulp Friction, Done in 60 Seconds, and Free Willy.* None of those were the work of Milo, but they were the standard of greatness he aspired to.

No. Milo's triumph, if you could call it a triumph, and then only by redefining the word beyond the bounds of all rationality—nevertheless, his triumph, such as it was, was his creation of a website of erotic science fiction which he oh-so-cleverly called *Dangerous Virgins,* narrowly avoiding a lawsuit only because no one was courageous enough to show it to the copyright holder of a book series with a somewhat similar title.

Some of the titles Milo authored were *Star Trick, Land Of The Lust, The Man Who Fondled Himself, When Harlot Was Won, Humping Off The Planet, A Master For Me, A Gay For Glam Nation, A Rape For Revenge*, and *The Trouble With Nipples*.

It turned out that Milo actually had a small talent for erotic fiction. It was a very small talent, but it was large enough to attract enough of a following that he was actually asked for his autograph by three people at an Adult Entertainment Convention in Los Angeles.

Emboldened, he went on to write *Brave Nude World, The Handmaid's Tail, Stranger With A Strange Gland, Time For Enough Love, I Sex-Robot, Rendezvous With Mama, Whore Goes There?, The Lust World, The Breast From 20,000 Fathoms, Whore Of The Worlds, The Miserable Lay, The Man Who Screwed Too Much, Been Her, A Sale Of Two Titties, Yankee Doodle's Dandy, On Golden Blonde, Beast Of Eden*, and *The Son Also Rises*.

He skipped *Moby's Dick*. It was too obvious.

When amateur internet porn finally devoured Milo's employer, Pink Taco Videos, his erstwhile employer, feeling that there was no more money to be extracted from Milo's labors, in an act of uncharacteristic generosity (he really didn't give a shit, he'd lost everything to his ex-wife anyway), released the publication rights to Milo, who promptly transferred all of his titles to Amazon's Kindle Unlimited Adult Library and soon found himself earning three times as much money in royalties every month. Okay, three times what he was previously earning at Pink Taco wasn't all that much, but it was still three times as much. For Milo, it was the difference between eating canned cat food and real tuna. Even Dolphin-safe tuna.

So Milo had a career. Sort of. And like all writers, he imagined success was inevitable. All he had to do was build up a fan base. He decided to expand.

Somewhere between *Whoreson Gets A Clue* and *The Cat In The Thong*, he stepped on a cultural landmine. It arrived as a subpoena. A lawsuit. Milo responded by going public, providing the estate the one thing they didn't want—publicity for how inept their lawyers were, that they were unable to recognize that no one is immune to parody, pastiche, homage, or satire.

None of that is especially relevant, the lawsuit died without resolution when the lawyers were fired, but the publicity it gained earned Milo the undying wrath of Randy Fanborg—not his real name, but when he reads this, he'll know who I'm talking about.

Randy was a terminal Trekkie—or Trekker. (Some of these fanborgs take themselves far too seriously.) He had sewn his own command-level costume—not very well. Omar the Tentmaker would have done a better job. His gold velour looked like an unwashed rumpled bedspread, even worse when Randy put it on. The high point of Randy Fanborg's life was having a photograph taken of him sitting in an inflatable replica of Captain Kirk's Command Chair in a shabby recreation of the bridge set at a local Trek convention. It was the inflatable chair installed in front of a poorly printed backdrop portraying the real bridge of the *Enterprise*. But, it was the high point of Randy Fanborg's life because for just that fleeting moment, he got to pretend he was Captain Kirk—a swaggering, overbearing, tin-plated dictator with delusions of godhood.

None of this would have been important to this particular narrative, except that Randy Fanborg was an aspiring wannabe troll. He didn't live under a bridge and he didn't eat goats, but he did still live in his mother's basement and he mostly survived on Pepsi and the five-dollar pizza special from Little Caesar's. Occasionally, he celebrated Taco Tuesday with a trip to El Pollo Loco.

Oh, and he also had a very small penis. So small, in fact, that when he was born the doctor assumed he was a girl. Randy Fanborg had indeed been raised as female until he was fourteen and his voice changed. He failed to menstruate and started developing a mustache instead. After a DNA test revealed him to have XY chromosomes, an endocrinologist prescribed massive doses of testosterone. It worked only to the extent that Randy Fanborg's penis was no longer inverted. It was small, but it was there.

Randy Fanborg's computer was a hand-built assemblage of parts scavenged from the local computer repair shop that had finally bellied up, and a few replacement parts he'd scrounged from eBay. He spent at least fourteen hours a day staring into an HD monitor he'd picked up at a local gaming tournament when no one was looking.

He had a complete collection of every sci-fi movie and TV show that had ever been uploaded to The Pirate Bay. If he wasn't watching the umpteenth repeat of an otherwise forgotten episode, if he wasn't playing the online game, he was checking the various websites and discussion forums where he had fairly earned a reputation as, "Oh, that guy."

Yes. *That* Randy Fanborg.

It didn't matter how much anyone might have liked a particular episode or film, Randy Fanborg was right there to explain why it was not a good episode, not a good film, and why the credentials of everyone involved were suspect. He disdained fan-theories and head canon. He knew better.

Randy Fanborg was The Expert on Canon, diligently pointing out every single contradiction in every episode and film. He was The Expert on Trivia, quickly annotating every jot and title of every script he had memorized—which was all of them. Even "Spock's Brain" and "The Alternative Factor." He was The Ultimate Expert.

But Randy Fanborg reserved his greatest enmity for those who wrote poems, parodies, filk songs, and satires of The Mythology of which he'd appointed himself. Randy Fanborg only needed ruby slippers, a white robe, a pointy hat, and a scepter to be recognized as The Holy Protector Of All That's Sacred In The Realm.

So of course, he focused his most aggressive attacks on those who wrote space-porn. Yes, he'd been annoyed by *A Private Little Whore, Charlie-SeX, The Naked Slime, What Big Girls Are Made Of, The Groom's Gay Machine,* and *Menage-A-Ree!* But it was *Titty On The Edge Of Forever* that finally pushed him over the edge.

In that moment on, he became Milo Twisling's mortal enemy.

His first act of cyber-revenge was to visit Amazon and leave a one-star review for every story that Milo had published. "This is crap. Don't buy it. This desecrates a sacred cultural landmark. And the author isn't very nice either." That last sentence was fictitious. Randy Fanborg had never met Milo Twisling, but in his infinite wisdom as a self-appointed online reader of minds and personalities, plus his experience accidentally reading a book on Transactional Analysis, Randy felt he was qualified to make the assertion.

(He hadn't intended to read the book on Transactional Analysis, and he hadn't read much past chapter three, but it was a long bus ride and he'd finished the paperback novel he'd brought with him. He'd found the book on the floor of the bus where it had fallen out of a bored student's laundry bag. The book smelled of unwashed underwear, something that Randy Fanborg did not notice, it already being a strong component of his own personal odor.)

Anyway....

When Randy Fanborg saw that Milo had not crept off into the woodwork in shame, he decided that stronger measures were necessary. It turned out that Milo Twisling not only had a website, a Facebook page, and a Patreon account, he also had a fan club. Randy Fanborg bit his lip, gritted his teeth, sprained his jaw, and joined.

For a long while—several hours, in fact—Randy did nothing at all He was too bitter. Reading through the slavering fannish adulations of Milo's exuberant readers did nothing to improve his mood at all.

In Milo's favor, his several years of experience crafting fictitious sexual adventures had given him enough experience to distinguish the difference between erotica and porn. Erotica uses euphemisms. While some people believed that Milo Twisling was a skilled practitioner, in truth he was cheating. He had written a simple database program for the creation of euphemisms. It was very much like a game of sexual Mad-Libs™.

The basic sentence was this: "He [verbed] her [adjective] [noun] with his [adjective] [noun]."

Milo would then choose a verb from column A, an adjective from column B, a noun from column C, an adjective from column D, and a final noun from column E.

VERB	ADJECTIVE	NOUN	ADJECTIVE	NOUN
conquered	delicious	abyss	burning	adversary
delighted	delightful	canyon	engorged	advocate
explored	dripping	cave	enthusiastic	campaigner
filled	deater	chasm	fleshy	champion
impaled	enthusiastic	gulf	furious	charger
invaded	fresh	honey-pot	hard	crusader
overwhelmed	hot	magic	helmeted	delight
pushed into	intended	mystery	hot	eagerness
thrust	inviting	opening	impatient	enthusiasm

Actually, he didn't choose anything at all. He'd written his database program to randomly create combinations and spit them out by the page-load. The more words he added to each column, the more variations his program would create. Sometimes he varied the sentence structure, but the basic idea remained the same.

Over time, Milo developed other simple programs for creating names of characters, situations, and settings. The stories practically wrote themselves.

Thus did Strong William invade the delightful mystery of Sweet Mary with his upstanding harpoon. And Brave Martin delighted Miss Marlena with his magnificent champion. And of course, Curious George impaled Little Joe with his impatient gladiator. Sometimes it happened in The Victorian Caves. Other times, the scene of sequestration was The Grotesque Cemetery. Once, the setting was The Terrifying Tower.

And this is how Milo Twisling became well-known as an erotic stylist. All he needed was a title and the rest was easy: *Dr. Yes, From Russia With Lust, Boldfinger, Thunder Balls, You Only Love Twice.* And James Blond thrust his hot eagerness into her open canyon.

Hey—it sold. And it sold well enough for Milo Twisling to upgrade his shopping from the dollar store to K-mart.

And while fame in the world of erotica is as fleeting as a one-night stand in West Hollywood, Milo had finally earned one of his fifteen minutes. He was invited to be an Author Guest of Honor at the West Coast's most prestigious Adult Entertainment Gathering—The Los Angeles SexCon held just south of downtown at the Los Angeles Convention Center, 720,000 square feet of convention space, filled with prostheses of all kinds—dildos, silicon vaginas, fleshlights (motorized and self-propelled), sex-dolls, sex-bots, a variety of costumes, lingerie, leather, whips, chains, handcuffs, massagers, vibrators, books and magazines, DVDs and Blu-rays, virtual reality goggles and software (several with bluetooth links to motorized sex-toys), and a variety of booth-babes, porn stars, and various young men and women whose affections were easily negotiable.

Milo, however, was not one of the primary attractions. The Guest of Honor at such an event was primarily a token speaker at a token banquet, a convenient pretense that the convention was actually about something. Nevertheless, the word "honor" was so alien to Milo Twisling's personal experience that he felt he had no choice but to participate. So, he packed his suitcase, loaded his yellow 72 Pinto and prepared for his long drive to validation.

He intended to speak at some length about how the continuing success of his website, *Dangerous Virgins,* served a specific health need for those whose sexual outlets were of a solitary nature. He was, if you will pardon the immodesty, performing a necessary service. The *Dangerous Virgins* website stroked the imaginations of those who for lack of a partner were reduced to stroking themselves.

Upcoming works would include *Sgt. Pepper's Lonely Hearts Club Blonde, Tales Of Mystery And Emasculation, The Rocky Whores' Picture Show, A Knight At The Opera, A Gay At The Races, Lest It Bleed, Mommy!, Singin' In The Pain, A Funky*

Thing Happened On The Way To The Forum, and his magnum opus, a seven-book trilogy to be called *The Civil Whore*. (A thematic sequel to *Fanny Hell*.)

All of these were already written and scheduled for publication. It was Milo Twisling's goal to have *Dangerous Virgins* become the premiere outlet for those who had no other outlet.

The avalanche of publicity given to Milo Twisling's upcoming appearance in Los Angeles—most of it generated by Milo Twisling—served primarily to attract the ugly attention of Randy Fanborg. By now, Randy Fanborg's hatred of Milo Twisling had evolved into a mortal vendetta that could only be satisfied by a conclusion of Sicilian magnitude.

Unfortunately, Randy Fanborg was neither Silician nor anything else. Randy Fanborg was one cheek shy of being half-assed. There were no candy canes on his Christmas tree. He was not the sharpest cheese in the fridge. To say that Randy Fanborg was stupid would have been a compliment. He approached stupidity only from the far side.

But Randy Fanborg was coherent enough to write a letter. Coherent enough to put a stamp on the envelope. Coherent enough to find a Post Office. And send that letter. To the Los Angeles Police Department—the most feared collection of men (and women) in black since Tommy Lee Jones and Will Smith.

In his letter, Randy Fanborg warned of a devious, depraved, dangerous degenerate who intended to commit dreadful deeds upon the unsuspecting citizens of legendary Metropolis. Randy Fanborg imagined himself a stylist. He also imagined himself the chosen one, and often checked the front porch to see if an owl had arrived from Hogwarts.

But the LAPD is not known for its sense of humor. Or anything else, for that matter. Those red lights in your rear view mirror almost always signify an unhealthy dent in your gross personal product. Running a city is expensive. The Department of "If you see something, say something" took Randy Fanborg's letter seriously. Quietly, very quietly, an all-points bulletin was issued for any yellow 72 Pinto crossing the border into the state on either I-40 or I-10 or I-15—which is why somewhere south of Barstow, Milo Twisling was pulled over by no fewer than seven flashing, screaming police cruisers. His battered pinto was immediately surrounded by fourteen armed officers all pointing their weapons at him. A stern voice on a bullhorn advised him to put his empty hands out the window, then slowly exit the vehicle. Meanwhile, traffic backed up on the I-15 for seventeen miles in both directions as the onlookers slowed to see what the excitement was about, most of them hoping to see poor Milo shot down like the rabid dog in *To Kill A Mockingbird*. (Milo had not yet figured out a suitable title for that retelling.)

To make a short story even shorter, Milo spent the weekend in the Barstow jail. Because it was Labor Day Weekend, he would not see a judge until late Tuesday afternoon, by which time SexCon would have evaporated into the haze, much like Brigadoon. Milo Twisling wouldn't just be known as the no-show Guest of

Honor—he'd be the GoH who stood them up. The backlash was considerable—including a wildcat boycott of *Dangerous Virgins*.

Randy Fanborg would have wet his shorts in glee had he known—had he not accidentally electrocuted himself when he spilled a Pepsi into the second-hand keyboard he had partially dismantled for refurbishing, producing a lot more sparks in his mother's basement than were normally seen on the bridge of the starship *Enterprise,* even after the impact of a Klingon photon torpedo on its rapidly deteriorating starboard shields. ("Oy, Keptin, I kent giff you no more power. The engines are all farpotshket." In Milo's version, *Star Trick*, the chief engineer was Morris, who could repair the engines without all the Scottish kvetching. Plus, he could get replacement parts from Cousin Hermie a lot faster and cheaper than going through those Starfleet momsers.) Never mind that. Randy Fanborg died as he had lived, with one hand on the mouse and the other in his underwear.

Disgraced in the eyes of his colleagues, Milo Twisling had to give up writing porn. Instead, he turned his attentions to science fiction and fantasy, where he became far more successful as the author of—

Never mind. That's a whole other career and that story will not be repeated here. Milo Twisling has already had one career destroyed by a fanborg. In the current climate of hyper-sensitivity, with various outrage committees roaming the public landscape, nobody, least of all Milo Twisling, wants to be the subject of another internet pile-on.

And what of his unpublished works in the *The Lost Dangerous Virgins* series? They remain unpublished, mere strings of ones and zeroes on his hard drive. His last few desperate fans insisted that they deserved to read what was promised to be his greatest work of all, *Atlas Fugged*—they even created a hashtag.

But no, Milo had left that world behind, and this one as well. (That's the subject of another peripatetic tale for another time. But as his last act, instead of responding to the frenzied demands of his readers, he used their hashtag as the title of an anthology. *#ReleaseTheVirgins*.

THE GREAT MILO

His former employer called him a joyless little squirt.

His ex-wife said that sex with him was a joyless little squirt.

His father said that the sex that produced him was a joyless little squirt.

But despite all that, everyone called him Milo.

Milo's spirit animal was a tick. (The leech had already been claimed.)

Milo was small. Milo was round. Milo was sallow. Had he been any more sallow, he would have looked like an audition for *The Simpsons*.

Milo had squinty eyes set too close to each other—so close that stereo vision was impossible for him. If he went to a 3D movie, he could look through one lens of the polarized glasses with both eyes.

Milo had large protruding ears. Very large. Paint them black and you don't need to buy him a Mickey Mouse hat at Disney World. Milo could hear people thinking about how ugly he looked, even if they were in another room. In a building across the street.

Milo had a nose that had apparently decided to make a U-turn at some point in its development and had inadvertently backed into itself. Milo's nose was a crumpled fender looking for an accident. Milo's nose had been the inspiration for the award-winning makeup design in the first *Noseman* horror film and its three sequels.

Milo had a bald spot. He'd had a bald spot since he was three years old. He'd had a comb-over since he was four. It didn't work. Milo had an albedo. The reflection of sunlight on Milo's head could be seen from space.

Milo did not have an Adam's apple, he had an Adam's cantaloupe. It bobbed up and down when he spoke, as if it was trying to escape. And it had good reason to. Milo was squeaky. Milo was nasal. Milo enunciated every syllable at least twice in a word. His dialect was vaguely British, halfway between Nerdspeak and Asperger's— and his focus on minutiae would have bored even Marcel Proust. Listeners had been known to gnaw off appendages to escape the sound of his voice.

Milo had the posture of a hunchbacked hedgehog. As many times as his disheartened parents had told him to stand up straight, that was how many times he had replied, "I *am* standing up straight!" X-rays of his skeleton eventually demonstrated the discouraging truth of his assertion. Milo was a human box of corn flakes, his contents had settled in transit. He sagged like an overripe pear, like a Ziploc bag filled with soggy oatmeal, like a beer belly flubbering over the despairing belt of a morbidly obese couch potato.

It wasn't that life had handed him lemons, it was that life had *made* him a lemon—allegedly a fruit, but also a joyless little squirt.

As if small, round, sallow, and bitter wasn't enough, Milo's choice of attire...well, attire is the politest euphemism for an appearance halfway between *faux couture* and corn-on-the-slob. To say that Milo was a walking fashion crime was several orders of magnitude deeper than understatement.[*]

It wasn't that he was ugly, it wasn't that his mother dressed him funny—it was that he was colorblind and chose his clothes based on what didn't show the spaghetti sauce stains. It didn't help that (for reasons unknown in this narrative) most of his T-shirts, as well as all of his underwear, had lost their laundry tags, so Milo was never sure which side of the garment was the front. That he occasionally had his boxers on backward often made trips to the urinal an adventure. His tighty-whites did not present the same problem—not as long as he remembered "yellow in front, brown in back."[†]

Milo needed to get laid in the worst way—which, since his wife had left him, was probably the best he could hope for. But even that was beyond the realm of possibility.

In short...

All the separate atoms in Milo's body had spent more than a billion years coming together in just the right way and at just the right time to become Milo. If this was the best that the universe could do in all that time with all those atoms, then this has to be seen as evidence that this is a pretty sorry excuse for a universe.

But Milo did have one remarkable skill—he was able to remain blissfully unaware of reality. He could not recognize the unbridgeable chasm of evidence between himself and the kind of human being who gets enthusiastic thank-yous from the staff when leaving a Japanese restaurant. Milo believed he was a superhero—or at least one overdose of gamma radiation away from that condition. For unexplainable reasons and without any evidence at all to support this belief, Milo had nevertheless convinced himself that he was destined for greatness.

That this opinion was not shared by the universe at large[‡] did not trouble him at all. It was Milo's conviction that success was inevitable. He'd read it as a meme on Facebook. "People who don't know it's impossible are the ones who accomplish

---

[*]   Red Nikes. Knee-high black and white striped tube socks. Possibly stolen from Chuckles the Clown.

[†]   It was possible that Milo had removed the tags himself. He had an extreme case of Obsessive Compulsive Disorder, a condition so severe that he himself referred to it as Compulsive Disorder Obsessive—the words had to be spoken in alphabetical order.

[‡]   Actually, that's redundant. Any time you talk about the universe, "at large" is a given. If anything, it's insufficient. Even the word "insufficient" is insufficient to evoke the scale of things we're trying to discuss.

great things." The meme had been given its gravitas because the words were inscribed in the Papyrus font over a picture of a cat.

Coming as it did, on the day he lost both his job and his wife,[*] Milo had no choice but to assume that the meme was a personal message from the Cosmic Badger.[†]

Nevertheless, Milo would occasionally quote Carl Sagan. "I am—" he would announce, "– made of star stuff."

Well, yes. But so is that unidentifiable substance found between the tiles behind the toilet. And you don't hear it bragging.[‡]

Milo did have one claim to greatness—had anyone ever pointed it out to him, it would not have pleased him, at least not until he could have recontextualized it as a virtue. He had a great case of paranoid narcissism, not as bad as certain politicians, but certainly malignant enough to earn him an honorable mention in the *Guinness Book of Assholes.*

He assumed that everything was about him. Even things that weren't about him, were about him. And because he was The Great Milo, or the Milo Destined For Greatness, it was therefore his job to sit on the Pedestal of Unconditional Truth and pronounce judgment on all that passed before his peculiar bubble of awareness.

Milo had come to this unfortunate condition because he took everything personally. He had not yet gotten his participation trophy for life, the awards and honors that were duly his for successfully escaping from his mother's vagina.[§]

This wretched lack of acknowledgments and tributes from a deliberately oblivious world was the primary reason why Milo had become a joyless little squirt— in appearance as well as personality.

Why am I spending so much time describing Milo before proceeding to the rest of this narrative?

To prove a point.

Never piss off a writer.

Never piss off a man who buys ink by the barrel.

Never piss off a man who rearranges electrons by the gigajoule.[¶]

Writers are the Research and Development Division of The Human Race, occasionally researching the highest aspirations of the species, but more often detailing the procedures necessary for executing the most exquisite forms of revenge.

Writers specialize in two kinds of revenge.

---

[*]   At his sparsely-attended funeral, someone asked her why she'd married him in the first place. She said, "I needed the goddamn green card."
      Milo apparently had a very small penis. On their wedding night, his ex-wife had pointed, laughed, and asked, "Who the hell do you expect to satisfy with that thing?" Milo had responded hopefully, "Me…?"

[†]   Milo had some very strange religious convictions, but so do most people. Talking snakes, burning bushes, virgin births—why not a cosmic badger?

[‡]   Mostly it says, "I am Grout."

[§]   Milo assumed that the world owed him a living—forgetting for the moment that it's a lifetime job to collect.

[¶]   Or to put it another way, plowboys should not pull on shootists.

The first is putting you into their book, describing you horribly, and then dropping a house on your sister, throwing cold water on your dreams, and stealing your shoes.

The second is leaving you out of the book entirely—which should have happened here, except even that would have given Milo too much credit.

You may have noticed that Milo hasn't actually done anything in this story, nor should you expect him to. Milo has no agency, not in this story, not in this life, not in this universe. In fact, it's pushing it just to tell you about him.

Which is why this story is not about Milo.

Milo is completely irrelevant to this tale.

This story is about That Pesky Dan Goodman who is a much more interesting character—character being the operative term in both fiction and meatspace.

That Pesky Dan Goodman is a nexus of the improbable and the unlikely.

I shall elucidate.

Imagine a universe so vast that your imagination is insufficient to imagine how vast it is.

It's the math.

Imagine a hundred billion galaxies.

That's already beyond the ability of your imagination. The number itself is incomprehensible, but imagine it anyway. That's the current best guess of how many galaxies there are in the universe. But that number is still insufficient. The astrophysicists are still thinking too small. There are probably a trillion galaxies in this universe, maybe even a smidge more. Maybe even an order of magnitude more.[*]

Now imagine that each of those galaxies contains a hundred billion stars.

Imagine that each of those stars has ten planets. (It's easier on the math, bear with me.)

So on the small end that's 10 (planets) multiplied by 100,000,000,000 (stars) multiplied by at least 100,000,000,000 (galaxies), and you get at least 100,000,000,000,000,000,000,000 planets in the universe—100 quintillion. If you assume the larger number of galaxies, one trillion, then there might be a sextillion or septillion number of planets in the universe, give or take a few.

What this means should be obvious.

If the odds against anything happening are even a few quintillion to one, then somewhere out there, it's not only possible—it's inevitable.

Think about it this way.

If the odds against you winning the lotto are 292 million to 1, then somewhere in the universe, it is inevitable that you will win the lotto—not just once but at least 342 billion times. Probably not in this iteration, but somewhere out there, more than a few of your other selves are right now doing the happy dance.

---

[*] I'm not even going to estimate all the galaxies that formed and died in the 13 and a half billion years since the Big Bang and all the galaxies yet to form in the billions of years still to come before entropy has its way with this universe.

But in this universe, your lotto ticket is a Schrodinger event—as long as it remains in your pocket it's either a winning ticket or a losing ticket. As soon as you take it out and look at it, it's a losing ticket.[*]

And in this universe, That Pesky Dan Goodman was a nexus of improbability—because this is the location within this universe where all those improbabilities collide and become inevitabilities.

Some people think That Pesky Dan Goodman has fallen into this universe through a Vonnegut Singularity, a chrono-synclastic infundibulum. Others believe he is an agent of chaos, a recovering fallen angel, a forgotten piece of eldritch substance left over after Cthulhu and Yog-Sothoth were conceived, a mistaken afterthought of creation, or perhaps even a half-breed of some kind—half human and half something else, still unknowable.[†]

Whatever.

The fact remains—That Pesky Dan Goodman has developed an unpleasant habit of wandering into narratives in which he has no right to be present, complicating the lives of people who would much rather be the bystanders who capture the occurrence of horrific events on their smartphones instead of being the unfortunate victims of the tornado, the fire, the earthquake, the tsunami, or the stampede of customers when the Walmart doors open on Black Friday.

Such is the case here.[‡]

Unfortunately, there is no main character in this story. Whoever it might have been, he left the narrative before it began, so while Pesky is generally a side character in any other narrative, this time the searching spotlight of literary attention falls on whoever has wandered too close to the author's keyboard.

On this particular morning, a morning unlike any other, because if it were like any other, we wouldn't be paying any attention to it at all—on this particular morning, That Pesky Dan Goodman was seated comfortably on the Orange Line bus[§] between Woodland Hills and the North Hollywood subway station.[¶]

Pesky was reading a book. An old-fashioned book. A book printed on paper. Paper that had been made from the bodies of murdered trees, shredded, pulped, and stirred into a soupy mass, churned in a broth of noxious chemicals, so the lignin

---

[*] If it were a Heisenberg event, even if you knew your ticket was safe in your pocket, you still wouldn't know how fast it was traveling.

[†] That Pesky Dan Goodman was known to visit the local science fiction club from time to time, mostly for the free refreshments occasionally provided. One of the club's more suspicious members managed to secure a sample of Pesky's DNA and quickly took up a collection to have it tested. The lab sent back a curt note, "Your rhinoceros is diabetic. And she's pregnant." After that, no further attempts were made to determine the ancestry of That Pesky Dan Goodman.

[‡] Notice, we have now gotten nearly 2000 words into this exercise and nothing at all has happened. Even Jane Austen was able to set the stage for her narratives faster than this.

[§] Ironically, the Orange Line buses are painted gray.

[¶] Yes, Los Angeles has a subway. This is one of the six impossible things you are asked to believe before breakfast.

could be leached out of the cellulose fibers — the fibers then bleached to an eye-blazing whiteness, pressed flat into mats, then pressed again into great acid-free rolls, sprayed with more chemicals just for the hell of it, and then cut into sheets of various sizes, depending on need, and upon those sheets little crawly insect marks had been impressed with a quick-set ink, a resin-oil-solvent mixture. All the separate sheets of paper had then been bound together for portability, and pressed between two stiff pieces of paperboard, with a garish illustration on the front and some identifying nomenclature, ie. a title.

Upon viewing these crawly little insect marks (as you are doing now[*]), That Pesky Dan Goodman was able to decode meaning and hallucinate the experiences of the individual who had initially coded this specific stream of linguistic symbols.

Pesky liked books. He liked the ambition. He liked the idea that persons long removed from any attainable circumstance could still send their experiences careening outward through time and space to infect the minds of unsuspecting others. Centuries might have passed since these thoughts were inscribed, but here was a gift from a mind that aspired to share itself. Pesky liked peeking into other possibilities of existence and this was one way of achieving that adventure—one that did not involve any specific risk to his own corporeal existence.

On this particular morning, riding the bus eastward, That Pesky Dan Goodman was continuing his latest literary adventure—no, not quite. He was not reading the book as much as he was trying to read it. It was a book well worth reading, not quite a classic in its genre because it did not exist in any specific genre, existing solely in a class defined by itself.

The book was an autobiographical memoir involving a talking dog, a fabulous redhead, Charles Manson, a Judeo-Christian interpretation of God (portrayed by the archetypal sassy black lady), and an odd assortment of little-known historical figures and murder victims, all in a branch of literature that would someday be called Recursive Peripateticism.[†] What made it remarkable was that the book had not yet been written, let alone published in this specific timeline.[‡]

However—

Pesky was unable to concentrate on his book because of a deliberately unpleasant individual looming over him, yammering loudly into his cellphone. What makes *this* remarkable is that Pesky had actually found a seat on the bus.

---

[*] Or would be if you weren't viewing these crawly little insect marks on some kind of electronic screen, in which case you are staring into a large flat light bulb on which crawly little insect marks have been simulated by specific sets of blacked-out pixels.

[†] A self-referential, plotless narrative that wanders from place to place without apparent purpose. Like this one.

[‡] How Pesky had obtained this volume might have had something to do with his unauthorized access to an experimental trans-dimensional para-lithonic resonating transceiver, containing a 64-core multi-fractal array of entangled particles. Call it a quantum empathizer for short. I can't say more than that without violating a very rigorous Non-Disclosure Agreement. If after publication of this story, I die under mysterious circumstances that will be evidence that I've already said too much.

Pesky had claimed a seat near the front of the bus by the singularly clever tactic of boarding at the initiating terminal of the line. Otherwise, he would have been standing, and would not have been able to read his book. In that situation, the book would no longer have any relevance to this narrative.

In a less mundane circumstance, Pesky would have assumed the unpleasant man to be a professional prankster and that he had been chosen as the target of a hidden-camera television stunt. But no, this was just someone whose social skills had gone into remission shortly after he bought his first cellphone. For the purposes of simplifying the rest of this narration, we shall call this individual The Asshole.

The Asshole was tall and athletic. He had dark hair and good features. He was well-groomed. His attire was casual, not slobby, and moderately affluent.

And he was loud.

The Asshole had no indoor voice and apparently no awareness that he was on a crowded city bus with lousy acoustics and that his annoying yammering was audible all the way to the rear seats of this double-length, articulated bus. But it was particularly annoying to Pesky because The Asshole was standing right over him, facing him, and his mouth was less than an arm's length from Pesky's right ear.

If perhaps The Asshole's conversation had been even moderately entertaining, it would have served as impromptu street theater. Certainly, the people in the rear seats of the bus would have been entertained. But no—The Asshole was orating loudly in a foreign language—Pesky assumed it was Spanish*—and the full force of his enthusiastic proclamations were hitting Pesky dead on.

Sighing to himself, Pesky put his book back into his man-purse, pulled out his tablet and asked Google to translate, "Please be quiet. You are too loud."

Google flashed these words on the device display: *"Por favor, silencio. Usted es demasiado ruidoso."* He held it up in front of The Asshole's face.

The Asshole blinked, read the words, then leaned in to shout at Pesky, "No—no Española. Portuguesa!" He then returned to his conversation, but was apparently now explaining to his distant listener why he'd had to interrupt their talk to explain to *el stupido* that he was having a very important conversation, but not in Español.

Pesky returned to his tablet and asked it to translate the same phrase into Portuguese. He held it up to The Asshole again. *"Por favor fique quieto. Você é demasiado alto."*

This time The Asshole had a harder time of pretending not to understand, so he handed the phone to Pesky. A woman's voice demanded to know, "My friend wants to know, what is your problem?"

Had the question been delivered with a smidge more courtesy, Pesky might have considered answering politely. But the last four words had conveyed a sense of arrogance that triggered Pesky's mad monkey impulse. He said, *"Un momento, por favor."*

---

* Living in Los Angeles, everyone picks up a few Spanish phrases, like, *"Hola," "por favor," "gracias," "quesadilla,"* and *"pendejo."*

Pesky then popped open the back of the phone, removed the battery and handed it to the person in the seat behind him, one of the archetypal sassy black women that Hollywood scriptwriters love to include as side-characters, as a way of demonstrating their commitment to diversity. The sassy black woman had been watching these events with varying degrees of annoyance and amusement. She was happy to receive the battery and passed it to the high-school aged Latina behind her, who, because she was plugged into her own earbuds and did not realize what was going on, promptly dropped the battery into the depths of her cavernous purse.

Pesky handed the now-inoperative phone back to The Asshole, who grabbed it and began working his way back through the crowded bus in pursuit of the battery. The result was not only a passive voice sentence, but also a frantic conversation that might have been *Español*, or maybe Portuguese, but was probably a word salad of two different, but vaguely similar languages chattering past each other, the subject being a cellphone battery and who was the rightful owner—the original purchaser, or the recipient of the unasked-for gift.

How this confrontation ultimately resolved, Pesky never found out, because to Pesky's great relief, the bus had finally arrived at its terminus across the street from the North Hollywood subway station* and as if simultaneously launched from their seats by some hidden ejector mechanism, every passenger immediately rose and began pushing for the doors.†

Pesky's subway ride to downtown Los Angeles was much less eventful, and he was able to read far enough into his book to discover why the talking dog would not eat his salad until the parsley was carefully laid down upon the napkin next to his bowl.‡

After transferring to the Metro Expo Line, an above-ground light rail system, Pesky was once again able to log onto the internet and study plans for a portable cellphone jammer. That such devices were illegal in the United States would not have been a deterrent to That Pesky Dan Goodman. He had not gotten his adjective by accident.

Pesky debarked at the Exposition Boulevard station, crossed the eastbound side of the avenue, walked through Exposition Park, and into the California Science Center.

Today, Pesky was on his way to examine their newest exhibits on polarized magnetism and also how global climate change was increasing the predatory range of venomous insect swarms. It was his own theory that some previously undiscovered species were the harbingers of an alien civilization's attempt to exoform the Earth, but as yet the evidence was sketchy and problematic.

---

*   Made you look.

†   We shall speak no more of The Asshole. (Unless it's necessary.)

‡   This is a true story. I'm not making it up. The dog had better table manners than most humans—except for his way of saying thank you. That was an enthusiastic jump into your lap, accompanied by an odiferous belch in your face. But this is good manners for a dog.

Today was actually Pesky's day off. Pesky's work ethic was a perfect NOR operation on the Genesis-derived calendar week. He worked one day and rested six—if he worked at all. In his current incarnation—this story—That Pesky Dan Goodman was a freelance assassin.[*]

So far, Pesky had removed from this timeline seven individuals whose continuing existence had become a sore point in his daily routine and thirty-seven others whose actions, both past and future, would significantly damage the stability of the continuing chronology. While Pesky had no particular loyalty to this time and space, he did enjoy movie theater popcorn (with butter) and was not yet ready for any existence where movies, popcorn, and butter were no longer readily available.

So the circumstances which warranted removal included (but were not limited to) a depression greater than the Great Depression, global climate disruption, biological blight wiping out agricultural monocultures, widespread famine, water wars, refugee swarms, asteroid impact, manic theocracy, a zombie apocalypse, and nuclear winter. Of these options, Pesky considered at least three of them hovering somewhere between probable and likely, although not yet inevitable.

No matter. Today Pesky was interested in polarized magnetism and venomous insect swarms, in particular the Beale Mosquito, which had somehow found its way to the western hemisphere from Godknowswhereistan.

Actually, the Beale mosquito was misnamed. It wasn't a real mosquito, merely a small biting fly with delusions of grandeur. It had first been identified as a nuisance at the Sedona Pride Parade, when several of the insects were found on the left buttocks of another of those archetypal sassy black ladies (only this one a lesbian), that populate the works of authors too lazy to realize that there are many other kinds of people on the planet as well as sassy black ladies.

The insect's name was a contraction of, "If that shit don't beat all—! Do you know how many hours I spent sewing these fucking sequins?!" Calling them "fucking sequin flies" was inelegant, even for a sassy black stereotype, so they were called "beat all flies," which was eventually shortened to Beale mosquitos by a short, near-sighted etymologist, who through a series of paradoxical events the author chooses not to

---

[*] (It's necessary.) That The Asshole had walked away from the Orange Line bus still capable of drawing breath has to be regarded as evidence of Pesky's general good nature, as well as his commitment to not working any day he didn't have to. Besides, he preferred to be paid for his wetwork—and there was still the slight chance that somebody, somewhere might actually have cared about The Asshole. Pesky had an unbreakable rule that clients should be carefully vetted to eliminate any possibility of a redeeming quality that would justify exemption. In this case, however, The Asshole had not become a candidate for peskivation only because Pesky had other matters on his mind.

Pesky's vetting of potential clients was conducted through the lens of an obscure branch of communication forensics called contextualism—the study of semantic structure as an access to the mental processes that produce an appalling avalanche of unhinged linguistic expressions, the best examples of which can be found in any unmoderated comment thread, especially political ones.

Pesky's specific area of study was the ideological ranch dressing and political croutons found on the word salad of various public speakers. It gave him no shortage of likely candidates.

detail here, had not turned left at Albuquerque as instructed, and having wandered into the Pride celebration by mistake, had been misidentified as a short, near-sighted entomologist. Anyway—somehow, the taxonomy stuck. Beale mosquitos.

By itself, a single Beale mosquito is a harmless bite, an annoyance too small to be considered even an annoyance, but during its annual swarming season, it becomes a buzzing cloud of noise, forewarning a season of almost-misery caused by the inevitable flurry of aggressive little pricks, each one less than nothing, but together, almost as painful as a *Lost In Space* marathon. Almost.

Most of the year, various affected communities dismissed the possibility of a Beale mosquito attack with a contemptuous smirk, but for a week or two each swarming season, the insects were a nuisance in the eyes and ears, and occasionally the rectum.* They were a burden to be endured. Flame-throwers only seemed to excite them.

None of this information was new to Pesky, but this was his first opportunity to see an actual swarm of Beale mosquitos, contained as they were in a closet-sized terrarium allegedly secured with fine-mesh filters.

The terrarium was a sealed, floor-to-ceiling, four-sided, glass case, two meters wide on each side. Across the top, there was more glass, also a frame containing two small fans designed for cooling the innards of desktop computers, but in place here to simulate the dry winds of a desert environment. The fans were fronted by very secure fine-mesh filters to keep the insects from escaping.

Inside the case was a half-meter of sandy soil and several small cacti. Spotted around the cacti, as well as scattered across the soil, Pesky could see a fine layer of tiny brown shells, the remnants of egg-sacs that had recently hatched. A few unhatched egg-clusters were still visible on the dark skin of the plants, but even as Pesky watched, more of the biting flies were chewing their way out.†

The terrarium itself was filled with a cloud of tiny dark bodies. If a cloud could have emotions, this cloud was pissed off. It swirled angrily and buzzed like an enraged vibrator. Several small children pressed their faces against the glass, leaving greasy trails of ketchup, relish, ice cream, and snot. This only enraged the cloud more.

Pesky took a few pictures with his own small camera, but it was insufficient to capture anything more than a blur. He finally gave up, realizing that his time might be better spent observing the effects of polarized magnetism.

Now having outlined the circumstances necessary to understanding what happened next, we must return to and expand upon the theme statement of this entire narrative: That Pesky Dan Goodman is a nexus of the improbable and the unlikely.

While on the surface, this assertion might seem to suggest that Pesky is the causative agent for unlikely and improbable events, there is actually much more to it than that. Pesky is rarely the architect of the unusual—no, his presence is more often the chrono-synclastic catalyst for events already possible. Pesky's personal

* Especially for nudists and men wearing assless chaps in West Hollywood.
† Not all insects have larval stages. This is a real fact, not a fact made up for this story.

morphic field simply increases the potential of occurrence. Even something as casual as a spontaneous wander through a crowded mall can be enough to trigger episodes both calamitous and whimsical—such as the serendipitous invention of coconut ash ice cream,[*] or the parachuting Santa accident,[†] or the husky who walked six miles to a supermarket, shoplifted a rawhide chew toy, and then walked home again with it.[‡]

This is the point.

In this self-referential, plotless narrative, Pesky is merely a bystander. But his presence—well, you remember those allegedly secure fine-mesh filters on the fans at the top of the closet-sized terrarium enclosing the swarm of Beale mosquitos?

They weren't.

Pesky didn't do anything. The mesh wasn't fine enough to stop the most curious of insects. What actually kept the flying insects inside the case was the downdraft from the fans. But those few bugs who were too lazy to fly, who had decided instead to walk, were able to make their way through the mesh and into the workings of the fans. When enough of them had made the journey that their bodies had been ground to a fine slushy substance on the spindles of the fans, the motors ground to a stop and burned out. This ended the downdraft that kept the rest of the swarm within the terrarium. Inevitably the rest of the swarm seeped out the top, attracted by the smells of ketchup, relish, ice cream, and snot. Especially snot.

But by this time, Pesky was already on the other side of the building, watching polarized magnets dancing on a spinning platter.

As the afternoon warmed, the swarm found its way out of the air-conditioned building and into the hot dry air of the Los Angeles basin, where a large flock of hungry house sparrows would have happily made short work of them and this would have been the end of it, except—

On this same day—

To be fair, it wasn't the pilot's fault—

SkyLifter builds the Heavy-Lift Air-Crane, a powered airship capable of lifting up to 150 tons of payload.[§] They were not at fault and nothing in this narrative is meant to suggest any failure of design or equipment on their part. In this totally fictitious situation, they had leased one of their vessels to a house-moving company for a proof-of-concept demonstration.

The area around Exposition Park and the University of Southern California is one of the city's oldest and most affluent neighborhoods. Houses of vaguely Victorian design are found on many of the better streets. They aren't just mansions—they're castles. These exuberant confections are usually large and sprawling, tall and elegant. Most have three stories, several have more. Almost all have wide porches and high verandas, deep basements, carports that used to be liveries, roomy attics and dormers, pointed gables, tall windows and comfortable window seats, expansive parlors, huge

---

[*]   This is a real thing too. Look it up.

[†]   This one is also true.

[‡]   Yep.

[§]   A real company. A real airship. I wish them success. They deserve it.

kitchens with connected servants' quarters, dumbwaiters, high chimneys, fanciful cupolas, a few brightly tiled domes, the occasional widow's walk—and enough architectural gingerbread to cause the hearts of studio art directors to palpitate in excitement.

Most of these houses are worth millions. But the land they sit on is worth even more because of its proximity to the university. A cluster of apartments would be far more profitable than a fraternity house or a student association. So...the obvious solution is to move the house.

The problem is that as wide as most of the streets in the area pretend to be, the houses are wider. None of these architectural wedding cakes can be moved by a truck. They just won't fit. Not even on Hoover Blvd. The alternative is to lift the house vertically and transport it by air.

The house in question—the house we are about to discuss—had once been painted in shades of purple and red, trimmed with pink and white and gold. Now, it was mostly a faded shade of maroon. It had once been a well-known Los Angeles institution, the home of Bubbles McGowan Horowitz, one of the most respected of all madams in the city's history.

Lady Horowitz had begun her career as a protégé of Lou Graham, owner and operator of Seattle's legendary brothel in Pioneer Square, but in 1902 when that institution finally fell victim to a sudden streak of Puritanism by Seattle's Chief of Police, Lou and some of her ladies relocated to San Francisco. Lady Horowitz retreated further south to Los Angeles.

Even though The University of Southern California was barely two decades old when Lou set up her establishment, the institution had already become notorious for the antics of its enthusiastic young collegians. Being that location, location, location was the defining factor in the success of any business, Lady Horowitz was certain that she would provide a very necessary service to this particularly exuberant and especially wealthy clientele.

She was not wrong.

The Bubble House, as it came to be known, became a favorite gathering place for the most elite ranks of administrators, professors, athletes, and favored students. Lady Horowitz would not allow her young women to service any student who was pulling less than a 3.5 grade average. During her tenure, the university graduated more students with honors than at any other time in its history.

Lady Horowitz retired in 1920, shortly after Prohibition became law. She is quoted as saying, "Enough is enough. I can only break one law at a time."

The boredom of retirement did not agree with her. Barely a year later, she died in her sleep, but she died with a smile upon her face, and those who attended her funeral had to acknowledge that the wages of sin were spectacular. After a lengthy probate process, the house was eventually purchased by the University as a study center, actually a private retreat for faculty members requiring discretion.

After the crash of '29 and the subsequent Great Depression, the house stood empty for a few years until it was finally sold to a Chicago businessman whose wife believed the house was haunted and intended to hold séances to communicate with the denizens of the world beyond—but no spirits ever responded to requests for contact, no matter how desperate and pleading the entreaties, and when she finally joined them, neither did she.

During the latter part of the thirties, a Mormon-based fraternity rented the house, but their parties were especially dull—no coffee, no tea, no sodas, no alcohol, and no women. But their lemonade was rumored to be exquisite.

When World War II broke out, the house became the center of a somewhat clandestine study group, whose actual purposes remain unclear even at this late date, but some historians theorize it was a center for the development of propaganda, or maybe code-breaking, or possibly a private retreat for high-ranking army officers and various suppliers of necessary military hardware. Or perhaps just a whore house.

It was still a whore house throughout the sixties, once again catering to the over-enthused libidos of the young fraternity men in nearby Fraternity Row. Despite several police raids—and the ensuing embarrassment to members of Zeta Beta Tau, but not Sigma Alpha Mu because most of their members were gay—this iteration of The House of Negotiable Virtue continued to thrive, except for those nights when *Star Trek* was on.

At some point, lost in history, but preserved in uncertain memory, the house became the property of a bank, then a real estate company, then a holding company, all of whom promised a total restoration to the structure's former glory—but of course, like all corporate promises, anything that might compromise the bottom line was repeatedly backburnered.

Eventually, the city decided that the house should be condemned and demolished. They were almost to the point of holding an auction for the various brass fixtures, some of which were over a hundred years old—when the Historical Preservation Society leapt for the bait, demanding that the house be declared a cultural landmark and preserved as an example of Los Angeles' lost culture.[*]

This alone would guarantee that the house would sit on its lot, untouched for at least another decade, inhabited only by hobos and crack users who had cut a convenient hole in the chain link fence.

Never mind all that. Cutting back to the present, despite all the legal efforts to save it, the house was now being rescued by a Silicon Valley billionaire with more money than sense. His plan was to relocate the house to a sprawling lot in San Mateo, some 333 miles north.

The only way to do this, of course, was to lift the house off its foundation and fly it. The billionaire had gotten the idea from a Pixar movie and had rented the SkyLifter Air Crane to do the job.

It took several months for the transport crew to slide the necessary supports beneath the house, testing them daily, ultimately creating a rugged framework, a

---

[*] The assumption here is that Los Angeles once had a culture to lose. The larger assumption was that if that culture could be identified, it was worth preserving. This is a question best left to those who have too much time on their hands.

travel-cage that would keep the mansion upright for its long journey to its new location.

When all was ready, the SkyLifter Air Crane was moved into position above the Bubble House, blotting out the sunlight for several city blocks. The SkyLifter was a huge disk-shaped object, nearly half a kilometer in diameter. Of course, the news media were present with vans everywhere, cameras pointing eagerly, and satellite dishes aimed at the sky—reception was difficult with the airship in the way, so several of the reporters had to connect via Skype.

Crowds filled the surrounding streets, and even the street directly beneath as well. Almost everyone was snapping pictures with their phones. The more industrious engaged in spectacular contortions to take selfies with the SkyLifter in the background. Instagram's local server crashed from the sudden onslaught of photos.

Although residents had repeatedly been informed of the event, there were several who had never opened their mail or turned on their TVs and who still had no idea what the internet was—at least a dozen of them called 911 to report an alien invasion. A monstrous super-craft was hovering over the city, what else could they assume? Two of them had heart attacks while waiting for an operator, one fatal.

As soon as the SkyLifter was holding steady against the slight morning breeze, the airship dropped an assembly of cables and wires, hooks and fasteners, and various electronic monitors. The transport crew rushed to connect these to the appropriate receptacles on the travel cage.

After several hours of testing, monitoring, securing, testing again, after every light on every console flashed green, after every screen on every tablet and smartphone showed satisfactory readings, after every go/no-go point was passed, the chief of the ground crew said to his headset, "It's a go."

The pilot of the SkyLifter, a big easy-going fellow named Travis Maltz, leaned out of his open window—he wasn't that high up, less than 20 meters—and waved at the crowds below. When the applause and cheering finally died down, he withdrew back into his cabin and worked his controls, releasing more helium from the internal tanks of the airship into the lifting bags.

Slowly, majestically, the Bubble House lifted off its foundation. This was the tricky part, getting it up into the air without it banging into any of the surrounding buildings. This would have been impossible without sophisticated computer software to compensate for the afternoon breeze. Fortunately, everything went off without a hitch and as the SkyLifter rose, the ancient mansion also lifted above the rooftops.

And yes, 911 did receive another call about space aliens—this one was a breathless report that the alien invaders were now stealing houses.[*]

To avoid the downtown area, the SkyLifter was going to head south, first passing over Exposition Park and the California Science Center before heading west to Santa

---

[*]   I should probably insert a snarky footnote here about 911 calls, but I can't think of anything. I've got nothing. But here's a footnote anyway.

Monica, and then north toward Santa Barbara. Despite the possibility of strong ocean winds, the northward route had been planned to avoid heavily populated areas.

That Pesky Dan Goodman had been aware of the SkyLifter effort for several months. It was one of the reasons he had planned his excursion to the Science Center on this day—so he could see the Air Crane ferrying the house across the sky.

At this point in the narrative, it's appropriate to acknowledge that Pesky is not always aware of the effect he has on probability. Because what happened next was not his fault.

As the SkyLifter passed over Exposition Park, it passed through the growing swarm of Beale Mosquitos, unnoticeable in the hazy afternoon—unnoticeable until they attacked. Sensing a corned beef sandwich in Travis Maltz' lunchbox, they flooded in through the open window of the flight deck—the same window that Maltz had opened so he could wave to the crowd below.

At first, Maltz didn't notice the Beale Mosquitos. He was concentrating on balancing the load against the vagaries of the wind patterns in the Los Angeles basin. As mild as the winds were today, Maltz still needed to keep the house absolutely vertical while driving steadily and meticulously west. So far, everything was *copacetic*. Everything was going according to plan. Everything was proceeding just like the hours spent in the simulator—

Until the Beale mosquitos started biting.

Maltz was allergic to insect bites.

He had a seizure.

In his flailing around, he accidentally hit the wrong levers on his control board. Oops.

Fortunately, only one person died in the accident.

Remember Milo? As it happened, he was also in Exposition Park that day. He had just come out of the Imax 3D theater, where he'd enjoyed a spectacular documentary on The Magnificent Wildlife of The Los Angeles River.

Milo was crossing through the park, heading toward the Expo Line station. His headphones were tight in his ears and he was listening to the "Immolation" movement of *Gotterdammerung* from a remastered 1969 recording of *Wagner's Greatest Hits As Performed On The Moog Synthesizer*, so he did not hear the groaning of the cables above, nor the snapping and crackling of the travel cage of the Bubble House.

Milo had also forgotten to remove his polarized glasses, so he was unaware of the half-kilometer shadow he was walking through. His attention was focused on his iPhone. He couldn't understand why the screen was so hard to read (it was the polarized glasses, try it sometime)—he was trying to check his email to see if the editor of *Dry Fart Magazine* had responded to his submitted article on the communist subtext of the latest Pixar blockbuster.

So he was caught completely unaware when the ballast tanks of the Skylifter emptied themselves, knocking him flat on his back with the impact of several thousand gallons of very cold water. From that position, he was able to see how the travel cage holding the Bubble House finally broke free from its moorings to come plummeting straight down on top of him. He barely had time to say, "Oh, shit," before he was instantly smashed into the sidewalk, splattering like a big bag of rancid strawberry jelly, leaving only his black and white striped socks and red Nikes sticking out of the mess.

That Pesky Dan Goodman heard the impact, but as he was on the far side of the Science Center, he did not see the explosion of dust and debris, nor was he close enough to be struck by the small pattering of wooden fragments that were hurled into the air by the impact.

No.

That Pesky Dan Goodman was preoccupied, frowning at his feet, realizing that the soles on his shoes were worn to an uncomfortable smoothness, and that it was time for him to go shopping for a new pair. Perhaps something glittery. But definitely not Crocs.

And that was that.

Cold water.

Dropped house.

Shoes.

Done.

THE OLD SCIENCE FICTION WRITER

"Grampa," he began, "did you have glimmers in the olden days?"

I reached over to tousle his hair, he twisted away. "The olden days, eh? You want to hear about how your Great-Gramma Jo drove a covered wagon all the way from St. Louis to the gold fields in Sacramento and how we were chased by Apaches across the Arizona desert? Of course, I was just a baby at the time, so I had to use the little gun, not the big rocket launcher, because I was too small to lift it. Or do you want to hear about Aunt Alice's heavy metal rock band, the Juicy Lucies, and how they started a riot at the Hollywood Bowl when they played bare-breasted? Or should I tell you about the time I wrote a script for the very first *Star Trek* series—?"

Danny-Marie made a face. "No, tell me a *real* story. Not one of your made-up ones." He settled himself on the couch, tugging at his skirt; he hadn't decided which gender he wanted to be for adolescence. He was still trying on possibilities and discovering that the freedom of an unbifurcated garment had certain drafty disadvantages. Meanwhile, I still called him *he*, because that was a lot easier than any of the invented pronouns.

"A *real* story, huh."

"Yeah, something I can goggle—to see if you're lying."

"I never lie. Let's see...." I scrabbled through the dusty shelves of memory. "Do you want to hear how I predicted computer viruses fifteen years before the first one was actually written? Or the day I testified against Charles Manson? Or how about the time a Shuttle astronaut asked me for my autograph? Or I could tell you how John Cusack played me in the movie about me and your dad? Or maybe you want to hear about the dog who liked salad? That's always a fun story—"

"No, Grampa! A *real* story!"

I thought about protesting. Those *were* real stories. The dog who liked salad was one of my favorites, but this was not an argument I was going to win. I sighed and said, "Okay, you tell me. What do *you* want to hear about?"

"I wanna hear about the olden days."

"Those were the olden days."

"The *real* olden days."

"Well, um. Let me think. That was a long time ago, you know. There were still dragons—"

"Grampa! Dragons weren't invented then."

"I'm not talking about the invented dragons. I'm talking about the real ones. Before the knights killed them all."

"Grampa! I'm not a little girl anymore. I'm old enough to apply for puberty—"

"Don't do it. It's a trap."

He gave me the teenager look. "Tell me about when you were little. A hundred years ago. What was it like?"

I muttered something about Father William. He had the right idea. "Be off, or I'll kick you downstairs."

"Who's Father William?"

"He was my priest when I went to Seminary school. Did I ever tell you about the religion I started? Spiritual Harmony Among Many. We went by the acronym. I was the head SHAMan...."

"Grampa!"

"That's a true story too, Danny-Marie." I stopped, took a breath. There's no such thing as patience, only exhaustion. I was too tired to argue. "Just what is it you want to hear?"

"What was it *like*?"

"It was like...like today, only a lot quieter." Another deep breath. "Our first television had a great big seventeen-inch screen."

"What's an inch?"

I held my hands apart, a soccer ball's width. "About like that. That was for the ladies. It was different for men. Never mind. That comes after puberty. But we had to sit real close to the screen. It would have been bad for our eyes to sit too far away. And it wasn't even black and white. It was green and white. And it was kerosene-powered. The only show we could get on it was *I Like Lucy*. They weren't even married yet."

Danny-Marie frowned, still suspicious, but didn't interrupt.

"This was before Big Think. A long time before. If you were a grown-up, you had to get up every day and go off to work—wait, I'll explain work in a minute. If you were still a child, you had to go to school so you could learn how to be a grown-up before it happened—and it happened whether you were ready or not, so you didn't have a lot of time, you had to learn fast, before puberty hit. Otherwise—"

"Yeah, I know about that. It's on the license exam. What did you mean about going to work?"

"I'm trying to figure out how to explain it. See, before Big Think, people had to do everything themselves. We called it work. Sometimes you liked what you were doing, so it was more fun than work, but there was a lot of stuff that needed to be done that wasn't fun. We called that stuff work."

"Like what stuff?"

"Like *everything*. If you wanted to eat, you had to grow your own food. You had to put seeds in the ground and water them and wait till they grew into vegetables. If you wanted meat—"

"I know how to grow meat. You took me to the meat farms, remember?"

"How could I forget? You ate yourself sick on dino-bits." He made a face. I ignore it and continued. "Anyway, work was necessary to keep all the different pieces of the world running. We didn't have bots, so people had to do all the hard things themselves, building houses and sewing clothes and repairing cars and everything else you can think of and a lot of stuff you can't. If you worked, people traded you money for your work—that is, if it was work they wanted or needed. If you didn't work, you didn't get money, so you couldn't buy food or live in a house or have clothes or anything."

"So everybody was naked and hungry?"

"No. Everybody went to work, because they didn't want to be naked and hungry. Some people built things. Others tore things down. Some people cleaned things. Others made them dirty. Getting things dirty was the job that teenagers did best, so it all worked out. Mostly."

"What did you do?"

"I wrote stories. People paid to read them. They gave me their money, sometimes a lot, so I ate every day and wore nice clothes and lived in a big house."

"People *really* paid you for your stories?"

"Yes, they did. Once they even gave me an award."

"No, they didn't!"

"Yes, they did. And they paid me a lot because I was good at it. Just like you're going to pay me for this one."

"No, I'm not."

"Then I'm going to starve. And I'll take off all my clothes and go live in the garden—"

"No, you won't. Daddy won't let you."

"I think I liked your daddy better when he was your mommy. Without all the testosterone."

"Thpffft. Tell me how Big Think happened?"

"Well, that's a tough one, kidlet. A lot of different things happened all at once, all together, but separately, and it took a while for everything to settle down. It was a very confusing time, because so much was happening and a lot of people were very upset because they didn't understand any of it, so it made them afraid, but not all of us. Some of us were even excited.

"See, back then, there were other people who wrote stories too, not just me. We wrote a special kind of story called science fiction. We wrote about all the stuff that hadn't happened yet. And some of us said that one day a Big Think was going to happen. So it wasn't a surprise to everyone. Just most people."

"Science fiction? What's that?"

Oof. That one hurt. Okay… "It's complicated. Hard to explain. Um, science fiction was…" Hmm. It really *was* hard to explain.

"Okay, let me back up a little. The reason we all had to go to work was because we hadn't built everything yet. And a lot of the stuff we had built was kind of clumsy—we didn't know how to make houses self-sufficient or cars that could drive themselves. We were just fumbling along because there was so much we still didn't know. Most of the time we were just patching things up as fast as we could."

"That's crazy. Was everybody stupid in the olden days?"

"Not stupid. We just hadn't learned enough yet to do better. It was a crazy time because people didn't like not knowing, so they made up stuff and pretended they did know. A lot of silly stuff—"

"Like what?"

"Like you wouldn't believe. People made up all kinds of weird stories that they used instead of real explanations."

"Like what? Tell me!"

"Okay, just one. Ready?"

"Ready."

"There were people who believed that the more money you had, the more important you were."

"No. Really?"

"Yes. Really."

"Dumb."

"Well, yes—we know that *now.*"

"And everybody was that crazy?"

"No. Not everybody. There were a lot of people who were trying to figure out the *really* important things—how stuff actually worked. They got a lot of it wrong at first, but they didn't quit and they got enough right that it was worth it to keep going. It was hard work, but it was the kind of work that was fun too, because the more they found out, the more they found out how much more there was to find out. So it was like solving a great big puzzle—until they found out just how big and infinite the puzzle really was."

"And then Big Think happened, right?"

"Well, not right away. Remember I told you that Big Think didn't happen all at once? There was a kind of middle period in there, where we figured out we had a way to figure things out, but we still hadn't figured everything out. There was still a lot of stuff we didn't know—like the umptillionth digit of pi, it's 1 by the way—but we had finally gotten to the point where we knew what we didn't know, so we could start thinking about what it would be like when we did know it. That was what science fiction writers did."

"Huh?" Danny-Marie made *that* face.

"Okay, let me try again. We tried to imagine what all those unknown things were and how they might work and how things would change after we found out. That was science fiction. And you know what…?"

"What?"

"It was a lot of fun. We got to think about all kinds of stuff."

"What kinds of stuff?"

"Oh, how spaceships would work and what bots would do? How do you get to Mars? What's inside a left-handed quark? And where does your lap go when you stand up? Things like that."

"But that stuff is so *easy*! Everybody knows that stuff."

"Well, now, yes. But this was a long time before flybois and glimmers and pheens. We thought about that stuff because we wanted to know how to build it."

"You didn't know how to print a pheen?"

"Kidlet, you asked about the olden days. There was a lot of stuff we didn't know back then. That's why we thought about it—that's what science fiction was. Big thinking before Big Think. A lot of it was silly, a lot of it was wrong, but there was also a bunch that started people thinking about what to do next and how to do better."

"And that's what you did?"

"Yep. And I wasn't the only one. Out of all the billions and billions of people, there were maybe only a thousand of us—if that many. It was a very special job, one of the best jobs in the world, and not a lot of people could do it well. But each of us was thinking about a piece of the *big* puzzle. The puzzle that Big Think came along to solve."

"Only a thousand?"

"Maybe a few more, maybe less. Hard to say. Not all of us knew enough science to get it right."

"What stuff did you think about? Did you get any of it right?"

"Well ... um, some stuff, yes."

"What stuff?"

"Well, I thought about Big Think before there was a Big Think. And portals—I thought about how portals might work. And shifting. And sex-bots too. I wasn't the only one thinking about sex-bots though. Back in those days, sex was very important. Really. And hard to do. If we wanted to have sex, we had to have it with each other. Or even by ourselves."

"Now, you're just being silly."

"I'm a science fiction writer. It's my job to be silly. Except nobody needs silly anymore. Not my kind anyway."

"Grampa...?" Danny-Marie looked across at me skeptically. "Are you making this up?"

"No, I am not."

"There really were science fiction thinkers?"

"Yes, there were. I would not lie to you about this. They were some of the very best people on the planet."

"Really, Grampa? Really?"

I spread my hands in surrender. "What do you think?"

"I think you're making it all up."

"Well, yes, I am very good at making things up. At least, I used to be. Just ask me. But not this. Not this time. See, it was Big Think that put us all out of business.

"First there was Little Think. And that seemed like a good idea at the time. Then Little Think helped design Big Think. And after Big Think, we didn't have to imagine anymore, we didn't have to make anything up—because Big Think had a Q-brain and could do all the science in minus-time and tell us how to make it real. We would ask Big Think how something worked or how to do it and Big Think would tell us the fastest, most efficient, and cost-effective way to the result even before we finished asking the question.

"It was a great time-saver. And a lot of fun—but only at first. Because after a while, we realized there wasn't anything to imagine anymore. Big Think would either tell us how to build it or why it wasn't possible. That, my dear, is how Big Think put us all out of work. Each and every one of us. I haven't written a science fiction story in...oh, my, over a hundred years. It was a very special time. But now it's over."

Danny-Marie frowned. An idea was forming behind those eyes.

"I have a question for you, Grampa."

"Of course you do."

"A lot of the stuff that Big Think says. We have to believe it because nobody is smart enough to understand the proof, right? Only Big Think. So...what if Big Think is just making stuff up too?"

"Hmm. Y'know, that's a very good question. In fact, it's even a good idea for a science fiction story. Do you want to help me write it—?"

"No. But you can write it and tell it to me. Next time."

He switched me off and I disappeared.

WHEN THE "MARTIANS" RETURNED

Well, they weren't really Martians, but everybody called them that, because it was a lot easier than calling them Xqrlt3ns. (The 3 is silent, but even after you know that, it's not much help.)

They were tall and green and spindly and had bug-like eyes, but not the kind that covered their whole heads, because that would have been too disturbing. Some people called them Sleestaks, but having evolved on a planet with much lower gravity, they were much too thin and much too tall for the resemblance to stick. So, Martians it was.

Their language, such as the linguists were able to understand, had no vowels, and only two tenses—too-tense and in-tense.

The Xqrlt3n ship was first detected by amateur astronomers, the usual way these things happen because the professionals are always much too busy looking the other way. This time it was an Australian hobbyist named Tim Knapp who first noticed a strange object approaching from sunward, one of the best places to look for unknown objects because most astronomers don't look there. The ship had slingshotted around Sol in a braking maneuver, and for much of its approach was lost in the glare. Knapp discovered the alien ship by accident. At first he thought it was a floaty in his right eye. He spent several minutes cleaning his glasses too.

Tim Knapp owned one of the world's most remote petrol stations, halfway between Alice Springs, a small town in South North Australia, and Coober Pedy, a smaller town in North South Australia.

It's a seven hour drive on the A87, also known as the Stuart Highway. Drivers are warned to have a full tank and plenty of water and sandwiches. It can be a grueling journey, but for those who need a break along the way, if they can't wait until they arrive at the world-famous Erldunda Roadhouse, they can watch for a weather-beaten little structure crouched beneath a faded sign proclaiming "Knapp's Sack. Ice and Stuff."

Here, tourists can buy gasoline at exorbitant prices, vegemite sandwiches, stale meat pies, and a variety of colored stones that have spent a year or more in the rock tumblers in the shed beneath the solar panels.

None of that is important to this story. The real reason for the remoteness of Knapp's Sack was the absolute clarity of the night sky. There were no city lights to create an atmospheric glare in the night sky, no people around to annoy or interrupt him, and a near-total lack of clouds and rain in the dry Australian outback.

Tim Knapp was a self-taught astronomer. Before relocating to this desolate part of the Stuart Highway, he had made and lost several fortunes and an equal number of wives—although he still missed Christine Marie, his first wife and childhood sweetheart. And perhaps she missed him too. They still exchanged emails and even phone calls on holidays. Neither one quite remembered why they had broken up, but it had something to do with Tim's impatience and a kidney soufflé.

Knapp's continuing failure at relationships had finally led him away from Sydney to the flawlessly clear nights of the outback, where he could gaze out at the Milky Way with a rapt sense of wonder and awe. He wanted to discover a comet, or something equally interesting. He fantasized about finding an object in the heavens that would someday be known as Knapp's marvelous discovery.

He had built for himself a fairly sophisticated observatory on top of a nearby hill, three kilometers east of his little store on the Stuart Highway.

At sunset, he would close up the store, pack whatever sandwiches had not been sold that day, plus a few bottles of beer, and drive his ancient Jeep up a winding dirt trail to his lair for the evening, a small dome-shaped building.

Depending on what part of the sky he wanted to observe or what celestial wonder had caught his attention, he would arrange his sleeping schedule around the hours of best visibility. His telescope was mounted on motorized gimbals and could be synchronized with the rotation of the Earth, so it could focus on any specific part of the sky for as many hours as the sky was dark.

Knapp kept scrupulous notes and took high-resolution photos, some with exposure times of eight or nine hours. His most recent passion was the possibility of a near-Earth asteroid encounter. Anything coming around from behind the sun would be almost invisible until it was only a few days away. While Tim Knapp was not hoping for an extinction-level event, he was certain that if he could discover a near-miss, it would give him that specific moment of astronomical glory that very few amateur sky-watchers ever attained.

He did better than that.

He spotted the Xqrlt3n ship before anyone else.

Of course, once he reported his discovery, the first reaction from almost every professional observer of the heavens was skepticism. Amateurs didn't discover things, and those six comets discovered by Terry Lovejoy were just lucky accidents, okay?

But then, one after the other, they turned their big eyes sunward and confirmed that Tim Knapp had actually seen something unusual. Tim Knapp was interviewed by three Australian news shows on two successive days, before the news media turned its attention to more photogenic subjects—also because "real scientists mean real ratings."

Tim Knapp did get a nice mention on Wikipedia, and for a few weeks he even displayed a sign at his station, "The first discovery of the Xqrlt3n spacecraft was made here!" Until he got tired of people asking him questions about the Xqrlt3ns that he couldn't answer.

And that's pretty much all we need to know about Tim Knapp right now. Events swept by him so fast he didn't have time to finish his meat pie. As it happens, he didn't even bother to finish it. (Australian meat pies are not known for their culinary excellence. Quite the contrary.)

By the time the alien vessel was visible to the rest of the world, it had already entered an elliptical orbit around the Earth, eventually braking into a geostationary position above the Atlantic equator. Several orbital telescopes were immediately focused on it, giving Earth observers a very clear view of the ship. (Also, a number of nuclear-devices were loaded onto an equal number of orbital boosters, just in case. This latter action was not a matter of public knowledge, but multiple governments were in contact with each other, all of them promising not to shoot first. So they all waited.)

Everybody waited.

Various scientists were immediately summoned to the studios of the news media to discuss what the alien arrival might mean to humanity.

So many scientists were recruited by so many news organizations that there weren't enough qualified scientists available to discuss the significance of the alien arrival. Fortunately, there was no shortage of people who could pretend expertise, so none of the news media lacked for punditry.

The short version of any of these conversations usually went like this:

"Who are these aliens?"

"I dunno."

"What do they want?"

"Dunno that either."

"Are they dangerous?"

"Dunno."

"What do you think we might expect?"

"Beats the hell out of me."

Complicating these conversations, the Xqrlt3n vessel did not respond to any signals beamed at it, nor did it emit any signals of its own. It simply hung there for the longest time, an unmoving point in the equatorial sky.

Unfortunately, it was out of sight for poor Tim Knapp, half a planet away. He was very frustrated. He could only watch the reports on the telly. Even worse, nobody wanted to interview him. He was already old news.

After an annoyingly long period of inaction, the Xqrlt3n ship separated into three parts. One piece rose, one piece descended. The middle piece stayed exactly where it was. High-resolution telescopes revealed that the upper and lower sections of the Xqrlt3n vessel were tethered to the main body. The ship was reeling out its upper and lower sections.

The entire process of unspooling took several days, until both of the tethers were thousands of kilometers long. When the lower end of the cable reached almost to the measurable boundaries of the Earth's atmosphere, the piece at the end detached, sped up, and began descending toward the surface.

This, at least, was something that the more knowledgeable scientists could actually discuss, and they did so at length.

The mechanics were fascinating. While an orbital elevator would be an extremely difficult undertaking, a skyhook would be much easier to establish and it would be just as practical, if not more so. A skyhook would be an energy-efficient and cost-effective method of launching and reacquiring a landing craft. So why hadn't NASA thought of it?

Actually, NASA had, but the challenges of creating a strong enough, long enough cable and getting it into space had not yet been solved. Never mind, that's another story.

Meanwhile, the Xqrlt3n shuttle was flying through the ionosphere, or maybe the troposphere, one of those spheres.

The specialists at NASA's mission control were quick to predict multiple possible landing zones for the alien shuttle, but their software was designed for the physical limitations of human technology. Unfortunately, the Xqrlt3n landing craft had abilities that were not factored into their models.

Let us now turn our attention to Carl Dershem.

Dershem was a mad scientist—not the proverbial mad scientist as in malevolently deranged, but the other kind of mad scientist—terminally outraged at the stupidity of the human race, especially those too invested in Dunning-Krugerrands to recognize, let alone understand, the superior achievements of his massive intellect.

In a previous tale (still unwritten), Dershem had invented the Pelzer Ray, but because he couldn't figure out what a Pelzer Ray actually did or what might happen to a target that had been pelzed, he finally gave up on the whole project. Despite that, he still secretly hoped that someday some serendipitous accident of science would rescue the entire work from oblivion. (Meanwhile, don't worry about the Pelzer Ray, unless you're pregnant, prone to migraines, or have irritable bowel syndrome. It has no further significance in this tale.)

Nevertheless, Dershem was good television. All an interviewer had to do was ask the right question and Dershem was a self-starter, winding himself up into a frenzied, near-apoplectic rage at metastatic stupidity in general and malignant incompetence in specific. He didn't hesitate to name names, so he was always good for a spike in the ratings, despite the usual complaints from the legal department.

But, in this situation, he outdid himself.

Beautiful Jo Choto was the anchorwoman for the National News Network Nightly National News—yes, that was her full name, her parents had named her Beautiful Jo, but as soon as she was old enough to be embarrassed, she shortened it to Jo. She invited Dershem to be a guest on her nightly roundup any time she needed either a scientist or a controversy, which was at least once a month. With the arrival of the alien spacecraft, Dershem was on almost every night—in no small part because no one from NASA wanted to lend credibility to any show that would regularly feature Carl Dershem.

Dershem's appeal was obvious. He was willing to speculate. He was willing to extrapolate. He was willing to elucidate. Put a microphone in front of him and get out of the way.

For example:

"So, Doctor Dershem, the alien spaceship has just landed in central Africa. A United Nations Contact Team is en route to meet them. What do you think will happen?"

"Good question, very good question. Excellent question. Some of the best scientists in the world have been considering this question. It's a huge question, very significant. And right now the best answer is that we don't know, we can only speculate—but speculation is important because it's a consideration of possibilities. Possibilities, you ask? Well, it's the question we should all be asking. Because it allows us to consider our responses. Preparedness, this is all about preparedness. Are they a threat or are they a menace? We don't know. But let's consider, what do they want? What could they want?

"What do they need? What do we have that they might need? Nothing, really. If they want minerals, they can mine the asteroid belt. If they want oxygen, they can extract it from water, they can find plenty of water on Europa or in Saturn's rings. If they need methane, they can help themselves to the atmosphere of any of our gas giants. So they're not dipping into our gravity well for anything freely available anywhere else. Of course not. So they have to be coming here for something that's unique to this planet. The obvious thing is something that no other planet has—life. Yes, that's what they're here for. Obviously, they want to meet us.

"But why? This is a question that some of the best thinkers on the planet are working on. It's the question you asked at the beginning. But we won't know the answer for sure until we actually establish some kind of communication, will we? That has to be the first step. When the United Nations Contact Team arrives in central Africa, they will have to spend a lot of time just learning how to talk to these alien visitors. Then we'll find out what they want, won't we?"

"Thank you, Doctor Dershem. That's all the time we have tonight. I'm Jo Choto and you're watching the National News Network Nightly National News. Thank you for tuning in and be sure to stay tuned for Tim McKenny's Sports Roundup with all the latest news about the heartbreaking situation in Florida."

(Don't worry about Florida either. Whatever it is, it's not going to be heartbreaking as much as it's going to be bizarre. But "heartbreaking" works better than "bizarre" for keeping viewers from changing the channel, so that's why Jo Choto said "heartbreaking.")

Meanwhile, down in Africa. . . .

The Xqrlt3n shuttle landed twenty kilometers east of Yalinda in the Central African Republic. The exact coordinates were 6°31'05" North 23°32'15 East. (You can look it up on Google Earth and see how remote it is.) Why they chose that landing site, when there was a perfectly nice meadow in Hyde Park, London, a beautiful mall in Washington DC, an attractive set of lawns adjacent to the Eiffel Tower in Paris, a huge open space in front of St Peter's Basilica in the Vatican, a broad open square adjacent to the Kremlin in Moscow, and, of course, the Forbidden City in Beijing also had plenty of space. These were all suitable landing sites, according to any number of filmmakers. Yet, the Xqrlt3ns chose to land instead in one of the remotest regions of the Central African Republic, a country that had otherwise managed to escape the attention of nearly everybody except its immediate neighbors: Chad, Cameroon, and South Sudan.

The government of the Central African Republic was not equipped to deal with the influx of scientists, reporters, attention-seeking politicians, their various assistants and aides, and a variety of groupies and wannabes that descended on the capital city of Bangui. Nor did they have the facilities to transport this small army of chronovores to the landing site of the Xqrlt3n spaceship.

Fortunately, the United Nations Contact Team had arrived in six well-equipped C-5 cargo planes conveniently borrowed from the United States, carrying several helicopters and enough scientific and military gear to overthrow a small government and then analyze the DNA of its demise. Fortunately, the Bangui international airport had a runway long enough to accommodate such gargantuan planes. The Contact Team promptly set up their base station in nearby Le Mônjur Square— inflatable structures filled with humongous crates marked with numbers and symbols and warnings.

As soon as the helicopters were unloaded from the C-5s, assembled, fueled, and checked for readiness, nearly fifty scientists, observers, reporters, politicos, deputies, various aides, and several expendable generals boarded their respective aircraft and lifted off, heading noisily eastward.

They flew low and landed three hundred meters west of the Xqrlt3n landing craft. They all donned self-contained hazmat suits, with oxygen tanks on their backs, and plodded painfully across the remaining distance. The Xqrlt3n ship was shaped like a giant pumpkin. It was parked on three slender legs. A wide ramp lowered from its belly. A gaggle of Xqrlt3ns were already exploring the area immediately around the base of their shuttle.

They were tall and spindly. There were seven of them. They had greenish-gray-blue skin. They had dark, multi-faceted eyes. They smelled vaguely of lavender and chocolate and seaweed. They did not appear to be sexually variegated. Their clothing was not much more than knee-length gauzy scarves or fluffy boas, draped casually around their shoulders, and mostly designed to hold a variety of instruments, geegaws, doodads, whatchamacallits, and thingamabobs. But no widgets or doohickeys.

A delegation of three scientists approached slowly, arms spread wide, palms open, while behind them the rest of the contact team furiously photographed, measured, scanned, and recorded. Others made sure that everything photographed, measured, scanned, and recorded was broadcast to the rest of the world.

The three approaching scientists were Dr. Kier Salmon, Dr. Christy Davis, and Dr. Robert Newell. In preparation for this mission, their obituaries had already been written. The only thing missing was the date and cause of death, but it was presumed that these particulars would be available shortly.

The Xqrlt3ns barely noticed the humans. They were too busy examining a type of bush so uninteresting that neither the BBC nor David Attenborough had ever given it a second thought. But finally one of the aliens turned around and made an annoyed waving-away gesture at the approaching humans.

Dr. Kier Salmon, Dr. Christy Davis, and Dr. Robert Newell all stopped where they were, puzzled. They looked at each other through the transparent face masks of their hazmat suits. They frowned, they shrugged, they shook their heads in confusion. Not sure what to do, they waited and watched and waited some more.

At last, the Xqrlt3ns finished their examination of the otherwise uninteresting bush. Four of them wandered away to examine another uninteresting bush. Three of them turned to face the humans. The shortest one spoke in perfect English, although with a noticeably British accent, "Please go away. We have work to do here."

Dr. Salmon said, "Welcome. Welcome to Earth. We greet you in peace."

And then, Dr. Davis said, "We'd like to talk to you."

And Dr. Newell added, "We have so many questions to ask."

"Yes, yes, we know all that," replied the alien. "But we have work to do. So please go away. If we have time, we'll talk to you later. But don't count on it. We must stay on schedule." The Xqrlt3n pronounced it "shedjewel." And then all three of the Xqrlt3ns turned away to join the rest of their companions in their study of the next totally uninteresting bush.

"Well," said Dr. Salmon. "That was . . . unusual."

"Unexpected," agreed Dr. Davis.

"And rude," said Dr. Newell. He added, "After all, we came a long way to meet them—"

"They came an even longer way," said Dr. Salmon.

"And apparently, they must stay on schedule," said Dr. Davis. She pronounced it "shedjewel" too. She wasn't British, so perhaps she was mocking the alien's pronunciation.

"Yes, that's what they'd like us to believe," said Dr. Newell. "But look at them. They're just standing there, staring at that totally uninteresting bush."

For a moment, none of them spoke. They stared at the Xqrlt3ns staring at the bush. But nothing happened.

Finally, Dr. Salmon said, "We're going to look like idiots, aren't we?"

"Absolutely," agreed Dr. Davis.

"That's already established," said Dr. Newell. "The cameras have been rolling this whole time."

"Well, there's nothing for it, is there?" said Dr. Salmon. "Let's head back."

And the three unhappy scientists turned around and trudged back to the others.

In the interests of brevity, this narrative will skip the obvious scramble of consternation at all levels of science, politics, and uninformed punditry. Instead, we'll summarize:

In the three weeks that followed their initial landing, the Xqrlt3ns lifted off and traveled to additional locations in Africa, Northern Asia, Canada, Mexico, South America, and finally New Zealand. They did not visit any national capitals. In fact, they avoided all major human settlements in favor of remote areas of wilderness. Whenever and wherever humans sought them out, they were waved away in annoyance. The Xqrlt3ns were insistent about staying on shedjewel. They had a lot of totally uninteresting flora to examine.

Of course, once they had examined the totally uninteresting bushes and one particularly ugly banyan tree, none of these were ever uninteresting again because human curiosity demanded an explanation. A multitude of researchers followed the Xqrlt3ns' examinations with even more detailed studies of their own. Whatever it was about these plants that required the study of the Xqrlt3ns, it was immediately a whole field of intense research for human beings. Unfortunately, except for a slight increase in their ability to hold carbon dioxide, a side effect of global climate disruption, there was nothing in any of the plants that merited an increased level of examination. These bushes really were totally uninteresting.

But the mystery continued, because the essential questions remained unanswered. Who were these Xqrlt3ns? Why were they here? What did they want?

Which was why Jo Choto's Nightly National News on the National News Network was also pulling big ratings because Carl Dershem was saying exactly what everyone else had been carefully (and very strongly) advised by their respective governments to not say.

By now, of course, most people were calling the visitors "Martians" because "Xqrlt3ns" was too hard to pronounce and more than one commentator had injured himself trying. Others, pretending to a more professional demeanor referred to the Xqrlt3ns as aliens, visitors, or beings. But "Martian" was a convenient shorthand for most lay people.

Except for Carl Dershem. "Well, it's obvious these creatures, whatever they are, have not come here to invade us," he said. "Or they would have unleashed their Pelzer Rays or whatever weaponry they might have aboard their orbiting dreadnought. Perhaps they don't find us appetizing. Maybe we taste bad. I don't know. We'd have to ask a cannibal about that. But if we tasted all that bad, then why would anybody be a cannibal? Unless they had no other choice, like the Donner Party or those Uruguayan Rugby players who spent seventy-two days in the Andes after their plane crashed. But I don't think that's it either. How did we get on this subject anyway? It's distasteful."

He bent to his notes, shuffling through his various papers. "I don't think they're here to quarantine us. That's obvious. They would have said something by now, wouldn't they? And you have to wonder, how do they speak such perfect English?

And with that damned annoying British accent too—what's all that about? What are they, snobs? They must have been listening to our radio and television broadcasts all the way in, decoding and decrypting and translating—what do they think of us? Maybe they have to go somewhere and report? No, I don't think they're tourists. They're too busy studying all those totally uninteresting bushes, although obviously they're not totally uninteresting and we should be taking a much closer look at everything they're looking at closely to see what's so interesting. Maybe it's a new source of fuel or food or those bushes have some hallucinogenic property and we're going to have to pass new laws to keep our young people from smoking or eating the leaves, and then of course, we'll end up with cartels and smugglers and a black market selling drugs to innocent children outside the schoolyards, right?"

Dershem found another page and ranted on. "Obviously, they're not here as ambassadors, they haven't said one word to us that was diplomatic, not one word. And isn't that strange? We're the obvious owners of this planet, aren't we? Aren't we the intelligent species? Why aren't they talking to us? Aren't we important? Obviously, these aliens don't think so. They're not here for any reason we can understand, are they? They're not talking to dolphins or whales or giraffes. So why are they here? Nobody knows anything."

Jo Choto finally had a chance to get a word in. She said, "Well, yes—if they're not here for any reason we can understand, then we don't know why they're here. Nobody knows anything. And that's it for tonight. Please stay tuned for Tim McKenny's sports roundup and the real tragedy of the Green Bay Packers—"

In truth, there was no real tragedy of the Green Bay Packers, but Tim McKenny's ratings were still sagging and the programming executives at the National News Network were beginning to realize that Carl Dershem was a hard act to follow. Reruns of the abortive *Gilligan's Island* reboot would cost them less to broadcast and would probably pull an extra half-percent of market share.

Finally, one afternoon, one of the Xqrlt3ns approached the watching throng of human observers. "Where are the dinosaurs?" it asked.

The humans looked at each other, not sure how to answer. Finally, Dr. Kier Salmon spoke up. "They're all gone." Dr. Salmon had been tracking the Xqrlt3ns across all the separate continents since they had arrived, and despite being ignored across all the separate continents, still felt comfortable enough to answer. "They died a long time ago."

"How unfortunate. Well then, we'll be leaving now."

"Wait! Can we ask you some questions?"

"Maybe next time. We have to stay on shedjewel."

And with that, the Xqrlt3ns boarded their ship. A moment later, it lifted off and disappeared into the bright blue sky. Eventually it linked up with the lower end of the orbiting skyhook and was reeled in. Shortly after that, the Xqrlt3ns accelerated out of Earth orbit and headed outward toward interstellar space.

Earth was alone again. One question had been answered. Yes, there was life elsewhere in the universe, presumably intelligent. But another, more puzzling question, had been left behind. Just what the hell had they been doing here? And why did they ask about the dinosaurs? Had they been here before? They must have—

There was only one clear answer.

Carl Dershem had said it. Jo Choto repeated it. And eventually it became a cultural mantra.

Nobody knows anything.

Three days after the Xqrlt3ns had left, an Australian reporter phoned Tim Knapp to ask if he was following the "Martian" ship.

Annoyed at being treated like yesterday's news, Knapp hung up without saying anything. But he was no longer alone. Excited by the short flurry of publicity that Knapp had enjoyed, Christine Marie had caught a bus all the way out to Knapp's Sack.

Perhaps she had finally realized that Tim Knapp was her one true love—or maybe she had returned to him in the vainglorious hope that one day there would be a movie about his discovery of the Xqrlt3n ship, a quick rush of fame and fortune. Or perhaps she was now hiding out from a spurned boyfriend. Whatever the case, it's not part of this story. Her secret remains safe. We will leave it at that.*

Meanwhile, after slamming down the phone, a very old landline, Tim Knapp headed into the kitchen for a beer. Christine Marie was at the sink washing dishes.

"Mm," he said. "Something smells good. Kidney soufflé?" He opened the oven door to take a peek.

"Close the oven door, Tim," Christine Marie said. "It's not done yet."

Carefully, Tim Knapp closed the oven door.

---

*   Coincidentally, the spurned boyfriend's name was Milo. Not that one. Another one.

FOLLOW THE OTHER BRICK ROAD

OR

IN THE LAND OF THE WURLIKINS

Much less traveled is the red brick road.

It goes north and west, first past a few tiny farms, then through rolling hills, some of them covered with sparkling yellow flowers. Beyond the farms, there are stands of trees, then woods, then a creeping wilderness where the road wanders through dark overgrown forests, seemingly without direction or purpose, until it finally climbs high into the range of mountains that protect the land from the hot winds sweeping out of terrible deadly desert on the other side.

Up here, the road is broken and unrepaired. The surface is cracked and uneven. There are muddy holes where the red bricks have fallen away – if you follow the road long enough, eventually it disappears, puttering out into nothing more than an uneven dirt path, unsuitable for carts and barely passable for horses of any color.

But if you persist, if you follow the path far enough, all the way to the shadowed valleys, where the surrounding mountains are as tall and sheltering as they are difficult to traverse, you will eventually reach the village of the Wurlikins.

It is not a big village, there is little to distinguish it from any of the neighboring townships. The houses are well-maintained, but simple in construction. The Wurlikins paint their homes in simple colors, they are not given to extravagant decoration. The inn is clean, the meals are nourishing, the ale is hearty, but otherwise all is unremarkable. What commerce obtains focuses mostly on necessities. There is nothing particular to attract the traveler in search of curiosities, novelties, or distractions. There are no adventures to be found here. Nevertheless, from time to time travelers do pass through on their way to other, much more interesting lands.

If there is anything at all to distinguish the Wurlikins, it is their high spirits. They are generally a happy race. They are not what the casual traveler would call a beautiful people. They are mostly small and like flowers, they come in all colors – pink, brown, yellow, and red. Some are wiry, some are stout, others are round and stumpy.

The women tend to be tiny and sprightly, with dark eyes and intricate ornamentation decorating their close-cropped hair. The men are shorter than the women and rounder. They wear their hair in long ribboned braids that fall to their waists. The women wear intricately embroidered vests and high boots, the men wear flowing robes and sandals – except at festivals, when the men wear yellow vests and the women crimson pantaloons.

Most have big ears, many have long noses that bend upward at the end, but all of them have big brown eyes that flash when they laugh, which is almost all the time. The Wurlikins say that life is a jest – if you're not laughing, you're not getting the joke.

Despite the isolation enforced by the troubling passage through the high dark mountains, travelers will find a joyous welcome, eagerly greeted and festively treated. The Wurlikins are always hungry for news and a wanderer who has a marvelous tale to share will find himself invited to dine at many tables. Great mugs of bright cider will be thrust into his hands, tall flutes of the finest green wine as well. And the sausages? Baked into a sourbread bun, slathered with sweet onions and mountain mustard, washed down with a hearty beer, the sausages alone are worth the journey.

Even though they may have already heard the news, the Wurlikins will happily attend any retelling, ever ready to hear new details. "Is it true a house fell from the sky? Did a wizard really fly away? We heard that a boy turned into a princess –?"

Of course, every wanderer who arrives at the village of the Wurlikins will have their own version of the most talked-about events, as well as those not commonly known, so every retelling further embellishes the tales, burnishing even the smallest and simplest of far-off events with magnificence, until every bit of news glows like the stuff of legend.

This is why travelers are greeted so warmly. Visitors are welcome all year round, not just at the time of the spring jubilee or the autumn harvest. Many choose to stay, some for the sausages and beer, others because the rest of the journey no longer seems as immediate as it felt at the beginning. The northwest trails are known to be perilous, where travelers are often beset by wild beasts, angry spirits, and occasional flying monkeys – and if a traveler tarries too long, the ferocious storms of winter will pile the mountain snows so high that only the very tops of the trees poke through.

But by summer, when the spring snows are melting steadily, feeding gurgling mountain streams and sparkling waterfalls, the forests will be bright with colorful blossoms and new life everywhere. The village fountains will send bright cold sprays high into the air – and everywhere, the Wurlikins will be preparing the town for the joyous Solstice Celebration.

This year, however, it happened that a band of scraggly travelers appeared some distance from the town, all looking grim and dangerous.

There were five of them. They had not come up the red brick road, they had come the long way around, scrabbling across the mountains where no roads ran. They appeared abruptly, stepping out of the forest onto the sheep meadow where a small flock grazed in peace. The animals scattered in fear, bleating as they ran. While most of the shepherds ran to retrieve their flock, one of the younger ran for the mayor, hollering excitedly, "Visitors! We have visitors! Visitors from the Dark Hills!"

Big and broad were these visitors – they all wore the same ferocious expressions under their thick beards. All five were clad in long dark cloaks, roughly made from the thick-furred skins of various animals who had been unwise to cross their paths – lions and tigers and bears. The men lumbered out of the forest, speaking to each other in low rumbles that sounded like grumbles, but just as easily could have been growls. Hard to tell at a distance.

The men regarded their surroundings with narrow eyes. They approached the village with a wary suspicion. They bore deep scars of past encounters and even deeper scars invisible. They had come from the other side of the eastern reaches and had little knowledge of the Wurlikins and their ways. What they were seeking, they did not say – perhaps they traveled to a strategic relocation.

They were enormous, bigger than ordinary men, so they towered over the Wurlikins. They moved with an ominous gait and a wary demeanor, as if unknown dangers stalked them everywhere.

Regardless of their appearance, they were weary travelers and they should have marvelous stories to tell. Mayor Wurlikin stepped forward, eager to greet them, certain that his enthusiastic welcome would ease any fears the travelers might have brought with them. A crowd of onlookers gathered behind him, growing by the moment as the villagers abandoned their daily tasks and rushed down to the edge of the meadow, anxious to meet these strange brooding men.

"Welcome!" said Mayor Wurlikin, looking up at the men, looking from one to the next. "Welcome to the land of the Wurlikins! You must be tired. We have sausages and beer for you, hot baths and warm beds! We are eager to hear of your travels."

A sly-looking traveler stepped forward first. "I am Carrion," he announced, looking down at the assembling crowd. "I began my journey seven years ago. I travel with men who are worthy of my company. We have journeyed far and intend to journey farther."

Mayor Wurlikin nodded happily. "Welcome, welcome, and welcome. Stop and rest awhile. The mountains are steep and rugged. You must rest awhile before you journey on."

Now, the second traveler stepped forward. He was stouter than the first. He had a chest like a barrel and legs like tree stumps. His arms were as thick as his neck. He pounded himself proudly and announced, "I am Partisan the Unbeaten and I will gladly prove it to anyone who doubts."

"Of course, you are," said Mayor Wurlikin. "And of course, you will. There isn't a Wurlikin who would dispute that. You have come here unbeaten, and I am certain you will leave the same way. We are not a fighting people. We settle our disagreements by dancing. He who can last the longest is the winner, and everybody enjoys the contest."

The third traveler declared himself then. He was the tallest, but also the one with the most profound stoop. "You may call me Victor, because that is what I am. Unlike others, I do not seek glory. I have already earned it. I do not seek fame, I am already famous. You must have heard of me."

Mayor Wurlikin was too polite to ever disagree with any traveler, so he nodded in simple agreement. He stroked and stretched his magnificent mustaches. "We do not get many travelers, so we do not get much news. But even so, we have heard of many Victories, and many Victors, but none to match yourself, of course –"

"You see...?" said Victor. He accepted the Mayor's acknowledgment with an expression that might have been satisfaction, but was hidden behind a thick black beard. He nodded and moved aside, so the fourth traveler could step forward and speak.

This man's hair was gray where it wasn't patchy. His skin was dark where it wasn't sallow. He had seen far more winters than any of the others. He said, "I am Loose the Interpreneur. I am a Mage and I share my visions wherever I go. What I speak is real, because when I speak, it becomes so."

"Ahh," said Mayor Wurlikin. "What a marvelous skill indeed. I am sure that everyone in the village will be eager to hear what you have to say." Finally, he turned to the last traveler. "And you sir? Who might you be?"

The last traveler opened his cloak, throwing it back to reveal the burnished red breastplate of his heavy armor. It was immediately apparent that despite his silence, he was the real leader of this band. He had bands of black and crimson paint across his face, outlining his eyes with a ferocious mask. He had bone trinkets braided into his long black hair. He carried a sharp yellowed staff, ancient and carved from the tusk of some gigantic beast, perhaps one of the legendary behemoths of the desert. "I am Boilsore," he said, and nothing more.

"I am Mayor Wurlikin," said Mayor Wurlikin. "Because it is my time. It is a difficult job, so it is passed around every year, so that everyone can wear the mantle. But this time is my time, so it is my privilege to welcome you to all the hospitalities that our village can provide. Did I say that you are welcome here? If I did not, let me say it now. Travelers are always welcome. Come to the Wurlik Inn, sit in our most comfortable chairs, put up your feet and put yourselves at ease. We shall provide for your every need. When you are rested and recovered from your journeys, you can fill our ears with your best tales and we will fill your bellies with our best ales. Who can say no to an invitation like that?"

"We could," said Partisan. "We do not need gifts. We are the dark men of the Grimmly Wood. We take whatever we want."

"But of course," said Mayor Wurlikin. "You will find much for the taking here, and you are welcome to it. We have more than we need and we are happy to share it. Come and recover from your travels."

He led the newcomers to the Wurlik Inn, a sturdy log building joyously decorated for the Solstice Celebration. Most of the year, the inn stood rugged and alone on the south side of the village square, dark and dusty, seemingly forever in need of paint, but now as every summer, it was festooned with ribbons and banners and giant confections of bright fabric, all sewn to look like wildflowers of many shapes and colors, cornflowers and queen's lace, red blankets and white daisies, bluebuttons and buttermugs – a display that dazzled the senses. The fountains had been perfumed to match and their sprays flavored the air with sweetness.

Boilsore grunted and frowned. He waved his staff, a thick and sturdy club, at the hanging veils and ribbons, ripping them down into a tumble of silken folds. Behind him, Carrion and the others flailed at whatever other decorations remained in their reach.

Mayor Wurlikin and the other townsfolk were not startled. They did not receive visitors often, but they knew enough to recognize that every stranger could be strange, some stranger than others. If the newcomers found the decorations odious, then the decorations must come down. Immediately, all the nearby Wurlikins began ripping down whatever banners and ribbons they could reach, all the gaudy flower confections and hanging veils, all the decorations they had worked so long and hard to assemble came tumbling to the ground where they were quickly kicked into dirty piles of fabric and from there to someplace out of sight.

"There," said Mayor Wurlikin. "That is so much better. Simpler. No longer so hard to look at. No longer too bright."

Inside, in the cool shade of the inn, Boilsore and Carrion, Partisan, Victor, and Loose, unburdened themselves carelessly, with little regard for any of the resident Wurlikins. The men dropped their gear to the floor, they shed their heavy coats, and moved to settle themselves into the largest and most comfortable chairs. "Beer!" shouted Carrion. "Bring us beer. Beer and bread." The others echoed his demands. "And great platters of roast beast as well."

Immediately, the Wurlikins rushed to please their guests. They filled huge mugs with sparkling ale – still dripping with foam, they carried them quickly to the burly men. The huge dark travelers gulped the ale faster than they could taste.

Deep in the kitchen, where the fires burned high even on the hottest of summer days, the cooks carved thick slices of meat from the flanks of the roasts they had prepared for the Solstice Celebration. They slapped them onto heavy wooden planks, poured thick gravy over each slice, and sent the serving women hurrying out to fill the bottomless appetites of the five voracious visitors.

Others brought in huge loaves of dark bread, fresh from the oven and steaming with flavor, followed by platters of fresh-churned butter. The hungry travelers ate with gusto. They pulled great handfuls of bread from the loaves, slathered them with butter and sweet sauce, piled on slabs of dark juicy meat, and banged their now-empty mugs on the table to demand more beer, eating and drinking as ravenously as if they had not seen food in a fortnight.

The Wurlikins applauded the appetites of their guests, even if they didn't share the meal. There wasn't enough beer or bread or beast for all. But no matter. The important thing was the well-being of their guests. Once satisfied, they should have great tales to share.

Impressed by the gusto of their guests, the Wurlikins began singing songs of joy and welcome. The melodies were high-spirited and bouncy, the lyrics a confection of word-play and surprises, a spontaneous burst of enthusiasm.

Partisan was the first to finish. He was big of build and well-armored in thick rolls of meat and muscle, abundantly wrapped in generous layers of meals made flesh. This was a man unbeaten in his appetites as well as in his battles. He belched his satisfaction as he wiped his mouth with his wrist, then grumbled his annoyance at the noise around him. "You sing like wailing badgers," he said. "I have heard death rattles that sound better."

The Wurlikins looked at him, surprised. They looked to each other. "Oh? We didn't know." They turned to each other, all of them shushing. Then they shushed each other for too much shushing – until finally, Partisan shouted, "Enough shushing! Can we not have quiet? I cannot hear myself drink!"

Embarrassed, the Wurlikins shushed until they hushed and finally fell into a vaguely embarrassed but very sincere silence.

Loose looked to Partisan, grinning. "These Wurlikins are very cooperative. There will be no trouble here."

Carrion laughed aloud. "That is disappointing. I was hoping for a little excitement." There was an empty wooden platter in front of him. As if to emphasize his words, he brushed it to the floor.

Loose nodded his shaggy head in agreement. Noticing that his own serving board was almost empty, he picked it up, hefted it, judging its weight, then flung it at the opposite wall where it broke into three pieces against the wooden frame that held the log walls firmly in place.

Boilsore stood up then. "My friend, you are right. This food ain't fit for eating. It's only fit for throwing." He picked up the wooden plank that bore his third, still unfinished helping and hurled it at the same wall. The plank hit square on and bounced off, leaving various bits of meat and bread and gravy hanging on the wall, dripping and sliding to the floor.

The other travelers laughed heartily, shouting their agreement, and began tossing their own serving boards at the wall, each one hitting it with great thunking noises.

"Ho!" shouted Mayor Wurlikin. "Our guests have spoken. This food ain't fit for eating!" He picked up an empty plank, a remainder of Carrion's first or second serving, and tossed it at the wall himself. Lacking the same strength and fury in his pitch, the plank did not break, it made only a feeble thud, but it was enough.

Immediately, the other townsfolk grabbed whatever serving boards remained. Those who could not find planks threw other loose objects at the wall, whatever still remained on the heavy wooden tables of the inn. For a few moments, the air was full of flying objects, boards, planks, spoons, mugs, half-filled bowls, salt grinders, pepper mills, and even the occasional shoulder bone that had been left for the dogs. Everything banged and bounced, a few things broke. Bowls and mugs clattered and splattered and splashed their unfinished contents everywhere, leaving dark liquid stains on the log wall and spreading puddles on the rough wooden floor.

This sudden unexpected clamor brought frowns of puzzlement to the huge dark men. This was not a behavior they had seen before.

Then, abruptly Victor laughed. "All right, then." He picked up a nearby stool and hurled it at the log wall. The wall shook, but it was still stronger than the stool, which broke apart as easily as if its pieces had only stayed together out of courtesy. Not finding a stool, Carrion grabbed a chair and hurled it. The wall shuddered. Boilsore lifted a long bench and heaved it like a javelin. This time, the wall broke, the logs crackling and groaning and fracturing outward. Dusty bars of daylight appeared where gaps had opened up in the broken frame.

Almost immediately, the Wurlikins did the same. Everything they could lift – stools, chairs, benches, and spittoons went flying across the room. The wall did not resist the assault. Now that it had been fractured, it fragmented, eventually revealing a well-framed view of the village beyond. Above, the roof of the inn groaned, complaining loudly at the sudden lack of support from its eastern wall. It sagged.

Boilsore laughed. Carrion guffawed. Victor and Loose and Partisan hooted and roared. Of course, the Wurlikins joined in the merriment, chuckling and chortling, sniggering and snorting. Outside, a small crowd had gathered. Looking through the broken wall, seeing what was happening, they too began to laugh.

The burly men eyed the failing roof with suspicion. One by one, they eased themselves to their feet. They grunted with the effort – they were somewhat exhausted from the labors of the feast, but they gathered their cloaks and baggage, and relocated outside the building.

There, they surveyed the broken frame of the inn. The eastern wall had shattered outward, the support for the heavy roof was gone, the entire building leaned inward. Boilsore laughed at the poor construction and gave the doorframe a vigorous thrust with his heavy boot.

The building groaned. It creaked. It protested loudly its own failure to stand – all the separate noises of crackling logs and mortar served as prelude to the mighty crash as the Wurlik Inn collapsed in upon itself. As the dust rose, Carrion laughed. Partisan laughed. Loose and Victor laughed. Boilsore grunted in satisfaction, then he laughed too.

All around them, the Wurlikins laughed as well. They applauded Boilsore's strength and laughed at what was left of their prized Wurlik Inn.

Boilsore turned to his companions. "They do not build very well here, do they?" To the Wurlikins, he said, "Your buildings are shabby." To prove his point, he strode to a nearby building, the town meeting hall, a proud and ancient structure that had endured longer than any Wurlikin could remember. Boilsore gave it a mighty kick. The building shuddered with the impact.

The Wurlikins cheered and Boilsore kicked the town hall again, this time even harder. A gigantic crack opened up in the side of the forward wall, spreading from the big front windows all the way up to the ornate gabled roof. Boilsore surveyed the damage. "See?" he said to the other men. "This building is weak and unworthy. It does not deserve to stand." He gave the building another kick.

Quickly, the Wurlikins joined him, shouting enthusiastically. "Weak and unworthy! Undeserving!" They kicked at the walls, the doors, and the sturdy beams at the corners of the structure. The town hall complained loudly, but withstood their tiny efforts.

Carrion and Boilsore looked to one another. Boilsore snorted. "You are all too weak. I'll show you how to kick down a building!" And with that, he kicked in the door of the town hall. He kicked the door frame, once, twice, a third time – and the town hall groaned and began to lean.

All this clatter was loud enough to attract a much larger crowd of citizens, they laughed and applauded and rushed to join the activity. In no time at all, the town hall was surrounded by tiny attackers. And in less time than that, with dozens of Wurlikins kicking it every which way, the tired old building broke apart, it cracked and crumbled and crashed in upon itself. There was a dreadful noise and a great cloud of dust rose up from the rubble. All the Wurlikins laughed and cheered and clapped their hands in delight.

Still caught up in the frenzy of destruction, several of the Wurlikins moved on to the next building, a granary, and began kicking at its walls. Soon, others joined them until a large laughing crowd had surrounded the entire structure.

Boilsore and Carrion frowned. Victor and Loose and Partisan looked puzzled. The behavior of the Wurlikins was not what they expected – they were supposed to be scared. This was not right. Definitely bizarre.

"These people are mad," muttered Carrion.

"Perhaps it is the altitude," suggested Partisan. "The air is too thin and weak for them."

"No, it can't be the air," said Loose. "Or we would be feeling it too. It must be something else."

"Maybe it's their food. Or their beer."

Victor shook his head. "But we ate their food. We drank their beer. I feel fine. Do you?"

The others grunted their agreement.

"So then, what is it?" asked Boilsore. "Why are they behaving like this?"

"Perhaps..." Carrion started to say, then hesitated. There was fear in his voice. The others looked to him, concerned. "Perhaps," Carrion said, "They are demented. Perhaps they have been bitten by stingflies or jitterbugs. Perhaps it is an infection. And perhaps, if we remain here, perhaps we are at risk as well."

The five dark men fell silent, each considering the possibility. Strength was one thing, madness another.

Boilsore started to shake his head, then stopped. "It could be something like that," he admitted.

"Perhaps we should leave this place," said Loose. "Before whatever curse befell these fools attacks us as well."

"We do not flee like cowards," said Carrion.

He would have said more, but he was interrupted by the cheers of the Wurlikins as the wall of granary crashed down in a huge cloud of dust. A few sacks of grain went flying as the shelves collapsed. Several barrels of flour went rolling downhill, where they crashed and burst against the stone fence surrounding a cluster of houses. A crowd of Wurlikins went shouting after them and began kicking the nearest house, all of them laughing joyously.

"No," said Boilsore, "we do not flee like cowards. But there is nothing here for us. Or if these fools keep this up, there will be nothing soon enough. There is no profit here. We will advance to the next town and conquer that one instead."

The others grunted, nodded, and reached for their heavy coats and heavier packs. They hoisted their burdens onto their shoulders and headed further up the road, higher into the mountains.

The Wurlikins stopped what they were doing to watch the departure of the men. Without an audience, it wasn't much fun to kick down a house, so the Wurlikins stopped what they were doing and returned to the center of the town. Several of them began singing a joyous song of farewell.

"That was too short a visit," said Mayor Wurlikin. "Too too short. I guess they weren't having fun. Not enough fun to stay and share their stories." Mayor Wurlikin peered up the road. "There's not much up there, not much at all – unless you count the Biggins. And not the little Biggins either. The bigger Biggins. I don't know what kind of fun these fellows are looking for, but I don't think they'll find it up the road."

"Why do you say that?" Several of the younger Wurlikins gathered around him. "Tell us about the Biggins."

Mayor Wurlikin took out his pipe and puffed it to life. "Well, I can't say all that much. I won't go anywhere near the Biggins myself." Seeing both curiosity and skepticism on the faces of his listeners, Mayor Wurlikin added, "It ain't that they're unfriendly. They're kind enough folk. But I won't eat any of their sausages, and I don't think you want to either."

A MILD CASE
OF DEATH

Death—after the fact—feels just like a bell, like a great giant gong struck with a silver hammer. *Bdooonnnggg!!*

While I stood there wondering just what the hell had happened, a voice materialized beside me.

IT'S TIME TO GO, DAVE.

"Dave's not here, man—" I said it without thinking.

PLEASE DON'T MAKE TROUBLE, DAVE.

I turned to look at the intruder. "Who are you and what the hell—" The rest of the sentence died in my throat. Or what would have been my throat, if I had still had a throat. But yes, it died.

To tell the truth, I felt disappointed. I had expected, hoped that Death would appear as a tall sepulchral figure in a black hood and cloak, carrying a transparent scythe of mysterious power. If I squinted just right, I could sort of imagine Death as that kind of figure, but mostly he manifested as a polite blurry darkness.

IT'S TIME TO GO, DAVE.

"I already told you, Dave's not here."

The figure hesitated, appeared to check its PDA, or maybe a clipboard. I said it was blurry.

THE SCHEDULE SAYS DAVE. 11:37, SUNDAY EVENING.

"And I told you twice already, Dave's not here."

YOU'RE DAVE.

"No, I'm not."

YOU'RE HERE. IT IS 11:37, SUNDAY EVENING. 11:38 NOW.

"But I'm not Dave. Dave doesn't even live here. He was supposed to stop by earlier, but he never showed. He didn't call either. I don't know what happened to him. Tell you what, if he calls I'll tell him you're looking for him—"

THE SCHEDULE SAYS DAVE. 11:37, PACIFIC STANDARD TIME. AND HERE I AM AND HERE YOU ARE, SO YOU MUST BE DAVE.

"I'm not Dave."

ARE YOU SURE?

"I'm sure."

The figure hesitated. It's hard for a blur to look confused, but it did.

"What's the problem?"

YOU'RE TRYING TO FOOL ME, AREN'T YOU?

"No, I'm not. I'm not Dave. You made a mistake."

NO, I DIDN'T. YOU'RE DAVE.

"Listen, it's all right. Everybody makes mistakes—"

Death checked its clipboard again. I HAVE A SCHEDULE TO KEEP. I HAVE OTHER APPOINTMENTS. WHY DON'T YOU JUST PRETEND YOU'RE DAVE AND COME ALONG LIKE A NICE CHAP. THAT WILL SAVE US BOTH A LOT OF TROUBLE.

"No, I don't think so. That doesn't sound like a good idea to me."

BUT I'VE ALREADY COLLECTED YOU.

"You did *what?*"

LOOK DOWN.

"Eh? Is that me?"

NO. THAT'S YOUR BODY. YOU'RE RIGHT HERE. NOW IF YOU'LL JUST TELL THEM THAT YOU'RE DAVE, EVERYTHING WILL BE ALL RIGHT FOR BOTH OF US.

"No, wait a minute—! I know how Dave lived. He was a liar, a thief, a cheat, a fraud. He was a television producer, for God's sake. If I tell them I'm Dave, they'll send me to the bad place—"

IT'S NOT THAT BAD. IN FACT, IT CAN BE QUITE PLEASANT. EXCEPT FOR THE COMPANY, OF COURSE.

"You've been there?"

NO. BUT I'VE READ THE BROCHURES.

"It's full of lawyers, isn't it?"

NOT AS MANY AS MOST PEOPLE THINK. THEY DON'T LET LAWYERS IN, BECAUSE THEY BRING DOWN THE PROPERTY VALUES. BUT THERE ARE A LOT OF TELEMARKETERS, EVANGELISTS, USED CAR SALESMEN, AND BARRY MANILOW FANS.

"Barry Manilow?"

Death sighed. IT'S A LONG STORY.

"Like we don't have all eternity...? Look, can I ask you something?"

YES?

"Do you have to talk like that?"

LIKE HOW?

"Like that."

OH, THAT.

"Yes."

"Well, not really. But it's sort of expected, so—well, you know."

"That's better. Listen—you seem like a nice fellow, a hard worker, just trying to do the best job you can. I'm sure you call your mom regularly, floss your teeth every day, you don't jaywalk, right?"

"Well—"

"But you get my point. So, why don't you just put me back and let me get on with the rest of my life and I tell you what—if you'll give me your pager number, as soon as I can track down Dave, I'll beep you, okay?"

"I can't do that—"

"Sure you can—"

"No, I can't. I don't know how."

"You don't know how?"

"We don't do reinsertions. Once you're decanted, well—that's pretty much it."

"Decanted? Like you can't get toothpaste back in the tube, eh?"

"Actually, you can get toothpaste back in the tube. Would you like me to show you how it's done?"

"Toothpaste you can do. People, you can't."

"Yes, that's right."

I felt like I should sit down and sink my head into my hands and feel something. Anger? Outrage? Grief? Except I couldn't feel anything. Dead people don't have feelings. Great. Just great.

"Y'know, this is really crappy. All that exercise, all that healthy living, all those goddamn pills and herbs, look at me, I'm so goddamn healthy, vitamins take me. Look at what I missed. All those cheeseburgers and fries and Cokes, all the beer and pizza I never put away. All the booze and dope and fatty foods. This is not fair." I turned to the blur, realizing I towered over it, well maybe not *towered*, but I had at least a good two inches, maybe three. "Do you have a supervisor?"

"Yes, but it won't do you any good?"

"Why not?"

"He's on vacation."

"I'll wait. Right here."

"That's probably not a good idea."

"Why not?"

"Because, well—do you really think you'll want to be reinserted after two weeks?"

"This is a done deal, isn't it?"

"Pretty much."

"Somebody owes me, big time."

"You're very convincing, you know."

"Thank you."

"You even had me going there for a minute. Now, come along, Dave."

"I'm not Dave."

"Have it your way." The blur gathered itself together. IT'S TIME TO GO NOW. Then it added politely, DAVE.

"I'm not Dave."

DON'T BE DIFFICULT. YOU'RE DAVE NOW.

"I will too be difficult. I'll be any damn thing I want. I'm going to tell them I'm not Dave."

IT WON'T DO ANY GOOD.

"Why not?"

HUMANS SAY ANYTHING TO AVOID THE CONSEQUENCES OF THEIR ACTIONS. THEY WON'T BELIEVE YOU. IF I SAY THAT YOU'RE DAVE, YOU'RE DAVE.

"This isn't fair—!"

DEATH HAS NEVER BEEN FAIR.

"But I'm not Dave!"

THIS WAY, PLEASE. MIND THE STEP—

It was a long step. Down. *Down?*

"Excuse me?"

WHAT?

"Down?"

YES, DOWN.

"This is really not right. I mean it. You got the wrong guy and now you're taking me to the wrong place."

THEY ALL SAY THAT.

"Would you please stop talking like *that?*"

IT'S PART OF THE JOB.

"Well, it's freaking me out, and I'm already freaked out enough."

EXIT THROUGH THE GIFT SHOP, PLEASE.

"The what—?"

Souvenirs

"Hello, welcome to the gift shop!"

The young man was as bright and smiley as a high school cheerleader, and every bit as cute—bubble-butt and all. He wore a crisp red and white uniform. The insignia was shaped like a Star Trek badge. His name badge identified him as Michael.

Great, just great.

"Where am I? Is this—?"

"This is the gift shop of course. There's always a gift shop at the end of the ride, so you can pick out souvenirs."

"Souvenirs—?"

"Of course!" he sparkled. "You don't want to leave life empty-handed. Take your time, look around. You'll find all kinds of wonderful mementos—"

"Mementos...?"

Michael gestured proudly, pointing with his whole hand. His posture, his smile, everything—he'd obviously been trained by Disney. "Over here, to your right, we have action figures. "And over here, to your left—" Another open-palm gesture. A wall of screens.

"Here we have a display of photos taken at all the most surprising moments in your life—here's where you pooped your pants in first grade, *that* was embarrassing, you look like you're going to cry, what a cutie you were. Oh, I like this—here's one of you learning how to masturbate, looks like you were having a lot of fun there, humping your pillow while watching the Mouseketeers. And here's that auto accident where you were almost killed, that was a close one, look at how scared you were, that's such a great expression! Oh, here's my favorite—your first time having sex with another person—oh my, he was handsome, wasn't he? Look at how amazed you were when he took off his underwear. Let me suggest that you order the whole collection, it comes in a beautiful red leather folder with your name engraved in gold, plus your birth and death dates, no extra charge. Oh—and look, here's your death already—ooh, that's a much better expression than most people make. That's quite nice. You should have that one framed—"

"I, um—okay, this wasn't what I was expecting."

"Yes, I understand. You were on the ride a long time, longer than most—we're seeing that more and more these days, a lot of guests are staying on the ride for decades, sometimes as long as a century. Getting off so suddenly can be a little disorienting." He brightened. "Maybe you'd like to see the action figures—?"

He led me across the aisle, where the racks were filled with stacks and stacks of boxes, each with a different figure, each one appropriately dressed—each of them attached to a colorful cardboard backing, all of them posed and mounted behind form-fitted, stiff transparent plastic. "On this rack, most of these just have you typing, there's a lot of those—but over here, there's even more of you just sitting and staring out the window, I guess you were thinking, right?"

"So those are the *in*action figures....?"

Michael shook his head disapprovingly. "Oh no. We would never insult the guest. Those might have been your most interesting moments, that's when you did your best imagining—"

I was already moving to the next counter. "Hey? What are these—?" I held up a couple boxes. "I was never in the Navy. Not the army either. And what the hell is this? I was never a drag queen. I never did drag in my entire life—I would have looked like my mother."

Michael hurried over to explain, "Oh, those are your alternate lives—who you could have been, what you could have done. I'm afraid you were a disappointingly good person—okay, there's a little shoplifting when you were a kid, some tax evasion as an adult, but those hardly count. Some people, their alternate lives—they've been drunks, abusers, junkies, child molesters, thieves, televangelists, and a lot more murderers than you would believe—but that's a contextual possibility as much as a personality thing—"

Michael indicated the shelves with another of those professional gestures. "But you—the worst you'll find on the Bad Lives Shelf is lying to your parents, a little bit of early plagiarism—you covered that one well, I'll give you credit for that—and that time you went out driving drunk and stoned and whiplashed that old lady. Tsk tsk. But that's hardly very exciting, I mean, compared to some of the things you could have been—"

"So, all the bad things I've done are—?"

Michael waved it off. "Negligible in context. Compared to some people who've come through here—never mind, that would be tattling."

I looked around. "Is there a Good Lives Shelf? Are there better lives I could have had?"

Michael shook his head. "Well, yes and no—there are better lives you could have had, but you don't need to see them. Some people find them depressing. And in your case, oh my, yes. We don't want you breaking down and crying, collapsing in anguish, smashing things in rage—it disturbs the other guests."

"I'm not that kind of person."

"No, but you could be."

"Really? That's the first piece of good news I've gotten here—"

Michael said, "The whole point of the Alternate Lives Section—to show you some of the other possibilities of the ride. For the next time you do it."

"The next time?"

"Oh yes. Just go around to your right—"

"Uh, no. I don't think so. Not right now. Which way is the exit?"

Michael pointed to the left. "Right out there. Remember, the afterlife is the happiest place after life." He twinkled at me. "Would you like a pair of complimentary wings and a halo?"

"Not really."

"Well, some people expect it so, we make it an option—" He handed me a pair of sunglasses. "But do put these on. It can get pretty bright out there. It's full of stars."

After Life

Eventually, I found myself in a room.

Well, not a room. A space. Not very well defined. In fact, not defined at all. So I wasn't sure how I knew it was a *space*. But I knew.

There was a person here. Sitting behind a desk. There was nothing on the desk except a thin black vase with three white lilies sticking out of it. The person behind the desk was indeterminate, dressed in something that could have been white, or maybe gray, but wasn't quite enough of either.

"Please sit down. Be comfortable."

"Sit where?" I looked behind me. There was a chair there. Now. I sat. It was neither hard nor soft. Neither comfortable nor un-.

"Excuse me?" I said.

"Yes?"

"Is it necessary for this whole place to be so ... so indeterminate?"

"Mm, yes. I see your point. Just a moment. Is this better?" The space was now identifiably a room. Bare blank walls. No door.

"Um, no. It isn't."

"Something wrong?"

"It's—it's very stark. Institutional. Not very comfortable."

"You think this place should be comfortable?"

"Is there any reason why it shouldn't be? And you did tell me to be comfortable."

"Point taken. How's this?"

I looked around. Now the space was defined by Grecian pillars that stretched infinitely upward. Long silky-white drapes wafted in a soft breeze. Beyond, summer-blue sky with soft cumulus pillows here and there. "Nice," I admitted. "A little bit of a cliché, very Warner Brothers, but—"

"I can change it, if you wish—"

"No, no thanks. This will do."

"You're sure."

"Quite."

"Can I get you something? Water? A soft drink? Iced tea?"

"No, I'm fine. Really."

"Good."

I waited. He waited. We waited. He still seemed indeterminate.

Finally, I asked, "Are you God?"

"I'm an aspect of the universe."

"You don't look like an aspect."

"Oh? How do you think an aspect should look?"

"I don't know. Like God, I guess."

"And what does God look like?"

I shrugged. "Like God. Unmistakeable."

"I see. Do you prefer the George Burns or the Morgan Freeman iteration? Or perhaps something more in the Charlton Heston or Michelangelo mold? Or maybe Hattie McDaniel?"

"Hattie McDaniel?"

"A very popular aspect."

"Um, no. I just—"

"How's this?" Gregory Peck. The Atticus Finch version. "Will this do?"

"Yes. That's fine."

Gregory Peck looked at me across the desk. "Is there anything else?"

"Is this where I get judged?"

"No."

"I get judged somewhere else?"

"No."

"Well, where *do* I get judged—?"

"Being judged is important to you?"

"No. Yes. I mean, I thought it was part of the deal."

"No, it isn't."

"No judgment at all?"

"No. Are you disappointed?"

"Well, sort of. I thought I did pretty good. Didn't I?"

"I don't know. Why don't you tell me—"

That stopped me for a moment. "I have to tell you?"

"It's a start."

"Oh, I see. This is all self-service. Like a cafeteria. I'm supposed to sort it out for myself, argue both sides of the case, all my good works versus all my sins, right? I get to undertake a self-examination of my entire life, however long as it takes, and then finally pronounce my own judgment. Right?"

"No," said Gregory Peck.

"No...?"

"No."

We waited some more. He waited while I sorted it out in my head. No judgment. But if there's no judgment, then what is this place? What am I doing here? "Is this Heaven or Hell?"

"What do you want it to be?"

"Look, you're the aspect. You're the one who knows what's going on. Not me. So could we just get on with it?"

"We are getting on with it. This is it."

"This is it? *This* is it? This is *it?*"

"Yes."

"What about eternal reward? Eternal punishment? Judgment day? Heaven? Hell? God? St. Peter? Pearly Gates? Satan? Fiery pits of agonizing brimstone? Demons? Pitchforks? Are you telling me none of that is here? If it's not here, where is it?"

"Is that what you want?"

"No, I don't—"

"What is it you want?"

"I want an explanation. I think I deserve an explanation, don't you?"

"What I think is irrelevant. This is *your* space."

"Did I end up in some kind of purgatory? Limbo? Is that it? This is a waiting place, isn't it? How long do I have to wait? Ten thousand years? A million? That really doesn't seem fair. I only had 72 years on Earth. Why should all of eternity be determined by a mere flick of time. I didn't even have enough time to—to live a whole life, to learn enough to—to be wise. I didn't have enough time to do all the things I planned to do."

"You had 72 years, 4 months, 3 days, 22 hours, 14 minutes, 33 seconds. Wasn't that enough?"

"No, it wasn't."

"It was a lot more than most people get. And you had your health."

"Fat lot of good that does me here."

We waited some more.

"So okay, fine. I get it. What happens next?"

"Nothing."

"Nothing?"

"That's right."

I inhaled. I exhaled. Mostly for effect. That was interesting. I could breathe here. I did it again. "Nothing," I repeated.

"That's right," said Gregory Peck. "Is there something you would like to have happen?"

"Can I ask you something?"

"Ask anything you want?"

"Will you answer honestly?"

"Of course."

"How long does this go on?"

"As long as you want."

"Where is God?"

"God is here."

"Here?"

"Yes."

"Where?"

"Here."

"Do I get to meet God?"

"If you wish."

"When?"

"Whenever you wish."

"How about now?" I said.

"All right."

Nothing happened.

I looked across at Gregory Peck. He did not seem antagonistic. In fact, he seemed very nice. He wasn't doing this deliberately.

"So, where is God?"

"God is here."

"Are you God?"

"I'm an aspect."

"Yeah. I got that part. So, let's see. There's no Heaven. There's no Hell. There's no Day of Judgment. There's no reward, no punishment."

"Do you want any of those things?"

"No, I don't." I got up from the chair, went to the edge of the room—the *space*—and stared out into the eternal blue. I scratched behind my ear.

"Is it this way for everybody?" I asked.

Behind me, the aspect answered. "No. It's this way for you."

"Hm." Well, that was useful. The afterlife was a personal experience. A puzzle that each person had to solve for himself. "So how much time do I have here?"

"As much as you want. We create it as we need it."

"Yes, of course. I should have known. Thank you."

"You're welcome. Are you sure I can't get you anything? Water? A soft drink? Iced tea?"

Something went click. Or *klunk*. Or whatever sound a small epiphany makes inside your head—if you have a head.

But I was starting to figure it out. I walked back to the chair and sat down at the desk. The aspect sat across from me. He waited patiently.

"You work for me, don't you?"

"Yes, I do."

"You didn't tell me that."

"You didn't want me to. You wanted to see how long it would take for you to figure it out for yourself."

"Well, this is embarrassing."

"Every time."

"Right." I scratched behind my ear again. An interesting sensation. I'd have to remember that one.

"I like playing jokes on myself, don't I?"

"Yes, sir, you do. Who else do you have to play jokes on?"

"Yes, there is that."

"That was a good one with the redhead, though. Nicely orchestrated."

"Yes and no. It didn't seem like fun from the inside."

"I guess not."

"I'll have a cappuccino, please."

"Right away—"

And there it was. Coffee was one of my better ideas. Almost as good as sex. I put the mug back down on the desk. "So," I said. "I guess I'm ready for the next life."

"Very good, sir. What would you like to try this time?"

"Well, I'm just brainstorming here, but how about this—"

THE SHADOWS OF ALEXANDRIUM

First there was a sound—a grinding, whooshing sound.

Then the door dilated.

"Isn't that a little gaudy?" a woman asked.

"Of course. That's the point."

The Proctor stepped through first. He was giddy with delight. He clapped his hands once, then spread his arms wide, whirling to indicate the vast dimensions of the institution. His voice echoing like a symphony, he announced to the small cluster of visitors behind him: "Behold, the Alexandrium!"

The woman was the first to follow. Her name was Sharon Henderson and she carried a camera and a bag of chocolate-filled candies and cucumber sandwiches. She busied herself with her belongings, but once inside, she halted in astonishment, her eyes wide, her mouth caught in mid-word. The rest of the tour group filtered in behind her, also hesitating, clustering in stunned silence.

Pillars of rose and gold stretched impossibly upward, gleaming with polished light. Above, almost lost in the distance, the glass ceiling revealed a sky of painful brightness, a lustrous dazzle so intense the startled visitors had to raise their hands to shield their eyes against the incandescence. They blinked away the purple spots in their vision until their tears finally turned all sight into a watery blur. Everything around them glowed and sparkled with ecstatic radiance.

When they could finally see again, still careful to keep their eyes shielded, the Proctor gathered them close. "There it is," he announced. "The center of the Khandalorian Galaxy! Well, not quite. The center is an enormous black hole not too far beneath us—it's the biggest black hole in the known universe. Don't panic, we're well outside the event horizon. Well, mostly outside. Never mind, try not to think about it. But all of that, everything you see out there, all that howling luminosity, all those stars and all the planets that circle them, they're dancing to their inevitable deaths, everything spiraling inward to oblivion. Thirty-four billion years from now, they'll all be gone, one after another, nothing left except the glowing Cerenkov radiation that still blazes around the singularity. If you look down—yes, the floor is transparent, too—you can see it lurking there, like a gigantic shadow across reality.

It isn't, of course. It's something worse—it's the place where reality collapses in on itself, vanishing forever—or at least until forever ends. Magnificent, isn't it?"

His listeners, an assorted gaggle of otherworldly tourists, except for a pair of hooded Crimson Monks, made appropriate noises of amazement and fear. Sharon Henderson reached for her camera and started to focus on the blaze above, but the Proctor stopped her before she could snap the shutter. "You might as well put that away. The Alexandrium can't be photographed. This is a nullity nexus." Before anyone could ask, he added, "It's all right. We're perfectly safe. Well, mostly safe. The Alexandrium is—well, it is. Until it isn't."

Sharon Henderson took the picture anyway, then stuffed her camera back in her bag. The Proctor was probably right.

The round woman, the one in the red hat and purple dress, still careful not to look directly up, not at the overwhelming glare, once was enough, raised her eyes from one level to the next. Her name was Tracy Blackstone and she was descended from royalty—if not in fact, then certainly in her own mind.

Tiers and tiers rose upward in graceful repetition, every level a row of marvelous invitations, each revealing their tall and roomy corridors, every corridor lined with busy shelves, and every shelf overflowing with artifacts from a multitude of worlds: books, scrolls, tapestries, paintings, displays of all kinds, and things that were simply indescribable. Ms. Blackstone blinked in confusion. "But it's all just a big library, isn't it?"

"Oh, no, no, no." The Proctor recoiled from the thought. This time, he was an angular man, a gangling man, a sloppy man, a something-or-other man, whatever, perhaps he hadn't quite solidified yet—but he was definitely a man. This time, anyway.

"A library?" he said. "To call this a library is to call a single-celled amoeba an entire civilization. Well, yes—but no. That's backward. Let me try it another way. Saying the Alexandrium is only a library is like saying an entire galaxy is no more noteworthy than a single small asteroid. No, no, no—the metaphor is insufficient. Argh, my brain hurts, doesn't yours? You must all be in agony."

The Proctor pushed his hair back off his forehead, an unruly sand-colored thatch. He frowned, considering the enormity of the idea. "Consider. Consider this. Consider everything. A planet has a civilization, it has an ecology, that's how we think about it—what it is and what it isn't. But it also has all the possibilities we don't see, the multiple potential variations of its civilizations and the even vaster multitudes of potential ecological variants. You cannot talk about it until you include the meta-planet, all the different possibilities that could have happened on that world and didn't. What if the comet hadn't wiped out all the mammals, giving rise to the Dinosoids? What if there had never been the collision with a Mars-sized object that ripped off the planet's mantle and created its three moons—what would the tides on that planet have been and what lives would have developed instead in those vast, swirling seas? What if the planet had developed shadow-rings instead of moons? What fantastic creatures would have evolved under its ice-glittering skies?

And what beautiful poetries would they have created for themselves? Think about that—and all the other possibilities I didn't mention. You can't. Your brains aren't big enough. Annoying, isn't it?"

The Proctor brought his focus back to his rapt crowd of listeners, all eleven of them.. They all wore name badges. "What if—?" he demanded of Jeff Levine, the tall man. He had to look up, high up—Levine stood nearly twice as tall as the rest of them. "What if? But that is the question, isn't it? The essential question. The question that underlies existence itself. To be? Or naught to be? That is the dilemma. Let that think in." The tall man frowned as he let that think in.

Now the Proctor shifted his attention to the second man—his name tag identified him as Dave Weiner, but that was a false identity. Weiner was really a sleeper agent of the Zorganite Encumber, sent to observe the methodologies of the followers of the Scarlet Affectation. Right now, he was pretending to be on holiday, but in reality, he intended to examine certain ancient tablets that had been destroyed in the Twelfth Declination of Bloor. The Proctor knew all this, of course, but he wasn't going to let the being pretending to be Dave Weiner know that he knew. It was part of the plan—if there was a plan, that is. There probably wasn't. Plans are annoying.

The Proctor continued, whirling around and pointing enthusiastically, "What never will be, will be here in the Alexandrium! All—and I mean *all*—of the infinitely infinite possibilities of time and space, and all the smaller infinities between them— that's what the Alexandrium is!" He whirled again, pointing at the multitude of tiers, stabbing at the shelves, at all the separate passages and corridors rising toward the dazzle above, then turned back to Blackstone. "A mere library? Never! This is more, so much more, far more than all the heavens and earths dreamt of in your insufficient philosophies.

"Here are all the books that were never written, all the paintings never painted, all the symphonies never composed, all the sculptures never carved, all the great works that never happened. Shakespeare's *The Comedies of Fortinbras*. Kubrick's *Napoleon*. Beethoven's Tenth and Eleventh—and oh yes, the Twelfth as well. The Twelfth—what a glorious noise! And Dickens' *Christmas Cake*." He clapped his hands again. "Oh, I love Christmas! Don't you?" He stopped, looked at all of his companions with genuine interest. "Doesn't it always make you smell of oranges?"

Blackstone's companion, a man named Westfield, a mere wisp of a soul hidden behind thick glasses, stepped forward then. His full name was Ser William Westfield, the "Ser" short for Serial. He was the forty-third William in the line of cloned Westfields. He could have been called Jack, barely escaped being called Jill, and while most of his clone-family called him Willy, he preferred Bill, usually insisting "this Bill has come due." Unfortunately, that pun never worked well in the High Ghaloodian dialect of his current homeworld. But right now, Bill Westfield cleared his throat timidly.

"But how does it work?" he asked. "I mean, all the things that were never written or created—how can they be here?"

The Proctor smiled politely. He'd heard this question before, or some variation of it, probably several thousand times, he'd long since lost count. "I'm sure you've heard the theory that a million monkeys pecking away at a million keyboards for a million years would produce all the great works of literature? Have you ever wondered about the cost of housing and feeding and training all those monkeys? I don't think it's a practical effort."

He pointed at Westfield's bony chest. "Let's consider something else. Perhaps you're familiar with the idea that if you follow pi out for a trillion to the trillionth decimal places, eventually you'll find all the great works of art embedded in its numbers? Or maybe you have some experience with quantum exponential theory— the postulate that a meta-core quantum extrapolator can generate an infinite number of possibilities instantaneously? Maybe all of those theories are true. Maybe not. Do you really care? The Alexandrium is here. Is that explanation enough? Or do you need me to go on?"

The timid man shook his head. "No, no, that's all right. Thank you." Westfield stepped back into the tentative safety of the very small crowd, certain that any further explanations were going to be more than he wanted to hear.

"The Alexandrium isn't just infinite," said the Proctor, adjusting his bow tie, patting his fez, and immediately forgetting the timid man. "It's an infinity of infinities, each one called into creation as fast as it can be postulated. In theory, the Alexandrium is bigger than the entire universe, bigger than the entire meta-universe that contains all the universes. In theory."

The Proctor paused for effect—a necessary bit of dramatic looking around— before answering the obvious question, the one that hadn't been asked yet but was certain and inevitable. "Yes, that does suggest a rather interesting inquiry. How can the meta-universe contain something bigger than itself? How can anything be bigger on the inside? Because it is, that's how it works. Because it's only an index, a nexus of infinite possibility, creating, sorting, discarding, and recreating as necessary. It's very annoying, all those choices. Never mind that now, here we are. Here *you* are. What would you like to see? Feel free to look around—"

"But there's so much, it's too much—" That was Sharon Henderson again. She was a bookish young educator, encumbered with facts and baggage, traveling on an industrial sabbatical. She had trained for employment as a professional companion for Temporal Royalty but had failed the swimsuit competition. Now she was unhappily reconfiguring herself for more pedestrian efforts. Still turning slowly around, staring in astonishment, and noticeably dazed at the sheer size of the Alexandrium lobby, she seemed unable to grasp any of the complexities of what she was seeing.

"Yes, it is huge, isn't it?" said the Proctor, as proud as if he'd designed the foyer himself. "And this—this is just the index! Well, the index to the index to the index. The actual works . . . well, depending on what you're looking for, you might have to take a lift, or even a train. There are stations on every fifth level. Try not to pick a destination more than ten or twenty hours away. We only have a short time here, two days at most, maybe three—" He glanced at his watch. "That is, if we want to get to the Palace of Infinite Sorrows in time for the Hexecution. The buffet is not to be missed. But here you are, be here now. Enjoy." He waved the crowd into the Atrium of The First Question, where the galactic light poured down like golden fire.

The group shuffled forward slowly, a little bit eager, but also a little intimidated—their curiosity muted by their caution. They spread out slowly, as if unsure about leaving the safety of their companions, but they weren't really companions, just a group of people riding the same tourist shuttle.

Wanda Beers, a woman of indeterminate color—she hadn't yet picked one for today—touched the Proctor's arm. "May I ask you a question?"

"Of course."

"Where would I go to look up information about—"

"The Legend?"

"You read my mind?"

"No. Sorry. I don't read minds, most are fizzy and disjointed. Mine, especially It's just that everybody asks that question."

"Really?"

The Proctor nodded. "The Legend is the single most studied subject in galactic history. Some people think the Legend is a delusion or a wish fantasy or maybe an attempt to explain any miraculous survival in the face of certain doom. The Legend shows up in almost all the cultures represented here. He—or just as often she or it—appears to exist throughout all time and space. But the Legend does tend to favor human and humanoid societies, so there's a theory—actually a very well-documented idea—that the Legend is an artifact of mammalian evolution and that the presence of a strong, protective parent during the early formative years fosters the belief in a larger parental force, one that is invested in the survival of the entire species—I'm not boring you with this, am I?"

"No, no, please go on."

The Proctor realized that several others of the group were gathering around, so he continued quickly. "The Legend is often a man, but depending on who's telling his story, his age and appearance can vary. There are at least a dozen different descriptions—both consistent and contradictory. He's a man, she's a woman. He's tall, she's short. He's dark, she's pale. He wears a long coat, she wears a short one. He wears a hat, she doesn't. Sometimes he travels alone, sometimes with a companion, sometimes two or three. Sometimes he carries a towel. Everybody has their own favorite interpretation, of course. Some see him as a warrior, others as a savior. He's neither, but whatever he is, there's one consistency in the stories: The Legend only shows up where he is needed."

The Proctor paused for effect, then added with a sly wink, "Let's hope he isn't needed here. It's almost always—well, not always, but often enough—a little messy. But to answer your question, it's that way—" He pointed Ms. Beers toward a nearby corridor. "There's a whole wing of the Alexandrium dedicated to the exploits of the Legend, real and imagined. And you can find a large variety of cast-resin homunculi in the gift shop as well, from shelf-size to life-size. Batteries not included. It's right next to the food court."

"Excuse me, sir—?" That was Sharon Henderson again. She pointed past the Proctor. "That dark corridor? What's that?"

The Proctor turned to look. Looked twice. Frowned. The dark corridor shimmered uncertainly in silver and blue waves, as if it had not yet decided whether it wanted to be corporeal. "Hm," he said. "That's new. But it's nothing to be concerned about, I'm sure. The Alexandrium isn't dangerous. Not at all. Not usually."

As if to bely his assertion, the dark corridor flickered with streaks of unrealism. The Proctor studied it with a raised eyebrow and then a perceptive squint. Finally, he resolved his doubts. "Ah, yes. It's simple. Well, the explanation is simple. The actuality is so far beyond comprehension, I'm not even going to try to explain. No, I will try. It's a function of the expanding universe. The universe is will someday become so vast, so large, that no light from any star or galaxy will be able to reach any other star or galaxy in a finite amount of time, so every sky everywhere will be dark—and the universe will still keep expanding. Any intelligent species that develops in such darkness will never know that there are other possibilities for life. They will look to the dark sky and believe that they are alone in time and space—how unbearably sad, right? But that's the advantage the rest of us have. We can look at the stars and know for certain just how alone we really are in this cosmos. But never mind that now—that's a different discussion."

He turned to his audience, the seven or eight who remained. "But yes, this explains the dark corridor. As the universe expands, so do its possibilities—and so does the Alexandrium. New possibilities are always creating themselves. Or being created. I really don't want to have to explain creation. Unless I must." He turned to study the dark corridor again. Even in the few short moments since he had begun talking, its appearance had changed. The corridor no longer shimmered. It looked much more solid now.

The Proctor scratched his ear in thought. "This must have occurred fairly recently, obviously since my last visit." He squinted as he peered into the distance. "Looks like it's still opening up, still expanding, still sorting itself out—still filling itself up. Of course, it'll never be full, that's the problem with infinity, you know. It goes on forever and forever, not just the big infinities, but all the little infinities as well, all the tiny micro-infinities inside and between the big ones—very troubling to mathematicians, philosophers, and just about anyone else who tries to think about these things. Our brains are finite. Possibilities are not. Anyway—let's have a look and see what this corridor is about. Who's with me?" He looked to Sharon Henderson. "Are you game?" She nodded reluctantly.

Not every member of the group followed him, only the five most curious. The others had wandered off in search of Gershwin's 1951 Berlin Concertos, The Beatles' 1995 Reunion Tour, and the last twelve volumes of The Lost Chtorran Cycle.

The new corridor was still solidifying, its details becoming ever more distinct. The towering entrance was now revealed as a set of seventeen nested gothic arches, each one decorated with satyrical devices that suggested a variety of desires without specifically picturing any of them.

Beyond the opening, the depths of the immense hall were lit with indistinct orange flickers—Cocteau Torches high on the walls. The group paused for a moment at the entrance while the Proctor studied several intricate decorations. The pillars here were thick and somber, but with an inner translucence.

"Hmm," said the Proctor. "This looks like Hellarian black quartz, but the size of these crystals—I'd say they're impossible, except here they are."

By any standard the work was magnificent. The pillars were engraved with silver and crimson runes, a lacework of ominous elegance. The Proctor traced the inlaid hieroglyphs with a delicate touch. "This is wonderful! I thought this language was lost. I haven't seen pictographs like this since . . . never mind. It must be a residual resonance of an earlier timeline." He turned back to his companions. "The universe is a palimpsest, you know—multitudes of new realities written indelibly on top of old ones every quantum tick of time. But sometimes traces of the past are still visible in the underlying strata—"

"Yes, yes. We read that in the brochure," said Westfield. "But what is this— this place?" He glanced around nervously, waving his hands as if afraid to point at anything in particular. "This isn't in the brochure. What is it?"

"Hm. I don't think you read the whole brochure," the Proctor replied. He spread his own hands to include everything around them in a metaphorical rebuttal. "This—all this—is just another possibility. Everything—everything is a possibility." He paused, taking another deep survey of the entrance to the hall. "This one—it isn't new. Not with these petroglyphs. It's always been here. Well, sort of. It was just waiting to be created. Possibilities always need someone to imagine them to make them real. Perhaps one of you . . . ?" He looked around at the members of the group, eyeing each one meaningfully. He squinted at Sharon Henderson in particular.

"No, no—" protested Westfield. "I would never. *We* would never." He looked to the round woman, the one in purple, Blackstone. She wasn't his wife, but they were indentured members of the same contract family, so technically she was. Or he was. It all depended on the jurisdiction, except there wasn't any in the Alexandrium, so it didn't matter. "We wouldn't do a thing like that, would we, dear?"

She nodded. "Of course not. We're High Ghaloodians."

The Proctor was unconvinced. "Yes, that's what you'd like me to believe. But that's how possibilities work—someone has to consider them first. The more a possibility is considered, the more real it becomes. Eventually, it becomes a probability, and after that, it can even become an inevitability. That must be what happened here. But what," he mused, "was anyone thinking that called this into existence? I wonder what dark ruminations slouching toward Alexandrium, waiting to be borne . . . ?"

He clapped his hands together excitedly. "Well, nothing to be done about it but to investigate, right?" He pointed toward the foreboding entrance and the darker depths beyond. "Exploration and discovery await!"

"Um . . . ?" suggested Sharon Henderson. "Do you think it might be dangerous. Maybe we should just . . . I don't know . . . leave it alone?"

"Ahh, Sharon. Where's your sense of adventure?" The Proctor lifted his fez long enough to brush back his unruly hair, a useless gesture as it flopped right back into place. "Besides, the Alexandrium never hurts anyone. Well, hardly ever. Not often enough to be statistically significant. Let's go see—" The Proctor strode eagerly into the dark. His companions hesitated, uncertain—but only momentarily. They were probably safe in his wake. One by one they followed.

A few paces inside, they stopped, all of them startled. They turned around and around in amazement, staring at the sheer size of the hall. The corridor had become immense and sprawling, spotted with nooks and crannies inside every nook and cranny.

In places, the walls glowed with amber flickering light, the reflections of hidden flames. But high above, bars of slanting golden brightness shone, carving through areas of deep distinct shadow, diagonal shafts of lustrous illumination, the dust within sparkling like stars.

"This is incredible," exclaimed the Proctor, forging ahead. "Simply incredible! The enormous scale of this! Look! You can't even see the ceilings. This might be the biggest annex of all—"

He put one hand against the wall to support himself and leaned far back to look directly overhead. The upper levels rose endlessly on thick pillars, towering huge and high until they finally vanished into the clouds that filled the uppermost ranks of the chambers. Spiral staircases wound around the pillars, also disappearing upward.

"Isn't this wonderful? What grandeur! Come on now!" The Proctor led his companions deeper into the passage, exclaiming with excitement at every new detail, marveling at the intricacies that were still coming into being around them. He moved from display to display with growing enthusiasm.

"Look!" He pointed. "Look at that! A complete sea-gryphon skeleton. And over here, a gelatinous snark! Isn't this marvelous? Did I say marvelous already? Have I used that word too much? Have I worn it out? Oh, look over here—what is this? What a funny little furry thing, I wonder why it's here—oh, here's the plaque. It says it's the worst ecological threat in the Sevagram. How curious. Let's not touch it. No trouble at all—" He backed away carefully, raising his hands against any imagined contamination.

He darted to the opposite wall, barely glancing at the marvels there. He bounced away like a pinball, heading diagonally deeper into the grand passage where strange sculptures stood on pedestals—they looked like figures caught writhing in confusion and pain. Deeper still, baroque frames revealed eloquent paintings where distorted and disturbing images flubbered into being. Further on, more nooks opened up revealing glaring frozen heads. Display cases containing unfinished objects bristled and blustered into existence. And everywhere towering ranks of shelves sagged with rows and rows of volumes, some bound in black leather, others in red, a few in silver. There was no discernible order to any of it.

The Proctor stopped to run his fingers over the spines of the volumes on the nearest shelf. "Oh, this is wonderful, wonderful—just wonderful. Here's a mint-condition copy of the *Catalog of Unnameable Horrors*. First edition, oh my—" He turned the pages in delighted fascination. "Oh, yes. I remember this one. And this one, too. Oh, here's a new one—"

Sharon Henderson raised a tentative hand. "Sir . . . ?" The Proctor looked up from the page he was studying. "If they're unnameable, then how can they be catalogued?"

"That's exactly the right question to ask—and the answer should be obvious. As soon as you name them, they disappear from the catalog." He pushed the heavy book back into place on the shelf, brushed at it with his fingers, and blew away a bit of imaginary dust.

Blackstone, the round woman, held up her hands in puzzlement. Her purple dress had darkened to indigo and appeared to be darkening even further—so dark that the details of the fabric were becoming ever more difficult for the human eye to resolve. Her husband of convenience, Westfield, hadn't noticed. He was studying the row of books at his eye level. He frowned in puzzlement. "I can't read any of these—"

"Of course not. They're written in languages that haven't been invented yet."

"Well then, what good are they?"

"They aren't good for anything. They're simply possibilities. They may never be real. They just need someone to—well, believe is the wrong word, but it's the closest in your language. Maybe create is better, but creation implies consciousness, and I would hazard a guess that a great deal of all this is coming from something unconscious. So not create, either. Your language is insufficient. This way now—" The Proctor pointed deeper into the expanding passage.

Further on, additional corridors branched off in all directions, seemingly haphazard and unplanned. Some angled upward, with steps rising up and up, as if leading to distant altars. Others slanted down, as if heading into unknown depths of discomfort below. A few branches opened onto a vague, uneasy brightness. Most disappeared into faraway gloom.

The woman who hadn't spoken at all until now raised a polite finger. Her name was Janet Welter and she was a janet-welder from the JaneT Construction Cartel. Many of the employees of the cartel were janet-welders; most of them were also cloned from the original Janet Welter, but since the demand for synthetic Janets had collapsed after that regrettably well-publicized event at the Imperial Colludion, she had been preemptively retired along with most of her clone-sisters. None of that is relevant to this story. Nor is it important to know why she was part of this tourist group. She's just another possibility. Carry on.

"Excuse me, but . . ." Janet pointed. "This, all this—it's physically impossible. I mean, all those branching corridors, they'd have to intersect with some of the other corridors we saw in the entrance hall, wouldn't they? And I can see that they don't. So this is impossible—"

"Yes, of course it is," agreed the Proctor. "But you're thinking in terms of Euclidean geometry. The Alexandrium does not. It's one of the side effects of fractal infinity. Oh, here, I just noticed this. Look at these reverse faces carved into the walls. Isn't that remarkable, see how their eyes seem to follow you everywhere? Hmm—" He stepped forward to study one, then frowned at the descriptive plaque below. "I thought I recognized him. But why would anyone want to honor *him*? The man was ignorant, incompetent, corrupt, and totally lacking empathy. And he never owned a dog. Oh, wait. I get it. He's a very good example of a very bad example. Yes, I get it now." The Proctor stepped back, looked up and down the great corridor, finally understanding the larger context, right on schedule. "Yes, I see. Hmp. This was inevitable. Unfortunately inevitable."

"Inevitable?" asked Tracy Blackstone. Her dress had long since become totally light-absorbing. She was a bright pink face hovering over a shapeless splotch of darkness—literally a black stone, topped by a rosy red-hatted blob. "This? But it just appeared, didn't it? We saw it. How could it be inevitable?"

The Proctor looked annoyed and unhappy, not at Ms. Blackstone, but at their surroundings. "This corridor. This part of the Alexandrium. It's an unfortunate side effect of . . . well, side effects."

"Why do you say that?" asked Westfield, her unhusband.

"Because . . . if I'm right, and I usually am, except when I'm not, this is the acknowledgment, the recognition, the realization of all the things that people don't want to think about. I should have seen it coming. My bad. So many people, so many fears. All that wallowing in dark possibilities brings them into being. This—" The Proctor paused for now unnecessary dramatic effect. "This is the library of discomfortables."

He paused in thought. "Hmm, now that I think about it, I'm surprised the whole Alexandrium hasn't turned into this. This is very likely infectious." The Proctor turned around slowly, looking at the stark space as if seeing it for the first time, surveying the seemingly infinite depths of the towering black hall. He frowned. Were the unseen torches flickering out? Had the higher shafts of light gone dim?

The floor creaked unexpectedly beneath his feet. It sounded like old boards straining under a great weight. "That's odd," he said, looking down. "But certainly in character."

"What is?" asked Westfield.

"The floor. It creaks. But look at it—it's solid marble, beautiful marble indeed, some of the very best. Like you might find in an exquisite mausoleum. But marble doesn't creak like this—" He danced around to demonstrate, and the floor obliged with additional groaning noises. "Of course it doesn't. It should clatter with a marbleous resonance. This is an unforeseen event, definitely an unusual possibility. I wonder if—no, never mind. I'm probably wrong. I've been wrong before. I'll be wrong again. Sometime. Maybe. This could be one of those times." The Proctor abruptly pointed them onward. "We'll keep going—it's safe. I mean, it should be safe. Really."

Further along the corridor, the walls appeared to be rougher-hewn, but when the group looked closer, the surfaces of their surroundings became just as intricately embellished as before. Before Westfield could ask, the Proctor explained, "It's still forming itself. As soon as you look, it crystallizes." Abruptly, he turned to the tall man. "You have a question, Mr. Levine?"

Levine shook his head. "I'm listening—"

"You can hear it, too?"

Levine nodded. "I'm a Lethetic."

"Oh, yes. Of course. I should have recognized it by your eyebrows. You've had some work done?"

"It was a requirement of the job. So I could pass."

"Unfortunate, that. Did it affect your knoggling any?"

"Unfortunately, yes. It was reflated."

"Oh, that's not good. So sorry to hear that. I hope they compensated you well."

"It was sufficient. I am now retired."

"Ahh, well, then it's all good. I guess."

Levine shrugged. "I can't complain." He added, "No one wants to listen—and besides, they placed an injunction, so it would be both irrelevant and inconsistent..."

"Yes, of course—"

Wanda Beers interrupted then. She had also chosen a color, but in this dim light, no one could tell which one. "What in the name of the Seventh Insertion are you two talking about?"

"No, wait—" That was Sharon Henderson. "This is more important. What were you two hearing?"

"That—" said the Proctor. He pointed forward, frowned, then pointed back. "Or maybe it was that way? I'm not sure."

They all fell silent then, listening to the distant emptiness.

"It's the wind," said Westfield, timidly. "It has to be the wind. Right? Because this corridor goes a long way, doesn't it? So that would make wind, wouldn't it? Isn't that right?" He didn't look certain.

"Yes, it goes on forever," said the Proctor. "Because that's how infinity works."

"Oh, yes, of course. Maybe we should head back now?" Westfield turned around as if to encourage the others to follow, then stopped himself and stared at the distant entrance. It was far behind them, very far, only a faintly glowing brightness. "Have we really come that far—?"

"Oh, no. The corridor is growing. Stretching. The more we explore, the more real it becomes."

"That sound," said Sharon Henderson. "It's not the wind—"

They all fell silent again, listening harder. This time, the sound was perceptibly closer.

Finally, Sharon spoke. "It's like a chorus, very faint and far away—"

"No. It's something moaning—"

"It's water. Rushing."

"It's just the wind—"

The Proctor interrupted. "It isn't anything. Until it is. It's going to be whatever you make it."

"It sounds like something growling—" said Wanda Beers.

"Yes, that's a possibility," agreed the Proctor. "You would have to think of that, wouldn't you," It wasn't a question.

"It's getting closer," said Levine.

"We should head back," said Westfield. "Let's go back. Okay?"

"I'm not sure that's possible," the Proctor replied. He pointed. They looked.

Far away, far more distant than even a moment before, the last bright glow of the receding entrance . . . winked out.

They were left in murky gloom. Overhead, the unseen torches flickered unsteadily. Uneasy patterns of shadows danced on the walls. And far overhead, the sky-blue glow receded, becoming an even more distant blur.

The Proctor said nothing. That was unusual. He almost always had something to say. Instead, he seemed uneasy. The group looked to him, curious. Levine cleared his throat and asked slowly, "Did you know this would happen?"

"It was . . ." said the Proctor slowly, ". . . always a possibility."

"So now what?" demanded Blackstone. "How do we get out of here?"

"Can't we just walk back that way until we get there?" asked Westfield.

"I'm afraid it won't be there," said the Proctor. "I'm fairly sure this corridor is now infinite. In both directions." He glanced around the group. "It happens sometimes."

Sharon Henderson rearranged her bag on her shoulder. It had gotten quite heavy. "Can't we just, I don't know, create a possibility of return?"

"Sorry. It doesn't work that way."

"So there's no way out—?"

"I didn't say that."

"But there's no way out, is there?"

"No. Not at the moment."

"But there will be—?" Sharon persisted.

"Um—I'm not sure about that."

"I thought you said the Alexandrium never hurts anyone," said Beers. Of all of them, she was the angriest. She had chosen a new color—furious red.

"Yes, I did say that. And it's true. But sometimes people do get lost. It is infinite, you know."

Tracy Blackstone started to say something, but the Proctor held up his hand to stop her. "Wait. Let me think on this."

He turned around slowly, once, twice, a third time, examining the circumstances of their situation. He studied the branching corridors—except they were no longer branches, but forks. The original corridor was now just one of many, indistinguishable from the rest. Finally, he looked up, his thoughtful gaze rising slowly and deliberately toward the upper levels, the levels above those, and the even higher levels beyond.

Sharon sniffed and looked around. "What's that smell?" she asked.

"Brimstone," said the Proctor, without looking over. He was still focusing on the highest reaches above. "And a trace of sulfur," he added.

"Brimstone and sulfur!"

"Nothing to worry about. It's not a volcano."

"Nothing to worry about?" Wanda Beers snorted. "Really?"

Levine pointed down one of the hallways. "That's a very solid-looking nothing."

That brought the Proctor's attention back down to the group. He squinted. He frowned. He considered.

"It's moving," said the blot that was Blackstone.

"It's growling," said Westfield uncertainly.

"It's coming this way," said Sharon Henderson.

"I don't like the look of this—" said Levine. He was knoggling now, despite his reflation.

The Proctor shook his head. "It's only a possibility. It isn't real. Not yet, anyway. Don't think about it."

"What if you're wrong?" said Beers. "It looks real. It sounds real. It even smells real."

"I told you not to think about it. Now I have to." The Proctor paused to consider it. He shook his head. "No, I'm not wrong. Not very often, anyway. What you need to know is this: There are specific limits regarding what the Alexandrium can manifest. Otherwise, the whole place would be overrun with ghoulies and ghosties and long-leggety beasties—and things that go bump in delight."

"But what about this place?" said Westfield. "Where we are now—this isn't anything like the brochure promised."

"Ah-ha! I was right. You didn't read the whole brochure. There's a whole section on exceptions."

"Speaking of long-legged beasties," said Sharon. "That thing is getting closer."

"It looks like a bear," said the Blackstone blot.

"Bears don't have eight legs," said Levine. He was taller, so he had a better view.

"Or glowing red eyes," said Westfield, stepping behind Blackstone.

"Bears don't make clackety-slobbering noises like that, do they?" asked Sharon.

"Well, if discretion is the better part of survival—" The Proctor pointed to the nearest spiral staircase. It was made of overwrought iron. "Who's up for a climb?"

"Huh?"

"Up there?"

"Is that the way out?"

"I don't know, but we'll have a better view, won't we—?" The Proctor started up the staircase, bounding the first seven steps skyward with excitement. He stopped to look back. "Well, come on now. You don't want to get eaten, do you?"

"Is that a possibility?" Westfield stared nervously toward the noise.

"What do you think? You're the one creating it."

Timidly, he looked to the round woman, a nearly invisible blot now, only a floating face. She looked to the tall man. He shrugged and moved first. The others had no choice but to follow. Westfield glanced back down the corridor, listened intently for a moment, then hurried after the others.

"I do not like stairs," he said, puffing as he climbed. He held on to the handrail and pulled himself along with visible effort. "I really do not like stairs."

The face in the round black splotch called upward, "I thought you said the Alexandrium wasn't dangerous—"

"It wasn't. Not until you lot arrived—"

"Wait—are you saying this is our fault?"

"It's a Schrödinger substantiation. It can't manifest without an observer. Keep up, now—"

The staircase spiraled up around the pillar, delivering them onto the next level. It was much the same as the level below, a broad space with its own set of branching corridors and passages, the same sort of intricate carvings and obscure runes, the same brooding shelves and disturbing sculptures. As before, unseen torches flickered vaguely above. The Proctor shook his head in dismissal. "As I expected. Let's keep going." He headed up the stairs again. "This might take a while."

"Wait a minute! That Schrödinger thing you said. What's that?"

"Schrödinger is probably the wrong way to explain it. We don't have a cat. I meant that nothing exists until someone says it exists. No, that's not right, either. Try it this way. A possibility doesn't exist until someone creates it. One of you. Or maybe all of you together. Think about it—no, *don't* think about it. That's the problem. You all keep thinking. Never mind that now. We must keep going. If there really is something there, it can probably climb stairs."

His companions looked back down the spiral steps nervously. They couldn't see anything, but there were strange new noises to be heard. It sounded like chitinous claws scrabbling on rough iron plates. It sounded like something large panting heavily as it thumped its way up. It sounded like something moaning hungrily. It sounded like fear.

The Proctor didn't have to urge them upward.

At the next level and the next, the Proctor repeated his examinations, quickly studying all the gloomy corridors, all the dark nooks and murky passages. Nothing different here. And the noises from below sounded closer every time. He pointed the group back up the spiral. "Right. Let's push on."

Each level was a variation on the same theme: bleak intersections of multiple corridors, all leading into somber hallways and obscure chambers. Every level—again and again, each one another variation, all the same, but different. Their only course was to keep ascending the winding flight, keep climbing and climbing toward the distant light. More disturbing sounds rose up from below. Perhaps there were several things following them now.

"We're not outrunning it, are we?" said the timid man.

"It doesn't seem like it, no."

"All this climbing—it's bad for my knees."

The Proctor shook her head. "We can't stop here." None of them had noticed when she'd changed. They'd been too busy catching their breath. But it had happened rather quickly. For a moment, the Proctor had become a lot shorter, a lot rounder, a lot balder. He looked at himself and shuddered—"Oh, this will never do!"—a quick recalibration and she regenerated immediately. She took stock, counting fingers, ears, mouth, and nose. All in their proper places and functioning appropriately. "Ahh, much better. Well, close enough. But still not a ginger." She put her annoyance aside and pointed upward. "If we stop, the sky will keep getting farther away."

Her companions looked. "It's already farther away. This isn't working."

"Hmm. No, it isn't. How very annoying."

"So what are we going to do?"

"This is the Alexandrium," the Proctor said, "and there are always possibilities."

"Name six," said Blacstone.

"I can name more than six. They're just not possibilities here." The Proctor pointed at the floor. "I mean, not right here."

"Well, do something!"

The Proctor looked offended. "I *am* doing something. I'm creating a new possibility."

She paced a few steps toward one corridor, examined it skeptically, frowned, then turned to the next. She repeated this behavior with every passage, circling wide, looking into all of the different opportunities branching away. Here, there were no sculptures, no traceries, only the barest of runes. There were no busts. The nooks were devoid of displays. The surrounding shelves were either empty or sparsely occupied. "Don't like this," she said. "Don't like this at all."

"What will happen if we keep going up?"

"It'll become less and less. It will become more and more unresolved."

"Is that a good thing or a bad?"

"Yes." She faced them, straightening, reassuming the authority of leadership. "I'm sorry, we seem to have blundered into a—a thing that isn't anything. Not yet, anyway. And I don't think we should wait until it becomes something."

"Well, if we blundered into it, can't we blunder out of it—"

"It doesn't work that way." The Proctor scratched her head, thinking.

"You do have a plan—" Sharon asked. "Don't you?"

"I have many plans," the Proctor said, still scratching. "Unfortunately, none of them fit this situation. And I don't like planning anyway. Plans never really work out, do they? So why create them? But—" She straightened. "We can still be decisive. I told you there are trains, so there must be lifts as well. Stay together now. I think . . ." She cupped a hand to one ear, listening. "Ah, yes. This way—" She pointed. "We'll take the lift."

"The lift—?" Westfield protested. "Why didn't we start with the lift? Why did you make us climb all those stairs?"

"Because it wasn't a possibility then. Now it is." The Proctor led them to an ornate overwrought-iron cage, ushered them inside, and slid the metal door shut behind them. It rattled and clanked as it klunked into place. They could have been inside a large baroque cell of ancient design.

The Proctor stepped to the left side of the door, where a large square plate had conveniently appeared. It was thick iron, painted black, and in the center was an ornate iron lever, also painted black. It stood in an upright position. The Proctor pushed the handle to the right. The machinery groaned and shuddered, the cage lurched down—

"Whoops—that's not right." She pulled the controller back to its upright position. The metal framework shuddered again, then bumped to a halt. The riders looked around uncertainly—they were caught halfway between two unresolved floors.

"Let's try the other way." The Proctor pushed the handle to the left and this time something above the cage whined with organic grinding noises that grew into a howl of rusty protest until finally the machine jerked and started moving laboriously up.

"Ahh, much better," she said.

They rose slowly toward the light. The ancient lift grumbled, its movement rough and uneven. The group could have climbed the stairs faster, but at least their progress was mostly steady. They didn't have to stop and rest.

"How far will we have to go?"

"All the way, I suppose."

"How far is that?"

"How far is infinity—no, don't panic. We'll only go as far as we need to. It might take a while."

Around them, the darkened floors of the Alexandrium's unfinished passages continued to drop away, sliding downward, vanishing into the darker depths below. When the tall man pressed his face against the bars of the cell and looked down, the bottom was already lost in murk. When he looked up, the view was much the same, only brighter and less distinct. As part of his discipline, Levine had studied quantum disorders, so he considered what he saw as the differentiated expressions of asymmetrical fractals and wondered about the resolving power of the Alexandrium— but if all you have is infinity, there is no limit except the life-span of the observer.

A few minutes passed, then a few more after that. Many minutes passed—an hour passed. The lift still grumbled, though not as much. It had become resigned to its task. They rose and time receded. The Alexandrium receded. Everything around them became ever more vague.

Abruptly, the Proctor brought the lift to a halt and opened the door. "Stay there, please. Hold the door. I just want to check something." She stepped out of the metal cage but kept one hand on the frame as she looked around. There was not much to see—except for the other lift opposite theirs. Another Proctor had just stepped out. A female companion held the door behind him.

He was dressed like a baker, with a colorful knit scarf draped around the shoulders of his long brown coat. He had curly hair and a whimsical expression. "Ah, there you are," he said. "You're going up?"

"Yes. And you?"

"We're going down."

"So . . . you've been up? What's up there?"

"Nothing."

"Oh, that's perfect."

"What's down?"

"Didn't get a good look—but it was making growly noises."

"Oh, good. I love those things."

"Well, do be careful," the female Proctor said. "Don't go folding yourself."

"Oh, that's not me, I assure you. Although there are always possibilities. But you already know that." He waved and stepped back into his own lift. The Proctor returned to hers.

There is this about lifts and elevators. People become resigned and indifferent. They fall silent and stare at the numbers, unable to acknowledge the existence of any others who might momentarily share the same space—it is the latency spell of the enclosure. People retreat into their internal spaces as a defense against the collapse of personal boundaries.

But this machine cast a different spell. There were no numbers to watch, only the separate levels, all the shelves of brooding emptiness, each floor sliding down, all of them dropping into the gloom below, one after the other, next and next and next, an endless vertical panorama. Each succeeding story fell into view a little less distinct, a little blurrier, a little more out of focus and unresolved.

The group had been silent at first, but finally, as they descended into a boredom that matched the sinking stages of the Alexandrium, they began to complain.

"How long is this going to take?"

"Where are we going, anyway?"

"My feet hurt."

"Do you even know what you're doing?"

The Proctor ignored most of their comments and complaints, but to the last question, she said, "Of course not. Not having a plan is part of the process." She frowned as she studied the cloudiness beyond the bars of their cell. There was no longer anything distinct outside the cage, nothing specific to see anymore, just a few shadowy forms of fog drifting downward.

"Ahh," she said. "It may be possible—"

"What?"

"—that we've outrun the darker possibilities. Boredom can do that."

Even though the lift still appeared to be rising, the noise of its machinery had long since faded and the ride had become so much smoother, they might have been gliding. All sense of motion had disappeared.

"Look," said the Proctor. "See?"

Sharon Henderson pushed past her to look. "But there's nothing to see."

"Exactly." The Proctor looked surprised that Henderson would even raise the question.

"So we're there?"

"No. There's no there here."

"Well then, where are we?"

"Nowhere. There's no here here, either."

"So where are we going?"

"Where there's neither here nor there. Nowhere."

"Um—" Westfield pointed timidly. "I think we're already there."

The Proctor turned around to look. "Oh, yes. Here we are—we're here. Although I shouldn't say that. As soon as I name it, it becomes something, doesn't it? No, this is nothing. Definitely nothing."

She was right. This time.

Outside the cage, there was nothing. It was a very solid nothing, but it was clearly nothing at all.

The Proctor pushed open the metal door—but it wasn't metal anymore and it slid aside easily without a clank or a clunk. It was already losing form. Before the last of the Proctor's companions could step out, it faded away.

"Um—" The timid man looked at the nothing beneath his feet. "It's gone. How are we going to get back?"

"We're not going back."

"Well then, where are we going?"

"As I told you. Nowhere."

"Excuse me?"

"This is nowhere. We're here."

"How can we be here if it's nowhere . . . ?" Westfield flustered into silence.

"I can explain it to you," the Proctor said gently. "I can explain it at length. I just can't understand it for you."

"But there has to be some kind of scientific explanation—"

"Possibly. But that's not a possibility when you're nowhere—"

Blackstone put a hand on her unhusband's arm. He shut up.

The Proctor faced her companions. "Now, listen carefully. We don't want this to go all pear-shaped—" She steepled her hands in front of her face while she thought about what to say next, then abruptly stopped herself. "What does that mean, anyway? Pear-shaped? Pears are delicious. I like pears, don't I? Oh, wait. No, I don't." She scratched her ear, frowning as she tried to remember what she thought about pears. She finally decided it was irrelevant and shook the memories away. "Never mind. Just don't do anything stupid. In fact, don't do anything at all. Oh—and stay away from the shadows."

"Shadows?" asked Sharon Henderson. "What shadows—?"

The Proctor pointed.

Off in the distance—or what would have been the distance if there was any space to measure—there were vague, unformed semblances that might have been a darker form of nothing, but weren't enough of anything to be something.

"Oh," said Sharon.

"Those aren't really shadows."

"So . . . what are they, then?"

"They're not-shadows."

"If they're not shadows, what are they?"

"They're not-shadows," the Proctor repeated, then realized that was a conversational dead end, not much different from arguing over the names of fictitious demons. "Oh, go ahead, call them shadows. I mean, that's the easiest way to think of them, even though they aren't. If we were somewhere, they might be possibilities, but here where there's nothing, they're not anything."

"Uh, they seem to be very solid nothings—and they're coming this way, aren't they?"

The Proctor nodded.

"We should get out of their way, shouldn't we?"

"Well, yes—but there's no place to go. There's no there here, remember?"

The companions looked nervously past the Proctor. "Those not-shadows—are they dangerous?"

"They shouldn't be."

"What do you mean, 'shouldn't be'?"

"In theory, they're nothing, nothing at all. Because we're nowhere, everything is nothing. And nothing is everything. But . . ." She hesitated. "Just don't get into one, because that might make it something. And then . . ."

"And then what?"

The Proctor took a deep breath. "If we had the time—well, actually we do, because there isn't any time here, just like there isn't any space, except what we're creating by being here, all this staring around—that's making nothing into something. Perception is creation, you know—oh, you didn't know that, did you? Well, I could give you the entire doctorate-level set of theses on existence, nonexistence, and beingness, plus the allied philosophical discussions all the way down to the sub-quantum level where everything just collapses back into iggly-squiggly question marks." She glanced around at the dark nothings that had not only drifted noticeably closer but had also taken on a bit more solidity. "But we really don't have the time, do we?"

Her small group of companions looked around as well, then back to her for the rest of the explanation.

"You see, the problem is us. We're making this real." She stamped on the very solid nothingness beneath her feet. It clacked like stone. "See? Our presence here means we're not really nowhere anymore. We're somewhere—a very unique somewhere, but still somewhere. And all that nothing out there is trying to create something because—well, it's about creation. Sorry, I am going to have to get quantum-philosophical.

"One theory—or call it a hypothesis, an idea, a belief, a whatchamacallit—about creation is that it's the appearance of something out of nothing. Got that? Something out of nothing. Except it isn't. Except maybe if you're creating creation, that might be true—but in the physical realm, creation always—well, mostly—usually occurs as the synergistic synthesis of existing forms into new configurations, so it's not really creation at all, it's only the transformation of some previously existing material—and, see, that's the point. Transformation requires something to be transformed. That's why we're the problem. Because we're here, we're creating creation. The longer we're here and now, the more we're creating a here and now. So the nothing shadows are coming for us because we're raw material for whatever is going to be created from us. It's a function of consciousness and the way it perceives time. Oh, I do wish I could explain this better, but it's this—whole worlds pivot on acts of imagination. I said that somewhere before, didn't I?"

"Oh," said Sharon. "You're saying we're going to be changed?"

"I'm saying that transformation is inevitable."

"Oh, that doesn't sound good."

"It sounds uncomfortable," said the black blot with a face. Blackstone.

The crimson woman spoke next. "I don't want to be transformed."

Westfield shuddered. "Why can't we just go back?"

"That's the problem," said the Proctor. "There is no back. Consciousness is linear. There's only forward. I thought I explained that."

"No, you didn't."

"Well, I could, but I won't. There's no time. Of course there's no time. There's no space here, either."

"So you're saying nothing happens until we create it?" Levine looked down at her sharply. "And whatever we create, it has to be created out of us?"

"Yes. That's right. Mostly right. But don't worry. It doesn't hurt. Well, not painfully—"

"How do you know?" Sharon asked.

"Because I've done it." The Proctor frowned as she ticked off her past identities on her fingers. "I might have lost count around thirteen or fourteen. And I'm not sure if I should count that one. It doesn't matter. I still don't like pears. They're too juicy. They're sloppy. When did I decide that, anyway?" She looked up and glanced around at the group. "Yes, what?"

"You've done this before?" Sharon Henderson accused.

"Oh, not this—" She waved her hand at the nothing around them. "But transformation—reconfiguration, reconstruction, reidentification, whatever you call it—yes, I have. Once, I was a Scotsman. I had a wife, too. She was a ginger. But I've never been a ginger. Funny, that. Mildly annoying."

Her companions looked at her as if they'd never seen her before—as if she'd suddenly turned bright blue, sprouted wings and feathers, and begun speaking an indecipherable gibberish.

"Oh, right. I forgot. You people don't do transformation, do you?" She looked sad. "I guess that's on me. I should have explained." She brushed her blonde hair back. "But it's the only way out."

"How long have you known this?"

"Why didn't you tell us before?"

"What kind of a monster are you?"

"That depends on who you ask. I've been called—"

"Who—?"

"Yes. That's correct. But like I said, we don't have time for this." She pointed at the shadowy nothings. "They're getting closer." Even though they hadn't moved, the shadowy nothings were uncomfortably close now.

"How do they do that? They're not moving."

"Of course not. Because motion would have been something and these things are nothing. Oh, wait. Now I see."

"See what?"

"How stupid I am. I should have realized this sooner—"

"What—?"

"They really are just shadows."

"I thought you said they weren't."

"Well, I can be wrong. I thought I told you that." The Proctor sighed, took a deep breath. "Transformation is going through the shadow to get to the light. Well, yes, that's true whenever and wherever the shadows are something. A real shadow occurs when something tangible blocks a source of illumination, it's an artifact of time and relative dimension in space, but these shadows are nothing, so—"

"What are you talking about?"

"I'm talking about nothing. I should have seen it from the beginning. The shame is on me. Look around. Where are we? We're nowhere. No time. No space. There's nothing here, so there's nothing there—so these aren't shadows at all. That's what we've been doing wrong. We've been focusing on the darkness. We're making darkness real when we should be looking through it—to see what's blocking the light, except there's no light here, either—"

"So is there something there or not?" Westfield looked around nervously.

"Yes. No. In a way, they are shadows, but they aren't shadows of something else—those are our shadows. We're casting them."

"Wait? What?"

"We're the only reality here, so we're the only things that could have shadows. Even the light is an illusion. So that means—oh, fish custard and fingers."

"What, dammit?"

"No need for that. It's actually good news. Kind of. Transformation has to be self-created. It's like all we have to do is click our heels together three times and say, 'There's no place like home.' Except that's the wrong story. That won't work here. We'll need something stronger."

Suddenly, the sun went nova—

"No, wait. Stop. That's not it, either." The Proctor looked annoyed. "That's a possibility, yes—but not this one."

—fortunately, it wasn't this sun that had gone nova, it was some other sun, a hundred and thirty-seven thousand (and a smidge) light-years away. Nobody here (wherever here was) would know about it for a smidge more than a hundred and thirty-seven millennia.

"Here's the problem. We have to create from nothing. That's the hard one. So first we have to create creation. I said that, didn't I? And then we can create something." She looked to her companions. "I apologize in advance. This is going to take a while. Six days, at least." She spread her arms out wide and shouted, "In the beginning, there was the word. Then there were more words. Lots of words. Good words. Bad words. Silly words. Big words. Little words. Troubling words. Happy words. All the words. Up and down and all over everything. But listen up, all you nothings! Nothing is nothing, it has no power here. Because nothing is stronger than anything. No, let me say it a better way. Anything is better than nothing. And something is better than anything. So here's something now. The biggest words of all. The words of creation! *Let there be light.*"

And there was light.

And so on and so on.

On the seventh day, she rested.

"Okay," she said, "I admit that was a little gaudy, a little dramatic. Certainly more than just having the door dilate, yes? But why not? When you create, create big. You only have time to get half of it done anyway." She pointed. "Right. So there's an exit. Freshly made. That will take us back to . . . um, okay, not the Alexandrium. But there might be a shuttle. I might be able to create one—"

Sharon Henderson stared at the Proctor.

Then she stared at the doorway.

It was painted a dark shade of cyan-blue. (To be absolutely accurate, it was Pantone, PMS 2955C, with a hexadecimal color code of #003b6f. In the RGB color model, #003b6f is comprised of 0% red, 23.14% green, and 43.53% blue, with an approximate wavelength of 475.27 nm.)

"What is it?"

"You! *You're* the Legend!"

"Don't be silly. Anybody can be a Legend. If they really want to be. That's how it works."

"And that means I'm a companion!"

"Stop that. Everybody's a companion. If that's what they choose. Come along, now, I can't keep this up forever. Well, I could, but . . . that's not how this works."

The Proctor ushered them through the doorway towad a beautiful rolling hillside, everywhere carpeted with fresh green grass, knee-high and fragrant. Across the fields, fresh spring flowers sparkled with color. Overhead was a sky so blue it glistened. A gentle breeze sent rippling waves across the meadows.

Going last, the Proctor followed them through, and then stopped, herself surprised—"Oh," she said.

Sharon Henderson stood alone, looking around confused.

"Where are the others?"

"They were just possibilities."

"All of them?"

"Mostly, yes. The Alexandrium works that way sometimes."

"They weren't real?"

"No, they were real. All possibilities are real. But some possibilities go away after a while because they're no longer necessary—or possible. Or maybe you were one of their possibilities. Maybe I'm wrong. It doesn't matter. We're here now. This is a real here, not a there. Right?"

Sharon looked back through the open door—the door into nothing. "It's bigger on the inside, isn't it?"

"No, it isn't. Because there's nothing there." The Proctor closed the door, then opened it again to reveal only more meadow. "See? There's only the other side." But she took a key out of her pocket and carefully locked the door anyway. "Now. What would you like to see next?"

Sharon Henderson burrowed into her bag, bypassing her forgotten camera, and pulled out a cucumber sandwich. "Aren't you hungry? A bit of lunch first?"

www.ingramcontent.com/pod-product-compliance
Lightning Source LLC
Chambersburg PA
CBHW070219030726
47505CB00006B/1735